PRAISE FOR A... ....SSELL

"The Waning Moon is a can't-miss fantasy adventure with humor, snark, and fun banter. A must-read!"

The Waning Moon is the second in the Eleanor Morgan series and I think I can pay Cissell no greater compliment than to say reading this book inspires me to read the first book in the series and to continue with the entire series, as it is completed. This is a winner and one of the best in its genre that I've read of late.

Honorable Mention (Urban Fantasy) in the 2018 Readers' Favorites Book Awards

THE WANING MOON

AN ELEANOR MORGAN NOVEL: BOOK TWO

AMY CISSELL

BROKEN
WORLD
PUBLISHING

The Eleanor Morgan Novels

The Cardinal Gate
The Waning Moon
The Ruby Blade
The Broken World
The Lost Child*

*Forthcoming

THE WANING MOON
Amy Cissell

A Broken World Publication
PO Box 11643
Portland, OR 97211
The Waning Moon
Copyright © 2017 by Amy Cissell
ISBN 978-1-949410-04-4 (ebook)
ISBN 978-1-949410-05-1 (paperback)

Cover Design: Covers by Combs
Edited by: Colleen Vanderlinden

This is a work of fiction. Names, characters, businesses, places, events, and incidents are either the products of the author's imagination or used in a fictitious manner. Any resemblance to actual persons, living or dead, or actual events is purely coincidental.

For my two favorite people. L—you light up my life. C—you make it worth living.
Thank you.

ACKNOWLEDGMENTS

I'm grateful to my editor, Colleen Vanderlinden for her expertise, humor, and encouragement.

Special thanks to my cover artist, Daqri Combs for her excellent work bringing Eleanor to life.

Thank you to my proofreader Kari Furness—without your polishing, this book would be a lot less shiny.

I want to thank my beta readers, Nichole and Marci, for their time, critiques, and encouragement.

My first reader, platonic soul mate, and combination cheerleader and ass-kicker deserves her own call out. Without Cat, this book would still be sitting in a file somewhere.

The biggest thanks this time around are for reserved for Chris. My partner, my love, and my favorite reader. Without your patience, support, enthusiasm, and incredible eye for detail, I couldn't have done this.

CHAPTER ONE

ISAAC AND FLORENCE were sitting at the motel table poring over maps when I woke up. Three cups of Starbucks were centered on the table. I inhaled the scent and shuddered when I realized how good it smelled. This adventure was destroying my discerning palate. Before too long, I'd be willingly downing Folgers crystals and swearing it tasted like my usual roast

"Are you going to lie there thinking about coffee or are you planning on joining us?" Florence asked without looking up.

"I need you to teach me how to shield my thoughts better." I hopped out of bed and headed for the coffee.

"I'd settle for teaching you how to shield your body better," Florence said after a quick glance in my direction.

I looked down at myself. Yep. Completely nude. "Sorry." I hustled towards the bathroom only pausing long enough to grab my bag and snag my coffee.

I rewarded myself with a life-affirming sip of Americano after successfully putting on each article of clothing and weaponry. Properly caffeinated, dressed, and armed, I returned to the main room.

"What are you looking at?" I eyed the maps of Ohio, Illinois, and Tennessee covering the table.

"Mounds," Florence said.

I snickered. "Glad you two found a way to bond."

Florence glared at me, but the hardness in her eyes quickly gave way to an amused twinkle, and she snorted. "You are ridiculous."

"That's why everyone loves me. I'm fun."

"Barely-controlled chaos is not everyone's idea of fun."

I fluttered my eyelashes at her. "C'mon, Florence. You're having a little fun, aren't you?"

"Between harnessing powerful magic I never dreamed of, breaking ties with the coven I regarded as family, and fleeing my home with a wolf and a dragon?" She smiled. "Maybe a small bit of fun."

Isaac ruined my moment of triumph. "Did you know there are over seventy American Indian burial mounds in Ohio alone? I was wondering, Princess Pandemonium" — I stuck my tongue out at him — "if you could narrow it down?"

"I narrowed it down to mounds, didn't I? Why do I have to do all the work?"

"Because you're the only one who can find and open these gates. We're the sidekicks," Isaac said.

"I prefer minion," Florence said.

I rolled my eyes. "You guys are great sidekicks, but to graduate to full minionhood, you'll need to do a better job of anticipating my needs. Better coffee. Better beer. Maybe a foot massage every afternoon."

Isaac laughed. "Can you come look at the map?"

Isaac's map was marked with lots of large purple "x's." Florence had a tourism guide open with a list of mounds. I sat down and stared at the purple marks. Nothing jumped out at me. Not even a general pull of "start here."

"Ummm..." I said. Profundity, thy name is Eleanor. "Maybe I'll feel something when we get closer?"

"This area is bigger than the Black Hills," Isaac said.

"Bite me."

"Pressuring Eleanor to pick a location will probably have a detrimental effect on the overall results. We have over a month to find the gate and can get to Ohio in two reasonable driving days."

I tried to shake off the panic-inducing pressure and concentrate on the map, but I couldn't focus.

"Why don't we start driving? We can figure it out on the way," Florence said.

"Breakfast first?" I asked.

"Of course. No one wants to be trapped in a car with a hungry dragon."

"I'm not that bad."

"Yes, you are," Isaac and Florence said together.

We packed up and headed out. I gazed mournfully at the minivan. "This is a far cry from the beautiful truck you bought me in Portland."

"We'll trade it in again soon," Isaac said. "We'll need something older with no computer parts. We'll want to start collecting gasoline. Modern gas stations won't work if the grid goes down."

"By the end of this journey, we might not even have a working car," Florence added. "Be grateful for what we have now."

That shut me up. I'd mourned the impending loss of the internet, but hadn't thought through all the implications of throwing the world back to a pre-Industrial time. The minivan suddenly looked shiny and new.

"Fuck," I said.

"That about sums it up," Isaac said.

IT WASN'T until we were well on our way that I'd girded my loins enough to ask the question I'd been dreading. "What's the damage?"

"What damage?" Isaac didn't quite meet my eyes.

"You know what."

Isaac looked at me. "It wasn't as bad as last time."

"Mostly," Florence added. "In some ways, though, it was worse."

"Just tell me!"

Florence took a deep breath. "As you know, commercial air traffic was grounded. I called my friend at the FAA when we stopped in Murdo. The gate energy rendered my cell phone useless, and I had to use a pay phone. That was an adventure in itself—it's been a long time since I've made a long-distance call from a payphone. He thanked me for the tip, and let me know rather subtly I shouldn't contact him again. We are credible terrorist threats."

"I prefer to think we're incredible terrorist threats," Isaac interjected.

I ignored the admittedly amusing pun. "But no one died?"

The air in the vehicle grew noticeably chillier.

"The military is reporting no casualties," Florence said.

"We've talked about this, Isaac."

"Most of western South Dakota and eastern Wyoming lost power during the surge. There are no official reports of the effect that had on hospitals, nursing homes, or vehicles, but there are rumors."

"What about backup generators?"

"They'll work as long as gasoline supplies are available, but there won't be any new supplies coming into the area anytime soon."

I leaned back in my seat to process. There were a lot of aspects of what I was doing I hadn't considered beyond the immediate repercussions of a magical surge.

"We need to warn someone; let them know it's going to keep happening. They can stockpile supplies in the affected areas, and make alternate delivery arrangements."

"I agree," Florence said. "But I don't want to compromise my government contacts without reliable information. If they get in trouble or we get identified, things will go downhill even more quickly. We need to stay anonymous—and now that the media is reporting this could be terrorist-related, it'll be even more challenging."

"How do we stay under the radar? Is that even possible without hiding in northern Canada?"

"It's going to keep getting easier," Florence said. "Rapid City airport and the adjacent Air Force base are shut down. The effects of this gate are not intermittent as they were in Portland. There is a permanent bubble of circuit-destroying energy around the gate. In Portland, within a couple of hours, everything except what was caught in the pulse was back online. The power stations there were repaired in short order, and the outages were over in hours."

"And this time?"

"Hear for yourself," Isaac said and flipped on the radio.

"...the work of an electromagnetic pulse," the newscaster said. "It seems to be localized, and we're waiting on confirmation from the White House on whether they've traced this back to any terrorist groups. Communication into and out of the region is slow, but first reports indicate not only is the power out, but there is no estimated date when things will be back online. That means no television, no computers, no cell phones, and anything with computer circuitry— including cars, most appliances, thermostats, gas stations, credit cards, and many other everyday items. Authorities are recommending you fill up your bathtubs and any empty containers with water, open your freezers and refrigerators as infrequently as possible, and check on your elderly neighbors to ensure they're okay." Isaac flipped off the radio as it went to commercial.

"Are you saying this didn't happen the first time?"

"Not like this. The plane crashes were on the news, and there were reports of power outages, but since the effects were less widespread and things were better in a few hours, people dismissed it as a freak event. Now they're throwing around the "T" word with abandon."

"I kind of feel like a terrorist right now."

"We are not terrorists," Isaac said. "Terrorists have demands, or political aims, or something."

"I'm not a terrorist, then—just someone destroying the very fabric mankind has built its existence on."

Florence tsked.

I corrected myself. "Destroying the fabric of *human*kind to restore the earth's balance and unleash a horde of megalomaniacal supernatural beings who might want to punish those who have taken liberties with the earth. That sounds pretty fucking political to me. I am a terrorist."

"Well, when you put it that way," Florence said. "But I think you're doing the right thing."

"I'm pretty sure Timothy McVeigh and Osama bin Laden thought they were on the right track," I said.

"There is no way to talk about this without sounding like I'm rationalizing, but we have to believe in what we're doing. We have to believe what's happening is right."

"I do," I said. "I don't want to kill anyone in the process. I can't stop this without killing myself, and if I believed this truly was the wrong course, I would." Isaac glared at me out of the corner of his eye. "I'm not going to. The gates need to open. I wish there was a way to stop the loss of innocent life in the process."

"That's what separates you from Osama bin Laden and Timothy McVeigh," Florence said.

"Road to hell, good intentions," I said.

"Actions based on good intentions are better than no action at all. Sometimes great good looks, on the surface, like great wrong. We are going to change the world."

"I know agonizing over this does nothing. I am concerned, however, about the effects of the coming winter on the Black Hills and wherever we go next. If power is not restored and is indeed permanently knocked out, how will people survive? Without transportation, refrigeration, and heat, what will happen?"

"When it becomes apparent there is no salvaging the power system, evacuations will commence," Isaac said. "People survived before the advent of electricity and computers, and they can again."

"That was with smaller populations, less urban density, and a much, much lower dependence on technology. Today's people are helpless. The only ones left when I finish will be a bunch of supernaturals, crotchety mountain folk, and doomsday preppers."

"Once all the gates are open, and travel between planes resumes, you can take the throne and order your loyal subjects to help," Florence said.

"Sure," I agreed. "What are the chances that will be as easy as it sounds?"

"Nothing worth doing is easy."

"I don't know—Isaac is totally worth doing, and he's wicked easy."

"Hey!" Isaac said. "I can't believe you insulted my virtue!"

"I can't believe you insulted my eardrums," Florence said.

"Thank you," I said. "For everything. For helping rein in the full blast of power. For finding a way to release me from the bindings placed on me. For standing with us against your coven and your former lover. For being my friend."

"I knew you'd be the one to save us all. I will do what I can to stand with you, to protect you, and most importantly, to give you space when you can no longer control your ridiculous hormones."

I reached up and squeezed her shoulder. She was giving me an out to think about something else, and I took it. Tomorrow there'd be enough time to worry about how many people I'd kill next time. And the next. And the next.

CHAPTER TWO

DUSK WAS STARTING to purple the eastern sky when I saw the first building silhouettes thrusting upwards and interrupting the horizon.

I closed my eyes. The lights of the skyscrapers remained superimposed on my eyelids. I tried to imagine the city at night with scattered bonfires—in metal barrels, of course—to break the darkness. I shivered. I was going to destroy these people's lives. I was more than Florence's weapon—I was a nuclear bomb.

Isaac navigated the traffic with ease while I gaped at the skyline like the tourist I was. I'd never been anywhere larger than Seattle before and paid little attention to the direction the car was going. My view disappeared when Isaac pulled into a long, circular driveway and stopped in front of the biggest house I'd ever seen.

In answer to my unspoken question, Isaac said, "A friend lives here. It's safer than a hotel."

"What kind of friend? Another shifter?"

"Yes. The leaders of the Chicago Pride live here." We piled out of the minivan and headed to the house.

"We're not going to have to overthrow another asshole, are we?"

"I certainly hope not," someone said from the darkness. I jumped and turned towards the voice.

In front of me was the most unassumingly beautiful couple I'd ever seen. They were of average height—much taller than me—and their skin was so dark they seemed to detach from the shadows as they stepped forward. He was a hair taller than her, and his head was shaved. Her black hair floated around her face in a cloud of tight curls. They looked majestic, and I fought the urge to incline my head in acknowledgment of their dominance.

"Florence, Eleanor, this is Candace and Joseph," Isaac said.

I reached my hand out. Joseph shook it, but Candace stared at it until I dropped it. This was going to be fun.

"Candace is the leader of the Chicago Pride, and Joseph is her mate," Isaac continued, ignoring Candace's slight.

"One of my mates," she corrected.

"The best mate," Joseph said in heavily accented English. She smiled at him, and her white teeth gleamed in the near-dark.

"Joseph and I have known each other for a long time," Isaac said.

"Glad I am to see you again," Joseph said. "It has been too long. I see you have a mate of your own now. Your search finally bore fruit."

Isaac put his arm around me and pulled me close. I wasn't sure how I felt about this "mate" talk, and I opened my mouth to dispute things. It was one thing to say I was his mate to appease an asshole wolf, but another thing completely to start introducing me that way regularly.

"Candace, you look even lovelier than last time I saw you—something I didn't think possible." Isaac squeezed me even tighter, and I closed my mouth.

"Your tongue is as smooth as always. Please, come inside," Candace said. "I will have someone help you with your bags."

We followed Joseph and Candace inside.

I BOUNCED up and down on the bed and looked around the room. "You introduced me as your mate."

"Is that a problem?" Isaac asked.

"I'm not your mate. I'm your girlfriend."

"It saves a lot of unnecessary hassles and protects you from unwanted advances."

"I don't need that kind of protection."

"Shifter culture is different. An unattached female is fair game."

"I don't care what shifters think about my availability. I'm the only one who gets to decide how available I am."

Isaac looked at me but didn't quite meet my eyes. "Fine."

"Tell me about your friends?" I asked. I needed to assuage his pride without compromising myself.

"Joseph and I met during the Great War, and although I didn't spend much time with him after, we remained friends."

"Anything I should know about them or the Pride? I don't want to put my foot in my mouth."

"Candace runs this Pride with an iron fist. There were about twenty-five members last I heard, but only four or five males. The rest of the Pride shares the males, but I don't know if Candace shares Joseph. She's possessive."

"Sounds like an interesting place."

Isaac kissed me, but before things heated up too much, someone knocked on the door.

"Candace requests your presence in the library for drinks and hors d'oeuvres before dinner," the servant said.

"Do we need to dress for dinner?" Isaac asked.

The man's upper lip curled as he eyed our travel-stained jeans and t-shirts. "If you have something clean, it would not go amiss."

"We will be ready and appropriately attired in twenty minutes," Isaac said.

"Very good, sir."

"Where am I going to get appropriate attire? All I have is hiking clothes and blue jeans."

Isaac opened his duffel and pulled out a garment bag. He hung it in the closet and slowly unzipped it. In it were a suit—one of the sharpest I'd ever seen—and a dress. Calling it a dress didn't do it justice—it was approaching gown territory. Isaac pulled two pairs of shoes from the bag and started stripping.

"I feel like I should get an updo and a manicure to do this justice." The sleeveless dress was emerald green chiffon with ruched bodice and a V-neck that dipped enough to be tantalizing, but not enough to be a potential wardrobe malfunction. The skirt ended above the knee and flared out delightfully. It was gorgeous. I took off my jeans and t-shirt and glanced over at Isaac when he made a noise. He was staring at me, naked lust in his eyes, and my knees went a bit weak.

"Here." He thrust a small bag at me. Inside were a strapless bra and the matching silk G-string. After replacing my underthings, freshening up with a sink wash in the bathroom, and pulling my hair up into a messy—but hopefully elegant—bun, I slid the dress over my head and had Isaac zip me up. A near-stranger stared back at from the full-length mirror. I'd gone from mildly attractive to sixties siren. I practiced my most alluring smile but succeeded only in looking like I had indigestion.

I looked at the shoes for the first time. "Holy shit! Crystal-encrusted Christian Louboutins? These must have cost a fortune!"

"I'm surprised you recognized them. I didn't think you were much of a shoe person."

"I've watched the Oscars—and the red sole is distinctive. Otherwise, I wouldn't have."

My feet slid easily into the shoes and waited for the anticipated wicked discomfort—a four-inch heel does not inspire the expectation of comfort. They weren't bad, though. I wouldn't want to wear them for hours, and not because they cost more than everything else I owned combined.

Isaac pulled me towards him, and we looked at ourselves in the mirror. He looked amazing. From his black wingtips to his black suit —not even a subtle pinstripe to break it up—and his shirt was almost blindingly white. I touched the shirt—the material felt thick and rich and was nothing like the business casual shirts I was used to seeing. The only spot of color was his garnet-colored tie.

"You look gorgeous," I said.

"Right back at you."

I gazed at our reflection until we were interrupted again by a knock. "If you're ready, sir, madam." The servant didn't betray a flicker of surprise at how well we'd cleaned up, which was disappointing. He led us to the library where Florence waited. She, too, had dressed up in a floor-length, brilliantly blue off-the-shoulder gown. It flowed over her shape perfectly and sparkled here and there with randomly placed crystals.

"Wow! Florence! You look fantastic. When did you guys go shopping? And why?"

"It's useful being a psychic. Most people think it's all 'the world is in danger' or 'a dark man is stalking you from the shadows,' but there's a fair amount of 'bring an umbrella' and 'you'll need a cocktail dress.'"

"You're awesome," I said.

"I know." She smirked.

Joseph and Candace arrived hand-in-hand, followed by a server bearing a tray of champagne cocktails. After everyone had a drink, Joseph got down to business.

"Isaac, you and your people can stay for one night because we've been friends for a hundred years and my lady is generous, but you need to be straight with me. Why are you traveling with a mage and a Fae?" He made Fae sound like a dirty word. I opened my mouth to protest, but Isaac's hand on my arm stilled me.

"There are three reasons, and it is a long story. Would you like to hear it now, or wait until after dinner when we'll have time to sit and digest both the sure-to-be-excellent meal as well as this tale?"

"Let us talk only of light and bubbly things now," Candace decided. "A champagne conversation to go with our champagne cocktails."

We discussed the local soccer rivalry between the Chicago Pack and the Chicago Pride. Not a mention of the strange events in Portland and the Black Hills. No speculation about the probability of terrorist attack versus solar flares. I knew little about soccer and even less about the local teams, so I tuned out. Something was up with Isaac. He was hiding something from me. I thought we'd taken care of all this nonsense when he'd told me about Emma and Michelle. My stomach knotted with nerves and I gulped my champagne to try to soothe my agitation. I set down the glass and turned back to the group in time to see Florence eying me with what looked like pity. I didn't know if she was reading my thoughts, Isaac's thoughts, or the future, but whatever she saw wasn't good. The champagne I'd swallowed tried to make a reappearance and a line of sweat broke out on my hairline. She turned back to the others. Short of making a scene—which was not my style—there was nothing to do now. I took some deep, even breaths and attempted to slow my heart rate before the predators in the room noticed.

THERE WERE a dozen people already in the dining room when our small group arrived.

"Most of the pride lives in the neighborhood," Candace explained. I sat next to her at one end of the table. Joseph and Isaac were at the other end, and Florence was about halfway down. "The only ones who stay at the house are pregnant females, females who are in heat, and the males they've chosen to mate with."

I tried to discern which of my fellow diners were pregnant and which were in heat. Other than the two women who looked to be approaching the end of their terms, there was no way to tell unless I started asking questions, and I was savvy enough to know that was never a good idea.

Dinner was delicious, but I couldn't tell you after what we'd eaten. The wine flowed too freely to allow for stilted conversation, and I found myself babbling away to the woman seated next to me about coffee and beer. I was sober enough to guard my tongue when it came to more sensitive subjects, and when she poured me another glass of wine, batted her eyelashes at me winsomely, and asked if I had a sensitivity to iron, I was glad my metabolism worked as well as it did. I ignored the wine in favor of the glass of water in front of me and tried to catch Isaac's eye.

It looked like he and Joseph were arguing—which meant everyone in the room who was paying attention, except me with under-developed hearing, could hear them. I slowed my breathing and tried to hone in on Isaac's voice, ignoring everything else.

"...nothing more than a trap?" Isaac sounded angry.

"It's not like that," Joseph replied. "You are my friend. I would never do anything to would harm you."

"It's not me I'm worried about."

"She is Fae. You said on the phone she was your mate, but you left out the part where she was Fae—the Fae we're supposed to watch for. She's blinded you, enthralled you. The mage is in league with her—or possibly another thrall. Can't you see she's using you? She's certainly not beautiful enough to have caught your eye without magical aid."

I gasped out loud. Isaac looked across the room and caught my eye. He winked at me. It didn't look like Joseph had noticed I was listening.

"Joseph, my friend. I am not enthralled—at least not magically. The hold she has on me isn't unnatural any more than the hold Candace has over you. And if you ever insult her again in my hearing, we will have more than words. I was assigned by my Alpha to watch her when we realized who she was and what she was going to do. The first time she saw me, she threw a knife at me. I'm one of the oldest wolves on this continent, and even though I was not at my best, she shouldn't have been able to get a knife in me at all. If I hadn't been quick—and if her knife had been silver—she would've killed me. It was a perfect heart shot."

"Dammit!" I said. "I can't believe you let me think I'd missed all this time!"

Conversation stopped, and everyone at the table turned to look at me. I blushed. Busted.

Isaac laughed, and Joseph squirmed in his seat.

Candace clapped her hands, commanding the attention of everyone in the room. "Joseph and I will have brandies with our guests in the drawing room. The rest of you will retire for the evening."

Chairs were scraped back, and the other diners slowly trickled out amid a buzz of conversation.

I approached Isaac and Florence at the foot of the table.

"Are we safe here?" I asked. I didn't bother to whisper.

"I don't know," he replied.

"Of course you're safe here," Candace said. "We offered you shelter for the evening, and we won't break hospitality. But come now; this is not a conversation to have in front of the help."

I shot a sympathetic look at the people clearing the table. I wasn't impressed with people who weren't polite to those they deemed inferior. Real character manifests in how well you treat those who have no recourse against you.

In the drawing room, which didn't appear to be a good room for drawing at all—there was only one tiny window—full brandy snifters awaited us. Candace shut the door, took a snifter, and then sat in the almost throne-like chair, leaving the rest of us to follow.

"Tell us your tale now, Isaac," Candace commanded. "I would hear how you came to be traveling with a mage and a Fae. We know who she is and what she's been doing, and I want to know why I should let her go tomorrow."

I bit back a smirk. Candace obviously didn't know everything about me if she thought she could hold me. Our room had a fucking balcony. I wouldn't fly away and leave Florence and Isaac behind, but still. I could totally escape.

Isaac took a long sip of his brandy before beginning his story.

"Joseph, may I assume you've told Candace about Michelle?"

"I have."

He took another sip and then began. "When I was finally freed from Michelle after the vampire currently known as Raj Allred took over her territory and the territory of all vampire clans in the Pacific Northwest, I was returned alive but damaged to Charles. Charles had been the Alpha in the greater Portland area since my disappearance, having been my second when I had that role. Even in my brief years of freedom in the sixties, he maintained the Alpha role because my damaged control wouldn't serve me if I tried to reclaim my position.

"Charles tried to help me with my control, but as I was still stronger, he was unable to do so. He couldn't put a call out for a more powerful wolf to help me, because that would leave him vulnerable to a hostile takeover as any wolf strong enough to aid me would then, of course, be stronger than him. I spent most of my time alone in my house in the woods, close enough to draw on the pack's control to aid my own during the full moon, but far enough away to let Charles maintain the fiction of his dominance.

"Charles came to me when the local coven informed him the gates of magic keeping the Fae out of this world were weakening, and the first lock would break in Portland. He'd seen two Fae in the forest, looking for something not on any established trail. He wanted me to confront and take out these Fae.

"I waited until Eleanor appeared alone. I'd made great pains to hide my scent so she couldn't smell the wolf on me. Even though she was startled, she not only maintained her poise, she attacked. As you may have heard earlier, if I'd been any slower, her knife would've pierced my heart. It was steel, and the wound wouldn't have been fatal, but it would've hurt like hell. I retreated and shifted at the edge of the clearing. After that encounter, I knew I could never kill her.

"I watched. A few nights later, I followed her and her companion to a bar catering to supernaturals. Her companion was a regular attendee, but it was clear she'd never been there before."

I was startled. Finn hadn't said he'd been there before, but he certainly let me believe it was his first time, too. I'd be asking Isaac a few questions later. I had a feeling the more I knew about Finn's motivations, the better I'd be able to defend against whatever shit he sprung next.

Isaac glossed over the back hallway shenanigans and told the rest of the gate opening story. There were no more surprises for me, and I breathed a quiet sigh of relief.

When Isaac concluded his tale—ending it with the warning that everything was about to change—both lions turned their gazes to me.

I felt pinned for a second, and then remembered that although they were predators, no one was above me on the food chain. I pulled the dragon forward enough to feel the power course through my blood and smiled at them. Joseph looked away, but Candace did not. Interesting.

"Now what? Will you send an assassin after me when we leave?"

Candace ignored my questions. "What are your intentions? After you've destroyed the world, will you leash all shifters the way you've leashed your wolf? You must be powerful to have neutered him so thoroughly."

"My goal is to open the gates and allow magic to saturate the world again. There is only one shifter who holds my interest. He is free to stay or go as he wishes, and if he chooses to leave, I won't stop him. I don't know what to offer you that will appease you and not compromise my word. We will search for the third gate whether or not you approve. My question remains: will you send assassins after us tomorrow?"

"I suggest you leave at first light. I will not have the balance of my world upset because some Fae upstart has delusions of glory. William will show you back to your rooms." She pressed a button, and the door opened.

Our guide from earlier was in the doorway. "This way, please."

Florence followed us into our room. "Candace was telling the truth. If we leave at first light, no harm will come to us."

CHAPTER THREE

I T WAS TOO damn early the next morning when Isaac woke me up. I dressed blearily, wishing I could ring William for a cup of coffee. Less than a day with servants—and most of that asleep— had spoiled me. If I ever took the throne—something I still wasn't sure was plausible or desirable—I'd exalt the royal coffee bringer above all others.

We were dressed and ready to go way before first light. Florence was waiting in the hall, and William appeared at the end of the corridor.

"Joseph would see you in the drawing room before you leave. I've taken the liberty of having fresh coffee prepared to sustain you on your journey." William was definitely in the running for best servant of all time.

I hadn't been too excited to meet with 'Mr. She's Not That Good Looking,' but for coffee, I'd make the sacrifice. Joseph was waiting by the single window. A coffee pot, cups, and a basket of scones were on the side table.

I helped myself to a cup of coffee. The cups were way too small— who drank coffee out of something like these?—but the coffee was magnificent.

I took another fortifying sip as Joseph began to speak.

"Isaac, I can't pretend to understand why you're doing this, and I'm still suspicious of your Fae and the hold she has on you, but you and I have been friends for a century. If we forgot those ties every time one of us had a lapse in judgment, our friendship would've ended after the dance hall incident of 1917." Isaac and Joseph laughed uproariously. I rolled my eyes.

"Since we're all besties again, what's the deal with holding us up until sunrise?" I asked. "Are you supposed to make sure we're still here at first light so your mate can attempt to have me killed?"

"Of course not!" Joseph sounded outraged. I wasn't buying it. "I wanted to say goodbye to my oldest friend, let him know I'd secured the vehicle he requested, and give him some advice on how to avoid Candace's people."

"And you expect me to believe you're here without Candace's knowledge? I saw your relationship dynamic. You probably wouldn't wipe your ass without a permission slip."

"Eleanor, stop." Isaac's voice silenced me and a wave of shame heated my face. Joseph was one of Isaac's best friends, and I was treating him even more shabbily than he'd treated me. I was definitely not ready to grace the cover of "How to Win Friends and Influence People."

"I'm sorry, Joseph. I am suspicious of your intentions, and my tongue ran away with me. I hope you'll accept my apology."

Joseph bowed stiffly in my direction. "Of course. It would be ungracious in the extreme to not." He turned to Isaac. "Perhaps we could finish our conversation in private? I'll have William show your women to the new car. He can load the luggage for them."

I squashed the urge to put a knife in Joseph's back. You'd think someone who was essentially a favored plaything of a queen would be a little less misogynistic. I looked at Florence. The air around her was taking on a decidedly crystalized look. "Florence? Chill. Or, more accurately, don't."

Florence tamped down her temper and the lines in her face smoothed out again. She held out her hand to Joseph, and he took it.

She stared into his face for a second and then dropped it. "Thank you for the night's shelter. It's been interesting."

William came back into the room, grabbed our bags, and Florence and I followed him out. In the driveway next to the mini-van was another car. A weird-ass looking station wagon.

"What's that?" I asked. It was fascinatingly ugly.

"A 1956 Hudson Rambler," William answered. "They're extremely rare."

"Probably because they're ugly," Florence observed.

"I like it."

William placed our bags in the large trunk-region and I noticed there were six five-gallon gas cans strapped down as well.

"Do you know what kind of mileage this thing gets?" I asked.

"I believe the highway mileage is above thirty," William replied.

"Thank you. This car is amazing."

"It was a pleasure serving you. I wish you the best of luck in your future endeavors. Do not worry over-much about the wrath of Candace. She will be distracted today, and will soon forget about you."

I looked more closely at William. I'd known he wasn't human—an elderly man couldn't carry that many bags with ease—but I'd assumed he was a shifter. For a moment, instead of an old man, I saw a mahogany creature about three feet tall with pointed ears, too-long limbs, and an oversized nose. A pointed cap crowned his long, white hair and his only other clothing was a loincloth.

"Brownie," I whispered.

"Indeed, Your Majesty." He bowed and his human façade slipped back into place.

He disappeared into the mansion and I grinned. The day was definitely looking up.

"What did you see?" Florence asked.

"I'll tell you later," I thought at her.

We stood and waited. And waited. It was almost 6:30 now, and the sun would be up soon. I started to get nervous. Five minutes later, Isaac stalked out of the house. We all got into the car—I was driving—and left the estate.

"Before you yell at her, you need to know she was right," Florence said.

Isaac's lips pressed into a thin line. Our relationship was still shiny and new, and this was the first time he'd been mad at me. It sucked. I opened my mouth to apologize again, but Isaac spoke first, "Not now, Eleanor."

Knowing I was right wasn't enough to quell the sick feeling twisting my gut. My mind kept swirling over everything I could've done differently until I was ready to scream. I needed something to center me before I inadvertently lit the car on fire. "Florence, do you have the map back there? I need a little navigational assistance."

Florence gave me directions to the freeway, but other than that, the only noise was the traffic. After a couple of hours, I needed a break. Too much tension on top of the coffee left me with an urgent need to pee. I pulled off the freeway and into the nearest greasy spoon.

When I got back out to the dining area, Florence and Isaac were leaning into each other across a table. I couldn't hear them, but based on the rigid set of Isaac's shoulders and Florence's emphatic gesticulation, it was intense. I loitered near the counter until the waitress started giving me stink eye, then clomped over and slid in beside Isaac. After ordering coffee and second breakfast, Florence excused herself and headed towards the back of the diner.

Never one to beat around the bush, I decided to put on my big girl panties and start talking.

"I'm sorry. I shouldn't have been such an asshat to your friend. I could've found a more polite way to make my suspicions known. I handled myself poorly."

Silence stretched out between us and I sat on my hands to keep from fidgeting. I peeked at Isaac through my lashes, hoping to see his expression soften.

I was about to figuratively die from stress before Isaac said, "I'm sorry, too. I should know you well enough to know your instincts about people are excellent."

As long as we ignore Finn's existence in my life, I thought to myself.

22

"Florence filled me in on Joseph's thoughts while you were in the bathroom. She offered a few unsolicited opinions about my character while she was at it. As you suspected, he was trying to delay us until daybreak. He is helpless to Candace's whims, and his accusations of me being in your thrall are laughable after finding out you were right about his inability to do anything without express permission."

I opened my mouth to offer sympathy or empathy or a solid condemnation of his now presumably ex-friend, but he interrupted, "Let me finish. Maybe you were right about Joseph, but you were also right a moment ago. You handled it in a piss-poor manner, and I'm still mad at you. I'm angry you insulted my friend with no fucking evidence."

My mouth closed and my stomach dropped.

No one spoke again until we returned to the car after paying for brunch.

"I'm driving," Florence said. "You two sit in the back and make up."

I didn't want to, but it's impossible to argue with Florence. Isaac joined me in the back seat with zero protest.

After thirty minutes of charged silence, Florence said, "Since you're not ready to make up, maybe Eleanor could tell us about William?"

I filled them in on what I'd seen when he dropped his glamour—or when my eyes penetrated his glamour. When Florence confirmed she hadn't seen anything weird at all, it seemed like the latter was more likely.

"A brownie, eh?" Isaac asked. "I don't know much about them."

"My experience with brownies is confined to illicit foodstuffs," Florence said.

"What now?" I couldn't have been more shocked if she'd told me she ate babies for breakfast.

"Delicious and relaxing," Florence said. "You two should try them. You're both too uptight."

Isaac chuckled but refused to meet my eyes. The laughter that had been bubbling up inside me quickly dissipated. In the scheme of things, a lovers' quarrel wasn't a big thing, but it felt more insurmountable than finding and opening six more gates in nine months without the aid of electricity, indoor plumbing, and the internet. I charged onward, trying not to jump to conclusions with a single bound.

"William the Brownie who, as far as I could tell, was not made of pot offered his support, such as it is. I'm still learning all the Fae stuff, and without our resident Fae resource, a lot of this is vague memories and semi-educated guesses. Brownies are earth Fae tied to an individual family—like Dobby the house elf. They take great pride in keeping the house and grounds spotless and make excellent housekeepers and butlers. This one seemed loyal to me—or, at least he knew who I was and wanted me out of his sphere of influence alive. Either way, it worked."

ONCE WE'D SETTLED into our Cleveland motel rooms, I ordered a pizza, Isaac did a beer run, and Florence pulled out the maps and guide books.

When the anticipated knock came on the door, I peered through the peephole to ensure there was a pizza out there. I didn't care if a dozen vamps were delivering it, but if they didn't have pizza, I wasn't opening the door.

I paid the pizza delivery person and set our dinner on the table.

"When I finish knocking out the grid, what will happen to banking? Will what money people have be precious, or will these twenties be worthless?"

Florence and Isaac sported identical expressions of shock.

"Shit," Isaac said. "I hadn't thought of that."

"What currency will get us what we need to finish the trip? We might want to look into obtaining some while we still can," I said.

"What will be valuable in a post-currency world? I used to read a lot of post-apocalyptic novels, and in them, the economy usually reverted to a barter system," Florence said. "We should slowly withdraw all our funds and keep a large cash stockpile to use up before people realize it's worthless."

"Isn't that kind of...wrong? I don't want to cheat people."

"You can attempt to barter if you'd rather, but most people will think you're trying to cheat them. I've seen it in stories."

I shrugged. It was nothing but speculation now anyway. "What do we do when our worthless cash money is either gone or actually worthless?"

"Before that happens, we'll spend the cash on non-perishable but valuable items we can use to barter."

"Like what?"

"We'll want to think about our needs as well—we'll continue to need food even when there's no more access to take out."

I sighed melodramatically. "Destroying the world is no big deal, really. I mean, I'll miss the internet, but no more Taco Bell is an absolute travesty. I wish I'd realized that was a possibility." I was hoping my light-hearted black comedy would lighten the atmosphere between Isaac and me.

Florence said, "In addition to ensuring we have enough food, we'll need things with a high trade value: ammunition, gasoline, coffee, alcohol, and medicine. A stockpile of those items will help us barter our way across the country."

I grabbed a slice of pizza and took the beer Isaac handed me, mulling over a future without paper currency. A growing sense of unease had weighed me down all day, and it was easier to think about living in a pre-industrial era than to try to pinpoint what was wrong.

I'd assumed it was my fight with Isaac, but something in my gut told me that wasn't it. It wasn't until I'd polished off the last slice of pizza that it hit me. "We're going the wrong way. Something's felt weird all day, and it wasn't until right now that I figured it out. Before you ask, I don't know what the right way is, but this isn't it."

Florence finished her slice and unfolded the map, tracing a route in pencil. "I propose we take Route Three south through Columbus and Cincinnati. You will concentrate on your weird feelings. If we don't get a hit by the time we're in Cincinnati, we'll continue through Kentucky and then Tennessee. Hopefully, by the time we get to Memphis, you'll have a general direction in mind—either south to Mississippi or North to Illinois. If we make haste slowly, you'll pick something up, right?"

"Maybe? I didn't feel the second gate until I was about ten miles from it."

"But you didn't feel the first gate until you were within one mile," Isaac pointed out. "Your sensitivity and range are both increasing."

"Cities deaden it, though. There's too much iron and concrete. I can't feel it as easily here. I hate what I'm going to say next, but we need to camp as much as possible. I need to spend more time sitting in the dirt and less sitting in crappy motel rooms. Plus, if refrigeration is going away, I'd like to spend the next month eating Isaac's amazing camp fire meat creations."

"Perhaps you can drop me off in the nearest town every night," Florence said. "I can be in charge of stockpiling our post-apocalyptic stash."

"You don't want to camp with us?" I asked. "I thought you liked camping."

"What gave you that impression?"

"The two weeks we spent in the Badlands?"

"It was necessary to camp because we needed wilderness to practice your magic and flying. Not because I wanted to spend two weeks in a tent and drinking water from a questionable tap in the middle of nowhere."

"But shouldn't you like being one with the land?"

"Because I'm an Indian? Seriously?"

"I was going to say mage," I said.

"Fair point. I like connecting to the earth, but I also like sleeping in a bed. Speaking of which, that's what I'm going to do right now."

Florence returned to her room, and Isaac and I were finally alone. I looked at him, hoping he'd initiate a conversation that started with 'I'm over it,' moved to 'let's kiss and make up,' and ended with us in bed. He went into the bathroom and closed the door. I heard the shower turn on and opened another beer.

I'd finished two and was contemplating a third before the shower shut off. Either I was drinking extraordinarily fast, or Isaac was avoiding me. I checked the clock. Ninety minutes had gone by since Florence had taken her leave. Definitely some avoidance happening here.

I briefly considered stripping down before he walked into the room, but dismissed that idea as unnecessarily desperate. If he was still mad tomorrow night, I'd pull out the big guns—my boobs.

I dug through my pack and grabbed pajamas. I'd finished my third beer and was well into the book on Mound Builders of the Mississippi Valley before Isaac reappeared. I barely glanced up—this stuff was fascinating. I'd hoped something would reach out and grab me, but the photographs didn't exhibit any hidden power.

Isaac dropped his towel, and I dropped my book. I attempted to ogle surreptitiously but gave it up as a bad job fairly quickly. I congratulated myself for being the mature one and watched—maturely—as Isaac bent over to pull a pair of boxer briefs from his bag. I licked my lips then suppressed my groan of disappointment when he pulled them on.

He turned and caught me staring. I blushed, which pissed me off and made me feel belligerent. He raised an eyebrow at me, and since I still lacked the ability to do the same, I rolled my eyes back. Isaac grinned and sat down next to me. I held my breath. Was it finally kiss and make up time?

"I'm sorry," he said.

"Me, too."

He brushed his lips against mine. I wanted to press forward and throw myself into his arms, but held back, still a bit unsure of my reception.

I leaned back. "I don't know if I can do this."

He quirked that damnable eyebrow at me again. "Kissing?"

I punched him in the shoulder. "I hate that I'm not sure if you'll pull away if I try to take things further. I hate that I second guess myself. I hate that I spent all day freaking out about a relationship. This isn't me. I don't have relationships, and if I do, they're one-sided

—and it's not my side. I don't do relationship freak outs. I don't do fights. I definitely don't do sick feelings that make me want to simultaneously throw up and curl into the fetal position."

Isaac pulled away from me. "Are you saying you don't want this? One fight is all it takes for you to walk away."

"No!" I was louder than necessary. I tried to convince myself it wasn't because I was trying to convince myself. It had to be the truth because I was able to say it, right? "I want you. I don't want the crap parts."

Isaac exhaled forcefully, then pulled me into his arms. "Have you ever been in a relationship before?"

"Not one that's lasted this long, and never one I cared about."

"This long? We've only known each other for a couple of months."

"Your point?"

"My point is by the ripe old age of thirty-four, a lot of people have been in a relationship or two."

I tensed and tried to extract myself from his arms, but he didn't loosen his hold. "I'm not good with people. Are you trying to fight again?"

"No. I didn't realize how new this all was for you."

"I've never felt this way before. I've never let anyone hurt me this badly and then stuck around for what's next. You confound me."

Isaac dropped a kiss on the tip of my nose. "I'm sorry, Eleanor." He kissed each of my cheeks. "I'm sorry for not being able to drop my anger sooner." He brushed his lips against mine. "I'm sorry for making you doubt yourself and my love for you." His hands slid to my waist, found the hem of my tank top, and slowly slid it up. His thumbs skimmed my bare nipples, and I gasped. "I'm sorry I hurt you." He pulled my shirt over my head in one swift movement and leaned down to flick my nipples with his tongue—first one and then the other.

"Before we go any further, I have something to say, too." My sentence devolved into a moan as Isaac sucked my left nipple into his mouth. "Please?" I wasn't sure if I was asking him to stop or to keep going. He stopped, and I quelled my disappointment.

"I feel bad I accused your friend of having ill intent, and even worse that I was right. I was a jerk. A jerk who sucks at relationships."

Isaac's fingers resumed their journey over my skin, trailing over my hips and sliding under the material of my silky boy shorts. I grabbed his face and pulled him down to my mouth, kissing him like it was the last time I'd feel his tongue against mine. A ferocity I didn't recognize swelled in my chest.

Claim him. Mark him. I jumped. My inner voice didn't often surprise me. It was my inner voice, after all. But this was new.

"Are you okay?" Isaac asked.

"Yes. My inner monologue is a bit off today."

"Are you trying to get out of this?" He ran a hand between my legs, cupping my sex and rubbing his thumb over the growing wetness on the material. I lost my train of thought. He laid on top of me, forcing my legs apart. His hardness strained against the twin barriers of his underwear and mine, and I wanted those barriers gone. Now. I grasped him, lifted my hips, pressing myself even tighter against him, and started shimmying off my shorts.

"Are you going to share?" Isaac asked, helping me strip before removing his boxer briefs. He plunged into me and then held excruciatingly still. I tried to wiggle underneath him, but I was pinned down. Heat built in my center, but without a release, I was sure I'd explode. I tried to remember the question.

"Something about claiming and marking."

"Oh," he said. Then he started to move.

"Oh? What's that mean?" Isaac moved faster and faster, and I let go of my questions—for now. He brought me to the cusp of orgasm over and over, then stopped and waited for the fires to bank before starting over.

"Isaac Walker, I am going to murder you if you do that again," I said through gritted teeth.

He laughed, and this time when we reached the edge, he didn't stop. We fell together, and it was glorious.

A bit later, after some cuddles and clean-up, I asked again. "Why 'Oh?'"

"Do you know what claiming and marking mean to a shifter?"

"Do you know how obnoxious it is to answer a question with a question?"

Isaac laughed. "Fair enough. To claim or mark someone is to permanently designate them as your mate. It's a metaphysical sign to all other shifters—and any other supernaturals who care to see—that a person is mated and unavailable."

"Like a sign saying 'Keep Away—This One's Mine?'"

"More like a wedding ring."

"Oh."

We spent a few minutes not making eye contact, although that might have been entirely one-sided. I didn't want to look up to find out, but I was a grown-up, dammit.

Isaac didn't look nearly as terrified as I felt. In fact, if I were to analyze his expression, I might be forced to describe it as barely repressed excitement. I narrowed my eyes. He repressed a little bit more.

"There are benefits. The exchange of marks occurs by biting off and swallowing a bit of each other's flesh. For the bonding to take effect, both parties have to participate. The marks, once active, will stay active until one of the partners dies. It really is a "'Til Death Do You Part" joining, which makes it unattractive to most people. Few couples go through the claiming unless they're one hundred percent positive they've found a true soul mate.

"The marks alert you when your mate is in proximity and allows for a conversational telepathy between mates—even those that don't have psychic skills. It allows strong surges of emotions to get through the bond, which can be unfortunate if one person is in pain and can't control what's being exchanged. The proximity alert and the psychic bonds would allow one to find their mate if they had gone missing."

"Huh." I was definitely winning this conversation.

"Are you okay?"

"A little confused. A couple hours ago, we were fighting, and now we're talking about marriage."

"You brought it up."

"I wouldn't have if I'd known what I was bringing up," I muttered.

"Are you opposed to the idea?" Isaac asked. He was motionless.

I didn't know how to answer. I couldn't lie, but I didn't want to hurt his feelings. "It's a big 180 from where we were earlier today when I thought you were ready to pull the plug on us. It's fast, Isaac. Responsible and rational women don't think about marriage two months into a relationship."

"The magazines say I'm the one who's supposed to have commitment issues—not you," Isaac said. He pulled me into his arms.

"Magazines don't get me. I don't care much about clothes or shoes, I've never worried about how to keep my man, I don't spend a lot of time worrying about flat abs in advance of bikini season, and I don't need sixty sex tips to rock my guy's world."

Isaac kissed me. "You rock my world. I assumed it was because of your secret Cosmo subscription."

I laughed. "All home grown moves, baby."

"We're moving off subject."

"That was deliberate."

"Five more minutes, and then I promise to drop it," Isaac said.

"Deal."

"The words 'mark' and 'claim' popped into your head? Had you ever heard them before?"

"Not that I recall."

"It wouldn't be the first time foresight popped up. Could it be that?"

I mulled that over. "That's the most likely explanation. We should ask Florence tomorrow."

"Don't freak out," Isaac said.

"I'm not freaking out."

"I didn't mean right now." He got out of bed and rummaged through his bag. I enjoyed the view and tried not to freak out. It's much harder not to freak out when someone tells you specifically not to freak out.

Isaac climbed back into bed. He was holding a small box. I did not hyperventilate, but it was a near thing.

He opened it, and instead of the diamond solitaire I was dreading, there was a simple blue and brown band. I looked at Isaac, "What is it?"

"It's an engagement ring," he answered. "Will you marry me?"

I opened my mouth—I still wasn't hyperventilating—and asked, "What's it made of?"

"Petrified wood and turquoise. It won't trigger either of our metal allergies."

"How long have you had it?"

"Decades." Isaac tried to catch my eye, but I avoided it. I didn't know if it was better or worse that he hadn't gotten this ring specifically for me. Isaac tried to slip the ring on my finger.

I pulled back. "This is weird."

"Are you going to say yes?"

"I don't know. I'm not ready."

"But your spidey sense says you are."

"My spidey sense is not one hundred percent reliable. It said Finn was a good friend."

"The best time to do the ceremony is around the full moon."

"When is the full moon?" I asked. I was not freaking out.

"The next one is October 18—it's the Hunter's Moon."

"And today is?"

"September 25."

"That's less than a month." I swallowed. Hard.

"So, will you?" Isaac asked.

"I need some time." I'd never even told him I loved him. *I will not barf during a proposal.*

"How much?"

"We should stop talking about it now. Your five minutes are more than up." I said. A part of me died when hurt flashed across his face. "We can talk about it tomorrow. Let's get some sleep."

CHAPTER FOUR

W HEN I WOKE the next morning, I immediately felt the weight of Isaac's proposal and felt the ring taunting me from its box. It might not weigh much physically, but the emotional weight was greater than I'd ever felt.

"Ready to talk?" Isaac asked, handing me a cup of coffee.

I took a sip of coffee. It was too early to fight, and telling him I didn't want to get married would lead to a fight. Come to think of it, telling him I didn't want to talk might lead to a fight. The only fightless scenario I could think of involved accepting a marriage proposal I wasn't ready for.

I sipped my coffee and opted for an enigmatic smile. Then I grimaced. This wasn't coffee. I shuddered. "We should stock up on good coffee at the first available opportunity. I don't want to have to get through the rest of this year living on Sanka."

"Are you changing the subject?"

"Absolutely."

Isaac didn't even bother to hide the hurt my statement caused, and I felt terrible, but not terrible enough to agree to marry him when I wasn't sure that was the right decision.

His jaw tightened, and he started packing up his stuff. "A survival kit is our first priority. We'll need drinking water, and water filters."

"Good thing we have that big-ass car."

"Are we headed towards Columbus?" At my nod, he continued, "When we get there, I'll find someone to modify the trunk to conceal our goods. If I know anything about human beings, once resources become scarce, their vaunted humanity goes out the door."

"That sounded bitter," I said.

"Seeing Joseph stirred up a lot of shit. What happened to me at the hands of a vampire was horrific, but Michelle has nothing on what humans do to those they deem lesser. Human beings have as great a capacity for evil as anything else I've ever encountered."

"This," I waved my hands to encompass everything that was going on, "is going to bring supernaturals into the public eye, isn't it?"

"Yes. It might be feasible for them to stay hidden, but there will be fewer reasons and incentive to do so. Some will object to opening the gates because they don't want to be forced into the open."

"There have to be those tired of hiding, too."

"There likely are, but they might resent not being able to choose the way their presence is revealed."

"I'm providing a service. By generating this much chaos, there are bigger things to worry about than the existence of werewolves."

"You are such a public servant," Isaac said. His grin didn't hide the pain still haunting his eyes.

Fuck. Why couldn't I be what anyone needed? I shook myself and tried to stay light-hearted. "I will dedicate my life to the human race."

He snorted, and there was a knock on the door. "Is everyone decent?" Florence asked.

WE PULLED over for every historical marker, took every scenic route, and stopped for the night in the small town of Coshocton. I'd felt nothing all day other than the vague sense of wrongness, but I couldn't even tell which direction I was being pulled. As a compass, I was vastly overrated.

The next morning, we headed out early. We had only one stop planned before heading on to Columbus, but Florence thought it might be our best shot in Ohio. We arrived at the Newark Earthworks early enough to be the first car in the parking lot. It was a place of power, but not my place of power.

We drove from the Earthworks to Columbus. It was lunchtime, so I pulled into a Taco Bell—had to get my fix before they were gone. Isaac excused himself to make a phone call. Florence and I sat in silence for a bit as I downed my second burrito.

"I thought there'd be less tension today. Didn't you two kiss and make up?"

"Uhhh," I said, rather cleverly.

"What's scaring you?"

"Isaac proposed."

"Based on your lack of ring, I'll assume you said no?"

"I didn't say no, but I didn't say yes."

"Why not?"

"We've known each other for two months. I fell fast, and I fell hard, but I'm not marrying someone—especially not in an irrevocable shifter bonding—without being sure. We were thrown together in a highly stressful situation. That doesn't usually equal a lasting partnership."

"That all makes sense. But then why not say no?"

I heaved a dramatic sigh. "Because last night, when we were making up, my vaguely prophetic inner voice urged me to claim and mark him. I didn't think much of it, but Isaac knew what that meant. By the look on your face, you do, too. What do you know, Florence? Spill it."

"He loves you more than he's loved anyone in his very long life."

"That's not why you made that face. Do you know something?"

"Do you love him?"

"Ugh. I hate it when people answer questions with another question."

AMY CISSELL

"Do you?"

"I don't know." I'd all but shouted it.

Florence leaned back and steepled her fingers. I slumped in my seat, unable to eat anything more.

"Why are you angry?"

"If you know how I feel, you know why."

"Say it out loud. You need to know, too."

I rolled my eyes. "I am tired of being pushed every which way by fate, and the Fae, and men who want more from me than I can give. Maybe what I feel for Isaac will continue to grow into more than lust and friendship, and extreme fondness. But I don't know if I'm capable of love. Is any Fae?"

Florence reached across the table and took my hand. From the way she stiffened, I guessed she was picking up something I probably didn't want to know.

Focus returned to her eyes, and she looked at me. "I won't tell you what to do, but I will tell you creating a mate-bond with him will someday save each of your lives. However, it will not be without serious consequence."

"Can it be broken?"

"Do you want it to be?" Isaac asked from behind me.

I bowed my head. "How long have you been there?"

"Long enough."

"You didn't think it necessary to let me know?"

"You should've known I was there."

"Maybe I should've, but you should've told me when you realized I didn't know. I didn't want to hurt your feelings." I'd spent an awful lot of time feeling badly lately. "Did you find someone to work on the car?"

"A friend of Rebecca's agreed to do the work on the car. Rebecca said she owed me several favors for backing her during her Alpha challenge and giving the Black Hills pack fair warning about their mini-apocalypse."

"That's nice," I said.

"Changing the subject isn't going to be that easy. Don't you want a permanent bond?"

"Do we have to do this here? Now?"

"Why not? You're a lot more open with Florence than you are with me, so maybe now is the best time to have this conversation."

Fucking men and their tiny fucking egos. Age and experience didn't offset that at all. "Fine. I will do the mate-bonding with you under the next full moon."

"Don't do me any favors," Isaac bit out.

"If you heard the whole conversation, you know it'll be doing us both a favor. If this will save you, I will do it."

"Even though you're merely "fond" of me?"

My body temperature rose along with my temper. I needed to burn off some steam before I said something I'd regret. I didn't know if it was Isaac's alpha bullshit shining through or if I didn't know him as well as I'd thought, but either way, it was pushing all my buttons in exactly the wrong way.

Florence must have sensed the impending conflagration because she interrupted. "Let's check into a motel and stow our personal belongings. Isaac, you can take the car to your friend, then we'll meet up and figure out what to do next."

"Fabulous idea," Isaac said. He stalked off without a backward glance.

Florence cast a protection spell on our possessions, citing a "weird vibe," and then Isaac took the car to his friend of a friend.

"Let's find some green and earth," Florence said. "You need to work on your shields. They're a little too good right now. I'd like you to keep the quality of the current shielding, but learn how to let the important stimuli through. No one should be able to sneak up on you."

I tilted my neck to one side and then the other, stretching the tension out of my connective tissue. "I hope we can find a place where I can spread my wings. I need the release."

"A city park at one o'clock in the afternoon isn't the ideal place for that, but we'll find some place we can go in the dark. There should be something appropriately dense near the river."

"Thanks. I thought by now I'd feel more integrated with my other self. Isaac and his wolf don't seem separate, but I still regard my dragon as a separate being I seldom think about."

"Have you ever asked Isaac how he feels about his wolf? How they interact?"

"Nooo…" I said.

"And have you spent much time with Isaac in wolf form?"

"No."

"You may want to ask him about it. Earth-bound shifters like your wolf might relate differently to their beasts than a Fae shifter, but probably not as much as you think."

"But shouldn't she be more a part of me?"

"How long has it been since you've known she was there; since the tattoo set her free?"

I counted back. "A little over a month."

"It's easy to think more time has passed when your days are action packed. A month isn't long to get used to knowing you're sharing your skin, especially since you're not forced to deal with it during a full moon like the earth-shifters are. However, you should work on building a better connection. Your dragon brings a lot of things to the table you're going to need. Earlier, I saw more than the mate-bond." She closed her eyes. "The path thus far has been easy, but that is about to end. Three battles are coming. You will be pitted against the blood drinkers, the magic casters, and the animal spirits before the next gate opens. The bond between a dragon and a wolf will save the other. Loss will precede the final triumph, but it is not the end. A vampire will be the cause of your greatest sorrow, and a vampire will help you find your greatest joy."

Florence opened her eyes again. "Let's go to the park."

I mulled over her words as we walked, but didn't question her until we'd found a patch of sunlight away from the few people milling about. "Do you know what it all meant?"

"It's self-explanatory. We'll be attacked by vamps, shifters, and mages. Constant vigilance is the order of the next few weeks."

"I got that part. I'm more interested in your interpretation of the second half. You know: the parts about bonding, loss and triumph, and sorrow, joy, and vampires. What more can you tell me about that?"

"I don't get footnotes with my visions."

I narrowed my eyes. "You're prevaricating."

Florence shrugged. "I can tell you nothing more. Now, let's work on your shields."

I let it go. For now. Florence never said more than she wanted to, but if there was going to be more loss, then why couldn't I at least be prepared? Maybe Florence would say that if I knew too much, I'd make a decision that, in an attempt to mitigate the effects of loss would cause the loss. But I didn't want to be hurt again. Losing a friend was hard enough—how much harder would losing a lover be? I shook my head, straightened my spine, and concentrated on shielding my heart and my thoughts.

I was dripping with sweat by the time she called a halt more than an hour later.

"You're doing remarkably well for someone who's less than half a year into her magic, but there is much more to learn. Your physical and magical fighting skills need to move to the forefront of your training. If we're going to face more attacks, you need to be ready to defend yourself by any means necessary."

"Another damn reason to camp again. More room, less chance someone will wonder why I'm throwing knives, waving my sword around, and playing with fire."

"And that's before we bring the dragon and wolf out to play."

"Do you think Isaac will cooperate?"

Florence's phone rang. "Speak of the devil."

"What are we going to do when our cell phones don't work anymore?" I asked, feeling a bit panicked.

"I expect we'll find a way."

AFTER DARK, Florence led us to a thickly wooded area along the banks of the Olentangy River. I was practically vibrating with tension by the time we got there. Isaac was barely talking to me, and rather than fueling my guilt; it made me angrier.

Once we found a clearing large enough, I stripped and called the dragon to the surface.

Pain flared as my bones and tissue rearranged, disappeared, and regrew, but it was over in moments. I leaned forward and chuffed in satisfaction. Smoke puffed from my nostrils. When I was human—or Fae, or whatever—the dragon felt like a separate part of me. When I was the dragon, however, Eleanor didn't feel like a distinct entity. We were one. I was one. Language was not adequate to describe this situation.

"It's not a good idea to fly right now," Florence said. "Once we're out of town again, it'll be better. You never know who's watching."

I snorted again. Florence jumped, and I chuffed my amusement. Flying sounded divine, but her logic was sound. My wings stretched out to their full length, and I fanned them. I glanced behind me—my peripheral vision was amazing—and then flicked out my tail. I arched up like a cat and then settled down. I sampled the air with my tongue, amazed at all the taste/scents I could discern. I tasted something new. Vampires were approaching from the air.

I turned my attention inward and shifted. I ran to my dropped clothes and weaponry. I grabbed my silver throwing knives and made sure my sword was in easy reach. Isaac had smelled the vamps almost as soon as I had, and Florence picked up the warnings from our minds. They jogged to where I stood and prepared to stand with me.

Moments later, a half dozen vampires landed in the clearing. I wasn't sure if I should be insulted or relieved they thought two-to-one odds were sufficient.

One vampire rushed Florence and the remaining five split towards Isaac and me. Even though I was the only person with visible weapons, I still only got two of the vamps. The burly shifter must look like a greater threat. Fuck that.

I threw a knife at the vamp coming in on my right. It found a home in her neck, and the wet, meaty thunk sent a shiver of nausea through me. My shudder meant I missed the second vampire. He knocked me off my feet, and his fangs descended towards my face. I called on the dragon's heat and flung a small ball of fire right into his open mouth. The fireball muffled his scream. He shook his head like a dog with a mouthful of peanut butter, but the fireball wouldn't drop free. He was on top of me when his head exploded, spraying brain matter everywhere. The rest turned to ash, allowing me to stand. The first vampire knelt nearby. She pulled the knife from her throat and attempted to get to her feet. I grabbed my sword and decapitated her before she'd healed enough to attack again.

Florence had dispatched her vampire in short order and was helping Isaac with one of his two remaining attackers. I retrieved my knife from the pile of dust at my feet and sent two fireballs, one after another, at the remaining vamps. Seconds later, they exploded, and ash rained gently on our heads.

I didn't drop my guard. The woods around us were eerily silent.

Slow applause echoed through the clearing as another vampire strode forward, flashing a hugely ostentatious silver wristwatch.

"Well done. I did not think you would destroy my children so fast." I couldn't decide if his Russian accent was genuine or the result of too many cold war movies with KGB villains.

Isaac and Florence took positions flanking me. "Who are you?" I asked.

The vampire bowed with a ridiculously foppish twirl of his hand. "You may call me Grigori."

"What the fuck is going on, Grigori?"

"I know who you are and I will stop you."

The power emanating from him was palpable. He was old, but he wasn't as old as Isaac, much less Raj. What he lacked in age, he made up for with melodrama.

"Everyone knows who I am, but no one has stopped me, and it doesn't look like you did, either."

"You think those were all my people? That was advance forces to test defenses. If you go now, you will not see rest of my people. If you stay, we will fight. You will lose." He leered at me. "But whichever you choose, please do not get dressed."

I refused to let his appreciation for my nudity intimidate me. Between the jiggling and the tendency my breasts had to get in the way of my throwing arm, naked fighting was uncomfortable, but at least I didn't have clothing to restrict my movement. And, if it would prove to be a distraction, then I was going with it.

"You like what you see, Grigori?" I leaned forward to emphasize the size of my breasts. His eyes followed the movement, and I threw a knife as soon as he lost eye contact.

He held up his hand, and my silver knife went through his palm and stopped inches from his heart.

"You cannot kill me so easy. If it were easy, I would already be dead." He snapped his fingers and figures started appearing at the tree line. I gave up counting after two dozen, but if I had to guess, I'd say there were probably at least thirty vampires, not counting Ol' Mustache Russkiy who zoomed up to hover over the fight. I tried to keep one eye on him as the vamps rushed us in groups of threes and fours. The one nice thing about there being more of them was they couldn't take us all at once. The other nice thing was that vampires— at least these vampires—didn't take advantage of long-range weaponry and were relying strictly on their absurdly powerful hand-to-hand strength combined with the deadly fangs. Not easy, not by any means, but at least better than the three of us taking on an army of snipers.

I didn't bother throwing my back-up knives—they weren't silver and would only irritate the bloodsuckers. I held my rapier in a loose, defensive stance and concentrated on my tiny fireballs. Isaac took on the vamps hand-to-hand and was ripping their heads off. Florence did something involving decapitation, which was a lot messier, but equally effective.

I created a wall of fire around the clearing to keep the vamps enclosed and watched for open mouths. As soon as the flames glinted off the fangs, I tossed in a tiny fireball. A mouthful of fire caused the vampire to panic, which fueled the flames. It didn't take long for their heads to explode.

When the last vamp, with the exception of the Russian floater, was dispatched, Grigori floated back down to the grass, inside my wall of fire.

"Now I am very cross. Those were some of my favorite children."

I tossed a fireball at his mouth, but he was ready and batted it away. I tamped it down before it could set anything on fire and created a second circle of flames between Grigori and my panting companions.

"What else you got?" I asked.

"Nothing more for tonight. But you have not seen the last of me." He straightened, pulled his cloak around him like a bad film Dracula, and launched himself into the air. Before he disappeared, though, he returned my knife.

It pierced my skin and came to a stop as the guardless handle hit my skin. I took a deep, panicked breath and felt an indescribable scrape inside my chest. The blade rested perfectly between my heart and left lung. Blood oozed out around the handle, and I repeated to myself, *you're immortal, you're immortal, you're immortal.*

The knife was silver, but it still hurt like holy hell. My pulse increased, and a cold sweat covered my body—I was going into shock —but didn't want to move in case that caused the knife to puncture a lung or move into my heart.

"Isaac," I said, looking up. He stared at me in horror. "It's okay." I almost laughed. I was comforting him with a fucking knife sticking out of my chest. "Can you please pull the knife out?"

"I'm ready to staunch the bleeding," Florence said. She had my shirt and was tearing it into strips. "Is it puncturing anything important?"

"Other than my person? No," I said. I wanted to say more, but the pain was making me light headed.

43

"Okay, then. Isaac—focus. Grasp the handle firmly and pull it straight out. Don't yank it, but don't linger. If her lung isn't punctured, we don't need to worry about it collapsing."

Florence put one arm around me, bracing me for Isaac's pull.

"Ready?" he asked.

"Do it." In one smooth pull, the knife was out, and Florence had the t-shirt strips held against my chest to stop the bleeding. I took a deep breath, then another. Sharp pain sliced through my chest. "I would like to sit down now."

Florence pressed the bandages against my wound as Isaac guided me into a seated position. I reclined against him for a couple of minutes before I realized my protective fires were gone.

"That fucker! He made me drop my defenses."

"He stabbed you," Isaac said.

"But it wasn't even close to killing me. I can't believe I dropped both of my fires."

Florence pulled the cloths away. The bleeding had slowed to a trickle.

"You're going to be ravenous soon," she said. "You need water and food to help your body heal from this. Can you move yet?"

I pushed myself up with support from Isaac. I was still a little wobbly, but otherwise okay. I said as much.

"You should get dressed," Florence said. "Isaac can take you back to the hotel, and I'll find some more food. You'll sleep well tonight, and by tomorrow morning there will be almost no sign of injury."

Florence brought me my clothes, and I gingerly put on my panties and jeans. When it came to the bra, though, I had to call a halt. "No way is that going on."

"Here." Isaac handed me his t-shirt.

I pulled it on. It was already soaked through with blood from Isaac's wounds, and the sticky remains of my chest stabbing didn't help at all. "Ummm, we're going to have to be fast and discreet."

Florence handed Isaac one of the unstained remnants of my shirt which he used to wipe his blood from his body. He had no visible wounds, and only the faintest scars were still visible.

"I can't take you two anywhere." She closed her eyes, and a pulse of power washed over me. When I looked down, my clothes were free of pesky blood stains, and a glance at Isaac showed the same.

"Wow! How are you with grass stains?"

"C'mon," Florence said. "Let's get you some food before you wake the dead with a growling stomach."

Isaac and I returned to the motel, a little disheveled, but not enough to attract attention. Florence met us at the room with four fast-food cheeseburgers, a large order of fries, a milkshake, and a gallon of water.

It took every last scrap of food to assuage my hunger, and about a gallon of water before my equilibrium was restored. Florence kept an eye on me the whole time. When I finished my last burger, she stood up. "I'm going to my room. I'll see you in the morning. Make sure you get some rest."

She shut the door, and I looked at Isaac. He'd barely said two words since the entire evening. "Are you okay?" I asked.

"Shouldn't I be asking you?"

I went up to him and kissed him. He flinched back. My near-death experience hadn't been enough for him to forget what he'd overheard earlier. I backed off. "I'm difficult to kill."

"I don't think he wanted to kill you."

"Great! I don't want people to want to kill me. It keeps me alive much, much longer."

Isaac took two steps and closed the distance between us. His head burrowed into my shoulder, and he took a deep breath. I put my arms around him, and this time he didn't resist.

"Are we okay?" I asked.

"I don't know. All I know is seeing you with a knife sticking out of your chest...it doesn't matter that you don't love me the way I love you."

I opened my mouth, but he put his hand up, silencing me. I'd told him I love him before, I didn't know why I couldn't do it again.

"I heard Florence's prophecy. I won't push for marriage, but if your magical mind and hers agree the mate-bond will save your life, then we should do it. There's a way out when and if you want it. It's not an easy way out—one of us would have to bind ourselves to someone else—but it can be done."

I bowed my head and rested it against his chest. "I hate hurting you."

"I'm sorry I pushed."

We stood in each other's arms until the stench of blood started to turn my stomach. "I need a shower."

"Need any help?"

I smiled at him and hoped the sadness wasn't apparent. "Always."

CHAPTER FIVE

I WOKE WITH alarm bells ringing in my head. It took the barest second to realize that although they were in my head, they were pretty fucking real. I inhaled, and the scent of vampire overwhelmed me. I reached between the mattress and box spring, grabbed my rapier, and rolled over onto my back, swinging my sword up to meet the rush of air coming towards me. I opened my eyes and saw Grigori. My sword was against the front of his neck. He was smiling more than that fact should warrant.

I shifted in bed to adjust my leverage.

"You think you can defend yourself against me?" he asked. "That is false hope. No man can stand against me. Many tried. They are all dead."

I was alone with this vampire and fear overtook me. "Where's Isaac?"

"The werewolf I can scent all over you? He was good, but he has been tasted before."

That was the last straw. I sat up further and pulled the sword across his throat. He moved, but not fast enough. His throat was cut almost all the way through. His head flopped over, held only by the skin on the back.

I watched in horror as he reached up and put his head back into position. The skin knitted together quickly, and in seconds he was no worse for wear.

"You are not the first to try that trick. And you will not be the last. I let you see how useless it is to try to kill me. Now you know. If you lay down your weapon, I will go easy on you."

I snorted. "I'm sure you'll go real easy on me."

"I am not like the others to throw around the hints and the banter. You will be a guest in my home, but a permanent guest. You will service me as I desire. You will want for nothing but your freedom. It will not be a bad life."

"And what do you get out of it?"

"Power. Drinking from you will give me power. That govniuk in Portland is bragging about how one sip has eliminated his aversion to the sun. I will have more than that."

"You don't think an age difference is partially to credit there? He must be about 1000 years older than you."

"You think you know my age? Go on, tell me."

"You're barely more than 100 in undead years. You're powerful, but not old. You were witch-born, like my friend you encountered last night. In the vamp world, you're still a baby."

He bared his fangs. Age was obviously a sensitive subject for him.

"You seek to provoke me, to make me kill you instead of capture you."

Since that was not my goal, I kept quiet.

"It will not work. You will come with me." His eyes flashed, and a compulsion slipped into my mind. Part of me wanted to go with him with no protest. I tightened my grip on my sword and let the geas have control—for the moment. I stood up.

"Come to me now. You do not want to hurt me with your sword."

Since he hadn't commanded me to drop it, I didn't. I did, however, transfer it to my left hand. He looked at that movement approvingly, assuming that was my weak side.

When I got within a couple feet of him, I stopped.

"I think you will come with me."

Again, the words wormed their way into my mind, but this time, I didn't let them. This was my last chance. I shook a throwing knife into my right hand, whipped it at him, and when it sank home in his heart, I decapitated him. All the way this time.

"You cannot stop me," he said. I grabbed my silver knife and cut out his heart.

"I am invincible," he said as I carried his heart into the bathroom.

"You're a loony," I replied.

I put his heart in the bathtub and sent a small burst of flame towards it. It burned slowly at first but soon went up in a puff of ash and smoke. I heard a clatter and turned to see Grigori's headless body collapse right behind me—which was not where I'd left it. It turned to ash, too, and when I went back to the bedroom, his head, although not ash, looked pretty fucking mummified.

The eastern sky was streaked with light when I knocked on Florence's door. The smell of coffee was wafting from her room. I was absurdly proud for successfully defending myself pre-coffee. Florence looked me over, and for the first time since I met her, looked shocked. "What the hell has been going on?"

"Nothing much. Had a chat with our Russian friend from last night. Some of that chat happened after I cut off his head."

"Where's Isaac?"

"I was hoping you knew."

I heard a door swing open and an exclamation of quiet surprise. "He's back. I hope he didn't spill my coffee."

I ran to my room and saw Isaac standing there, staring at the mummified head I'd left on the motel table. "What's that, Eleanor?"

"That's Grigori. Or what's left of him. Did he bite you?"

"Are you asking me if that head bit me?"

I laughed, which judging from the looks I was getting from my companions, was not the right response. "No. I meant earlier when his head was still firmly attached to the rest of him."

"No, I left to go get you coffee about a half hour ago."

I peered at his neck. "He totally bit you. You have half-healed fang marks."

"That's probably why I skipped the first two Starbucks I saw." He seemed altogether way too calm.

"At least I wasn't naked this time." Isaac continued to stare at the head. "Isaac, are you okay? You seem excessively relaxed."

"It's not every day I find a severed head in my bedroom."

"Are you stoned?"

He finally tore his gaze away from the head and looked at me. "Maybe. I do feel mellow. He must have given me some of his blood, too. Good thing you killed him."

"What woke you?" Florence asked me.

"Bells." She looked smug. "Was that the alarm you set up? Nicely done."

I filled them in on Grigori's Monty Python-esque Black Knight routine. By the time I finished, Isaac was rousing from his stupor—at least enough for him to react when I said, "I'm going to call Raj."

"You want to talk to the pervert?"

"He's the only vampire I know, and he's really, really old. Grigori said Raj has been bragging about the power he got from a sip of my blood. I want to know why the fuck he'd do that if he's on my side."

"Fine."

I didn't know if Raj would be up, even if it was earlier in Portland, but I thought it worth a shot. I dug through my stuff until I found his card and borrowed Isaac's cell phone.

"Hello?"

"Raj?" I asked, suddenly unsure.

"Eleanor. What a pleasant surprise." His voice caressed me. I couldn't believe he had that effect on me over the phone. "What can I do for you, my sweet?"

"I have the head of a vampire sitting on the side table in my motel. Before I separated his head from his body, he told me he'd heard one sip of my blood was enough to give you complete sunlight immunity. I'm curious...why would you say that?"

There was a brief pause on the other end. "Interesting. My sunlight immunity is the product of great age, not your blood. There have been other effects, however. Someone in my household has been talking out of turn."

"What effects?" I asked.

"Nothing I will share over an unsecured line. But on to more interesting topics: tell me about the head."

"He was absurdly hard to kill, but his age didn't match his skill. He was maybe a hundred, not more than a hundred and fifty. He said is name was Grigori and he had a Russian accent. FYI—I don't think he likes you."

"You killed Rasputin?" Raj said. His voice changed from his usual whispering seductive tones to something much harder—and tinged with a surprise. "Are you sure?"

"Ummm, no. I have no knowledge beyond what I've told you. Rasputin was a vampire? That explains a lot."

"I am coming to you. Keep the head. I need to be sure." Raj hung up before I had a chance to tell him where we were.

IT WAS ALMOST CHECK-OUT TIME, and I had a mummified head and a motel room full of greasy ashes. The second problem was easy to solve. I called the front desk and asked them to send over a vacuum. After a brief argument with the front desk person about the possibility of borrowing a vacuum cleaner with a new bag in it, Isaac took the phone and told the man I'd dropped the urn containing my beloved grandfather, and wanted to clean him up.

Ten minutes later, a motel maid was at my door with a canister vacuum and a box of one-gallon freezer bags. I took both, promised to leave the vacuum in the room when I left and got to work. I sucked up the heart ashes first, dumped them into a bag, and then divided the rest of Grigori between three bags. Florence helpfully labeled the heart bag, and we each took one of the body bags to keep them separated. I wasn't taking any chances. I'd seen every episode of Buffy— way more than once—and there's always one asshole who can come back from anything. And, if this was Rasputin, he'd been burned—and survived—before. I wrapped his head in motel towels, left fifty dollars and a note behind, and dropped it in a plastic shopping bag.

"Let's not kill any more people in motel rooms," I said. "This is way too messy."

Isaac laughed. "Good idea, Princess. From now on we'll ask them to meet us in the clearing outside town at dawn."

"That might get rid of a lot of our vamp enemies," Florence said.

"We need to be farther away from the humans if this is going to be a regular occurrence. I don't want collateral damage."

I stopped by the front desk to check out and thank them for the use of their vacuum. I assured the clerk there was no trace of my grandfather left in the room and insisted he take an extra hundred dollars to show our appreciation.

ON OUR WAY TO grab lunch and pick up the car, I saw a pro bowling shop. It was fate. What better way to cart around the mummified head of one of the most famous modern undead?

The selection was a lot more utilitarian than I would've thought, and it took a while to find something that spoke to me. I finally settled on a hot pink ball bag—heh—with a skull and crossbones on it and handed over my debit card.

I was starving, so I forced the others to stop at the greasy spoon a few blocks away. After ordering—three pancakes, ham, and eggs over easy plus coffee, of course—I headed to the bathroom to transfer Grigori's head from the grocery sack to my shiny new ball bag—that was never not going to be funny.

I got back to the table as the waitress was pouring coffee.

"Raj is on his way?" Isaac asked.

"Yeah, although he hung up before I could tell him where we were or where we were going. He'll have to find us. Or call you, since he has your number."

"I'm sure he'll have no trouble finding us," Isaac said. "He drank from you. He'll be able to locate you much like you're able to find the gates. The closer he gets, the stronger the pull."

"Handy. Definitely a good reason to kill anyone else who tries to taste us. Right now, I'm more concerned about the side effects from drinking my blood he didn't want to talk about over the phone."

"How long will it take him to find us?" Florence asked.

Isaac considered the question. "He probably won't leave until dark tonight. Flights out of Portland are hit-or-miss these days. He may have to go up to Seattle. He'll arrive in Columbus tomorrow morning but will need to bunk down until dusk to be at full power. He may have partial sunlight immunity, but I've never heard of any vamp who can stand the light of the mid-day sun. So, if he arrives in Columbus tomorrow, but can't start looking until late afternoon, he might find us towards morning the day after tomorrow or early evening."

"That quickly?" I asked. I was kind of impressed.

"He'll realize almost immediately you're not in the city anymore and will be able to fly himself towards you once he's in the area."

"How will he even know to fly to Columbus?" I asked.

"I'm assuming he knows where Rasputin lives. If not, it'll take longer."

Our food arrived, and the conversation halted as we all dug in.

After brunch, we had some time to kill before we could get the car. I was getting sick of carrying a giant backpack—not to mention a head—and was hoping the car would make it through the rest of our journey. If not, I was going to have to figure out how to either travel lightly or use magic to carry my bags. Or hire a porter.

When I suggested that, as the most royal of our trio, the others should consider it an honor to carry my stuff, Isaac laughed. "You're going to have to suck it up, Princess."

"That's not necessarily true," Florence said.

When she failed to elaborate, I elbowed her, "More details, please?"

"This might be something else we can ask Raj about, but I was always told the ley lines, in addition to being magic sinks you could pull on if you were strong enough and powerful enough, doubled as supernatural highways. I don't know how you travel them safely. It's

53

tricky to attempt to even pull from the lines, and an inexperienced mage can fry themselves if they hit a line with too strong a current."

"Hmmm..." Isaac said. "I have heard of line ferries, but I've never seen one. By the time I made my way out into civilization—" his upper lipped curled as he said the word "—the Industrial Revolution was in full-swing and the magic was disappearing quickly from the world."

"Speaking of magic and things disappearing from the world, can we grab a paper or something?" I asked. "I'd like to check on the state of the Black Hills." Florence and Isaac exchanged sideways glances. "I'm gonna go ahead and ignore that look you two shared and pretend it doesn't mean you both know something I don't because then I'd have to be pretty fucking pissed off at you. Since I demonstrated this morning that I'm not only more than capable of taking care of myself," I shook my ball bag—heh—at them, "there is absolutely no reason to withhold information."

"No one is withholding information," Florence said. A wave of calm washed over me.

"Stop trying to sooth me with magic," I said. It worked, though. I was feeling decidedly less grumpy when she continued.

"Let's grab a paper, go sit in that park until someone comes to kick us out because they think we're vagrants looking for a camping spot and chat."

Isaac went into the next convenience store we saw and came out with three papers: The Columbus Dispatch, USA Today, and The New York Times. We headed to a park a couple blocks from where our car was and dropped the packs. I placed Grigori's head on a bench, grabbed the local paper, and stared at the front page.

"Black Hills of South Dakota Still in Darkness!" the headline read. I scanned the article. There was still no power, and the perimeter of the power kill was, according to experts, spreading. There were two maps: One showed the initial perimeter as determined the day after the incident, and the second showed the new boundary, drawn three days after the first. It was roughly twenty miles further out, and experts—although the article was quick to point out expert was a strong word to use in such an unprecedented situation—believed it was spreading about five miles a day. As the perimeter hit transformers, it knocked out power to all who relied on that as an energy source. They had military personnel in the dark zone trying to assess the situation and arrange for evacuation. Horse-drawn carriages were being brought in to help with the evacuation, and a state of emergency, complete with martial law, had been declared within the zone.

The only known casualties from the initial blast were two Air Force pilots who'd been returning to Ellsworth Air Force Base. The cause was still unknown. No terrorist groups had come forward to claim responsibility, scientists were unable to find evidence there'd been a solar blast to cause the EMP, and no nuclear detonations had been detected.

Cars driven into the dark zone cut out after crossing the perimeter, except for earlier models without onboard computer parts. The article mentioned possible links between what happened in the Black Hills and the situation in Portland, Oregon which was now being called a gray zone to both link it to and distinguish it from the dark zone.

Portland's perimeter was spreading at about the same rate, but the power outages were more sporadic. However, they were happening often enough now that electric company personnel were not able to fix the outages before the next pulse came. Portland airport was shut down, and the FAA banned air traffic in a 150-mile radius around Portland. Seattle was beginning to get nervous, and SeaTac officials were on high alert. Amtrak was suspended. River traffic on both the Columbia and Willamette Rivers was shut down—the drawbridges were mostly down, and the ships themselves lost power when they got too close. The governors of Oregon and Washington had declared states of emergency and residents of Portland, Vancouver, and the surrounding areas were being evacuated in advance of the coming winter. The hospitals had been the first to be evacuated, followed by nursing homes, but a couple of dozen people died before they could get them out.

The article went on to talk about the economic implications of the

Port of Portland being shut down and what would happen if the creep totally took out Portland and hit Seattle as well. The markets were tanking, and there were already hints of unrest as well as some rioting happening in Portland.

"Well, fuck," I said.

"That sums it up," Isaac said.

"It's weird being the only people who know what's happening and not being able to tell anyone. We can't, can we?" I asked.

Florence said, "I can tell my friend at the FAA, but he did warn me all calls are being monitored after the pre-equinox warning before. He knows the whens, but not the wheres."

"There have to be supernaturals in the government. We need to contact them to start making plans. If the next gate takes out the eastern power grid, what will happen to the nuclear power plants? I don't want to create a Chernobyl-type situation."

We sat silently for a moment.

"You know," I said. "When I first found out I was supernatural, I kind of thought I'd be out changing the world, making tough decisions and either saving or destroying the world. I assumed I'd have to make sacrifices to keep the Hellmouth closed or something. I never thought it would be like this, though. I'd like a little more fantasy Dungeons and Dragons type action. More beheading vampires and less worrying about what happens to our nuclear power plants without any electricity and how many planes I'll bring out of the sky next time I open a gate.

"This," I waved my hand, trying to encompass the "real" world, "is the only thing most people know. I want to be unwavering in my decision to keep opening the gates, but is the magical backlash of not opening them any worse than the technological backlash of actually opening them? There has to be a way."

"There might be," Florence said. "You will need to play on the reason the Fae want back in this world at all."

"What do you mean?"

"Many of the Fae are distressed about the depredations visited on this world by humans, right? They want to halt—and even reverse—

the advancement of technology to restore the natural balance. You once said mages draw power from the Earth, but you Fae are of the earth—you feel her pain. The mother loans us power, but she doesn't have to loan it to you—it flows into you naturally.

"The fallout from radiation leaks caused by improperly shut down nuclear power plants—and whatever other weird nuclear shit the government has been lying about—will make it even harder to restore the balance."

"Good point and amusing nuclear pun." Florence bobbed her head and grinned. "I need to get in touch with Arduinna."

"Christ," Isaac said. "First the vampire, and now the Green Lady? We are going to end up with quite a menagerie."

"Says the wolf." I leaned over and kissed him. "I should've asked Arduinna how to get a hold of her. I suppose I could call Finn and ask."

Florence and Isaac stared at me like I'd lost my mind.

"Kidding. Relax. Although if I do find Arduinna, I'm going to ask if she knows how to break the bond Finn created—the bond Finn said Arduinna told him how to create. Finn said he wasn't told how to break it, but did allow it could be broken. I don't want a permanent link with Finn—not if it means he can listen in on my thoughts and appear out of nowhere. I feel like I've been lo-jacked by that mother-fucking elf."

"Leave the link in place," Florence said. It was my turn to look at her like she was insane.

"Give me one good reason."

"You can use the link to get to wherever he is, too. It's not a one-way link. Once you learn to use your abilities a little better, you'll be able to reverse the effects. Maybe not to listen in on his thoughts—your skills do not include telepathy…"

I pointedly ignored Isaac's muttered, "Thanks be to all that's holy."

"…but you should be able to find him due to the link. And you never know when you might need to find him."

I narrowed my eyes and looked at her. "Do you know a reason why I might want to find Finn?"

"I cannot think of anything you should know," she said. Her eyes flicked to Isaac so fast I wasn't sure if it had happened, or if it was a trick of my imagination.

"You lie with the truth almost as well as a Fae."

"That wasn't a compliment, was it?" she asked.

"No, but I trust you. I will keep the link, but I'd like to use it to my advantage for once."

"We can ask Arduinna for more information, and then I will do my best to teach you. Any ideas on how to get in touch with her?"

"Yes. Let's get the car, raid my seemingly bottomless bank account, buy a little pop-up trailer, and get out of town. I want to camp from now on."

"I distinctly remember saying I wouldn't be joining you on any camping expeditions," Florence said.

"I heard. I'm ignoring. It's good to be the queen." I said.

"You're not my queen."

"Not yet. But if you're good—and really, really lucky—I will be."

"Fine," she said. "At least a camper will be more comfortable than the ground."

"As long as there is propane, we can have heat."

"Good call, Princess," Isaac said. "There will be more storage for food, too."

"And beer. Let's keep our priorities straight."

We stood up, grabbed our gear, and walked to the auto body shop. The woman who greeted us, wiping grease from her fingers with a filthy rag, was incredibly gorgeous. I saw Florence look her over appreciatively, and had to keep myself from seeing if Isaac was doing the same. She was tall—nearly six feet—and athletically lean. She had a pixie cut, and her chestnut skin glowed. I couldn't decide if I hated her or wanted to be her.

I held out my hand, "Hi, I'm Eleanor. Thanks for working on our car."

She took it and shook. Raw power emanated from her. Definitely a shifter.

"Mary," she said. "Jaguar." She turned back to Isaac. "All the modifications you requested have been made. My payment?"

"I can pay," I said. Isaac looked at me, and I shut up. I didn't want to get in the way of a weird shifter dominance thing.

He pulled out a sealed envelope—too thick to just be cash.

"The information you requested."

Mary opened the envelope and pulled out several pieces of lined paper. The handwriting was cramped and slanted and covered both sides of each page. Mary skimmed the first couple of pages, gave me an appraising look, and folded the missive up and returned it to the envelope. "Paid in full," she said. "Will you run with us on the full moon?"

"No. We are leaving town today. If you would consider throwing in a freebie, I would like to know if there is a close, reputable place to buy a camper."

"That information will cost you nothing more." Mary moved over to a messy desk and found a post-it note. She wrote down a name and address and handed it to Isaac. "Tell them I sent you. You'll get a discount, and I'll get a referral bonus."

"Thank you. Be careful."

"I'll take it under consideration."

We took a moment to look over the modifications, then threw our packs in the back and gently placed the bowling ball bag under our new smugglers' panel. Isaac looked up the address of the RV dealer on his phone, and we were off. I stood silently while Isaac haggled the purchase price of our new little camper and held out my debit card when asked. I hated feeling like a helpless female, but whenever I opened my mouth, the salesman looked at me as if I was a new and mildly odd species of insect. I consoled myself by imagining turning into a dragon and, after making him piss his pants in fear, lighting him on fire.

WE STOPPED in Cincinnati for dinner, and I made quick work of a hot roast beef open faced sandwich with mashed potatoes and gravy. I considered ordering seconds but decided against it when I saw Florence's mouth quirk. Why did everyone think my appetite was weird? Dammit! I was feeding a dragon.

"You're right," Florence said, startling me. I hadn't realized I was projecting. "Your appetite shouldn't be amusing. Even if you weren't feeding a dragon and continually shielding us—which burns a lot of calories—your appetite shouldn't be noticeable or remarkable. I've never noted how much Isaac eats, and he has to be eating at least as much as you—especially around the full moon."

I was slightly mollified. When the waitress returned, Florence ordered me apple pie a la mode, and I forgave her.

The sun was low in the sky when we exited the diner and Florence got in the driver's seat. She drove south out of town, then pulled into a campground at Big Bone Lick State Park.

After setting up the camper, we built a fire in the pit and watched the stars come out. There were only a few other campers in the park, and we'd parked as far away from them as possible. When it was fully dark, and the park ranger had made his last round, I headed into the trees, found a clearing, slipped off my clothes, and shifted. After stretching out my wings, I took flight. It had been a while since I'd flown, and it felt amazing. I was mindful of the lights of populated areas, and stayed away, not wanting anyone to see me silhouetted against the sky.

As I flew, I thought about how to get in touch with Arduinna. Even though I'd ordered her to stay away, my father, whoever he was, had commanded her to keep an eye on me. She had to be nearby. The realization was a lot more comforting than I would've thought, considering how we'd first met. I'd had fantasies about beating Finn up lately, so I understood the urge.

After an hour of flight, I winged my way back to the Ohio River and tried to remember exactly where I'd taken off from. There were a lot of wooded areas around. Cincinnati's lights were to the northeast. I was in the right vicinity, but couldn't find the clearing from which I'd left. I flew lower, looking for a campground surrounded by fiberglass mammoths. I wasn't relishing the idea of asking for directions—especially since my clothes were still in the clearing.

Finally, after flying for too long much too low, I saw displays marking the Big Bone Lick State Park. I flew back towards the river to the trees and looked for a clearing. I landed, looked around, and realized I wasn't in the right one. Dammit. Now I was going to have to walk around naked until I found my clothes and my companions.

I reached out with my mind. "Florence? Can you hear me?" I didn't hear anything back, but I wasn't always the best at receiving. "If you can, please grab my clothes and come find me. I'm close, but don't know exactly where I am."

While I was waiting, I tried to expand my senses. I should be able to smell them. I remembered tasting the air yesterday and opened my mouth, letting the cooling night air flow over my tongue. I could taste the trees and the river. I could taste campfire. And there was Isaac. I headed towards him and soon heard voices. I stopped and called out as quietly as I could without whispering, "Isaac?"

The voices changed directions and came towards me. Moments later, two shapes emerged from the darkness, and Florence held out the bundle that was my clothes.

"Thanks for coming to find me," I said.

"You're welcome," Isaac said. "Did you get lost?"

"Yes. My nighttime navigational skills need some work. For a moment, I was worried I was going to have to land on a highway and ask for directions."

Florence unsuccessfully attempted to stifle a laugh. "That would've been a sight."

"I don't know what would've been more newsworthy—the nude girl wanting to go camping or the big green and purple dragon scaring the crap out of the drivers."

"I know what I'm more intrigued by," Isaac said.

"No," Florence said. "We are all sharing a camper, and that is the end of that line of thought, Isaac Walker."

He grinned, bowed, and said, "As you command." We went back to the campground, and I told them my theory about calling Arduinna.

"Should we do it now, or wait until Raj finds us?"

"I can solve that dilemma for you."

A grin crept over my face. Damn vampire, why was I happy to hear his voice?

"*Because you and I are inevitable,*" his voice caressed me.

"Stop reading my mind," I replied.

"Not when you're thinking such complimentary things about me."

"*Asshole,*" I thought at him. His soft laugh made my toes curl.

"Hey, Raj," Isaac said. "So glad you found us."

Raj laughed out loud. "Your joy at seeing me is almost frightening."

CHAPTER SIX

AN HOUR LATER, fully dressed and sitting at the campsite picnic table, I was ready to talk. Before I could ask how he'd found us so quickly, my thoughts were hijacked by worry. *Where will he sleep? In the camper with us? What about daylight? Should I get a coffin?*

"Do not trouble yourself about my sleeping arrangements," Raj said. "I don't sleep at night, and I won't be sharing your little recreational vehicle." His lip curled.

"Not much of an outdoorsman?"

"On the contrary, I enjoy the outdoors. I don't want to be cooped up in a primitive camper with a bunch of delicious smelling supernaturals. You never know what my…instincts…might drive me to taste."

I blushed and was pissed at myself. And Raj. "Stay out of my head, Raj."

"Make me," he challenged.

I stopped walking and assessed my shields. They looked strong enough from inside, but there must be a crack if Raj was able to worm himself into my mind.

"I'm not worming, you're projecting."

"It's true," Florence confirmed. "The more you try to lock it down, the louder it's getting. Relax. Don't worry about it for right now. You dropped your shields when you got lost, and it might take a bit to rebuild them. You'll get better at this, I promise. Soon it will be second nature."

I told myself to stop worrying about what Raj was going to pick up from my mind. Instead, I spent a few moments thinking about Isaac and all the delightfully nasty things I was planning on doing with him next time we had some privacy.

"I'm sorry I told you to quit working on your shields," Florence said. "Please, for the love of the Goddess, stop."

Raj laughed, "I'm rather enjoying it."

"Pervert," I said.

He projected back at me the same image of Isaac and me entwined in the heat of passion as I'd imagined, but this time, there was another person in my fantasy—a second pair of lips burned kisses across my body. Heat simmer low in my belly and I had to concentrated to control my thoughts. Florence stalked off into the night, muttering about uncontrolled libidos, leaving me with two men who both knew how turned on I was. Raj was picking it up from my mind and Isaac could smell my arousal.

Isaac, who had only been getting half of the conversation, was glaring at Raj.

"Okay, everyone," I said before Isaac could say anything to further deteriorate this conversation. "Let's get it together. We need to talk about Grigori. We need to discuss plans. I need to call Arduinna. And we need to pick up a coffin for fang boy over here since he won't fit in a ball bag."

"There's one other thing we need to do," Raj said.

"We're not having a campground orgy."

"It's hardly an orgy if there are only three of us. Trust me."

I rolled my eyes. "No sex."

"You put a stake in my heart. However, that's not what I was going to suggest. Instead of finding me a coffin, which I do not need, I was going to suggest I take a drop of blood from each of your companions. I was able to find you quickly because your blood runs in my veins. If

I had more—not that I'm suggesting a second taste, of course—I could have found you even sooner. A third taste would allow me to appear at your side. It would allow us to communicate at a distance. Then the only thing that could separate us would be the veil between worlds.

"A taste of each of your companions would allow me to find them, too, if they were lost or we were somehow separated on this quest."

"You're not coming with us," Isaac said. "So, it's not necessary."

"I'll be joining your merry band. I'm going to need upgraded accommodations, though. This is all rather...barbaric."

"You must know, based on what's going on in Portland, that this is going to be high living in a year's time," Florence said, reappearing with an armful of firewood. While she worked on the fire, I hit the cooler.

"Anyone else want a beer?" Isaac and Florence replied in the affirmative, Raj declined. I opened three beers and took them back to the fire.

"Okay, conversation time. Where should we start?" I asked.

"Tell me about Grigori," Raj said.

"Do you want me to get the head now?"

"Not until you finish the story."

I related our first encounter with Grigori and then talked about how he'd waited for Isaac to exit the motel room, bitten him and sent him on a long errand, and then attempted to compel me to go with him. When I got to the battle scene, Raj leaned forward. "How did you know to burn his heart after you decapitated him?"

"The first time I nearly decapitated him, he flipped his head back onto his body and laughed at me. Told me he was invincible."

"The Black Knight always triumphs," Raj said.

I laughed. "Isaac can quote Buffy at me, and you can quote Monty Python? You guys are awesome. Florence—can you pull some geeky quotes out to make this group perfect?"

"I'll work on it."

"Anyway, after I told him he was a loony—my exact words, of course—I cut out his heart. He verbally expressed his displeasure, which was creepy as fuck. I decided burning his heart would stop him, or at least slow him down long enough to get some help. I burned it in the bathtub. His headless body kept coming until his heart disintegrated. Then his body turned to ash, but his head did not. After Isaac returned, we borrowed a vacuum and a few Ziplocks. We have three bags of body ashes, a baggie of heart ashes, and his head in a bowling ball bag."

"Show me the head."

I grabbed the ball bag—heh—from the secret compartment and brought it back. Raj raised an eyebrow at the garishly pink and skull covered bag and unzipped it.

"This is Rasputin. Do you know how many people have attempted to kill him over the years?"

"Not exact numbers, but he did brag a bit about how a lot of people had tried to take him out and failed. Is he dead?"

"I've never seen a head survive, even on the oldest of vampires, but you say the rest of him is ashes?"

"Yes."

"We should probably scatter the ashes in different bodies of moving water as we continue on this trip, but let's keep the head as insurance."

"There is no 'we' on this trip, vampire," Isaac said.

Raj looked at him. "You are going to need me," he said. "You will end up in New Orleans at some point. There is a gate there. You will need me to navigate the territory of the vampire queen."

"How do you know there is a gate in New Orleans?" I asked. "I don't have that information, and I should be the only one who does. I don't even know where the next gate is, although I do know it isn't in New Orleans."

"Have you ever been, any of you?" Raj expanded his gaze to include Florence and Isaac.

"I haven't," Florence said.

"Shifters aren't welcome in New Orleans," Isaac said.

"The rumor is one of the cemeteries has a magic leak. It's a trickle now, but those who are sensitive to such things can feel it. Things are moving that haven't moved in centuries. Our queen is nervous, and she is never nervous. I haven't been there recently, but I went to the site of the last gate before you opened it, and I could feel it leaking when I was on top of it. It felt like sunbathing—warm and deadly."

"Maybe you could fly around to all the burial mounds in this region and look for another leak," I said.

"And miss the fun of the road trip?"

"We travel during the day. You could zip around at night while we're sleeping, and then rest in your coffin during the day."

Raj's eyes narrowed. "I do not sleep in a coffin. And I'm not a zippy errand boy." I laughed. "Are you teasing me?" he asked. I had the sense people didn't tease him often.

"A little," I admitted, holding my finger and thumb close together.

"You're not serious about letting him come with us," Isaac said.

"We'll work out the accommodation issue," I said, "but we'll need him in New Orleans. He's right about that."

"We could call him when we get there."

"Only if the cellular network is still active. Who knows what technologies will still be working when we get there?"

"I could drink from you twice more to seal our connection, then you could call me without technology," Raj suggested.

"No thanks," I said at the same time Isaac offered a much stronger no. I looked at Isaac, hoping my glare was enough to remind him he didn't get to fight my battles for me.

"Ah, well. It was worth a try. Your companions should let me taste them in case we are ever separated."

Isaac's no was even more emphatic this time. Florence, however, offered up her wrist. Raj looked surprised, then took her hand, bent over it as if he was going to press a kiss to the inside of her wrist, and then it was over. I didn't see any blood.

"Of course not," Raj said. "I'm not a messy eater."

That reminded me of what Grigori had said and what Raj had promised to talk about when we were no longer on the phone. "What did my blood do to you? You said your sunlight immunity is the product of age—you're about a thousand, right?"

"I am almost 1100 years old."

I wanted to hear more of the story, but I sensed—probably due to the warning look from Raj that was apparent even in firelight—questions about his past would not be welcomed now.

"Maybe someday," Raj said in my head. I redoubled my efforts to shield.

"By the time one reaches their first millennium, most vampires have decent sunlight immunity. I prefer not to be out during the middle of the day as the sun makes me uncomfortable, but unless you staked me out in the Thar Desert at high noon—and it would be difficult to convince me to cooperate—I will not expire."

"And the effects of my blood? What are they and why did Grigori think sunlight immunity was one of them? Surely he should've known that was an age thing."

"Rasputin was a bit different," Raj said. That earned three contemptuous snorts from his audience. He held up a hand. "I mean, you have discovered some of the ways in which he was different, but he did not have a sire. No one knows who turned him. Rasputin himself claimed to be born the way he was. He said he was Koschei the Deathless and no man could kill him."

"You are no man," Florence intoned. "Can I stay in the Nerd Herd now?"

"It's good to know you're a Lord of the Rings fan." I smiled and reveled in the fact that although I was burdened with an overabundance of obnoxiously old immortals, they were geeky.

"Back to the subject at hand," Isaac said.

"Yes, of course," Raj said. "Grigori claimed to be Koschei, a true immortal with no vampiric sire. No one ever came forward to claim him, and it was widely assumed either whoever was responsible was too afraid of the retribution that would be visited upon him when the rest of us found out he'd turned someone so insane or Rasputin killed his sire upon rising for the first time. Either way, Rasputin spent his first years mad with power and blood lust, and no one can quite tell when in the timeline he was changed since he was a product of madness and blood lust for much of his known life. He knows nothing of our ways, of our history, and has resisted—rather force-fully—any attempts to educate him."

"So that's why he wouldn't know sunlight resistance was a benefit of living for a long time?" I said.

"Exactly."

"But then who in your household was spreading rumors? Who knew you'd tasted my blood and there were, as you say, side effects?"

"That is an easy question and one I have answered before coming here. If you don't mind, I would like to partake of one of your beers now."

I nodded, and he fetched himself a drink and another beer for the rest of us.

"After we finished talking, I called my household together to tell them the news—that you'd done what no one thought possible. You'd killed Rasputin. No one reacted to the news in an unexpected way, and I'd locked on to each of their minds looking for a hint of betrayal. Then, I shared with them the rumor Rasputin had imparted to you before you dispatched him. One of the youngest in my household betrayed himself in his thoughts. He had good intentions. He'd bragged I was immune to sunlight and I'd drunk from the world-breaker. He wanted all to fear me and had been taunted by a visitor to our territory about my impotence."

My eyes, almost of their own volition, traveled from his eyes downward.

"Not that kind of impotence, my sweet," Raj said. "It is well known I don't kill if I don't have to. I prefer to use my reputation and dashing good looks to get what I want. I want people to join me, to give over to my power. Killing others might achieve my short-term goals of taking their territory, but if they surrender willingly, then I have indeed won because they refused to stand against me. I do not sanction the killing of our meals. Yes, mistakes happen, but we take care of it. No one should linger forever in the missing person database. Not knowing if someone you love is dead or alive is worse than knowing they're dead.

"I regard these habits as strength. Some see my reluctance to kill as a sign I am incapable of killing when necessary. Those that have challenged me over that mistaken belief have found otherwise. I might not kill first, but I am nearly 1100 years old, a vampire, and definitely a killer." His eyes glowed red for a moment before returning to their normal chocolatey brown color.

I cleared my throat when Raj turned his heated gaze on me. "About the side effects of my blood? You are an expert at misdirection and avoiding the question."

"You already know I am old and powerful. I'm the second oldest vampire in North America."

"The oldest is the Queen in New Orleans?" Florence asked.

Raj nodded. "I can fly, and I can read minds and project thoughts into anyone I choose. I am a vampire, and we all have some skill with compulsion. I can make people do things they wouldn't want to do and then forget they've done it. One thing I cannot do is cross the threshold of a private residence if the owner regards the space as theirs."

"My blood gave you the ability to enter homes without invitation?" I guessed.

"Yes. And that's not all. One small taste of your blood has not only eliminated that restriction, but has given me immunity to silver."

Holy shit. I decided that needed to be said out loud. "Holy shit. I can't believe you told anyone."

"None but you three know about the silver. I discovered my threshold restriction was gone by accident. When I returned to Portland after seeing you in South Dakota, I called my clan together to tell them how to prepare for the upcoming changes our world will see and let them know you were under my protection and no one should misinterpret my...private musings as an invitation to capture you or kill your companions. One of my clan—Joshua—did not appear, which is a grave insult. I found him holed up in a house with his human lover. Only when I was in the bedroom where he was hiding did I realize—through his thoughts—he was in his lover's home because he didn't think I'd be able to get him.

"Joshua immediately assumed he'd been betrayed by his lover—

that I'd seduced him, too—and killed the human before I could register what was going on. He staked me with silver, fled, and was immediately caught by one of my more loyal children. Joshua recounted the events before his sentencing, and although I backed up his suspicions that his mortal lover had invited me in, there were a couple who suspected the truth.

"The silver didn't burn me, and silver always burns. I was lucky no one saw that part. I staked myself near the heart with a wooden stake to create a slower-healing wound before returning to my people and told them he'd missed."

"Holy shit," I said again. "Everyone's going to want a taste of me if they find out the truth."

"They cannot have you. I've laid my claim. Only someone more powerful could challenge me for a transference of ownership."

I ignored the ownership thing. We'd discuss that later. "Or someone crazier than you, like Grigori."

"You will be a target, though, which is another reason I'm coming with you."

"Okay," I said. "But you and Isaac need to go work things out. I will not have two alpha males poking at each other all the time."

That would be even more fun, Raj whispered in my mind.

Raj stood. "Isaac, shall we take a walk? I promise to never poke at you without consent." He held out his hand. Isaac ignored it and stood up, and they disappeared into the darkness.

I grabbed my toiletries bag from the car and headed to the bathroom. I changed into some shared accommodation worthy pajamas, washed my face, and brushed my teeth. Isaac and Raj were not back yet when I returned to the camper. Florence was in her end of the trailer with the curtain drawn. I quietly crawled into my bed.

"Tomorrow, we work on your shielding," she said. The sudden break in the silence startled me, and I yelped. She laughed, and I formed a picture of a hand with the middle finger pointing up and thought it at her as hard as I could.

"I'm trying, Florence. I'm sorry I'm not doing better. I don't mean to make you uncomfortable."

"You're doing well for being new at it. It's only the sexual thoughts that bombard me. Unfortunately, those are the ones I'd like to do without."

"I'll keep trying. Good night, Florence."

"Good night."

I closed and my eyes and felt sleep pulling at me; it had been a long day. My eyes opened wide. Raj had arrived an entire day earlier than expected. I didn't know if I was frightened or relieved by that knowledge, but before I decided, I fell asleep. I woke briefly when Isaac crawled into bed. I snuggled into his side, and he pulled me close.

WHEN I WOKE the next morning, it was still dark. I heard Florence and Isaac talking quietly outside and smelled coffee and bacon. There were a lot of things I did not enjoy about camping, but smelling fresh-percolated coffee, bacon, and crisp, clean morning air almost made up for it. I rubbed my eyes, pulled on a sweatshirt, and slipped my feet into my sneakers before heading outside. Isaac met me at the door of the camper with a cup of coffee, and I took a long drink before kissing him.

We finished breakfast, packed everything up, and left as the sun was rising. As we got in the car, Isaac turned towards me and asked, "Do you feel the gate drawing you anywhere?"

"Nope, which means we keep to the plan. Where are we headed next?"

"Towards Louisville," Florence said.

"It'll only take us a couple of hours to drive to Louisville without stopping," Isaac said. "Even going slow, we'll be there by lunchtime. Do we want to stay in that area tonight, or keep on traveling?" He pulled out of the campground and onto the highway.

I grabbed the map tucked into the glove box and looked at Kentucky, homing in on the southern part of the state. "There," I said, placing my finger over Mammoth Cave National Park. "Let's look at the caves. That seems like a fantastic place for a gate."

"I thought we were looking for mounds?" Florence said.

I thought about it. I still felt strongly about the mounds. "Maybe they're a geographic marker?" I offered. "Something to identify this part of the country?"

"Or maybe you like playing tourist," Isaac said.

I grinned. "Maybe. Can we go to the caves? Please?" I fluttered my eyelashes at them, and they both laughed.

"Unless you get a better idea of where we're going, I don't see why not," Florence said.

Once again, we stopped at every historical marker. Although reading them all was fun, and exactly my idea of what a road trip should be, getting my bare feet on the ground was almost as important. At every stop, the vibrations of gate energy were a little bit stronger. We stopped in Louisville for lunch, and after we ate, I finally felt like it was time to ask the question that'd been hanging over us all morning.

"How'd your chat with Raj go last night?"

"I can't believe it took you this long to ask," Florence said. "The suspense has been killing me."

"Can't you pull it out of his mind?"

"His shields are excellent. I would've had to break them; I wouldn't do that to a friend unless I needed to save a life."

"Hmmm...an ethical witch," I said. "Who would've thunk?"

She reached out and smacked the side of my head. "Like you'd ever even heard of mages until three months ago. Don't get lippy with me, little girl." We exchanged grins, then turned back towards Isaac.

"I killed him and left his ashes in the forest," Isaac said.

"No, you didn't."

"Fine. We talked. I asked him to tone it down a little. I told him we were performing the mate-bonding ceremony at the next full moon. He asked to be the best man. I told him to bugger off. He expressed delight at the proposition. We agreed to work together for the common good. He said, and I quote, 'I vill try to do as you vish and stop attempting to seduce the sweet Eleanor.'"

73

"Did he really pull out a Dracula accent?" I asked. "Because that is awesomely weird."

"He didn't. That was for dramatic effect."

"How do you feel about this?"

Isaac looked at Florence. "You're our companion and privy to all of our secrets, but would it be okay if I talk to Eleanor alone?"

"Of course. I'll meet you back at the car in half an hour. Will that be long enough?"

Isaac nodded, and she took her leave.

"I am going to try to get through this without being totally obnoxious," Isaac said. "Please bear with me."

I reached out and grabbed his hand. "There are bears now? It's a zoo!"

His smiled warmed me to my toes. "So funny, Princess."

Isaac squeezed my hand and said, "I was never jealous of Finn. You were mine from the minute my lips touched yours, even if you didn't feel the same way. But Raj—something about him triggers all these ridiculous over-protective jealous feelings. You desire him, and he clearly desires you, too. His belief that you and he are inevitable bothers me. I told him all of that last night, threatened to kill him if he touched you, and generally acted like an all-around asshole."

Isaac stopped talking and looked at me from under his half-closed eyes. The silence stretched between us. He deserved a response. Relationships are hard.

I squeezed his hand. "Raj is ridiculously pretty and incredibly powerful," I said.

"As an opener, that's not as reassuring as you maybe meant it," Isaac interrupted.

"Shush. Let me go on. I cannot deny he stirs up feelings of desire. However, a lot of that is not springing unprompted from my own mind. He is sending me images meant to do that, and I don't know how to shut him out." I stopped, trying to figure out where I was going with this. Not being able to fudge the truth sure was an impediment at times. "I agreed to bond with you. I have not changed my mind. If the assurance of monogamy is what you need from me, I have no problem committing to that. I will not do this if you're unable to contain your jealousy. The last thing I need is another Finn issue."

"I will do my best. I trust your loyalty and your honesty."

"It's easy to trust my honesty. I can't lie."

Isaac kissed me. "You know what I mean."

"One more question. Where exactly is Raj now?"

"He was going to find the nearest town, grab a bite to eat, check to see if Rasputin had a nest he should take over or disband, and said he'd meet us tonight. Now that he's tasted two-thirds of our little party, he'll be able to find us quickly."

"Did you notice how fast he found us yesterday? He got from Portland to our campground in about fourteen hours—a full day before we expected him."

"He has a private jet on an airstrip near Salem and was able to fly directly to Columbus."

"I wonder if it would be possible to pick up a coffin as a joke," I mused.

"Do you have any idea how much those things cost?" Isaac asked.

"Yes. I buried my parents, remember?"

Isaac squeezed my hand. "Sorry, Eleanor. Do you think it's worth the expense and hassle to play a joke on the vampire?"

"Why not? My money will be worthless soon anyway."

"I'm not sure you can walk into a funeral parlor and purchase one," Isaac said.

"I can try."

I filled Florence in on my plan. She snorted but didn't argue. I found the nearest funeral parlor on Isaac's phone, donned a pair of oversized sunglasses, and headed over. After heating the air around me long enough to dry out my eyes, I headed inside with Isaac at my back. An average-looking, polite young man came over to help. He was nothing like the Gomez Addams character I was hoping for, and I almost lost sight of my script. I introduced myself as Nora Walker, ignored Isaac's inappropriate grin of pleasure at my appropriation of his last name, and removed my sunglasses.

"Thank you for helping, Mr...," I said.

"Doug. Doug Kaplan. But you can call me Doug."

"Thank you, Doug. I need to buy a casket. A friend of ours is the victim of a rare disorder and isn't expected to live through the day. He doesn't want to be brought to a hospital or, god forbid, a morgue." I tried to sound like I was stifling a sob, but wasn't sure how successful I was. "I will make sure everything is taken care of at our home, that all the necessary authorities are called, but was hoping I could bring home a casket today so we have a place for him to rest if he should pass on."

Doug looked flabbergasted. I guessed he didn't get requests like this often.

"I have cash," I said, and that weakened any further objections he might have. He led me into the showroom, and I picked a mid-priced model. Isaac helped Doug load it into the car. I climbed into the driver's seat and drove off. I waited until we were out of sight before howling with laughter.

Florence was in the back seat. "I hope the delay was worth it."

"That's the most cash I've ever dropped on anything. Ever."

"Nice to have the fairy princess trust fund to finance your practical jokes."

"It really is. I was hesitant about spending the money at first, and I don't think I'll need to go on shopping sprees like this often, but it's nice to live the high life for a day."

"I find it interested that in your version of the high life, you go coffin shopping," Florence said.

I sniffed. "We wealthy royals are known for our eccentricities."

WE'D SET up our campsite and finished dinner before Raj appeared again. I stifled my grin, did my best to shield my thoughts, and said as casually as I could. "Raj, we got the inside of the camper modified in case you need a place sleep."

Raj gave me a suspicious look but opened the camper door. Right there—front and center—was the coffin open to show off its white satin lining.

I started laughing hysterically, and even Isaac and Florence cracked grins.

"This is a joke?" Raj asked.

"Yes," I was wiping tears from my eyes.

"You bought a coffin as a joke?"

"She did," Isaac confirmed.

"You are a strange woman," Raj said. "What are you going to do with it now?"

"It'll be handy if you ever need it. We should keep it."

"I do not sleep in coffins," Raj said.

I rolled my eyes. "Relax, Drac."

"I can, however, think of other things to do in it. It does look…luxurious."

"Are you ever not thinking about sex?"

He pondered the question. "There are times when my mind wanders away from the subject. When I'm hungry. Or when you insult me by calling me Dracula, like that upstart deserves the publicity."

My mouth gaped open. "He's real?"

"And such a sucker for attention," Raj said.

"Sucker. Heh." I always appreciate a pun.

Before I could make further inquiries about Dracula, Raj interrupted. "What did I miss today?"

CHAPTER SEVEN

AFTER DINNER, I talked the others into a cave tour. The gate wasn't nearby, but I didn't want to miss out on some actual touristing. I was surprised when Raj agreed to join us. "I didn't realize they let people wander into the caves without a guide," Florence said. "Isn't that a liability?"

"Probably," I said. "Our tour isn't officially sanctioned."

"We're breaking into a cave?"

"Yep."

"And this cave is in a National Park?"

"Yep."

"Aren't you afraid of getting caught?"

"I'm breaking in with a vampire, a werewolf, and the most powerful mage I've ever met. Even if we did get caught, what are they going to do? Park rangers aren't prepared for us. Plus, this is probably traditional American Indian land, so you wouldn't really be trespassing, right?"

"I see you've thought this through," Florence said.

I grinned at her, and she rewarded me with a slight up tilt to her lips. "C'mon, Florence. Be bad with me." Before anyone else could say anything, I turned and glared at the men and held up a finger. "Nope."

We piled in the car and drove to one of the entrances and then snuck down the stairs and into the cave. Once in, I handed around flashlights, and as soon as we were out of sight of the entrance, we turned them on.

"Anything?" Isaac asked.

"No," I said. "I didn't really expect there to be anything here. I feel confident we're looking for mounds, but it was worth a shot."

We hiked until we came upon a smooth body of water. I consulted my map and announced we were at Crystal Lake. It was eerie in the dark, and since I couldn't see much, I turned to move on. The hairs on my arms prickled to attention and I halted.

"What is it?" Raj asked, picking up my unease from my mind.

"We're not alone anymore."

"I don't hear anyone else," he said. It took a second before I realized he meant mentally. I turned to Florence for her telepathic confirmation.

"Neither do I."

"I must be creeped out by the dark," I said.

"No," Isaac said. "I feel it, too. Something malevolent is stirring."

"Drop!" Raj and Florence said at the same time. The four of us fell to the ground as a barrage of energy shot overhead. We turned off our flashlights almost simultaneously.

"Witches," I said. "Dammit."

"Where are they?" Raj asked. "I can't see them or hear their thoughts."

"They're blocked," Florence confirmed.

"I can smell them now," Isaac said. "They're at our two o'clock."

"They can probably hear us," I said.

"They obviously already know we're here, and at this point, they know we know they're here. Identifying their position won't do any harm," Isaac said.

Florence crawled between Isaac and me, and Raj crept forward until we were crouched in a rough circle. Florence grabbed my left hand and Raj my right, and a circuit formed.

"*Now we can talk without being overheard,*" Raj said. "*Concentrate on projecting your thoughts, and we will all hear them.*"

"*I didn't know you could do something like that,*" I thought. "*I'm impressed.*"

"*I can't on my own. I can hear your thoughts and place mine in your mind, but I cannot create a link like this. I am only a small power boost for your witch's formidable skills.*"

"*Gifts of the mind are my area of strength,*" Florence said. "*But we can talk more about how great I am later and how much I hate it when bat boy calls me a witch. For right now, we must get rid of these magicians since they're standing between us and the exit and don't seem to be in the friendliest of moods.*"

"*Okay, how do we do that?*" Isaac asked.

"*Does anyone know how high the ceiling is right here? I could turn into a dragon. A couple bursts of flame and they'd probably run away.*"

"*I'd rather get out of here without damaging the cave system too much. It's a delicate ecosystem,*" Florence said.

"*Nature lovers always ruin the good plans.*"

"*Does anyone know how many there are?*" Isaac asked.

Florence reached out with her mind. "*Dammit. There are thirteen—a full coven.*"

"*Is our goal to escape without harming them?*" Raj asked.

"*I don't want to cart thirteen bodies out of here,*" I said. "*Sounds like a pain in the ass.*"

"*Isn't there a bottomless pit somewhere? We could cart them that far and drop them in. I bet they don't check it for bodies frequently.*"

"*I don't remember exactly where, but it's probably still quite an obnoxious hike from here. Maybe Raj could fly them over in pairs. Maybe he'll make a new friend!*"

No one said anything, and I pictured the large colonies of bats we'd seen earlier in our self-guided tour.

I could hear Raj grind his teeth. "*I do not turn into a bat. I do not sparkle in the sunlight. I have a reflection, I don't mind garlic, and I don't sleep in a coffin.*"

I suppressed a giggle. He was fun to tease.

"*Children,*" Florence chided us. "*What are we going to do about these conjurers?*"

"*Can you hold them with your mind?*" I asked.

She reached out and found their essence. "*For a short period. But not if we're all linked.*"

"*You freeze them. I'll shoot up a ball of flame to illuminate them, and Isaac and Raj rush them and take out as many as they can before Florence is unable to hold them any longer. I'll follow with my sword and take care of anyone who tries to get away. We can take one with us to question.*"

"*Sounds like a plan,*" Isaac said.

"*Florence? Raj?*" I asked.

"*I concur,*" Raj said. "*I'll break the link, and then project a countdown. We'll go on three. Isaac, will you be going as you are, or would you like to change first?*"

"*They'll feel the energy of the change and attack,*" Isaac said. "*I'll change as we charge.*"

"*You can do that?*" Raj sounded impressed.

"*You've no idea what I can do, vampire,*" Isaac said.

Raj chuckled, and I rolled my eyes.

"*Let's do it,*" Florence said.

We dropped hands and broke the link. A few moments later, I heard Raj start the count, "*Three, two, one...go!*" The last word echoed through the cavern. I sent a fireball up as high as I could to illuminate the cavern and finally saw the witches. They appeared young, but looks are deceiving when it comes to the magically inclined. Florence's hold was not complete. Three of them—likely the maiden, mother, and crone—were still moving.

"We need to question one of them!" I called, pointing at the women leading the charge. I wasn't sure if anyone heard, but seconds later the three women were unconscious in a heap. Raj and Isaac in his wolf form moved on the rest of the group. When they saw their leaders downed with such efficiency, the remaining mages stopped struggling. Isaac and Raj rendered them all unconscious, but from the looks of it—and from the sounds of their breathing and heartbeats, they were all still alive. Five minutes and no deaths. The coven hadn't managed to land a single blow on us.

"Not bad, team!" I said. "Shall we leave them here?"

"All but these three," Florence said, gesturing at the women closest to us. "Let's grab one of them, kill the other two, dispose of their bodies, and get out of here."

I stared at her aghast. I'd joked about a bottomless pit, but hearing Florence order the deaths of the two witches in front of us with ease was chilling.

"I heard their thoughts at the end. They were here to capture you, torture you, and use you as bait to do the same to more Fae. I might have an issue with the Fae as an overall group, but I do not hold with torture."

"I'll dispose of the young one," Raj announced. "She looks delicious." He picked her up, fastened onto her jugular, and rose up into the air with her. A few minutes later he returned alone. "I'm full, and she was powerful," he said. "Which would you like to keep? I'll take the other to the pit I disposed of the first one in."

"Take the crone," Florence said.

Raj took off with her and was back even faster this time. He grabbed the remaining witch. "I'll meet you back at the campsite."

Florence and I gathered our flashlights and began the long trek back to the entrance. Now that it was over, I was pissed. Stupid witches and vampires always attacking when I was trying to sightsee. I squashed down the part where I was also a little scared—mostly of Raj and Florence.

The others let me stew for a bit, and then Florence interrupted my bad mood. "I'm sorry the evil magicians ruined your illegal tour of the cave," she said.

"Whatever, cold-blooded Florence. You need a nickname as badass as you are." I willed myself to not think about how casually she'd ordered the death of three people.

"Evil people," she said. I must have been projecting. "The others are sheep and will hopefully recover their good sense without a corrupting influence. But the leaders? They were beyond redemption."

"Do you think that's possible? Can people move beyond redemption?"

Florence stopped abruptly, and I ran into her back. "He is beyond redemption. Any hesitation you show because you don't believe me will bring the end of your happiness. He cannot be saved." She continued walking without further explanation.

"Florence? Wanna unvague that up for me?"

"You know I won't."

"What good is traveling with my own personal prophet if I never understand her prophecies? And why can't anything ever be straight forward? Who can't be saved? When will I hesitate? And for what?"

"You'll find out. Eventually."

I rolled my eyes at her in the dark and followed her out of the cave.

WHEN WE FINALLY MADE IT back to the car, Florence got in the driver's seat. I opened the back door for Isaac, grabbed some clothes out of the emergency stash we kept in back and tossed them in after him. A couple minutes later, power rose from the backseat. I turned and watched as Isaac shimmered in and out of his wolf form until finally the man solidified and the wolf was gone.

"Are you okay?" I asked as he pulled on a pair of loose shorts. He was breathing heavily.

"Give me a minute."

I did as he asked and used that minute to not-so-subtly admire all the parts of him on display. The taut abs, powerful thighs, and amazingly muscular chest and arms.

"For the love of the Goddess," Florence said. "Shields up, girl."

I hastily erected the shields I'd taken down during the cave battle. "Better?"

"For now. There's a hotel close to the campground I'll be availing myself of tonight."

"Will you be okay on your own?" Isaac asked.

"I'm safer on my own. The only times I've been attacked have been with you."

Remorse stabbed through me. It was true. In addition to bringing about an apocalypse, I was putting my friends in danger.

"You can stop that line of thought right now. I knew what I was getting into. You're the only way to achieve my end goal, and I'm not letting you out of my sight—at least not for any length of time. We'll go question the magician, and then I'll take the car back to the hotel to give you some privacy and me a break."

We pulled into our campsite and saw Raj sitting on top of the picnic table. He'd bound the witch's hands and propped her up next to the fire pit.

"You could've at least started a fire," I said.

"I'm extremely flammable. I try not to start fires unless I have no other choice."

Isaac climbed out of the back seat, still wearing nothing but the loose, silky shorts. Raj and I both followed his movements as he stacked the kindling and logs expertly and then grabbed some matches.

"I can do this part," I said to keep my mind on the task at hand.

Isaac smiled at me and said, "I know." He struck a match, cupped in his palm until the flame brightened, and then held it gently to the loose moss and wood shavings in the protective circle of the logs. It caught quickly, and moments later a merry little fire was burning.

I looked at Raj who he was still eying Isaac speculatively.

"*Mine,*" I thought at him.

He tore his eyes off my boyfriend and grinned at me. "*I can share.*"

"*Not my style.*"

"*We'll see.*"

I was not going there. "Can someone wake the witch? Let's see what her deal is—besides torture."

Raj scored his wrist with his teeth, and a drop of blood appeared. I licked my lips and felt a flaring of heat. Raj looked at me knowingly, and I glanced away, glad the darkness hid my blush.

Raj dripped his blood into the witch's open mouth, and seconds later she stirred.

"What is the meaning of this?" she asked. "You cannot hope to hold me. My sisters—"

"—Are dead," Florence said. "At least the two that could've helped you. You're on your own. I won't kill you if you answer our questions."

The witch looked around but said nothing.

"You're a little outnumbered, and a lot outclassed," Florence said. "Either answer my questions willingly and earn my promise to not kill you, or I'll make you answer, and we'll see what fate has in store for you after."

I saw her swallow. "Ask," she said.

"Name?"

"Crystal."

"Real name," Florence said, a hint of impatience coloring her voice.

"Andrea Jenkins."

"Okay, Andrea. How old are you?"

"Twenty-three."

"She lies," Isaac said.

"Did I forget to tell you some of our companions know when a human lies? Your pulse increases, your breathing changes, the blood rushes about, and there's a smell."

"What kind of person can smell a lie?" Andrea said.

Isaac bared his teeth, still a little elongated from the change. "A werewolf," he answered.

She scoffed. "Werewolves aren't real."

"You're playing with elemental magic and trying to take out a Fae, and you don't believe in werewolves?"

"Everyone knows those who call themselves Fae are witches using magic for evil."

"Attempted kidnapping with intent to torture makes you a good guy?" I asked.

"Taking out one person to save the world is worth it," she said.

"And the torture bits?"

"To find your associates."

"She thinks she's telling the truth," Isaac said.

"She was looking forward to the torture far more than anyone doing something for the good of all humanity would," Raj added.

Florence took back control of the interrogation. "If I understand correctly, you were going to kidnap my young friend over there," she pointed at me, "and then torture her for information regarding other known associates to prevent the gates from opening and to save the world. Correct?"

"Yes."

"Who told you we'd be in the cave?"

After a brief pause, "No one. We could sense her."

"I don't even need the wolf to tell me you're lying this time. Someone must have told you what to watch for."

"Nope. We figured it out on our own."

"How'd you know about her existence in the first place?"

"There's an entire website devoted to her."

"Interesting," Raj said. "What's the URL?"

"www.fairybitch.com," Andrea said.

"Seriously?" I asked. "That's stupid."

"She's lying again," Isaac said.

"Is this the part where we get to torture her?" I asked.

"Must you always sound so enthusiastic about torturing?" Isaac asked.

"It's part of my charm?" I didn't want to reveal that the thought of torture turned my stomach and I was in danger of barfing on our captive.

"We won't torture," Florence said. "But we will get the truth. Raj?"

Raj strode forward, opened his mouth, and I watched in horrified awe as his canines elongated and his eyes lit up with an unholy red glow. Andrea's breathing quickened, and she whimpered. Raj grabbed her and whispered, "Be still." He licked her neck before biting. She struggled but didn't make a sound. After a couple of swallows, Raj released, and then licked her neck again.

"Now," he said, looking into her eyes. Her pupils were dilated, and she was shaking. "You will answer all of my friend's questions."

Andrea nodded.

"Name," Florence said.

"Andrea Jenkins."

"Age."

"Seventy-five." Wow—talk about well-preserved.

"Place in the coven."

"Mother."

"Who told you we'd be in the cave?"

"I don't know," she repeated.

"How'd you know where to find us?"

"I don't know."

"Who is your contact?"

"I don't know." Andrea was nearly sobbing now.

"Be careful," Raj said. "Too many questions she can't answer will cause her mind to fracture."

"How does your contact deliver instructions?"

"Email." Andrea seemed to relax now that she'd been able to answer a question.

"When did you get your instructions?"

"Two hours ago."

"How did you know they were legitimate?"

"Martha confirmed it."

"Who's Martha?"

"Our maiden. She said this action would make us heroes. She has the most power of us all. She's the one who brought us together. If you have more questions, you should ask her. She'll be able to answer anything."

"Shut up," Raj said. Andrea closed her mouth.

"We'll not get much more out of her. Too bad you killed Martha," Florence said.

"She was powerful," Raj said. "I haven't had my fill of witch blood in ages. Between that meal, and the sips I've taken of you and our Princess here, I might be spoiled for regular food."

Andrea's eyes had widened more with every word Raj had uttered until I was half-convinced they were going to pop out of her head.

Raj looked back at her. "If you have a question for me, you may ask," he said.

"What are you?" she whispered.

"The stuff of which nightmares are made," Raj answered. He glanced over at Florence, and she nodded. Raj smiled, and a shiver made its way up and down my spine. He turned back towards Andrea.

"You promised," she said. "You promised you wouldn't kill me."

"I promised *I* wouldn't kill you," Florence said. "I made no such promises about the others."

"Now hush," Raj said. And then he struck her neck. This time, he didn't bother to coat the site with his analgesic saliva. He drank her mercilessly. Soon she lost consciousness and then, shortly after, I heard her heart falter and then stop. Raj released her, and she fell to the ground.

"Can you dispose of her?" Florence asked.

"Or are you too full to fly?" I asked, rather more snarkily than I meant. I was trying not to let the death get to me, but this was harder than killing in the heat of battle or self-defense.

"It's okay to feel conflicted. It will pass," Raj said. "I'll put her with the others and see you at sunset tomorrow." He grabbed Andrea and took off, disappearing into the darkness.

"I'm off, too," Florence said. "Need anything out of the car before I go?"

"Nope," I said. "See you. Be careful."

I didn't know what to say after Florence left. I grabbed two beers and sat next to Isaac.

"What's on the agenda tomorrow? Shifter battle at Graceland?"

I laughed, managed to mask the note of bitter hysteria that was trying to take hold, and took a long swig of beer. "Sounds like a plan, wolf."

We finished our beers in silence, then put out the fire and went into the camper. I desperately needed Isaac to fill the hollow in my center that grew with every death but didn't know how to ask. He fell asleep next to me, and I stared into the darkness, trying not to cry.

CHAPTER EIGHT

W HEN I WOKE the next morning, I remembered that somewhere in the excitement of the last couple of days, I'd forgotten to call Arduinna. Although Isaac wasn't enthusiastic about the idea of talking to another Fae, he did reluctantly agree it would be a capital idea to see if there was something we could do to prevent a series of Chernobyl-like events along the Eastern Seaboard.

"I'll call her when we camp tonight. We should probably prepare to stay a couple of days in case it takes her a while to appear."

"If we're close enough to Nashville, maybe Florence will want to stay in town again. And with Raj off doing his creature of the night routine, we'll be alone. I can think of a few ways to keep busy," Isaac breathed into my ear. I shivered.

"Actually," I said, straightening up and trying to look serious. "I wanted to talk to you about that."

Isaac cocked his head and looked at me. "Yes?"

"Since we're not married, but I did agree to be your mate, we should probably hold off the sex stuff until it's official. You know, come to each other from a place of purity?"

Isaac stared at me, and I struggled not to crack a smile.

"What do you think?" I prompted.

"That is the worst idea you've ever had."

"It's only eighteen days away," I said, trying not to let the proximity of a semi-permanent bonding cause me to hyperventilate.

"Place of purity? Who are you and what have you done with Eleanor?"

I couldn't hold in my laughter any longer. Isaac's face relaxed, and I realized he'd started to believe I was serious. That made me laugh even harder.

"You are quite the prankster lately," he said. "Care to explain?"

"I enjoy teasing the people I love," I said. "And I feel comfortable enough with you to mock."

"You tease the ones you love, huh?" he said.

Well fuck. I didn't want to explain the difference between loving my friends and love-love. And then he took it in the complete opposite direction I'd expected.

"The coffin prank was teasing someone you love?"

"Nope. Not doing this. I don't want a replay of Finn."

Isaac ran his right hand through his hair. "I'm sorry."

"I know. But we can't have this discussion again. Raj is here. We'll need him—especially if he's right about New Orleans. I can find someone attractive without it diminishing my feelings for you."

"I'll rein it in. I promise." Isaac kissed me then, but before his apology could get too far along, I heard a car pull up behind us.

We broke apart and started packing up the camp. Florence got out of the car with coffee and breakfast sandwiches. She looked between us and sighed. "Good morning. I've said it before, and I'll keep saying it until you get it down. Eleanor, you need to work on shielding your thoughts automatically. Your other shields—the ones that prevent anyone from seeing or hearing you unless they're looking at you—are automatic, aren't they?"

I thought about it—which was the first time I'd done that in ages. I reached out with my mind and realized the shields I'd worked on with Finn were not only always there, but being unconsciously extended to cover everyone in my group when we were together.

"They are there, and I haven't thought about them in ages."

"It's past time to shield your thoughts with the same instinct. The benefit would go beyond saving me from your sex drive; it will protect you from unscrupulous psychics who could use that openness to launch a mental attack."

"How are Isaac's shields?" I asked. *I am not feeling defensive.*

"Shifters have a natural immunity to mind-reading. I can read his mind, especially when he's thinking about you, but I have to work to get more than impressions. You broadcast everything. If you're up against a psychic in battle, that will be devastating. They'll know what you're going to do as soon as you think of it."

"I only dropped my shields yesterday when we linked up in the cave."

"I know, but you shouldn't have needed to drop them all the way, and they should've gone back up to their former strength as soon as the link was broken. Instead, you dropped them altogether and left yourself exposed until I reminded you."

I bowed my head to acknowledge the legitimacy of her criticism. "I'll work on it."

"Yes, you will," Florence said.

"Can I have coffee now?" I looked up at her through my lashes.

"Your puppy-dog eyes have zero effect on me. Here's your hazelnut latte."

She didn't even crack a grin. "You are a goddess among women."

"I really am." She turned to Isaac. "Americano, extra cream."

"What did you get?" I asked.

"Earl Grey with honey and lemon."

"Tea? You drink tea?"

"I plummeted several points in the Eleanor opinion polls, didn't I?"

"Of course not. It's…tea. I don't really get tea."

Florence tossed me a bacon, egg, and cheese croissant. "Eat your disgusting fast-food breakfast and let's get this show on the road. Where are we headed?"

"Nashville," I said around a mouthful of food. I received two point-edly disgusted looks and swallowed before continuing. "Let's go slow and find a place to camp close to the city. I want to call Arduinna today. We might have an entire month before we open this gate, but I'd like her to have as much time as possible to think about how to keep the nuclear power plants from blowing up."

"Thoughtful of you to want to stay close to the city. I'm sure you have no other motivations other than wanting the Green Lady to feel comfortable near her natural environment of concrete jungle?"

"I was thinking of you. I know you don't enjoy camping."

"Save it for someone who can't read your mind. Truth be told, I would like to visit the Grand Ole Opry."

"Aren't you afraid we'll get attacked?"

"Only by men with fringed shirts."

THE CLOSER TO Nashville we got, the more uncomfortable I felt. "We're getting farther away. I'm uncomfortable now, but if we keep going too far in this direction, it'll be painful."

"You're sweating," Florence said.

"This is not my all-time favorite feeling. How close are we to Nashville?"

"We can be there in half an hour."

"We need to go west."

"Will you be okay tonight? We can skip Nashville and head west."

"I want you to have your Grand Ole Opry night, Florence. I'll be okay as long as I don't have to stay in the city."

Isaac did an exaggerated double-take. "Did I hear you correctly? You're finally giving up your city girl ways?"

"Woman," Florence muttered.

"My apologies. I certainly do not see Eleanor as a girl." He waggled his eyebrows at me suggestively.

"You two will be the death of me," Florence said.

"Are you being prophetic? Or are you annoyed with having to travel with us?"

"Neither. I was teasing. I've never seen my own death, nor do I typically see the deaths of those whose lives intertwine with mine for extended periods of time. That's how I know the level of involvement I'll have with someone. It makes dating kind of depressing. The first time I kiss a woman, if I see her die, our relationship won't last."

"That sounds lonely," I said.

"It is a bit. But, when I don't see someone's death, then we have a good chance of having a decent run. Of course, then it's confusing when we break up, because wow, did I not see that coming. And I should, you know."

"So Savannah?"

"Is none of your business." I didn't miss the way her eyes tightened a bit as she broke eye contact. I wished there was a way to reach Savannah to let her know she was a giant jerk face. "It's over. My heart aches for her, but I don't want to rekindle that relationship. You can stop thinking of the various ways you could deliver her—with or without her heart—for my birthday."

I hastily shored up my mental shields and tried to look astonished. "Florence, I don't even know when your birthday is!" Then I had a horrible realization. "Oh my god, I don't even know when Isaac's birthday is!"

Isaac looked at me. "January tenth. More or less. I'm not 100% sure, but that's the date I picked."

"You're a Capricorn? Crap!"

"Is that bad?"

"I'm a Pisces! We're terribly incompatible."

"We'll muddle through."

I rolled my eyes at him. "Florence, when is your birthday?"

"November 15."

"Oooh—soon. We'll have to do something super fun for your birthday!"

"Can I have a stripper cake?"

I couldn't decide if she was kidding or not until one corner of her mouth quirked up. "Why not? Of course, we already have this coffin. We could have some kind of theme party with vampire strippers."

"I approve of this plan," Isaac said.

"Why am I not surprised?"

All the teasing had taken my mind off of Florence's weird relationship conundrum as well as my growing discomfort. When the car slowed, I looked up—Nashville was right in front of us.

Florence left us in front of the Grand Ole Opry.

"Have fun," I said. "Don't do anything I wouldn't do!"

"I don't even know how I'd find something to fit that bill."

Isaac and I ended up at a pretty camping area on the Cumberland River near the dam. We set up the camper, and I made us sandwiches —it felt like a lifetime since I'd done that. We were the only ones in the campground—Tuesdays in October are not prime camping season.

I sat on the riverbank, staring at the water. Isaac sat beside me but didn't break the silence. I reached out and grabbed his hand and said, "I'm going to try to find Arduinna."

"Do you want to be closer to the trees?"

"This will be all right."

I formed a picture of the essence of Arduinna as I understood her. Once I'd fixed her firmly in my mind, I dropped some of my mental shields and tried to send my picture out into the ether with a plea to find me.

"I've made the call. Hopefully, she'll get it and will find us. Otherwise, I'll try again tomorrow."

"It's only about 2 o'clock," Isaac said as we walked back towards the camper. "We are practically the only ones here." Isaac reached out, grabbed one of my belt loops, and pulled me towards him. I stumbled into his arms. He bent down and kissed me hard, nipping at my lower lip until I opened my mouth to let him in.

I ran my hands up Isaac's chest and locked them around his neck. He slid his hands down my back to my ass, lifting me up. I'd closed my eyes at his initial incursion into my mouth but opened them now. His remarkable eyes—more green than yellow today—were looking back at me. The intensity in his gaze caused surges of electricity through me, and I tried to slide down his body a little further. Isaac grinned through our kiss and pulled back.

"Eager, aren't you?"

"You drive me crazy, wolf."

"It's all part of my dastardly plan."

I nodded my head as I smoothed out my features and tried for officious. "As far as a first run at the plan goes, it's not a bad one. However, I can see some room for improvements, especially in efficiency, at a few key points along the project timeline."

Isaac growled at me and started walking forward. A few steps later he stopped and dropped me. I wasn't expecting him to let go. My butt hit the picnic table—I'd only fallen a couple inches. I glared anyway.

"I was hoping to prove that although my plan doesn't involve getting from point A to point B the fastest way I know how, there are merits to taking the scenic route." He unzipped my jacket and pushed it off, then pulled my T-shirt over my head. When I reached forward to return the favor, he stopped me. "This is my show, Princess." He pushed me back until I was lying on the picnic table, then removed my shoes and jeans. I sat up, reached around behind me, and unhooked my bra. I stopped it before it fell off and held it up to cover my breasts. Isaac seared me with a predatory grin, and a fission of fear jolted my system before I could remind myself not only was he never going to hurt me because he loved me, but I was a dragon and could defend against all comers.

Isaac pushed me back down and slowly inched my panties down.

"You're a little overdressed for the occasion," I said before coherent thoughts were lost in a wave of pleasure as he bent down between my legs and delivered a long, leisurely lick. He moved up my body, tasting and biting until he got to my breasts. I was still clutching my bra over my breasts, and he pulled it away, cupped my breasts in his hands, and took my left nipple into his mouth. He rolled it around on his tongue, biting down gently while his left hand gave a similar treatment to the other one.

He went back and forth between them until I was gasping in pleasure, and then one hand slid down and found my wet and aching core. He slid his hand down to cup my sex and rub my clit with his thumb until I was writhing under his touch. He slid two fingers inside me and brought his mouth back down to continue the onslaught. Mindful that we were only *almost* the only campers, I tried to mute my screams of pleasure, not sure how much my automagic shields would contain.

In minutes, I was limp with pleasure as Isaac brought me to the brink of orgasm over and over again. Finally, when I was nearly mad with pleasure, he bit down gently on my clit as he slid three fingers inside me. My world grayed out a bit, and when I came back to myself, Isaac was standing in front of me, completely nude. I'd totally missed the stripping. I let my gaze roam over his body, and when he stepped closer, I reached forward. "I want to return the favor."

Isaac stepped back out of reach. "Not today. Lie back."

I did as he asked, and he stepped forward and plunged the entire hard length of himself into me. I gasped. For a second, when he was fully encased, we reached the fine line where pain and pleasure meet. "Okay?"

"Don't stop."

He didn't. He moved against me slowly, but before long, he lost the slow, careful rhythm, signaling he was close to the brink. I lifted my hips up, allowing him even more access. Seconds later, we came together. After a moment of recovery, Isaac pulled out and helped me off the table.

After getting dressed, I sat on the ground and pulled him down next to me. "You're my favorite wolf."

"You're just saying that because of the amazing sex."

"That's only part of it."

"I'm honored." Isaac planted a gentle kiss on my lips.

"I'm nauseated."

Isaac and I jumped. Arduinna was standing at the edge of the campsite. She did look a bit nauseated, but although that might be due to the green cast of her skin, she couldn't lie. Maybe we did make her ill.

"Glad you could make it." I fought the urge to stand. Royalty does not stand in the presence of servants.

"Next time you ask me to visit, could you not immediately go into rut? This place reeks of congress."

Isaac growled. "She is not an animal."

Arduinna waved her hand.

"It matters not. What do you want?"

Isaac stood and stalked off. I had a moment of giddiness when I realized he was trusting me to take care of myself with this formidable Fae. I watched him walk away, unable to take my eyes off that ass.

"Please, Your Highness, tell me what you want."

"Three things," I said. I counted them out on my fingers. "One: A report on how things are with you, including any contact you've had with my father. Two: information on how to break the link you told Finn how to forge in my mind. And three: Your word you will recruit some Fae to protect the world's nuclear power plants as the gates open."

Arduinna sank to the ground in front of me in a cross-legged position. She mimicked the counting I'd done. "One: I'm well, thanks for asking. I haven't talked to your father of late, but the flow of time is different here than in the Fae Plane, and it hasn't been long since last you and I talked. Two: That will not be possible. And three: I don't understand."

I smirked at her admission. I bet she didn't say that often.

"I have a question for you," she said. "How come this place reeks of vampire and witches?"

"It's been a few weeks since last we chatted, hasn't it?"

"You need to tell me everything."

"You need to tell me why you think it's okay to sit in my presence without permission."

She sprang to her feet looking furious and mortified—and a little scared. "I beg your pardon, Your Highness. I forgot myself."

"You're forgiven." I was feeling magnanimous. "Please, sit."

She eyed me carefully and then sat again. "Your father would have removed my head for that."

"And the Dark Queen?"

"She would not have removed my head. She would've started elsewhere and saved decapitation for last."

"Let's talk."

I gave her the Cliffs Notes version of the last month. I started with the deal I'd made with Raj the evening after I'd last seen her: his assurance he and his would leave me alone in exchange for the life of his blood servant, Salem. I glossed over the opening of the gate and brought her up to speed on the hunt for gate number three, along with the information Raj had shown up to assist us with a future gate in New Orleans and Florence was along to provide assistance, protection, and coaching.

I didn't mention my upcoming bonding, Florence's ulterior motive, or Raj's agreement to help us find and kill Michelle once this was all over. No reason to share intimate details with a servant—or whatever she was.

Once she was up to speed, I went into a little more detail about the effects the gate openings were having on the world. At first, Arduinna was delighted modern technologies were being rendered null by the overwhelming outpouring of magic, but when I explained about nuclear power plants to the best of my abilities, her look of subtle amusement was replaced with an expression I found inscrutable.

"You're concerned they'll explode?"

"Not only that, but they'll poison the surrounding area. The people and plants in the region will sicken and die."

"Why would humans build so many things that could kill an entire region if disaster struck?"

"You'd be surprised at how little humans consider the future when they're exploiting the earth for the present. When I Googled it—Googling is a way to search for information using technology that will soon be absent from this world—I found 500 active nuclear power plants. That didn't cover any that are no longer creating energy but still drawing on energy to keep from blowing up. We can provide you with a map. There are another two or three hundred that don't make energy for the masses."

"What do you expect me to do about this?" Arduinna asked. "How do you suggest we keep so many things from exploding? There aren't many of us in this world yet, and those who are here don't have the training to prevent nuclear fallout."

I narrowed my eyes. Her use of the term nuclear fallout made me think she understood better than she'd let on. I replayed her earlier words in my head. "Arduinna, earlier when you said you didn't understand, did you mean you didn't understand *why* you should protect the nuclear power plants, *how* to protect them, or *what* I meant when I made that statement? Please clarify."

The flash in her eyes was gone too quickly to interpret. "I specifically meant I didn't understand why you were recruiting me to save a bunch of humans from the follies of their race."

"But you knew it'd render the surrounding areas uninhabitable for decades if not centuries, which is beneficial to the Fae. Will you help?"

"I will get in touch with my contacts in the government to see where they are regarding plans to protect the power plants from the initial surge and do a controlled shutdown of the reactors and cooling ponds so when the power sources go offline, they will not explode."

Obviously, she'd been playing me if this was something that had come up, been discussed, communicated to her, and was well into the planning stages. In retrospect, it was arrogant of me to assume that I was the first person to think of something like this. I persisted, nevertheless. "Might I make a suggestion?"

"Of course, Your Highness. Serving you is an honor I don't deserve."

I burst out laughing. "Bullshit. But that was funny. I'm glad you have a sense of humor." I wasn't sure if it was my imagination or not, but it looked like Arduinna had almost smiled for a second. "I don't know if this is possible, but your reference to the flow of time being different on the Fae plane than here made me think of it. Would it be possible to create bubbles around the nuclear power plants that would move them into a faster time stream? That way the spent rods could be cooled appropriately in days instead of years, then moved to long-term storage before it became a real issue."

Arduinna looked at me. "I'm impressed, Your Highness."

"I've been doing some reading."

"I could wish you were more tractable—it would be easier to deal with you after—but I begin to believe you are what we need, if not what we want."

"Thank you, I think."

"If I may, Your Highness. I have one additional question."

I nodded my head in acquiescence.

"What of the half-breed?"

"Excellent question. Before I answer, I have a clarifying question. When you said it would not be possible to give me information on how to break the link Finn forged in my mind, did you mean it was impossible to break the link, impossible to tell me, or an impossible situation all around?"

Arduinna did grin this time. The narrow band of teeth visible had a faintly greenish tint to them, causing an uncomfortable twinge in my stomach which I refused to admit might be trepidation. "You learn quickly."

I waited.

"In this case, it is an impossible situation. The only ways to break the link are for the half-breed to do it himself or for one of you to die."

"That doesn't sound like such a bad option," I muttered.

"Forgive me, Your Highness, but when first we met, you seemed rather enamored of the bastard. What has changed since then that has you casually wishing for his death?"

"He kidnapped me and had iron bands tattooed on my dragon." I didn't think Arduinna would care he'd threatened Isaac.

Arduinna grew so still, I was beginning to think she'd taken root.

"And he is still alive?"

"For now. I haven't seen him since."

"And the bands?"

"Broken by a coven associated with the witch you smelled earlier."

"Did they know what you were?"

"Only the one that came with me into my mind to break the bands."

"It appears we miscalculated the half-breed's usefulness. He was to fall in love with you and give his life to protect you."

"You got it half right. He fell in love with me, but when I didn't return the sentiment, he decided if he couldn't have me, no one else could. He tried to make me weak. He bound me. He betrayed me. And he was the protector named by my father and cleared by you. This makes me wonder where your loyalty lies."

Arduinna paled from forest green to a lighter fern color. "My loyalty is with the king by birth and with you by command."

"Even if I am not the Fae you wish I was? Would you attempt to manipulate events to remove me to make way for someone more pliable?"

"My oath, sworn to your father in front of his Queen and the assembled court, was to protect you. I would never knowingly do anything to bring you harm."

"That leaves a lot of room for plausible deniability, Arduinna."

Her skin was now a celery color and I took pity on her.

"Swear to me now you have never, nor will you ever, do anything, overlook anything, or order anything that will lead directly or indirectly to my death, dismemberment, mutilation, weakening, kidnapping, etc. if it is, in any way, in your power to stop it."

"I do swear, Your Highness. I will never make a choice I see leading to your disadvantage."

I stopped myself before I thanked her. "What do we do about Finn?"

"Is Your Highness determined to see his death? I do not want to hear later that you are angry with me because I had him killed because you were irritated."

"I want the bonds broken, but you are correct. He was my friend for long enough that the thought of his death does cause me pain. I would rather he repent, break the bond of his own will, and then go live in a bog."

"A bog? Why a bog?"

"It sounds nasty. All damp and stinky and full of bugs."

"Are you ordering me to have him killed, or to capture him and relocate him to a bog?"

"Right now, I'd rather you capture instead of a kill. If he refuses to remove the bond, we can explore other options. I do want to see him before his relocation, though."

"If you agree, I will make safeguarding this land from the poisons harvested by the humans the priority and after that has been taken care of, I will put more energy towards finding the half-breed."

"That sounds like a capital plan."

"Your animal is coming back," Arduinna said.

"His name is Isaac."

"If you take the throne, you'll have to stop rutting with beasts."

"If I take the throne, I'll take that under consideration."

I stood up, and Arduinna flowed to her feet as well. I held out my hand and she looked at it.

"Thank you, Arduinna."

She took my hand, but rather than shaking it as I'd expected, she brought it up to her lips and kissed it as she bowed.

"Your Highness."

"Stay in touch."

"You authorize closer contact, then?"

"As long as you hold to the clause of not reporting my every move to my father unless under direct questioning."

"I gave my word."

"Then yes. Please report in regularly."

She dropped my hand, bowed again, and backed towards the tree line.

"You can turn your back on me. I won't stab you in the back or have you disemboweled for failure to show proper respect."

She turned and strode off into the trees. Isaac stood next to me and slipped an arm around my waist. I leaned into him and he kissed the top of my head.

"Did you get the outcome you wished?"

"I did. For the first time since I realized what the magic was doing to technology, I feel this won't be a complete catastrophe. I really am going to miss the internet, though."

Isaac laughed and hugged me again. "What did she say about Finn?"

I got him up to speed on the salient points of the conversation, leaving out the animal insults.

CHAPTER NINE

S UNLIGHT STREAMING INTO the camper woke me earlier
than I'd have liked, but later than I should've been up. After a
cup of coffee and a cold toaster pastry, we were on the road to
pick up Florence. The tugs of magical energy grew more uncomfortable the closer we got to Nashville. The gate was behind me and I had
the sensation of being torn in two—like the worst menstrual cramps
ever.

Florence was waiting out front with her overnight bag. She looked
radiant.

"Good night?" I asked as she climbed in the back seat.

"The best," she said.

"You got laid," Isaac said.

"Whoa! Did you bag a cowgirl? Nicely done."

"You two are crass."

"Spill, lady."

"I'm don't kiss and tell."

"It's unfair that you know all the details of my love life and you
won't share with me."

"I don't want to know the details of your love life," Florence
pointed out.

"Pleeease," I begged.

"There is nothing you can do or say that will induce me to give up private details of my personal life."

"Was she pretty?"

"I found her attractive. I seldom sleep with people I find unattractive."

"Fair point." I opened my mouth to dig further, but she interrupted.

"There are more important things to discuss. Did you get in touch with Arduinna? Did you talk to Raj? What's going on in our supernatural quest?"

"Whatever. This isn't over." I updated her on my conversation with Arduinna. "Raj didn't show up. Has he seemed weird lately? He hasn't tried to seduce me in at least a week."

"Hmmm, that is weird."

"I'm serious. His need to spew double entendres is like my need to eat. It was odd to have a conversation devoid of innuendo."

"Maybe he realized his attempts to get you into bed are futile."

"He told me we were inevitable the night we met. I'll be insulted if he's already given up. It's obvious something is bothering him."

"Since there's no real way to know what's bothering Raj until we see him again, let's table it and make a directional decision," Isaac said. "I know you need to go west, but do you want to head straight west towards Lexington, or northwest towards St. Louis?"

"Can you point in each of those directions?"

Isaac did, and I oriented my body in those directions as best as I could confined by the seat belt. "St. Louis."

"Positive?"

"Absolutely."

Isaac pulled away from the curb. Once we were on the Interstate headed northwest, the discomfort I'd been feeling released—further confirmation we were going in the right direction.

By the time we hit St. Louis that afternoon, power surges battered me at regular intervals. I wondered if the Arch was the gate—it had the physical presence.

"Can we drive by the Arch? I don't think that's it, but we should check it out."

Isaac handed Florence his phone and asked her to map us to the Arch.

"How come you never let me do that?" I asked.

"You're hard enough on my electronics when you're not vibrating. I don't want you to fry the circuitry."

Twenty minutes later, Isaac pulled into a parking spot near the arch. This wasn't it, but maybe a ride would give me the information I needed. I bought tickets and we went up to the top. The energy tugged at me and I pointed. "It's that way."

Isaac pulled up a compass app and asked, "Any idea how far?"

"Not exactly. It's close, though."

When we got back to the car, I looked at my companions. "Now what?"

"I need to get in touch with the pack, convince them I'm not a threat, get an invitation to run with them on the full moon, and see if they'll witness the mate bonding that same night."

I forced a smile and picked the least threatening part of his statement to respond to. "It'd be great if we could get out of here without assisting in another pack coup."

"It was for the best," Isaac pointed out.

"No arguments from me. I like Rebecca, but I don't want to watch you fight again."

"Now you know how I feel when I hear about battles to the death with crafty old vampires."

I dropped a kiss on his cheek. "That was not my idea of a good time, either.

"Let's find a camping spot outside of the city before it gets too dark, have dinner, wait for Raj to show up, and figure out next steps." I felt commanding and decisive.

We got in the car and followed the GPS's directions to a little state park across the river in Illinois. The campground had shut down for the season, but the campground host was still there. He said we could pull into one of the RV spots for the night as long as we didn't need hookups, promised to find us an open campground for the next month, and gave us a large bundle of firewood.

"Will you stay tonight?" I asked Florence after dinner.

"Yes. You're vibrating like a tuning fork and I'm concerned you might attract the wrong sort of attention."

"We're really, really close. I can feel the gate's rhythm. My body is trying to match the gate's vibrations to bring us in sync. It feels...," I trailed off.

"Yes?" Florence prodded.

"Like a powerful vibrator."

"Sorry I asked."

"I'm not," Raj said.

"Hey! A little warning next time!" I said.

"Sorry. It took me longer to find you than I thought it would. I wasn't really paying attention and thought you were going to be in Memphis. It was only after I got there I realized I was too far south. It's a good thing I tasted Florence, though. Right now, you're hidden from me—like you're on a different frequency."

"We're really close to the gate." I felt giddy.

"This is our home base, then?"

"Yes. We're going to find the local pack tomorrow," Isaac said. "The Alpha is a cousin of Rebecca's and she sent a letter of introduction. I need to declare my intentions within seventy-two hours of entering his territory, or they'll assume I'm here for a hostile takeover."

"It is the same for me, although I have only forty-eight hours."

"You guys are all so territorial," I said. "Florence, do you need to find the local coven and do the same?"

"No. As long as I'm here on my own and not traveling with twelve others, they won't consider me a threat."

"Raj, do you want a beer?" I asked.

"No. I'm really not much of a beer drinker. I brought a bottle of wine, though."

"Is it actual wine?" I asked as he uncorked the bottle and poured it into the glass Florence offered him. It was dark red but didn't look thick enough to be blood.

"Of course. Bottled blood would be disgusting. I prefer to drink from the source."

I covered my neck with my hand before I realized what I was doing.

"I don't need to take it from your neck. There are other, more...intimate...veins with more appeal."

"Glad you're feeling better tonight," I said, trying to will away my blush.

Raj stilled—and when an old vampire stilled, they were perfectly still. He looked like a sculpture, a work of art. "I'm not sure what you mean."

"Last night, you didn't make any lewd comments. Since you flirt every time you open your mouth, I made the logical assumption."

"You know me well."

"Well enough to know you're avoiding the subject."

"Indeed."

Goddamn supernaturals and their refusal to answer questions.

FLORENCE AND ISAAC were already up when I regained consciousness the next morning. I heard them talking to someone I identified as the campground host from the night before. I homed in on his voice.

"...month if you don't need hook-ups for a hundred dollars. I'm heading out this weekend, so there won't be any maintenance done, but if you promise to clean up after yourselves and report if there are any disturbances, you can stay."

"That sounds like an excellent deal," Florence said. "Let me grab the cash."

I heard a car door open and shut, and after a bit more conversation, the man left. I sat up, stretched, and got dressed before heading out to find coffee.

By the time I filled my mug, I was feeling uncharacteristically grumpy. Today seemed like a good day to stay in, curl up under a blanket—maybe not a blanket; it was already almost eighty degrees—drink cocoa, and watch geeky television.

"What's going on, Princess?" Isaac asked. "Is everything okay?"

"I don't wanna be a princess today," I grumped. "I want to stay in and watch old Monty Python episodes in my pajamas."

"C'mon, today is the day we meet the local pack!"

"Because that worked out the last couple of times."

Isaac stiffened, but didn't give up on trying to jolly me out of my bad mood. "Joseph and Candace were not pack," he said. I could hear the sharp edge in his voice and knew I was on thin ice. I grimaced. I hated mixed metaphors, even when they were only in my head.

I turned up the corners of my mouth and took a drink of coffee. "Let's go find some wolves!"

"That was a valiant effort," Florence said.

"What's wrong?" Isaac asked.

"I don't know. I feel out of sorts and bitchy. I don't want to meet the pack. I don't want to think about gates. I don't want to worry about vampires and witches and werewolves, oh my. I want spiked cocoa, a misty greenish-gray morning, a blanket, and a BBC marathon."

"How did you sleep last night?" Florence asked.

"Okay, why?"

"You had some fairly intense dreams, and I wasn't sure if they disturbed your sleep."

"You can see my dreams?" I was shocked and a little embarrassed. I'd had some spectacular dreams since meeting Isaac.

"Only if they're particularly intense. That's one of the reasons I prefer to sleep alone."

"But if you're in a hotel, don't you get everyone's dreams? How do you sleep?"

"If there are a lot, it's easier to tune them all out—like background noise. But if I'm close to someone, or in an isolated area, or both it's harder to ignore. I usually don't catch anything coherent."

I mulled that over while sipping my coffee. "I don't remember anything particularly disturbing last night."

"You probably need a day off," Florence said. "We could go shopping."

I looked at her, lowered my shields a smidge, and said with as much fake sincerity as I could muster, "That sounds delightful, Florence." I hated shopping. From the evil glint in her eyes, she knew.

"The pack Alpha probably has a television." That was much better than shopping.

"Okay. I'm still grumpy, though."

"What if we stop for breakfast on our way?" Isaac asked.

Ahhh...the recipe for instant cheer. "Will there be eggs?"

"And pancakes."

I beamed. "You're the best, Isaac Walker."

"Because I know food is the way to a better mood?"

"Even better—you know which foods. That's the key."

AFTER BREAKFAST, we dropped Florence downtown for some mysterious errand she wouldn't share. Everyone had too many secrets for my liking. It was almost enough to bring back my grumpiness. I practiced brooding in the passenger seat until Isaac flipped on the blinker and turned into a driveway. "We're here."

Isaac stopped where the driveway ended. We got out of the car and he waited for me to take his arm before striding purposefully towards the door. I tripped over my feet and broke into a light jog to keep up.

"Wait," I said. Isaac paused, hand on the doorknob. "Shouldn't we like, you know, knock?"

"They know we're here."

He opened the door, took my hand, and we walked in.

The house opened up to a large, airy foyer. Two men stood in the middle of the space and nearly a dozen more ringed the edges of the room.

Isaac and I approached the couple in the middle.

"I am Isaac Walker, second in the Pacific Northwest pack. I am passing through your territory and request permission to stay in the area until after Samhain. I am not seeking new lands, nor am I interested in testing your dominance. I come to you on the recommendation of Rebecca Driver, newly instated Alpha of the Black Hills pack." Isaac pulled me forward. "This is Eleanor Morgan, my mate."

I didn't say anything as all eyes turned towards me.

"She's human," someone whispered. The man found himself the center of attention. His cheeks flushed and then turned an ashy gray. If he'd been near an open doorway, he probably would've fled. For some reason, someone else's gaffe cheered me up immensely.

I turned back to the shifters in front of me.

"I am Christopher Driver, Alpha of the Mississippi Valley pack. This is my mate Luis Rodriguez. You are welcome to visit our territory for as long as you wish. Please, consider our home your home and do us the honor of running with us at the full moon."

Christopher held out his hand to me. "It's nice to meet you, Eleanor." I shook his hand, and then exchanged shy smiles with Luis.

"Thank you, Christopher. Your lands are beautiful, as is your mate. Anyone would be lucky to count you among their friends. I am honored to be welcomed and I look forward to spending the full moon with you."

The ceremony finished, the ring of shifters split up and left the room. I heard some good-natured teasing directed at the guy who'd interrupted the greeting to point out I was human to a room full of people who could smell another wolf a mile away.

"I have one more request," Isaac said once it was the four of us.

"I'll grant you almost anything if you'll tell me how Rebecca is doing and give us the story of her ascension," Christopher said.

"As long as that pendejo she married is dead," Luis added.

"He's dead. And I would love to tell you the tale."

"First, tell us the favor you'd like granted," Christopher said.

Isaac glanced at me and Christopher followed his gaze. He really looked at me for the first time—more than the cursory glance he'd given during the introductions. "You're the world breaker."

I tried to shrink into myself, but that was not part of my magical repertoire. Then I remembered I was a queen—or at least that I could be.

"Some have called me that." I stood up, put some steel into my backbone, and looked him in the eye. "I will bring the magic back. I will restore the balance."

"You will break our world."

"It will not be broken; it will be changed."

"You opened a gate in the Black Hills, didn't you? You caused that."

"Yes. The first gate was opened in Portland, the second on the Autumnal Equinox, and the third will be opened at Samhain."

"And the reason you'll be in this region until then?"

"The gate is here."

"You will destroy St. Louis."

I couldn't really deny it. St. Louis would fall.

"We'll give you the knowledge to prepare, to protect yourselves and your pack, and to survive successfully after," Isaac said.

"Is it inevitable?" Christopher asked Isaac.

Nice. Direct the question at the man, even though I was the one with the fancy world-breaking power. I didn't give Isaac a chance to reply. "If I don't open the gates in a controlled manner, they may implode and that would be much, much worse."

Christopher sighed. "I never thought I'd be around to see the world changed like this."

"Do you rescind your welcome?" Isaac asked.

"No, of course he doesn't," Luis said. "Let us know what you need, and we'll help."

"Will you perform the mate bond for us at the full moon?"

"You would bond with a non-shifter?"

"Yes."

"We would be happy to," Luis said. "Eleanor, if you have any questions about the ceremony at all, I'd be glad to help out. I've been through it."

"That would be nice."

"We will withdraw from your immediate territory now," Isaac said. "But tomorrow, I would like to talk."

"Come over mid-morning. You and I can discuss the future and Luis can entertain Ms. Morgan."

"Are there any good running trails in the area you can recommend?" Isaac asked.

"For two-legged running or four?"

"Two."

Christopher gave a few recommendations with directions, then we took our leave and went back to the car.

"That wasn't terrible," I said.

"Could've gone worse," Isaac agreed.

"Why does everyone calls me the world breaker?"

"Because of the prophecy, of course."

"It's weird being the subject of so many prophecies," I said. We were back on the highway and headed towards one of the running trails Christopher had recommended. "Not only do a lot of people seem to know more about me than I do, Florence popped out with another new prophecy a few days ago, too."

"She did? I don't remember you telling me about it."

"I was going to, but then we were attacked by vamps, and then I killed Rasputin, and then..." I let my sentence trail off. "I kind of forgot."

"Tell me now."

"I don't remember it exactly, but Florence wrote it down afterward. It was more specific than the one from when we first met. That one said I was going to be the instrument of destruction and salvation or something. And that I would experience loss. At the time, I thought it meant losing my friendship with Finn."

"And this one?" Isaac's prompting interrupted my musings.

"This one happened after we talked about the mating bond. I was talking to her about how I felt about my dragon. She suggested I talk to you about your link with your wolf. My shifting is probably different than yours, but since I don't know any Fae shifters, I'm hoping you can help answer some questions."

"I can, of course, try to answer any questions you have. The prophecy?"

"She said the easy days were over—which, since we've been attacked by witches and vampires since then has proven accurate. We haven't been attacked by shifters yet, but apparently that's coming. Yay!" I twirled my finger in the air. "She said we should complete the bond. The dragon and the wolf need to be united and my biggest loss will come before my final triumph."

"Anything else?"

"Yes. A vampire will be the cause of my greatest sorrow and my greatest joy."

Isaac went still. I probably should've left out that last part.

"What does Florence think it means?"

"She only would talk about the first part—the part about being attacked by every supernatural that comes around. She really pushed for completing the mating bond, too. She's explained that even if we're moving fast, it's the right decision." I cringed internally hoping he wouldn't ask how I felt about it.

"You'll still bond with me, even knowing a vampire is to be your greatest joy?"

"Maybe I didn't say it right," I said. "I'll need to ask Florence. But short answer is yes. Who am I to argue with the fates?" I didn't reveal my private fear that he would be the great loss the prophecies talked about and that we might not have the rest of our unnaturally long lifespans to spend together.

Isaac pulled into a makeshift parking lot at a trail head. I slipped into the back seat and changed into my running gear while Isaac changed on the other side of the car.

"How far do you want to go?" He was clearly not ready to move on to regular conversation.

"How hard do you want to work?" I asked.

"Hard." He locked the doors.

"Let's run an hour in at an easy pace and then return in less than forty-five minutes," I said.

AMY CISSELL

"Done." He took off before I could do anything. "Dammit." I started my watch and took off after him.

I never quite caught up to him, but I held my own. This was not an easy pace. When we hit the hour mark, I called ahead to let him know I was turning around. I didn't get an answer. I turned around anyway and started back to the car, pushing the pace until I reached that place where everything was hard but I wanted to keep running forever. The trail was as challenging as anything I was used to in Portland, and although it wasn't as pretty—I was biased towards the Pacific Northwest—it was reminiscent enough of the trail runs I did before everything changed that I was able to shed the stresses and worries of my new life and fall into the meditative rhythm of my feet.

Running had always been my peaceful place. The place I went to relax, to work through whatever problems I was having, to get away from it all. It'd been a long time since I'd been alone on a trail—and even though Isaac was out there somewhere, he wasn't close enough for me to hear.

The knots in my shoulders loosened and my gait smoothed out. The ups and downs over the rutted single track no longer felt challenging. I felt like I was flying over the dirt. Now that I knew what it was like to fly, I was comfortable comparing the exhilaration of flying as a dragon to a trail runner's high.

I was smiling, arms and legs pumping, when something hit my right side and knocked me down. With the extra momentum from running, I tucked and rolled and came up into a crouch with a knife in each hand. There was a large wolf in front of me. Its teeth were bared, although its mouth was closed. The eyes were almost glowing a yellowish color, and its dark gray and brown coat blended well with the undergrowth.

For a second I thought Isaac was fucking with me, and then I recalled the glimpses I'd had of him in his wolf form showed a much lighter coat. Saliva dripped from the teeth of the wolf in front of me.

I crouched down lower, trying to get my head below the wolf's head without losing my feet. I thought maybe showing it I recognized its dominance would help. When it kept growling that low, disturbing rumble in its throat, I decided that was a losing proposition. I really didn't want it to feel superior to me, anyway.

"What do you want?" I asked. I slid the knife in my left hand back into the wrist sheath on my right wrist and then grabbed two more knives from the sheaths on my thighs. I returned the knife in my right hand to a wrist sheath. Rearmed with the silver throwing knives Isaac had given me, I slowly stood.

The wolf took a couple of steps backward before catching itself and moving forward, growling even more aggressively. I was definitely winning this dominance contest.

"I don't have time for this shit. Either tell me what you want or bugger off."

The wolf's mouth opened and its tongue lolled out. A second later, I recognized it as a doggy grin. My stomach tightened. Soft, almost imperceptible footsteps padded behind me. I shifted my position to keep the wolf in my view and get a glimpse of what was coming. Three more wolves flanked me.

Fuck. I shouldn't have said we hadn't been attacked my shifters yet. This is all my fault.

Figuring I had little to lose by startling the wolves at this point, I took a deep breath and yelled, "Isaac!"

I didn't want to back up in case they misinterpreted it as submission. I met each wolf's eyes and then moved until my back was against a tree. There wasn't a lot of room in the clearing, but there was enough for me to shift. I'd be vulnerable for a few moments, so I'd need to take out a couple of my current opponents first, but once I shifted, they were toast.

I readied my knives and eyed my opposition closely. They formed a half circle and slowly closed in on me. My knife-throwing skills—while not terrible—were not such that I could count on kill shots.

I picked my first two targets: the wolf flanking me on the right and the one immediately to its left. I threw the first knife and without even checking to see if and where it hit, I threw the second. I grabbed the other two silver knives out of my thigh sheaths and threw them at the remaining two wolves. I scoped out the enemy and prepared to shift. I'd scored four hits, but only the first one appeared lethal. I'd gotten the first right in the throat and it looked like that wolf had already bled out. I must have hit the carotid and the silver kept it from healing fast enough.

The other three wolves I'd hit in the general chest region, but not anyplace useful. They were already getting up and shaking off the effects. They'd probably be a bit slower than before—especially the two that still had the knives stuck in them—but that wasn't going to be terribly slow.

I considered my options. If I was going to shift, I needed to do it now. I would be vulnerable as I changed. I'd have to kill them all. I didn't want my enemies to know I could turn into a dragon.

I dropped my steel knives into my hands and flipped them over to grasp the blades. I winced when my bare skin came into contact with the iron-threaded material. My sensitivity was definitely getting worse. I readied the knives, threw them, one at a time, at the two wolves who looked like they were recovering fastest and began the change. I formed the image of the dragon in my mind and pushed my essence into the picture, willing myself to hurry.

By the time I was stretching my wings out and regretting not having taken the time to strip off my running clothes, all three wolves were on their feet and charging. I didn't want to start a forest fire, and this place was the crackly dry of late autumn, so I held off on breathing fire at my attackers and went for brute force. I reared onto my hind legs and pulled my wings in close. I grabbed one wolf in each of my massive claws and the third with my teeth. I hadn't meant to bite as hard as I did. I'd wanted to hold it still while I disposed of the others, but I hadn't had a lot of practice doing that and misjudged. I'd cut the wolf nearly in half by the time I released it back to the ground. I was gagging on the taste of his blood—I like a rare steak as much as the next person, but raw werewolf was rank.

The other two wolves shook in my grasp and one let go of its bladder. Killing shifters was gross. I'd much rather kill vampires: minimal blood, a lot of dust, and, with the exception of Grigori, easy body disposal. A vacuum and a garbage bag, and before you can say "ashes to ashes" you've cleaned up your crime scene.

This, on the other hand, was not neat. The two dead wolves shimmered and slowly turned back to their human selves. I didn't recognize either of them—not that I necessarily would. I didn't know many shifters. I cocked my head and looked at the wolf in my right claw. Now that I had them, it was harder to kill them than I'd thought it would be. Killing in the heat of battle was easy. Killing once I'd neutralized the enemy and scared the literal piss out them was different.

I didn't know how to shift back without letting them go, and they were terrified. The second they were free, they'd either run or do something incredibly stupid like try to kill me again. I wished Isaac would show up and help out. Unless he hadn't turned around when I yelled turn, he should've only been a couple of minutes behind me. The fight hadn't taken long, but he should be here.

I panicked and one of the wolves made a hacking sound. I looked down and realized that in my own fear, I'd crushed its chest and caused it to slowly suffocate. I started shaking. This was not how I wanted things to go—I didn't want to torture someone. I dropped the wolf I'd broken and then reached down with my jaw, braced myself against the taste, and bit its head off. I spit the head out of my mouth and it rolled across the clearing. By the time it came to a stop, it was a woman with long, silvery-blond hair and an ethereally beautiful face.

The remaining wolf in my left claw went limp. I looked at it, but other than the knife wound caused by my first throw, there was nothing physically wrong. The wolf had fainted. Now was as good a time as any to turn back. I dropped the wolf and shifted. It was painful. Between the run, the brief fight, and the surges of adrenalin, I'd used most of my reserves. I rolled the wolf over and used strips of my ruined clothing to hog tie him. Then I walked back towards the trail and headed away from the car, looking for Isaac. I was naked and barefoot when I broke into a jog, one arm across my breasts to hold them still. I heard someone coming towards me, and I ducked off the trail. I didn't want to explain my naked jogging. Seconds later, Isaac ran into view. I jumped out of the underbrush and ran towards him.

He looked shocked.

"Are you okay?" I said. I ran my hands over his face and body, searching for injuries.

He raised an eyebrow. "Yes. Why?"

"Why didn't you turn around when I yelled out at the hour mark?"

"I wasn't quite ready to turn. I knew I'd catch up with you."

I punched him in the arm. "You asshole! What if you'd been attacked?"

"I can take care of myself."

"Against how many?"

"At least a half dozen before I'd need to even begin to think about worrying. Why are you naked?"

"Because I was attacked. I killed people. Shifter people." I burst into tears and he pulled me into his shaking arms.

I hated tears. I hated weakness of any kind but having him hold me while I sobbed out my guilt was nice. Eventually, I got a hold of myself.

"Sorry," I said, rubbing my eyes.

"It's okay," Isaac said. "Are you okay?" His eyes roved over my body looking for injury.

"I'm fine, physically. I'm not fine emotionally. I didn't mean to kill them like that."

"I'm still unclear as to why you're naked, though."

"You know me—I always fight in the nude." I tried to smile.

Isaac gave me the sideways look that comment deserved and cocked an eyebrow at me.

"I had to shift, and didn't have time to strip first. My clothes were destroyed. My ruined clothing is currently serving as rope for the fourth wolf. Can we go back to the scene? We'll need to call someone to clean it up. We can't leave a bunch of bodies in a clearing in the woods."

"Do you want my shirt?"

I eyed his sweat-soaked shirt and weighed the disgustingness of putting that on against the discomfort of being naked in the woods. "Nah, I'll stay like this unless we hear someone coming."

I led Isaac back to the clearing. Everything was as I'd left it except the wolf was now conscious and struggling against his spandex restraints.

Isaac growled at him. The wolf shrank in on itself and tilted its head back, offering Isaac its throat. Isaac reached out and snapped the wolf's neck. Its body melted into its human form—this one appeared to be a young man, barely on the verge of adulthood.

I gasped in shock and suppressed another wave of nausea.

"We couldn't let him tell anyone what you are," Isaac said. He didn't meet my gaze.

"Shouldn't we have questioned him or something first?" A note of hysteria was creeping into my voice.

Isaac looked around the clearing. There was a man on the far edge with a silver knife in his throat, another man in the center of the clearing who'd been bitten nearly in two, and a torso lying a few feet from that one.

"Where's the head?" he asked. I pointed to the far edge where the woman's head had rolled into the shadow of a stump. "How?"

I gestured towards the first body, "Lucky shot with a silver knife. The second there, was an accident. I was trying to hold him still with my teeth, but bit too hard. The headless one," I gagged and ran to the edge of the clearing where I emptied my stomach. I could taste the blood coming back up which triggered another round of gagging and vomiting. When I was finally done, I realized Isaac was standing next to me, rubbing my back. He handed me the water bottle he'd been carrying and I rinsed out my mouth.

I continued, without looking at the carnage. "The third one was an accident, too. I was holding her in my claws, and I squeezed too hard. She was suffocating, so I killed her to stop the suffering."

"That was good, Eleanor. Merciful. As was what I did. Once you shifted in front of him, you sealed his fate."

He was right. I knew he was right. But something was wrong, and I couldn't put my finger on it. "How do we clean this up?"

"I'll call Christopher. These might be his wolves, and if so, he has the right to know he was betrayed. If he sent them, his reaction will tell us if we were." He rotated me until I was facing away from the clearing. "Can you go back to the car and grab some clothes and my phone? I'll make sure no one stumbles onto this mess."

"How far is it?"

"About two miles."

"It'll be a slow jog for me without shoes or a sports bra," I said. "You could be there and back in less than a half hour."

"I wasn't sure you were up for staying alone."

"I made this mess; I can sit here until we get someone to clean it up."

Isaac kissed me and started towards the trail.

"Isaac?"

He stopped.

"Can you bring food? I'm starving."

He nodded and disappeared towards the trail.

I collected my knives and used the water I'd carried and my torn clothes to clean them. I gathered up the sheaths and examined them. They were destroyed as well. When I'd gathered and cleaned all the knives but the one in the first dead wolf, I sat cross-legged on the ground. I stood immediately. Naked cross-legged pose was not comfortable on the forest floor. I wished I had a watch to check. I'd been about twenty minutes since Isaac had left, but without a watch, my inner chronometer might be off.

I walked a perimeter around the clearing, carefully avoiding any blood puddles. A few minutes later, I heard someone coming. I tensed until I was able to scent him.

Isaac walked into the clearing and I went to meet him. He'd brought jeans, a lacy bra, and a low-cut t-shirt along with some socks and tennis shoes. "Really? This is what you were able to find?"

"That's it."

"Not the pile of clothes on the front seat that included panties and a more practical bra?"

"Didn't see them," he said.

I rolled my eyes and got dressed.

"Christopher is on his way. When he arrives, unless he looks guilty, we can leave him to it."

I tore into the energy bars Isaac had brought along. We waited in silence until Christopher and two others showed up. If the expression on his face was genuine, this was a shock to him—and he knew the wolves we'd killed.

"What happened?"

I recounted my story, leaving out the part about the dragon, which meant two of the dead were difficult to explain. He looked at me sharply and I returned his gaze with my best poker face.

"There's more than you're telling me," he said.

"There is, and Isaac can tell you the rest of the story tomorrow. But not now, when we don't know who might be listening."

"Fair point. Thank you for your role in uncovering the traitors in my house."

We were dismissed.

CHAPTER TEN

DINNER WAS OVER, Florence had gone, and I was contemplating going to bed when the air stirred near me.

Raj dropped out of the sky well away from the campfire and with no preamble announced, "I have news."

"So nice to see you, Raj," Isaac said.

"It's always nice to see you," Raj said. He stared at Isaac heatedly until Isaac dropped his eyes.

"I can't believe you let him out dominate you," I said.

"That wasn't a dominance contest," Raj said.

"You can't have a dominance contest with a vampire. They can ensnare you with their gaze." Isaac told me.

"And was he trying to ensnare you?"

"Since we met," Isaac said.

"He's such a jerk." I met Raj's gaze and I wasn't sure if I hoped he'd try or not.

His voice whispered in my head, *"I would not seriously try to ensnare either of you. I want you in my bed of your own free will. I always get what I want."*

"You have news?"

"I have found the gate. Would you like to come with me to confirm it?"

"How far is it?" Isaac asked. "Florence took the car already."

"It's close—only about a mile and a half as the vampire flies."

I looked around the campground. "You don't think anyone will see me?" I asked. Flying sounded delightful.

"It's unlikely. We'll be flying over mostly forested land. However, I thought it'd be better if I flew us there and then, if you feel comfortable, you can fly back."

"What about me?" Isaac said.

"You can wait here. We won't be long."

"It sounds like a good plan. I'll let you carry me because I'm already twitchy this close to the gate. I don't want to lose control of my dragon when we get there—who knows what kind of havoc I'd wreak. Side note: can you believe we found a campsite this close? How lucky are we?"

"Luck probably had nothing to do with this," Isaac said.

"Are you ready, my sweet?" Raj asked. He opened his arms.

Isaac dropped a quick kiss on my lips and pushed me lightly towards Raj. "Go."

I stepped into Raj's arms and he wrapped them around me. Before I could take another breath, he shot into the air. I was gasping and breathless in seconds. The ground zoomed away from us, and I felt vulnerable up here in my human form. I wondered if I could change before I died.

"You're immortal." Raj's voice in my head sounded amused.

"I can be killed."

"Not from falling."

"It'd really suck, though."

"We are not quite as high as a skydiver's plane. It would take you about a minute to hit the ground from here. How long does it take you to change?"

I'd never timed myself. *"Longer than a minute if I was plunging to my death."*

"I promise not to drop you."

I reached inside and found the spark that initiated the shift. I grabbed on, ready to change if necessary, and forced myself to relax into Raj.

We hadn't been in the air long when Raj descended. Vibrations overtook me, although I couldn't tell if they were having a physical effect or merely a mental one. Either way, I was nauseated. I was glad Raj had insisted on carrying me.

"I'm right about everything I insist upon," he said as we landed gently in a small parking lot.

I tried to laugh at his arrogance, but the unopened gate consumed me. I held onto Raj when he would've stepped away.

"Do you need me to carry you closer?" he asked.

I wanted to say no, but nodded. "I wonder why it was so hard to find the first gate? There's no ignoring this power—it's even stronger than the last one."

"You are more powerful now. You've honed your skills and you've had the magic of two gates pour over you. There's more magic in the world, now, too."

Raj picked me up. "Which way?"

I pointed to the northwest and he headed in that direction. It was dark, but I saw enough to realize we were in the middle of a circle of sticks. "Is this a henge?"

"It is."

"Holy shit. No wonder it's a place of power. Who built it?"

"This is a reconstruction, but the Mississippian Indians who lived here built it in about 1000 CE."

"This is younger than you, isn't it?"

"Yes."

"Holy shit," I said again. "That is crazy. I'm at an ancient archeological site with someone who was already alive when it was built. My life is insane."

"This is it? The gate?"

"It is. I wonder if any of these sticks mark the sunrise or sunset on Samhain?"

"It seems likely. I stopped in the visitor's center and read about markers for the solstices and equinoxes. Why not the cross-quarter days?"

"Can we leave?"

"Already?"

"It's too much. I want to do…things."

"What kind of things? Maybe we should stay."

I elbowed him in the ribs. "Not those kind of things, pervert."

He laughed. "Do you want to fly back, or shall I carry you?"

"You'd better carry me. I can't concentrate with all this music."

"Music?"

"It's the music of the spheres. Or the gates. It's beautiful, but distracting."

"Your wish is my command." He moved the arm supporting my legs and my body slid down the length of his until I was standing facing him, our bodies lightly touching.

"Raj," I said.

He smiled and pulled me closer. "Wrap your arms around my neck," he whispered. His arms tightened around my waist and he rose into the air. I yelped and did as he asked. Our lips were centimeters apart and when he opened his mouth and ran his tongue over his pointed fangs, heat flooded my body. Again.

"You're not playing fair," I whispered.

"Why would I do that?"

I barely noticed the air rushing by as he flew us to the campground. I concentrated on not running my tongue over his teeth.

He leaned forward and brushed my lips with his. I told myself it was only the fear of falling that made me tighten my grip and lean into him. It was a brief, gentle kiss, over almost before it started. Moments later, we dropped back into the campground, almost in the same spot we'd started from.

Isaac sat at the picnic table, pointedly not looking. He could probably smell my arousal, and the fact we'd landed facing each other instead of my back to Raj's front like we'd started must've looked suspicious.

Raj let go of me, and I stumbled backwards. Isaac jumped up and steadied me before I fell. I looked at him, breathed in his scent, and then used a tremendous amount of willpower to keep from pushing him back onto the picnic table and ripping his clothes off.

"Go ahead," Raj said. "I don't mind."

Isaac raised an eyebrow questioningly.

"She was thinking of taking you right here on the picnic table. I was going to enjoy the show."

"Beer?" I asked. I needed to put some distance between myself and these men if I was going to maintain a shred of dignity.

Isaac grabbed a beer from the open cooler. He popped the top on the table and handed it to me. Then he pulled the loosened cork out of the nearby wine bottle and poured a glass for Raj.

"Was it the gate?" Isaac asked.

"It was."

"So we're set now. Nothing to do for the next ten days."

"Lots to do, but the big things are done," I said. I turned towards Raj. "Am I right in assuming you're skilled with a sword?"

He opened his mouth, and I interrupted, "That was not intended to be a euphemism." Raj laughed.

"I am, as you say, skilled with a sword."

"Would you mind sparring with me every evening? My skills are dropping off, and I've not had a chance to spar with someone who is basically immortal and is as fast as I am."

"I'd be delighted."

"Great! I'll do magic practice with Florence, hand-to-hand with Isaac, work on the knife throwing skills, and then sword practice with you."

"Trying to lose weight?" Raj asked.

In my head, I punched him. Hard. He winced and laughed.

"You guessed it. I want to lose those pesky ten pounds and write a book. 'Lose 10 Pounds in 10 Days with Combat Training and Actual Combat with Supernatural Creatures!'"

Raj laughed, drained his wine, and stood up. "I'm off. I'm feeling a bit peckish, and since it seems unlikely either of you are going to offer to be my meal this evening, I'll look elsewhere."

He bowed and then shot up into the air and disappeared.

"Is there anything you'd like to tell me?" Isaac asked.

"It was intense and beautiful. Maybe we can drive over there tomorrow. It really is close."

"I meant about Raj."

"No. I mean, he does that sexual thing to me all the time, but he does it to you, too."

"Are you still feeling that heat?"

I looked up at him from under my eyelashes. "A bit. Maybe you'd volunteer as tribute?"

"I could give it a try."

I set down my beer and walked into Isaac's arms. He leaned forward and kissed me, then pulled back. "I can taste him on your lips."

"He kissed me when he was flying me back."

"Are your lips the only thing he touched?"

"The only thing that wasn't necessary. It's not a big deal. He's committed to his horny vampire schtick and tries the seduction techniques on everyone. Including you. If we weren't here, he'd probably be making eyes at the nearest tree hoping a dryad would pop out."

Isaac kissed me again, not lightly this time. I stepped backwards a few steps, pulling him with me, until my ass hit the picnic table. I let go of Isaac for a second and hopped up on the table. I pulled him into me again, and found when he was back in my arms he'd dropped his shirt along the way somewhere. I ran my hands over his bare skin, lightly scoring him with my nails. He gasped and then pushed me back onto the table, climbing on top of me. I tried to shimmy out of my shirt, but managed to get it stuck halfway off my head. It never happened like this in the movies.

Isaac was laughing uproariously by the time we managed to get me unstuck from my uncooperative clothing. I punched him lightly in the arm. "Laughing at my difficulties is not the way to get laid."

He stopped and arranged his face into a sober expression. "You're right. This is serious business."

I started giggling, and we laughed until we were out of breath.

When my laughter ran its course, I reached around behind me and unhooked my bra. Isaac watched with interest as I slowly revealed my breasts. He reached up and cupped them reverently in his hands, kissing one puckered nipple and then the other. He spent a great deal of time kissing and biting and teasing. I reached up, wrapped my legs around his waist, and pulled him tight against me. I tried to arch into him, but he disentangled himself and climbed off the table.

"What are you doing? That is not okay."

"I thought it might be easier if we were more naked."

I thought about it for a second. "You're right." I unbuttoned and unzipped my jeans, then lifted my hips. Isaac reached over and pulled them off and tossed them on the ground. I slid my panties off and tossed them in the direction my jeans had gone. He climbed back on top of me, and this time when I wrapped my legs around him, he didn't pull away. We kissed and teased until neither of us could stand it anymore. Finally, he rose up and plunged inside me. I gasped as he filled me, but before I could get used to the sensation, he was moving and everything intensified. I bit down on Isaac's shoulder as I came, and he howled, sounding more like a wolf than a man.

When it was over, we lay gasping with him still inside me.

"Are you okay?" I asked, examining the bite mark in the flickering firelight.

"Your puny teeth can't hurt me."

I bared my teeth at him and growled, but he laughed and disentangled our limbs. He rolled off me and just kept rolling. I heard a bump as he hit the bench of the picnic table and then a muffled whump as he hit the ground. I sat up and peered down at him. He was sitting on the ground shaking with laughter.

"Even covered in dirt, you are a beautiful man," I said. His nudity stirred the banked fires of my lust. I couldn't believe this gorgeous creature was mine.

He smiled, and his white teeth were a bright contrast in the darkness. "I'd better wash up, though. Sticky and dirty is not a good combination."

I nodded, "I'll come with you." I got off the table, grabbed a couple of towels from the camper, and followed him to the campground showers. We cleaned off, managed to avoid any shower shenanigans, and went back to the camper. Isaac banked the fire and we went into the camper to get some sleep. Eventually.

THE TEN DAYS leading up to the full moon were an exhausting blur. I worked on building an even more powerful magic weir with Florence. I practiced knife throwing and hand-to-hand combat with Isaac. And at sunset each evening, Raj came to me for our swordsmanship. I had my rapier and a couple of months of combat practice. He carried a khanda and centuries of practical application. He was fast and skilled, and it was all I could do to last five minutes against him without being "killed."

I practiced with my actual rapier, since, as he said, it was almost impossible to accidentally remove his head in combat practice. He used a practice blade. It was metal, but without a honed point or edge. It still hurt like hell every time he made it through my meager defenses and whacked me with it. Everywhere the metal touched skin, I developed a rash to go with my bruises. My iron allergy was growing the more I was exposed to it.

Each evening, after I was exhausted from sparring, I shifted into my dragon and flew closer and closer to the gate. I wanted to test my control while I was tired to make sure I could maintain it. Shifting forms had another benefit: when I shifted back to my human form, most of my cuts and bruises had healed.

My clothes were hanging off a frame that'd never needed help filling out a tank top before. There wasn't enough food in the world, and I was dreaming about taking naps.

"You need to rest," Florence said, interrupting me as I was about to nod off into my fifth meal of the day.

"I can't. I'm not ready."

"You'll never feel ready. That's life. There's always one more thing you could do to prepare. But for now, take a break."

I stretched and prepared to revel in the thirty minutes of alone time I would have before Isaac returned. Before I could get too used to the rare feeling, Arduinna appeared.

"May I approach, Your Highness?"

"Of course," I said, as regally as I could in my cut-offs and tank top. "What's shakin'?" I knew my informality would bug her. Sure enough, one muscle next to her left eye was twitching. I smiled, triumphant.

"I have people in place who can protect the nuclear reactors around the world. There are hundreds of places that need protection, and it was not easy to get them all here. They are not all in place yet, but the ones in this region of this country will be in place by Samhain."

"How will you do it?"

"We will construct time bubbles to slow down the effects of the reactors until we can figure out how to dismantle them safely. We cannot start, though, while there are still people who would notice and interfere. That is the other thing I am here to tell you. In order to protect the world from a sudden nuclear disaster, we need to tell the world why. Or at least part of why. Next week, there will be an announcement. The supernatural populations will no longer be living in secret."

I stared at Arduinna. That wasn't what I'd expected.

"This won't end well."

"What do you mean?"

"People will panic. There will be riots. We will be hunted."

"I do not think it will be that bad. There are several supernaturals in positions of power in this government and many others. They will keep order."

"I'm not sure that's true. Have you seen X-Men?"

"I do not know what that is."

"It is a movie—actually a series of movies—about how the American people react when they find out a portion of the population is supernaturally inclined. Spoiler: they don't react well."

"But if it is a movie, it is fiction."

"Technically, yes. But in reality? People are assholes. They're afraid of what they don't understand, and they shoot the things that make them afraid. It's how I feel about spiders. I don't understand why they need so many legs and lurk in my bedroom, so I squish them. I don't want to be America's spider."

"The only other way to make this work, then, will result in the death or modification of hundreds and thousands of people. Without announcing the boundaries that keep the magic from this world are breaking, we cannot convince people to stop flying their airplanes and to let us in to protect their nuclear power. Planes will crash. Again. You will not be able to stop air traffic in this area of the country like you did in the last. We will still be able to protect the nuclear reactors, but we will need to trap the workers inside as well. It is unknown whether they will survive that process.

"It will be your choice, Your Highness."

I stared at her, feeling helpless. I gathered my resolve, steeled my backbone, and thought it through. "If there are already supernaturals in several positions of power in the government, can't they give the orders, or push things through, to give us the results we want without alarming the public?"

"You would have your government take major actions like this, act secretive, and not share the information? Won't that alarm your countrymen?" I was beginning to believe Arduinna spent a lot more time on this plane than she let on. She was leading me by the nose and it seemed likely I would arrive at the same conclusion she and several others already had.

"Yes, but they could blame it on terrorists. That's what they do every time there's something inexplicable."

"It might be possible, but there are enough people who are not supernatural who would have to be involved in the process that leaks are bound to happen. And they will happen while it is still possible to broadcast their images across the world. People will want to be seen."

"So a controlled announcement, eh?"

"The president is Fae. A half-blood, anyway." Arduinna briefly looked like she'd smelled something foul. I guess her hatred of the half-bloods wasn't contained to Finn. "There are members of

Congress that are shifters, and a few top-ranked military officers are vampires, although I don't know how they manage."

"My name, my face, and my companions' identities won't be revealed?"

"No. We do not wish you further hindered."

"Fuck. My choices are to either let a bunch of people die and/or be trapped in radioactive time bubbles or to tell the world Twilight is real?"

"I hope you're team Edward," Raj said, appearing behind me.

"Not until you start sparkling in the sunlight, vamp. I'm not sure how to process the knowledge you've seen Twilight."

"I go to all the vampire movies. They make me laugh."

Arduinna was still looking at me expectantly.

"Can I have twenty-four hours to consider?"

"Yes. I will return tomorrow night for your orders." She turned to go.

"Wait." She turned back towards me.

"My apologies, Highness. I know I was not dismissed."

"I don't care if you leave before you're formally dismissed."

"I know, but if you ever take the throne, you would have to punish me for my impertinence, or else others would either assume we were lovers, giving me special rights or they would try to take advantage of your informal nature. And that would be bad. Better I retain good habits now."

"Are you asking me to bed?" I teased.

Arduinna flushed, although I suspected it was more ire than embarrassment. I guessed she wanted to say something ridiculously rude, but was holding back, due to the whole "power of decapitation" thing I had going on.

"I'm teasing. I wanted to ask if you'd had any word on Finn."

"I have not seen him."

"That's not what I asked."

She didn't elaborate further.

I heaved a melodramatic sigh. "Arduinna, have you heard any news or rumors or whispers about Finn's whereabouts or motivations?"

"You're getting good at this, Highness."

I was losing patience. "Answer the question."

"Yes. He was seen leaving the palace of the Dark Queen. Since he left with all appendages intact, it is believed he is allied with her, rather than with your father as previously believed. I do not know if he was always on her side and played the Light Court for a fool, or if your behavior drove him to this course of action."

"I didn't drive him to anything. His own insecurities and jealousy may have driven him places, but I won't take the blame for his short-comings. Even if I'd loved him truly and passionately, something would have happened that would've caused him to make inexcusably bad decisions. Perhaps he would've decided that, for my own protection, I needed to be part of the Dark Queen's court. He's not grounded in reality. I wonder how much of that is a character flaw, and how much of that was created while you and yours were "grooming" him for the task of being my keeper?"

Arduinna shifted on her feet and looked at the ground. Interesting. I'd struck a nerve. However he'd been groomed, it hadn't been pleasant. That might explain his lack of loyalty to my father.

"Any idea what he and the Queen discussed?"

"I have not heard anyone repeat their conversation."

"Let's assume I'm not an idiot and then you can answer the question." Raj moved restlessly behind me. I reached back and took his hand. Being between two powerful creatures was nerve-wracking. I needed Raj at my side, not my back. He moved forward to stand beside me and tension drained from my body. Another ally, and one this powerful, would hopefully make Finn think twice about fucking with me and mine.

"I will be by your side as long as you'll have me," Raj murmured.

"There was someone in the court while they met," Arduinna ground out. "He only revealed Finn was there. He has told no one of the conversation he overheard. He is a double-agent and is trying to maintain his cover. The queen believes him to be betraying your father, and we would like to keep her beliefs intact."

"Do you believe he would share information if that knowledge would keep me and my companions safe?"

"He would share knowledge if it would keep you safe. That is his prime directive."

"You're a Trekkie?"

Arduinna's lips curled up slightly and her greenish-tinged teeth flashed in what I could only assume was a grin.

"Fine." She visibly relaxed. Once again, someone I relied on knew more than they were letting on. At least Arduinna couldn't lie. I looked at her, trying to see where she'd led me astray with her words, but couldn't. I waved my hand. "You may go, Arduinna."

She bowed and disappeared into the trees.

I was still holding Raj's hand when I heard my car coming towards us. I tried to let go with casual indifference, but he tightened his grip. "I meant what I said, Eleanor," Raj said. "I will stand by your side as long as you will let me."

I looked up at him. "Why are you playing this game with me?"

"You're interesting. I haven't met someone interesting in a long, long time."

"Things are going to get dicey."

"You'll take the course that results in the least human casualties, even if it makes your life more difficult. I'm prepared for dicey. It won't be the first time I've stood at the front lines with the commander of a people."

I didn't get a chance to reply before Isaac approached. He looked at our clasped hands, took a deep breath, and ignored it. Pointedly. "I smell Arduinna. What's going on?"

I filled them in on the entirety of the conversation with Arduinna. Every couple of minutes I tried to free my hand from Raj without seeming like I was getting uncomfortable, but he wouldn't let go. Finally, I said, exasperated, "Raj! Can you please let go of my hand?"

He looked surprised. "But of course, my sweet! I had no idea you wanted me to let go. You had only to ask."

I rolled my eyes at him and he laughed. Isaac did not.

When I finished my narrative, Isaac looked thoughtful.

"I must inform you, Isaac, Eleanor is considering joining Team Edward."

Isaac looked confused. I started to explain the movie to him, and he waved his hand at me. "I've seen it. I tried to catch up on all the werewolf movies. They make me laugh."

I started laughing. He looked at me. "What?"

"That's exactly what Raj said."

"I'm confused," Isaac said. "You seem more like a Team Jacob kind of girl."

"This is the weirdest conversation I've ever had," I said. "Sorry, Raj. If it makes you feel better, I preferred Spike to Oz."

"I am content with this," Raj said.

"What do I do?"

"It's your decision, Princess," Isaac said.

"Okay. But you are two of my top royal advisors. What would you advise me to do?"

"What does your gut tell you?" Isaac asked.

My stomach growled. "My gut tells me it's time for dinner."

We ate, and chatted about movies and television shows. Raj and Isaac had a friendly argument about the realism of various supernatural creatures in the media, while I drank a glass of wine and watched their faces animate in the firelight. I wished Florence was here. I heard tires crunching on the gravel, and realized it was Florence.

"I wish I had a magical camper that was bigger on the inside and didn't require a gasoline powered car to haul it around," I said.

Raj and Isaac looked at me.

"I wished Florence was here, and now she is. I thought I should strike again while my wishing power was on."

Florence joined us by the fire. I caught her up to date on Arduinna's news, and then leaned back while the conversation turned to the mundane. I felt comfortable, secure, relaxed, even. I felt like I was home.

CHAPTER ELEVEN

I WOKE THE next morning wrapped in Isaac's arms. I'd gone to bed without making a decision about what I would tell Arduinna, but the reality was I didn't have a choice. If I looked back, all of my choices—with the exception of one—were non-choices.

I slipped out of Isaac's arms, showered and dressed, and followed the scent of freshly brewing coffee back to the camper. Isaac truly was the best thing that'd happened to me as a result of all the other crazy shit.

He smiled as I approached and as always, his intense gaze gave me butterflies and inappropriate thoughts.

I heard the crunch of gravel under car wheels. "Sounds like Florence is here with breakfast."

LATER THAT DAY, I headed into town to pull out my daily cash maximum from the ATM. I got back in the car and said, "My bank balance is not decreasing. In fact, it's increasing. I printed a receipt, and it doesn't show any transactions. No deposits. No charges. Nothing."

"That is not the biggest problem you've had on this journey," Florence said.

"I wish I'd had a magical bank account when I was in college."

"No one needs a magical bank account in college," Florence said. "People in college are too stupid for unlimited funds."

"There may be a run on the banks once Arduinna's people make the announcement," Isaac said. "People will panic, especially if the scope of the upcoming events is disclosed."

"This is going to suck."

"You could not make the announcement," Isaac said.

"I can't be responsible for any more deaths. Not if I can prevent them."

"There is no easy answer," Florence said. "If Arduinna's people make the announcement, people who would otherwise die in plane crashes will be saved and nuclear reactor personnel will have a chance to escape. On the other hand, if the announcement isn't made, the reactors will still be secured, but people might be trapped in the bubbles as they are dismantled, correct?"

I nodded.

"Some people will need to be in there to oversee the controlled shut-down. Those people ideally would be volunteers, but unless there's a bunch of self-sacrificing Fae out there, they'll use humans. The Fae can construct the bubbles at night when the fewest people are there and ensure one person at each site will have the correct orders. Surely the supernatural president and military brass can take care of that."

"What about the planes?"

"I'll give Arduinna my FAA friend's name, and he can receive his orders directly from the military to shut down air traffic around St. Louis. They can order an evacuation of the city, let them know there is a credible terrorist plot against the city—confirm the events in Portland and Rapid City were related, and blame it on some hitherto unknown group headed by a Hans Gruber-like fellow. We don't want armed idiots going after brown-skinned people."

"Florence, you are brilliant."

"I know. You should still load up on cash, and we'll keep buying supplies that will be worth more than cash once the country finally collapses, but it's in everyone's best interest to delay as much as possible."

I mulled over my options during the day. My choices weren't great, but after Florence's comments, I felt like I at least had choices. I'd suggested a similar course of action to Arduinna the night before, though, and she'd dismissed it out of hand. I thought back over that conversation, trying to figure out why the "blame it on the terrorists" course of action had been shot down—no pun intended.

Leaks, Arduinna had said. There were people who knew the truth who didn't want it to be a secret. They must be threatening to go public in a less controlled way or something. I'd have to ask Arduinna.

THAT EVENING BEFORE DINNER, I waited at the edge of the clearing until Arduinna appeared. Isaac and Florence stood a little behind me, content, apparently, to let me run the show.

When she was within hailing distance, she bowed before coming close enough to converse without shouting.

"Your Highness," she greeted me.

"Arduinna."

"Have you decided?"

"Yes."

"I will schedule the announcement with my contacts."

"That's not what I decided."

Arduinna froze. For the first time since I'd met her, she looked nonplussed. "You have decided to let events happen as they will? To kill thousands?"

"Arduinna, it's great you're pretending to care about humans for my sake, but you don't need to."

"They are irresponsible parasites who do not deserve this land they are destroying. It will take decades—maybe centuries—to restore the land. However, not all humans are guilty. Some are merely complicit."

"I have questions before I tell you my decision. Will you listen and answer true?"

Arduinna looked at me, weighing her answer. "As far as I am able without saying anything I am forbidden to tell you."

"Fair enough. How do you travel? You're always coming out of groves of trees." I thought about the first time we met, and began to understand even before she answered.

"I have an...affinity for trees. Where there are woods, or even an old, strong tree, I can travel. Well-established trees are in a...network, you might say. I merge my consciousness with one and reach out into the network to find my destination."

"You're emailing yourself through a tree network?"

"Treemailing would be an accurate term," Arduinna said, deadpan.

"I love it when you're funny. Maybe someday you'll loosen up enough to have a beer with me."

"That seems unlikely, Highness."

"We'll see." I grinned. I didn't think she despised me as much as she pretended. "Second question: How do you find me?"

"I am attuned to you in a similar way Finn is attuned to you," she said.

"At some point in my past, you not only created a mental connection between me and Finn but me and you?"

She nodded.

"Why tell me now?"

"I was not forbidden to tell you, and I can see no reason to hide the truth. At this point, you would prefer me to be your Fae on the ground, yes?"

I nodded.

"That means you will not attempt to kill me to remove this bond, especially since the only other Fae you are connected to is Finn."

"Fair enough. The only two Fae with this connection to me are you and Finn?"

"That I know about, yes."

"One last question. If the Fae cannot lie, how can they be spies and double-agents? How can someone work for both my father and the Dark Queen and not be caught?"

Arduinna took longer to answer this question. "It is not easy," she said. "The double-agent would have to be even more skilled than most in deceptive truths to never lie but to continue to serve two masters. If asked, "Are you a spy?" it would not be enough to answer, "Why would you think that of me?" or "How could you accuse me of such a crime?" because a competent questioner would continue to drill the person until they got a definitive answer. Instead, the person must be so successful the question of guilt would never come up—they would have to divide their allegiance and be loyal to both parties. Not many are capable of such things."

"How do you trust a double-agent knowing their loyalties are divided?"

"You don't."

What's the point then? I wondered, but did not say. I clearly had a lot to learn about politics.

"Thank you for answering my questions. Now here is my decision." I outlined the plan Florence had laid out earlier. I watched Arduinna carefully for any signs of disgruntlement, but she showed no emotion.

"You said there were opportunists who wanted the supernaturals to be exposed in a less-than-flattering manner?" I asked.

"Yes."

"If you know about them, then they have been identified. Is there a way to neutralize them for the time being?"

Arduinna grinned, and I hastened to add, "Non-lethally."

"I will think on it, Highness."

"What if you told them they could be the ones to make the announcement at a later date?" Isaac asked. "Let them have the glory at a time of your choosing."

"President Murphy and General Aldea might not agree."

"Why wouldn't they? If they're going to manipulate the timeline and the American public, wouldn't it be better to paint themselves in a more sympathetic light? They can prepare for the announcements by doing everything they can to ensure they—and by association other supernaturals—look good," Florence said.

I looked at her admiringly. "You are frighteningly good at this."

"You have a worthy advisor," Arduinna said. "She would be at home in the Fae courts."

I saw Florence stiffen and wanted to punch Arduinna in the face. I wasn't sure if she knew why the mage was with me and was going for a painful jab, or if it truly was a compliment.

"Thank you, Arduinna. Do you need anything else from me? Will you follow the spirit of what I want?"

She smiled, showing more teeth than I was comfortable with. "I understand your wishes."

"And?" I prompted.

"I will follow your instructions, adhering to the spirit of what you wish to accomplish."

"Please let me know if the President or the general have any issues with this policy."

"And if they do have...issues...what will you do?" Arduinna sounded genuinely curious.

"I'm not sure," I said.

"I can talk to Mircea Aldea," Raj said as he strode forward to stand beside me.

"I'm going to put a bell on you."

"You know General Aldea?" Arduinna asked. Her expression gave nothing away, but I don't think she was surprised.

"I've known him since before he adopted his uncle's surname to try to duck the assumptions and questions people made about his family."

It sounded like there was a story there, but I decided it could wait.

"Does President Murphy know what I'm doing?" I asked.

Arduinna nodded.

"And does she want me to keep on with that? Or would she rather the world stay as it is so she can maintain her position of power?"

"She has stated she would like the gates opened. I believe she is hoping to maintain her position and broaden her powers. She is extremely old and incredibly powerful. Those who will call for her to step down when it's revealed she's not human are the same people who already want her out of sight for having the temerity to be female. Her honesty makes her hated in many circles."

"People only want an honest politician if they tell comfortable truths," Florence said.

"Was George Washington Fae?" I asked. "He had that 'cannot tell a lie' going on."

Everyone looked at Arduinna.

"Not as far as I know."

I was surprisingly disappointed.

"With your permission? There is a lot to do in the next weeks."

"You may go." I waved my hand imperiously. She bowed low, straightened, and disappeared into the trees.

"I want to know more about General Aldea," I said to Raj.

"It will be a lovely campfire story at some other time. For tonight, I dropped by only to see if there was anything you needed."

"Would you stay and eat with us?" Florence asked. "I brought a lovely red wine for you."

"Thank you. I would enjoy that."

THE MORNING of the first day of the three-day full moon cycle started too early. Isaac left to meet the rest of the pack, leaving me alone with Florence at the campground.

I tried not to think about the bonding ceremony scheduled for the following evening. Luis had told me what to expect—there'd be words and an exchange of flesh. After that, Isaac would turn into a wolf and run with the pack, and I'd spend the evening with my non-shifter pals. It sounded simple, if a bit gross. My emotions weren't simple, though.

It was the latest weird situation in a string of weird situations, and I had a lot of mixed feelings. I only hoped no one asked me about them.

Of course, the minute I had that thought, Florence asked, "Would you like to talk?"

"No. I'd like to panic."

"What are you afraid of?"

I gathered my thoughts. "You won't tell Isaac?"

"Not unless what you're afraid of is him," she promised.

"I'm not afraid of Isaac. He would never hurt me." I immediately revised my statement. "He would never hurt me on purpose. Any hurt taken because of Isaac would be unintentional on his part."

"Talking to the Fae is weird. Does it hurt when you say something not completely true? Arduinna did the same thing yesterday when she realized she'd said something not completely true."

"It's uncomfortable but not precisely painful. You're an honest person. Do you feel uncomfortable when you tell a deliberate untruth?"

"Sometimes. Not if I believe my lie is justified, though. Telling someone an untruth that does no harm—like "You look wonderful in that dress,"—doesn't bother me. How would you phrase that?"

"I would find something both complimentary and true like "that color looks amazing on you!" I don't want to hurt people's feelings. If I didn't hate it with a fiery passion, I'd be great to take shopping. I will never lie to you in the store. If a color clashes with your complexion, I'll tell you."

We lapsed into a comfortable silence as the sun sank below the horizon.

I jumped when a hand landed on my shoulder.

"You're early!" I accused.

"You're jumpy and not paying attention to your surroundings."

"He's right. He shouldn't be able to sneak up on you all the time."

"He gets in under my radar."

"What do you mean?"

"I knew immediately when Arduinna arrived last night. I not only felt her pull on the earth, but immediately after, she hit the shields. It's my first line of defense. It has no real substance or use except as an alarm. I only use it when we're relatively alone because otherwise people would be jangling it constantly. It recognizes both of you and Isaac, because I don't want you jangling me, either."

"You would enjoy being jangled by me," Raj said.

I rolled my eyes. "The second line is my real shields. The one that keeps everything I say and do distorted to watching eyes. People can see us and hear us, but it's like we're under water."

Florence and Raj stared at me.

"What?" I felt defensive.

"That's amazing," Florence said. "I can't believe you set that up on your own."

"Thanks for the vote of confidence."

She waved my concerns away. "What I mean is that's advanced level shielding. Being able to create an alarm-only shield and key it to specific people is high level, and since you've only been working on shielding at all for the last two months, that is truly impressive."

"Thank you." I said, mollified.

Raj poured a glass of wine and asked, "Are you ready for your big day?"

I set down my beer, put my head between my legs, and concentrated on breathing.

"Damn it, vamp. I'd finally distracted her."

"Why should she be distracted? If she hyperventilates every time she thinks of forming a permanent mate bond, how will she get through the ceremony without making a fool of herself?"

Good question.

"What are you afraid of?" Florence asked again.

"Permanence."

"Nothing is permanent," Raj said. "Even for immortals such as us. Either of you could be killed at any time, even if you did nothing more with your lives than sit on the couch and watch television shows starring handsome vampires. You could be decapitated by a runaway semi-truck on your way to the grocery store for Cheetos. Since you're doing something a great deal more dangerous, that ups your chances of death considerably."

"So not helping, Raj."

"I sometimes forget how young you are. Once you have a couple lifetimes under your belt, death starts to lose its fear-inducing-quality. I've heard the theory the old ones start to long for death, and perhaps that is true for some. When you've outlived your family several times over and the mortals you know keep dying, it is hard to stay positive, but I do not long for death. I no longer fear it. Someday you will feel that way, too."

"That day is not today," I said.

"Fair enough. Let me try again. You are afraid of permanence?"

I nodded.

"Basically, you're having commitment issues."

I opened my mouth to protest. That sounded magazine article trite.

He kept talking, "You have prophecies that encourage an urgent, permanent bonding, both from your dragon half, which you should really work on fully integrating with your non-dragon half, by the way, and from your witch." Florence glared at him when he used the "w" word, but he kept going. "If you'd been allowed to get to this point without the urgency of the auguries, you probably wouldn't be tense about the whole thing. Isaac loves you. You love him—"

"—I don't know if that's the word I'd use..."

"I don't care what word you'd use. You love the wolf. You hate there's one more thing in your life not in your control. For the entire summer—maybe your entire life—you've never felt as though you've had a choice in anything. Am I right?"

I closed my mouth that was hanging open in shock. "Maybe." I certainly couldn't discount it, and maybe was a nice, equivocal word.

"You don't fear the permanence of the bonding as much as you resent the violation of your agency that brought you to this point. If you really were worried about the immutability of the bond, you'd have found a way to delay it another moon cycle or two, regardless of what the prophecies say."

"Plausible," I muttered.

Raj sat beside me on the picnic bench. He tipped my chin with his hand until my gaze met his. "Eleanor Jane Morgan, you are a wonder. You are smart, funny, courageous, and beautiful. You inspire love and loyalty from those who barely know you and you will fight fiercely to protect those to whom you have given your friendship. If I didn't know how much you loved that wolf, I'd be trying much, much harder to get in your pants.

"You feel you're not making real choices, coasting along making non-choices because of circumstances, but if you weren't who you were, you would be making different choices. You could've stayed with Finn out of obligation or complacency. You didn't have to apply yourself to the magical or martial arts. You could've asked Arduinna for more guards and protectors. You didn't have to agree to bring along Isaac or Florence. You could've had Salem killed when she and a group of rogue vampires"—he winked—"attacked without provocation. You didn't have to agree to dinner with me and you didn't have to call me when you killed Rasputin. You could've gone along with any of Arduinna's plans—either to let thousands and thousands die or to be exposed too early. In fact, you didn't have to worry about the nuclear power plants and ask for her help all. These are choices you've made. You."

He let go of my chin, but I didn't duck my head this time.

"If there's something else bothering you, spit it out, but don't hide from the truth behind the cheap veneer of half-truths. You may be Fae, but you don't have to adopt all of their customs right now. You love Isaac. You're not really afraid of being bound to him. You have the power to make choices, and just because it doesn't feel like a choice to you doesn't mean it's not. It means you have a strong conscience that eliminates some choices before you even consider them. Suck it up."

"Wow," Florence said. "That was quite the speech."

Raj looked slightly abashed. "I've lived a long time, and I know a lot about human nature. I was briefly royalty at one point as a human and know a little about the difference between the perception of a non-choice and the actuality. In fact, that comes up a lot when you're an awesomely powerful vampire, too."

"Feel better?" Florence asked.

"Yes. I appreciate you, Raj."

He stood up and bowed. "My pleasure, Your Highness." I held my hand out, and as he kissed it, he whispered in my mind, "It would be my pleasure, you know."

I rolled my eyes again. "Nice try, Dracula."

"Please don't invoke his name," Raj said. "If Mircea is involved in things it's likely Vlad is around somewhere, waiting to make trouble."

"Wait, General Aldea knows Dracula? Please tell me the story."

"Some other time. It's late. You need your sleep for your big day tomorrow. I'll see you in the clearing behind the pack house before moonrise. I'll be the one in the sunglasses looking for shade."

"It's ten minutes before sunset. You'll survive."

"If there was doubt about my survival, I'd skip it. Did you miss the part earlier where I said I wasn't looking for death?" He took a few steps back into the dark and then disappeared.

"So?" Florence asked.

"I'm okay."

"He's a handy fellow to have along, isn't he?"

"I rather like him. I'm glad he's here."

"Me, too."

CHAPTER TWELVE

T HE CLEARING WAS full of shifters I didn't recognize. Even after being in and out of the house for a couple of weeks, I'd really only spent time with Luis and met the wolves who did the cooking. I looked for familiar faces and found them dotted throughout the crowd. Not all of the faces reflected associative happiness, or even careful neutrality. I wondered if they were angry because I wasn't a shifter or if Christopher had told them I was Fae. Or because Christopher had told them after this month's full moon, they'd need to move out of the city or be prepared for a rapid downshift in technology. I shrugged slightly. Whatever was making them angry, hopefully they would manage to keep it to themselves during the ceremony.

"I will ensure no one causes any trouble for you, my sweet," Raj's voice said in my head. I spotted him on the edge of the crowd. There was a large empty space around him. Maybe he was the cause of the shifter's anger. I smiled at him before turning my attention towards the portion of the crowd we were quickly approaching. Luis and Christopher stood in the center of the clearing waiting for us. There wasn't much officiating that needed to be done, but as Alpha, Christopher

had the authority to keep his pack in line and declare our bonding a good one.

Finally, I looked to my left at Isaac. He looked as nervous as I felt, and for some reason that made me feel better.

"Are you ready?" he asked.

I couldn't answer in the affirmative, but I squeezed his hand and started towards the Alpha and his mate.

"We are here to witness the joining of this man and this woman under the light of the Hunter's moon," Christopher said. "We will bear witness to the words they say, to the flesh they exchange, and to the bond they create."

Isaac started, "Eleanor Jane Morgan, I choose you to be my mate. I ask you to share my life. I pledge to you my flesh to seal our bond."

"Eleanor?" Christopher prompted.

"Ishaq ben Ekkileb," I said. Isaac stared at me in shock for a second, and I tried not to think about how that name came to me. There'd be time to freak out later. Now, I had to get through this before the moon turned everyone present into animals. I tried again, "Ishaq, I choose you to be my mate. I ask you to share my life. I pledge to you my flesh to seal our bond."

"Words declare intent, but only flesh and blood can create an unbreakable bond," Christopher said.

I tilted my head, exposing my neck to Isaac. With the moon on the rise, his teeth were pointier than usual and I tensed for the pain. And it was painful as he tore the smallest possible piece of flesh from the side of my neck and swallowed it. He lapped up the blood and the pain dulled to a sting in moments. "Your flesh is my flesh, your blood flows in my veins. We are connected until death," Isaac said.

He tilted his neck, and I stood up on tiptoes to reach him. My teeth were regular and much less lethal. It took a little more work to get the small chunk of flesh from him, but I did it, swallowed, and licked up the blood. I tried not to think too hard about what I was doing. Barfing during the ceremony was probably a faux pas.

"Your flesh is my flesh, your blood flows in my veins. We are connected until death."

When I finished speaking, magic surged through my veins. The moon was a tangible presence in my life and I was restless and hungry. It quickly realized I was getting Isaac's emotions in addition to my own.

"The bonding is complete; the connection has formed."

"Witnessed!" yelled the pack.

"I can't hold on much longer," Isaac said. I looked up at the moon, partially obscured by hazy clouds, then at the shifters surrounding us. A few pack members had already gone furry, and the rest weren't far behind.

"I understand," I said. "Have fun tonight. I'll see you in the morning."

"Take care of her," he said over my head to Florence and Raj. I wanted to object to the notion I needed someone to do that, but felt the depth of his love for me at that moment and couldn't.

Florence and Raj stepped forward to flank me on either side.

"Of course," Florence said.

"Always," Raj said. "I give you my vow."

That was a little more than I was expecting, and from the surge of surprise I felt from Isaac, more than he was expecting as well. There was no time to dwell on it, though. He kissed me again and quickly stripped.

"You are a lucky woman," Raj said as Isaac removed the last of his clothes.

"She is, isn't she?" Luis said, eying Isaac appreciatively. He took off his tux, too, and in the blink of an eye, the only beings left on two legs were me, Raj, and Florence. Christopher and Luis led the pack off under the light of the moon leaving us alone.

"Ishaq?" Florence asked with a disingenuously neutral voice.

As soon as the name came out of my mouth, I knew there would be questions. These would at least be easier to deal with than Isaac's.

"Florence, do you ever open your mouth and have words that didn't make a full traverse through your brain come out?"

"Yes, when a prophecy hits."

"The same thing happens to me from time to time. When I'm

dealing with Arduinna occasionally, or talking to other Fae. And there are some other times when I think I'm going to say one thing and something else comes out. I'd been thinking I didn't know Isaac's middle name, and then when I opened my mouth, that's what came out. It was weird, but I'm guessing Ishaq ben Ekkileb was his original name."

"You are correct," Raj said. "His thoughts confirmed it when you said it, but it is a name he hasn't heard in a long time, and one he thought he'd left behind."

I felt terrible. It'd been inadvertent, but I didn't want to cause him pain.

"It was an old memory," Raj said. "It's that way with those of us who live a long time. It's hard to hold on to the early days and much becomes faded and buried unless there is a catalyst to bring those memories to the surface. I'll need to be careful to never be in a situation that might result in you true naming me. I'm not sure I want to know what would come up if I heard my original name for the first time in centuries."

Raj smiled, but I didn't think he was kidding.

"True naming is an interesting talent," Florence said. "And one that will be extremely useful as you continue to deal with more and more Fae. The Fae guard their true names closely. Generally the only people who know the true name are the parents and a life mate. They believe that information in the wrong hands would give someone power over them and it's considered rude to ask."

"Shit!" I said.

Raj and Florence looked at me.

"When I met Harvey, the tattoo artist, I asked him what his name was instead of asking him what he wanted to be called. He answered true. I thought maybe it was because I was royalty, but maybe it was more than that? Anyway, I made a mistake. He answered in front of me, Isaac, and Finn. I wonder if Finn compelled him later through the power of the name to tattoo on the iron bands."

"That is a possibility, I suppose. I always thought the fear of sharing one's true name was more of an affectation, but there are more things in heaven and earth than are dreamt of in my philosophy," Raj said.

I decided to change the topic of conversation before the subject of my true name came up. "Did either of you recognize the name?"

"Ishaq is the Arabic version of Isaac," Florence said.

"And 'ben' means 'son of,'" Raj added. "I don't know what Ekkileb denotes, though."

"Arabic, huh?" I asked. "So many questions! Like 'where were you born?' and 'how did you get to this country?' I'm hoping the answer to that second question is 'voluntarily.'" Power and heat rippled through my body. The thrill of the hunt was causing my adrenaline to pump overtime. I caught the scent of the deer ahead and moved to cut it off. I leaped out of the underbrush and toppled the deer, sinking my teeth first into its right rear hamstring to cripple it and then I tore out its throat. I felt the hot blood pouring over my muzzle. I tilted my face up and howled my victory to the full moon.

And then something cold dropped on my forehead and looked around. I was reclining on the sofa in the family room at the pack house. Raj was holding me, and Florence had placed a cold washcloth on my head.

"What the everlasting fuck?" I said.

"Excellent question," Florence replied.

"That mental bond must be a lot more powerful than I thought," I said. "I thought it was supposed to let us consciously communicate over long distances and give a general directional sense when I concentrated. I didn't think I'd get thrown into his mind when I was thinking about him."

"Perhaps it is because it's new," Raj suggested. "Maybe it will calm down with time."

"It might be because you are not a shifter," Florence said. "I'm not sure if there's another case of a shifter and a Fae bonding like this. Your bond may be more powerful."

My skin heated up as the urge to shift overtook me. "I need to fly. Getting the hunt though the mate bond is agitating the dragon."

"Are you going to join the shifters' hunt?" Florence asked.

"I don't want to cause a panic."

"You should hunt with Isaac tonight. It's traditional," Raj said.

"He needs to stay with the pack for control."

"Now that you are fully bonded, you will be all the control he needs."

"I am not an Alpha."

"Yes you are," Raj said.

"If he loses it, I can always sit on him until he changes back."

"Good plan B," Florence said.

"I'm going to strip."

"Good plan," Raj said.

"It's probably bad form to hit on me on me when I'm officially mated to someone else."

Raj didn't look even a tiny bit repentant. A row of white teeth shone in contrast to his dark skin and his grin widened enough that I saw his sharp canines. "The day I stop flirting with you is the day I'm staked through the heart."

"You can go now," I said. He mimicked crying, I rolled my eyes, and he left. I stripped down and found a robe to put on so I could get to the back yard without anyone seeing me naked. Once I was outside and alone, I shrugged off the robe and shifted. I flapped my wings a couple of times and launched myself into the sky. I circled slowly a couple of times while I determined Isaac's general location. Finally, I felt him to the northwest and took off in that direction. When I got close, I sent out a tentative thought.

"Isaac?"

"?"

"Hunt with me tonight, under the moon?" I tried to send him a picture of me as the dragon.

He didn't communicate back in words, just images and emotions. He sent me a vision of him out of control, ravaging my lifeless body. I replied in kind with the picture of my dragon-self sitting atop his wolf-self until he calmed down.

The next thing I received was a kind of wolfy laugh, and I knew I'd won. I saw him trot up to a large wolf I identified as Christopher and communicate with him, then he turned and ran into the forest towards me. I found a clearing and landed to wait for him. He ran up to me, then lay down in the snow and rolled over, exposing his belly and throat. Raj was right about me being Alpha. I nudged him with my snout until he stood again. I wanted to hug him, but with the wings and claws, I wasn't sure how.

"*Hunt?*" I asked silently.

He sniffed the air until he found the scent he was looking for. He tilted his head at me, then took off. I quickly rose to the air and followed. He chased down a deer and directed me to go into a clearing where I'd have space to land. When the exhausted deer entered the clearing, Isaac hamstrung it and I swooped down and finished the kill. We ate together and spent the rest of the night running until we were tired. We found a small clearing and I curled up with him next to me.

He sent back a feeling of contentment, and we fell asleep.

WHEN I WOKE the next morning, I felt oddly stiff in places I'd never been stiff before. I stretched out my arms and heard an "Oof!" before I remembered I was still a dragon and was sleeping in a clearing in the woods outside of St. Louis. I moved my head enough to see Isaac stretched out on the ground beside me. He'd changed back to human at some point and lay there gloriously nude.

"Good morning, mate," he said.

I grinned, which since I was still a dragon, probably wasn't as alluring as I'd like it to be. I pulled myself together mentally and shifted back. "Good morning."

He kissed me, and between the newly wakened bond intensifying our arousal and the fact we were alone and naked, it didn't take long for the kiss to become serious.

When I ran my hand between his legs to grasp his arousal, I felt the sensation twice and it left me gasping. I lowered my mouth towards him, determined to find out how crazy I could make us both, but Isaac stopped me.

"Eleanor, I can't take that right now," he said. His voice was at least an octave lower than usual. "Too intense, I won't last long."

"I'll bet you can find other ways to satisfy me," I said. My mouth was inches above his cock, and I blew out gently, teasing him. He quivered below me, but lost any resistance. When he let go, I took him into my mouth, sliding slowly up and down his shaft while I kept on eye on his face. His eyes rolled back in pleasure and the combination of the visual plus the mental feedback was incredibly arousing. I grew wetter and wetter. Letting him slide out of my mouth, I moved up his body and sank down on top of him, sheathing him in me. I had to stop. The sensation, stuck on a feedback loop, was almost overwhelming. When I got control of my breathing again, I started moving. Slowly at first, but it didn't take long to lose control. I rocked us to completion in seconds and fell against his chest gasping.

"That was incredible," he said.

"I had no idea it would be like that," I replied.

"It's much more intense than I expected. I can't decide if I hope our bond calms down a bit or if it stays like this always."

"It'd be nice if we could adjust the settings ourselves," I said. "Like keep it on low when we're in company or when you're hunting and turn it up when we're making love."

"Maybe keep it on low when I want to last longer than a teenage boy," he said.

I smiled and leaned forward and kissed him. When he nipped my lower lip, I wiggled. My excitement fueled his and he hardened inside me. He quirked an eyebrow at me. "Again?"

"Always with you," I said.

"Do you two ever do anything else?"

I sat up and whipped my head around. Finn stood at the edge of the clearing, his face set to a carefully neutral expression. I could tell, though, by the tightening around his eyes and the vein pulsing in his forehead that he was angry.

"Do you ever spy on anything else? Can't you find another way to get your rocks off besides watching something you can't have?"

"*What are you doing?*" Isaac asked through our mental link.

"Pissing him off, I hope," I replied the same way.

Finn's expression was no longer carefully neutral. He looked incensed.

"Is there something you wanted?" I didn't want to give Finn another show, but didn't want to move off Isaac and expose us both further. Neither of us had clothing available.

"I came by with a warning," Finn said.

"Okay, warn away."

"I'd rather talk to you alone."

"That worked out so well for me last time."

"I see you got that problem taken care of."

"Fuck you, Finn. Say what you need to say and get out."

My anger must have spilled over into Isaac, because when I looked down, his eyes were streaked with yellow and his teeth were elongating. I took a few deep breaths to calm my thoughts and my body, hoping that would calm Isaac as well.

"Your show of devotion hasn't fooled anyone," Finn said.

"Why are you still talking? Give us your warning and get out. I had other plans for this morning."

"Enjoy your time together," Finn said. "While you have it."

"That was your warning?" I asked.

"Sounded almost like well wishes to me," Isaac said. *"Should we tell him we're bonded?"*

"No. If he doesn't already know, it'll be better if we keep it that way."

Finn looked visibly frustrated. This was not working out the way he'd intended.

"Warning?" I prompted.

"You have until Samhain to surrender, dog," Finn said. "If you come with me willingly, we will let you live."

"Surrender to whom?" Isaac asked.

"Who's we?" I asked.

"Surrender to me. That's all you need to know."

"And what are you going to do with me next?"

Finn looked flummoxed. It wasn't like him to be unprepared. He was usually smoother than this.

"Samhain," he repeated, then vanished.

"That was interesting," Isaac said.

"Let's go back to the house. I'd like clothes and maybe a bloody Mary."

We were quite a few miles from the house, but rather than burn energy with two more changes, we walked back naked and barefoot. Almost two hours later, we stumbled into the back yard of the pack house. My feet ached and I bled from a couple of scratches I'd gotten, but mostly I was hungry. My stomach was growling; my midnight deer snack was already gone.

A few wolves and naked humans slept in the grass, but most of the pack was in the dining room chowing down. Isaac growled, and I gave him some serious side-eye.

"What are you growling at?"

"They're looking at my naked mate. Why wouldn't I growl?"

"How about if you stop and we go get dressed?"

He growled once more for emphasis, and we went inside and grabbed some clothes. After filling our bellies, we searched out Florence to give her the Finn update. She didn't look terribly surprised, and I started to feel a little suspicious.

"You know something," I accused.

"I know many things. I am not some ignorant fool you picked up on a whim. One of the things I know is when to share my knowledge and when to keep my mouth shut."

"Are you sure this is one of those times?" I asked. I was getting pissed.

"Yes. I can sometimes see two futures and the most likely outcomes if I have the ability to affect a change. Not telling you is the better choice."

"Most likely? You could be wrong."

"That is another one of the many things I know. But, if I worry and second guess myself, I will drive myself crazy. I make decisions based on the knowledge I have and then I am content. I suggest you content yourself with my decisions, too, as you will not be able to change my mind."

"A hint? Something I should watch out for?"

"Did you guys talk about the Ishaq thing yet?" Florence asked.

"Are you changing the subject?"

"I thought that was obvious."

I opened my mouth, intent on arguing, when Isaac touched my arm. Without warning, our bond surged again, and I was flooded with emotion: Arousal, confusion, anger—so much anger it staggered me—but also resignation. And hunger.

"You're hungry again?" I asked. The anger was more concerning, but I didn't know how to address that.

Isaac smiled at me. "I'm always hungry. For all sorts of things." The feeling of arousal intensified, and everything else faded into the background.

"Do you two want to be alone again?" Florence asked.

I took a couple of deep breaths and tried to focus. I stepped away from Isaac's hand on my arm, which helped me block out his emotions. "We're good."

I sat on the floor next to the door. Isaac moved towards me and I gave him a look. "Please sit a little further away from me. I have a question I need to ask, and you keep distracting me."

He smirked, but sat down across the room. Florence sat on the bed.

"I didn't sense Finn until he was in the clearing with us. Even if we were distracted, he should've triggered my warning system. The only people who should be able to get through the net are you two and Raj. Finn should never be able to surprise me. I do not want to be surprised by Finn."

Florence wrinkled her nose up until her brow creased. She stared at the floor between me and the bed. We sat in silence for a while. It didn't take too long until I was fidgeting. Finally she looked up. "How is your warning web shaped?"

"Like a large umbrella."

"A dome?"

"Exactly."

"If he's still connected to you—something that will last until either he dies or agrees to remove it, right?" At my nod she continued, "Then he can appear in your vicinity. He must have appeared within your warning dome instead of crossing the boundary of it and triggering the alarms."

"Dammit!" I was pissed at myself for not seeing it sooner and for building a web with such an obvious loophole.

"Don't beat yourself up," Florence said. "It's still an impressive shield, and it's likely he doesn't know it exists and that it was coincidental he appeared close enough to you to not trigger it."

"It's a weakness, though," I said. "You said the other night I wasn't paying enough attention when Raj snuck up on me, and it's true. Because I thought my warning system was going to be effective against anyone I wanted to be warned about, I haven't been paying attention. I relied too much on that shield, and now I've no idea how many times Finn has been within it, spying on us."

"If you were with me, I would've scented him if he were that close," Isaac said.

"Like you did this morning?"

"If you were with me and you were fully clothed, I would've scented him," he amended. "And if I was distracted enough to not scent him, then he was getting no information except we have a lot of sex."

I smiled.

"I can hear his thoughts," Florence said. "So if you were with me and we were not in a public place with lots of thoughts to tune out, I would know if he approached."

"And I'll bet Raj can smell his blood from miles away," Isaac said.

I felt a little bit better. "Okay, but no more discussing secret plans unless we've done a scan of the area."

"That seems like a good safety precaution," Florence said. "And, now that we've taken care of our security breach, can we talk about Ishaq?"

Isaac took a deep breath. "Can it wait?"

"Probably," Florence said. "But is there a reason it should?"

"Because I asked nicely? I am newly mated and would like to try my hand at romance today."

"Hey! There was plenty of romance. We killed and ate a deer together. We frolicked in the moonlight. I fell asleep curled up on a furry rug."

Isaac growled. "I am not a rug."

"You are furry, though."

"Give your real answer, wolf," Florence said as she stood up. "I'll drop it if you're honest."

Isaac stared at Florence, yellow streaking through his eyes. She met his gaze calmly. "You can't out-Alpha me, Isaac. Not when you're this uncertain of your own dominance."

"Just my luck to end up in the company of so many dominant women," Isaac muttered as he dropped his gaze.

"I'm sure you mean 'so many dominant people,' since our gender identity has nothing to do with our power," I said.

Isaac ignored my jab at his unconscious sexism and looked back at Florence. "Ishaq is long-dead. He was me, or I was him, so long ago. You've surmised, I'm sure, that I was born to that name. Either you or Raj will have also determined the general geographic area from which it springs. A man from North Africa, born when I was…I'm sure you can think of a reason I don't want to relive that part of my past?"

His meaning hit me hard and I gasped, nausea welling up to consume me.

"That is a good deal closer to honest than you were before, but as far as truth goes, something is still lacking," Florence said.

"Florence!" I was horrified that she was dismissing his revelation so callously.

"Will you drop it then?" Isaac asked.

"I will, but your ability to lie with the truth has been noted." She headed to the door. "Eleanor, will you run with the pack tonight?"

"No," Isaac said before I could answer.

"Apparently not," I said. "Do you want to stay at the campsite with me tonight?"

"That would be fine," Florence answered. "I'll come by an hour before sundown to pick you up."

"Have a good day!"

She left, and I looked at Isaac. "No?" I asked. He looked a little uncomfortable. "C'mon, Isaac. Our mate bond doesn't give you permission to speak for me."

"My apologies," he said. "Come sit by me?"

"You can't distract me that easily. Why no?"

"Most of the pack doesn't know your other form. Some don't even know you're Fae, although they will tomorrow, when the danger of accidentally shifting and trying to kill you passes. I'd rather not take any risks."

"They can't hurt me when I'm a dragon."

"I'm not worried about you. I'm more worried some idiots will attack you, you'll fight back, and Christopher's pack will be down a few members. I'd really like to retain the cooperation of the pack for the gate opening. We'll need a perimeter guard like we did in the Black Hills."

"That makes sense."

"Now will you sit by me?"

I crawled over on my hands and knees. "What did you have in mind for the rest of the day, Isaac Walker?" I asked as I slowly slid into his lap.

He kissed me behind my ear, "I was thinking I'd start here." He slid his hand down my side and then up and under my shirt, "And then make my way here." He pushed me off his lap and onto the floor, managing to remove my shirt at the same time. Then he unbuttoned my jeans and slid them off my hips, "Then eventually make my way here." I arched my back to push towards his mouth, and he laughed. "But only eventually."

A COUPLE OF HOURS LATER, we stumbled to the kitchen to refuel. We spent the afternoon alternating between eating and making love.

Evening—and moonrise—arrived too quickly. Florence showed up to collect me, and I kissed Isaac goodbye. "Have fun!" I said as he strode out into the clearing with the rest of the shifters. We left before they all started shifting, but I could feel Isaac's change through our bond. I'd been distracted last night, but felt every last painful second of it tonight.

Raj was waiting for us when we arrived at the campsite. "How was the hunt, my sweet?" he asked. He sat on the other side of the picnic table, sipping a glass of red wine.

"Satisfyingly bloody." Isaac was running with the pack, and joy from the freedom of four legs surged through our bond. I shook my head to bring my attention back to my present. "There was a bit of a surprise this morning, though." I told him about Finn and Raj confirmed he'd be able to sense if a Fae was close to us.

"Thank you, Eleanor," he said.

"For what?"

"For putting me on the trusted guest list. We do not know each other well, and I have done nothing for you but crash your party and flirt inappropriately."

"You helped with the witches at the cave."

"I wasn't necessary for that operation. Between you, your wolf, and your witch, you would've handled the situation fine."

I tilted my head and looked at him. "I'm not sure what you're getting at."

"I'm not trying to get at anything. I'm saying thank you for trusting me when I've done nothing to earn that trust."

"That's an excellent point. I mean other than flying out to confirm whose shriveled head I was carrying around, you haven't done much for us, have you? Our first meeting was because you sent some of your minions to kidnap me and kill my companions. Then you bit me without permission. Hmmm...maybe my trust has been misplaced and you are trying to lure me into complacency with your charm and good looks until you have a chance to kidnap me again."

"Tell me more about my charm and good looks," Raj purred. He was standing in front of me holding my hand. I looked at his wine glass which was ten feet away, where he'd been an eye blink ago. He raised my hand up to his mouth, turned it over, and breathed in deeply, his tongue reaching out to flick the vein in my wrist.

"You're incorrigible," Florence said, swatting him on the back of the head.

"The wine I brought is good, but this is a much finer bouquet. Kidnapping is no longer my goal."

"What is your goal?"

"I want to help you on your quest to break the world," Raj said.

"I wish people would stop using that phrase."

"Okay, then. I wish to assist you on your quest to return magic to this world, thereby rendering all technology useless."

I rolled my eyes. "Fine, call me the world breaker if you must."

"It is in the prophecies."

"Call it what you will, then. But answer me true. Why are you here?"

"You will need my help in New Orleans and by the time you need to go there, it is possible you would have no means of easily contacting me."

"And you want to help, why?"

"I'm bored. I've been kicking around this world for over a thousand years, and you are the first person in centuries to interest me. Ruling a little slice of the Pacific Northwest has been okay, but I don't really want to be a king—that hasn't turned out well for me. You, Eleanor Morgan, are interesting."

"You're here because you're bored? Seriously?"

"Seriously," he mimicked. "Never underestimate the power of boredom in the extremely old. It's what motivates us to do almost everything we do. Most who've lived more than a couple of hundred years would go to great lengths to have a new experience."

I eyed him skeptically. He was telling the truth, but not the whole truth.

"How about we leave it at that for now," he said. "Maybe I'll answer more at another time."

"As you wish," I said. "There are a lot of deferred origin stories happening around here."

"You want an origin story? That's different," Raj said. "I can give you my origin story. I was born in the mid part of the tenth century, the lesser son of great kings. I ruled our land for a number of years, and was considered blessed by the gods with divine beauty. However, I was conquered by the invading Muslim armies and lost my throne. Fortunately, they were not in a beheading sort of mood when I was executed. I decided to give up ruling and make my way in the great world, and here I am."

"Divine beauty?"

"Have you seen me? Blessed by Lakshmi herself."

I smiled at him. "You are a beautiful man. You were made a vampire while ruling India?"

"Only a small part of India. It wasn't a unified country then."

"And you were executed?"

"Ineffectively."

"Interesting. How did you become a vampire?"

"Ahh, my dear. That is a tale for another time. You are hungry and exhausted, and I will take my leave. Again, thank you for your trust in me. I will keep my senses alert for this Finn of yours. Should I kill him if I find him?"

"No!" Florence said.

We both looked at her. "Capture, but do not kill."

"Might I ask why?"

"No, you might not. Trust me."

"As you have trusted me." Raj bowed again and flew straight up into the air.

CHAPTER THIRTEEN

T HE NEXT MORNING, I woke before sunrise. I heard Florence still sleeping. I put on shoes and a hoodie to guard against the chill of the early morning air. When I went outside, there was a large, steaming cup of coffee on the table. I sniffed it. Vanilla latte. Fuck. Finn had been here.

I went to the out building to use the bathroom and wash my face and stopped to fill up my water bottle on my way back. By the time I'd lit the little stove and gotten the water boiling, Florence was up. I made coffee while she performed her morning ablutions. When she returned to the campsite, I handed her some coffee and then we both stared at the latte sitting on the table.

"Are you going to drink it?" Florence asked.

"Nope."

"Wow. I've never seen you turn down coffee before."

"Ha. Funny. Is he still here?"

Florence closed her eyes for a moment. "If he is I can't hear him. He was never good at guarding his thoughts from me."

"Or maybe he didn't guard them because he wanted you to believe he couldn't."

"I feel that there were things I picked up he'd rather I hadn't."

"Things like what?"

"There was a point he was seriously contemplating getting rid of his competition."

"It was never a competition," I said.

"I know and you know, but Finn honestly believed without Isaac in the picture, you'd choose him."

"By the time we got to that point, I wouldn't have chosen Finn if he was the only choice in the world." Something tripped my security web. I turned and saw someone running away from us.

Florence turned and looked, too. "Your hypothesis that his weak mental shields were a sham has new evidence. If he'd left in his usual fashion, we never would've known."

"Popping out doesn't work when he's pissed off."

"Or hurt," Florence said. "His emotions may have been equal devastation and anger. In his own way, he really does love you."

"It's too bad his own way is creepy as fuck."

"We've all made relationship mistakes and trusted those who didn't deserve it. You've done better this time, which is good, because it's time to pick up Isaac and learn to manage your mate bond," Florence said.

"Are you going to stay out here while we're gone? I worry about you being alone. I don't want Finn to hurt you. He knows hurting you would hurt me."

"I'm confident in my own power, but not stupid. I won't reject help. I'd rather not be alone with a crazy elf on the loose."

"Do you want Raj to stay with you?"

"He's not much use during the day. I'll ask one of the wolves."

"Do you have someone in mind or should I ask Christopher to pick someone?"

"I have someone in mind. I've spent a lot of time with the shifters lately."

"Make sure you impress upon him how dangerous Finn really is."

"I'll let her know. I'm sure she'll manage to stay awake."

I eyed Florence suspiciously. "Awake and alert?"

"Definitely alert."

"For danger?"

"Yes, mother," Florence said.

"I don't want you getting killed because you were making out with your bodyguard."

She smiled. "I'll be good."

I rolled my eyes. "I'm sure. Don't do anything I wouldn't do."

"Thanks for not putting any restrictions on me."

We headed out, leaving the cup of coffee on the picnic table.

FOR THREE DAYS AND NIGHTS, we stayed in a remote pack cabin working on stabilizing our new mate bond. Other than daily check-ins with Florence, we had no contact with the outside world. Our bond was strong, unpredictable, and liable to surge to full power at the most inopportune moments. After hours of frustration, I had an idea. "Isaac, what if instead of trying to make the bond work how and when we want it to, we work on not reacting to sudden surges of unexpected input?"

Once our focus changed, we made a lot more progress. Learning to filter through stimuli and decide what was mine, what was his, and what was important went a long way towards stabilizing the bond and left me confident I wouldn't fall over if Isaac scented a rabbit.

WE LEFT our refuge eight days before Samhain. One week and one day before I was going to further break this world. I spent the day working with Florence to eliminate the loophole Finn had exploited in my shields. I took inspiration from the campground bathrooms and added the mental equivalent of sticky fly paper hanging down—any movement within my shield would trigger the same alarm. It was hot, sweaty work and I had trouble getting my modifications to stick.

"Perhaps if you envision gluing the strands to your shield?" Florence suggested.

"If you think this is easy you can do it yourself." I closed my eyes and took a few deep breaths. "That was uncalled for."

"The sun is setting and you're exhausted. If your shields are going to stay up at all, you need rest and fuel."

We headed back to our campsite from the amphitheater where we'd been practicing and found a steak dinner waiting. Isaac opened three bottles of beer and a bottle of wine and we sat down to eat. As we were finishing up, Raj appeared and poured himself a glass of wine.

"Why can you drink wine but not eat food?" I asked.

"I can eat food, but I don't like to. It's not necessary to keep me alive, and it doesn't taste all that good. I still have a working digestive system—it just doesn't work well. A glass of wine before I eat my preferred food isn't enough to trigger any...systems I prefer not to be a slave to anymore."

"Thanks for being delicate about it."

"There are things you don't discuss with someone when you're wooing them."

I changed the subject before we could go any further down that path. "We have one week until the next opening. I'll check in with Arduinna tomorrow to see how her part of the plan is going. Isaac, is Christopher going to talk to the pack tomorrow, too?"

Isaac nodded. "He's going to offer them the chance to get the hell out of Dodge or stay and guard during the opening. My one concern is there may be some among those who offer to stay who would try to take you out during the opening."

"Do you have a sense about what time the gate will need to be opened?" Raj asked. "I can be there regardless, but I'll be much more effective if it isn't high noon."

"Sunset."

"That, I can do."

"Okay, team! We have a plan!"

I smiled at my friends, leaned into Isaac's arms, and took a sip of my beer.

THE NEXT WEEK passed so quickly I would've guessed magic was involved if I didn't know better. I spent each day working on further developing my shields. My physical training was relegated to the back seat for now, although I did try to get a run in every other day. This much stress and magical build-up could only be handled by physical exhaustion.

Arduinna stopped by every day for a briefing. Although General Aldea and President Murphy had originally balked at our revised plan, they quickly came around. Rumors swirled everywhere in the mortal world when Aldea and Murphy had a press conference to announce a credible threat to St. Louis of the kind that had hit Portland and the Black Hills. The National Guard came in to help with evacuations, and the whole city was in chaos.

Raj seemed to be enjoying it, but the rest of us—and by us, I mean me—were annoyed. We'd stocked up on enough water, fuel, and food to get through a month, but not having take-out readily available was destroying my morale.

By the twenty-ninth, St. Louis was greatly diminished. There were, of course, people who'd chosen to stay. You could bring irrefutable proof to some that staying put would result in certain death, and they'd smile and maybe lock the door.

That evening, the last plane took off from the airport. There was the occasional distant buzz of a faraway aircraft, but I'd never realized how much noise I automatically filtered out. Everything was muted.

It felt like we were preparing for war. People were ducking and covering, and I began to doubt my strategy. By associating the gate openings with terrorist events, it was going to make me a terrorist. Any magical beings were going to be associated with—motherfucker! —breaking the humans' world.

By sundown, I was positive I'd engineered the future attempted genocide of supernaturals. Even when President Murphy and General Aldea manipulated the big reveal, I didn't see how they could spin this to cast the magically inclined in a favorable light. I'd wanted to delay because I knew what humans did to things that frighten them; they'd spent a long time being afraid of things that go bump in the night. All you had to do is look around to see what they mock, what they try to lighten up, what they dress up as on Hallowe'en, and you could tell witches, vampires, and werewolves were not high on the trust list.

They liked elves, though. I scowled at the thought of Finn seeming more benign than Isaac. There was no hope for me. Dragons are almost never portrayed as benevolent.

I pulled some flames from the campfire Isaac had started to build and ran them up and down my arms. It was getting cold at night, and the warmth of the little fire elementals was soothing.

"Are you going to say anything" Isaac asked. "You've been sulking for hours. What's wrong?"

Harsh. Isaac wasn't usually a jerk, even when warranted. I wanted to answer like the sullen teenager he'd named me, but "nothing" wouldn't leave my mouth. Fucking not being able to lie. I hated being me.

My eyes widened. I opened my connection to Isaac and hoped I could project loud enough for Raj and Florence to hear, but keep my shields strong enough to block Finn. *"Is anyone else having a particularly shitty day full of doubt and recrimination?"*

Out loud, I said, "I feel like every decision I've ever made is wrong."

Isaac answered through our link, *"I'm not having much self-doubt, but I am having Eleanor-doubt."*

Aloud he said, "Have you considered that maybe it is?"

Switching between regular and mental conversation was hard, but I was sure someone was listening. *"Raj? Florence?"*

Raj said, "You children are whiny and self-absorbed. I've no idea why I attached myself to you and why I'm still hanging around." He followed up with, *"There is interference. Whoever is doing it is a fool, though. I've been alive over a thousand years and I know the difference between my own thoughts and someone else's. Mine have a lot more nudity."*

I almost grinned.

Florence looked around, "I don't know what's gotten into all of you, but I don't like it. Eleanor, you're doing the best you can with the information you have. Isaac, that was rude. Please apologize to Eleanor. Raj, you're free to stay or go as you like, but there's no reason to be impolite."

Florence couldn't project her thoughts, only read them, and Raj had trouble reading her thoughts. This was such a weird conversation.

"How do we get rid of the interference? It has to be Finn, but I can't believe he tried to make me think elves were the only class of supernaturals the humans would trust. What the hell, Finn? Way to be subtle."

I was fuming, and the campfire started flaring.

"Whoa, Eleanor," Isaac said. "Calm down. Don't burn down the campsite because you're in a bad mood."

"I am tired of this shit," I said. "I am tired of camping, and magic, and weapons, and supernatural shenanigans. I am tired of drinking inferior beer and vastly inferior coffee. I am tired of eating freeze-dried camping food. I am tired of it all."

"I'm tired of Isaac," I thought. I looked around. No way was that originating from me. Any lingering doubts I had regarding outside interference were gone.

Isaac looked devastated, and I realized our channel was still open.

I amended my thought, *"I'm tired of Isaac being fully clothed."*

I opened my mind as wide as I dared while still leaving some protections in place. I used my anger at Finn's interference and the energy from the fire elementals still dancing on my skin to fuel my fly paper shields. The "sticky paper" wasn't strong enough to hold him or even to let him know he'd been made, but I found him.

I faced the northwest. Raj and Isaac followed my movement and peered into the darkness. I grabbed my sword from the scabbard on the table in front of me. The flames on my arms danced down to the blade and lit it up. Give me a scanty leather bikini, and I'd look like a warrior in an online RPG. I marched towards Finn and when I sensed him move against the flypaper, I put all my energy into the stickiness of the strands around him.

"You fucking bastard." Isaac and Raj moved up behind me, but they gave me enough distance to swing my sword.

"Don't kill him," Florence cautioned.

I held my sword out. My hand shook with anger, but Finn's expression indicated he thought I was shaking in fear.

"Remove the link between us," I said.

"Or what?"

"Or I will start slicing off pieces of you. Florence says we need you alive, or I'd remove the link with your death. She didn't say we needed you whole, and I can cut pieces off until 'alive' is nothing more than a technical term for your existence."

"I don't believe you," Finn said.

I pulled one of my leather wrapped steel knives from a thigh sheath, pulled the fire elementals back from my sword, and handed it over to Raj. "Raj, if he moves skewer him."

"Your wish is my command, my sweet." He took my sword and pulled out his own. With a rapier and a khanda, he looked five kinds of deadly. Hot. I shook myself. Now was not the time for inappropriate vampire fantasies.

"Finn, remove the link."

"Didn't I tell you I didn't know how?"

"No. You implied it, but you never said you didn't know. Remove the link."

He crossed his arms, trying to call my bluff. Too bad I wasn't bluffing. I walked forward until we were almost touching, and then as quickly as I could, sliced off the tip of one slightly pointy ear with my iron knife. I maintained my impassive façade, although I really wanted to either pass out or throw up. Possibly both.

He gasped and his hand went up to his ear. Blood poured out through his fingertips. "You bitch!"

"I warned you. You know I can't lie. Remove the bond."

"When Arduinna taught me how to form the bond, she didn't teach me how to remove it."

"But you know how, regardless of whether Arduinna taught you or not. Remove the bond."

"No."

I grabbed his hand, and before he could pull away or I could think too hard about what I was going to do, I sliced off his pinky finger at the first knuckle. This time he was silent, his hand limp in mine. I could see the wound reddening and puckering up from the contact with the iron in my steel knife before his blood covered his hand.

"Look at what you've become, Ellie," he said. "You are nothing more than a killer now."

He was right, but I couldn't let my doubt show. "You mean torturer," I said. "I haven't killed you. Yet."

"You've killed, though."

"Yes, in self-defense. I don't feel guilty about that." I started to feel guilty about that. "Finn, stop. You're being too obvious. How do you think I knew you were here? You made me feel much worse about myself than I ever would, and your clumsy attempts to insert false thoughts made more than one person act out of character. You've known me for six years and have spent a lot of time with Isaac. You really should know both of us better than you demonstrated today. Even if Isaac is feeling crappy, he's never a jerk."

"He keeps secrets from you."

"Probably. We all have secrets."

"Big secrets."

"Big secrets like creating a connection without my knowledge or consent? Secrets like planning on kidnapping me and tattooing me to dampen my power? Secrets like whatever the fuck you're still doing here?"

"Bigger."

"Well that makes sense since everything about him is bigger." I let my gaze rake down Finn's body and then back up to his face. His insecurities were predictable. Finn flushed in anger. "Remove the bond."

Finn's voice lost the cool detachment. "He's created a bond with you, too! I can sense it!"

"Yes, it's true," I said. "The difference is it was mutual and I agreed to it ahead of time. Remove the bond."

"He's attracted to the vampire!" His voice had lost all detachment and he was bordering on hysteria.

"Have you seen the vampire? Of course he's attracted to him. I'm attracted to him. Florence probably is, too. You can't possibly mean that's the giant secret he's hiding." Finn deflated when his bombshell didn't have the effect he was hoping.

"I'm not, actually," Florence murmured.

"Finn. The bond."

"No."

I cut off the first joint on the next finger, and this time he couldn't stop the gasp of pain. He was almost hyperventilating, and I was afraid he'd pass out if I did any more damage.

"Remove. The. Bond." I said through gritted teeth.

"I need to touch you," he said. I took a step forward and then stopped.

"Finn, answer true. Do you need to touch me to remove the bond?"

"Yes."

"And will you remove the bond as soon as you touch me?"

Anger flashed in his eyes, and I knew then I'd been right to clarify. "Yes."

I handed my knives back to Florence and thought at my companions, "*I know I said I wouldn't kill him, and Florence says I shouldn't, but if he, for a second, looks like he's planning on popping out of here with me, I don't care. Kill him dead.*"

"*He won't leave with you again,*" Isaac thought back.

"You all want to have sex with me?" Raj asked.

"Eyes on the prize, Raj."

"They are," he said. I rolled my eyes.

I stepped forward and Raj and Isaac followed. Florence circled behind Finn and crouched, knives outstretched. She looked like a badass warrior goddess.

When I stepped into the circle of Finn's aura, he put his hands on my shoulders. Blood dripped down my arm and suppressed a shudder. I couldn't believe I'd done that.

Finn let go of my shoulder with his good hand and removed a knife from my wrist sheath before I could register what was happening. He slashed across my arm and then put his wounded hand on the cut.

"What the fuck are you doing?" I asked. Isaac was about three breaths from wolfing out and Raj had both swords out and ready. It was Florence, however, who had him by the short hairs. She'd moved up behind him and had one knife poised between his legs.

"I will cut off things you value more than a finger or two if you do not remove the bond and leave without creating any new ones. I don't want you killed, but I don't care if you're whole."

"It's a blood bond," Finn said. "I can't remove it without mingling our blood."

"And are you removing it?" Florence asked.

"I was until you threatened me."

"If you're going to be doing any more slicing and dicing, you may want to give a little warning first," I said. "We're all a little trigger happy, and cutting someone without a heads up is not a best practice."

"Fine. Can you get your pet witch to remove the knife?"

"I can ask my friend, who happens to be a mage of some power, if she will remove the knife without removing anything you might hold dear. Why should I ask her to do that?"

"I can't concentrate on removing the bond with a knife between my legs!"

"Florence, would you be a dear and back up half a step? You know his manhood is a delicate issue with him."

Florence smirked, but did as I asked.

"Okay. Remove the pre-existing bond and do not create any new ones."

Finn grimaced and put his bloody hand back on my wound. The bleeding was already slowing down, and since he'd grabbed a silver knife, it really didn't even hurt much. He closed his eyes and muttered something in a language I didn't recognize.

"Nire odolarekin, lotura hori apurtu dut."

Something popped in my head. It was like the time I dislocated my kneecap. I swayed on my feet and blinked a couple of times to clear my vision.

"It is done," Finn said.

"Be more specific," Florence said.

"The bond I created the night I met Ellie is broken. I didn't create anything new."

"Are there other bonds between you and Eleanor?" Florence asked.

"I've never created another bond between us." Finn said.

"That's not what I asked. Are there any other ties—created by you or anyone else—connecting you to her?" Florence sounded like she was losing patience.

Anger tightened his eyes, but Finn didn't reply. His actions were answer enough. He grabbed my bloody arm again and said, "Sever konexioa. Nire odol prezioa da."

Florence raised an eyebrow at Finn. "Does that take care of all of them?"

"There are no more bonds between me and Ellie," he said.

"If you did not create the second connection, who did?" I asked.

"That was not part of our bargain," he said. "Now, either kill me or let me go. I do not wish to stand here bleeding in front of you any longer. Your vampire looks hungry."

"I would sooner eat the leavings in an abattoir."

Finn flushed and the skin around his eyes tightened. This was not his best night ever, and I worried about how this was going to come back and bite me in the ass. He didn't have a good track record in handling hurt feelings, and I wasn't hopeful he'd suddenly matured enough to not seek revenge for this level of humiliation.

"As long as I am with you, he won't harm you," Raj said. "How were you able to stay close to him for so long? His mind is an abandoned maze, overgrown with dark, thorny thoughts."

"He was a pleasant diversion."

Finn flushed even deeper. "I was more than that."

"You were my friend, once. However, any claim you might have had to my friendship is long gone. Now you're a piece of my past that won't stay buried. You cannot even remain a fond memory."

"Leave," Florence said.

We all backed up a couple of steps to give him room. Finn backed away from us. I felt his movement as he hit all the fly-paper like magical extensions that survived the encounter. They'd worked!

Finn glared at me and then disappeared.

"The good news is my shields stayed up the entire time."

"Nicely done," Florence said. "And now, look to your mate."

I turned. Isaac's eyes were more yellow than brown now, and he looked incredibly stressed. I walked into his arms and kissed him. "Hey, baby, he's gone now. You can relax."

"He cut you," Isaac growled.

"Yes, but he broke the two bonds tying me to him, and my cut has already healed."

Isaac visibly struggled to get a hold of himself. "Do you need me to go?" I asked.

"No!" he shouted. Then more quietly, "No."

I stayed until his breathing slowed, until his eyes returned to brown, and until the extraneous body hair faded away.

"What do you think he'll do in retaliation?" I asked, trying to draw attention away from Isaac's lack of control. I wondered how much of it was because I'd been in danger and how much of it was a response to Finn's taunting about a big secret he hadn't yet shared.

"He won't slink away, tail between his legs?" Raj asked.

"He kidnapped me and had me tattooed in iron when I told him I'd never love him that way. He wouldn't know a strategic retreat if it bit him in the ass."

"Let's not worry about it now," Florence said. "The day after tomorrow, you'll open the gate. Nothing will happen between now and then. Rest tonight and tomorrow. Thursday will be here before we know it."

I didn't sleep well that night. I'd sliced fingers and a pointy ear tip off of Finn. I'm not sure I would've left him alive if Florence didn't think we needed him. In two days, I would take another step towards breaking the world. My lover and mate was keeping secrets. All I wanted was one, tiny thing under control. I rolled over and scrunched my eyes shut, trying to will my brain into stillness. A movie played in my mind: Finn's ear, him slicing into my arm, Isaac leaving me, Isaac dying in my arms, Isaac dying by Finn's hand. My mind didn't come up with any secrets that'd be big enough to change how I felt about

Isaac or juicy enough for Finn to gloat over. I buried my face in my pillow. The movie played again. And again.

I gave up any attempts to sleep when the first hints of dawn streaked the eastern sky. I tried to climb out of bed without waking Isaac, but an arm snuck around my waist and pulled me back into his body.

"Where're you going?" he whispered.

"Coffee," I whispered back.

"Not alone."

"My alarm system is still active. Nothing bigger than a raccoon has been through."

"He's seen your shielding now. He could adjust. I'll be glad to be gone from here and go somewhere he's not yet been. Hopefully it'll be harder for him to track us now."

"You guys can stop whispering. I'm awake," Florence said from the other side of the camper.

"Sorry to wake everyone," I said, peering out of the curtain covering our side of the camper and meeting Florence's eyes.

"This is actually what time we usually get up," Isaac replied. "It only seems early to you because you generally sleep another two or three hours."

I punched him lightly in the shoulder. "I don't sleep until nine."

"You did last week."

"Only because you kept me up all night—"

"Don't finish that sentence," Florence said.

"You're grumpy this morning." I said.

She glared. Grumpy Florence didn't enjoy being teased.

"I'll make coffee," Isaac said. I kissed him, sending my tongue out to flick across his lips. His desire surged through our bond and I smiled.

"Coffee, please," I said as I pushed him away. He growled and kissed me until I was gasping before leaving the camper.

Florence was shaking her head. "Why did I ever agree to share a camper with you two? Am I finally slipping into senility?"

"We're inspirational. You could write love songs about us and make millions."

"I'll keep that in mind." Florence crawled out of her bed and started going through her suitcase.

I dressed and went outside. Isaac handed me a cup of coffee and I breathed in the aroma before taking a sip. Perfection.

"I'm growing as a person," I announced after finishing the first cup and holding it out for a refill. "I am no longer the grumpiest morning person around."

"I told you mixing decaf in with the regular in increasing proportions was a good idea," Florence said.

"What?!" I looked down at my coffee and then at Isaac. I'd been betrayed. "This is decaf?"

Isaac looked a bit sheepish. "I thought we weren't going to tell her."

"I didn't want you to have any big secrets," Florence said.

"It's not 100% decaf," Isaac said. "It's about half-caf. We decided it'd be good to ensure none of us had a caffeine dependency in case we start having trouble getting coffee."

"Did you even look at the emergency stash in the trunk?" I stalked over and opened it. The hidden panel swung up to reveal water, a filter, cans of food, and dozens of bags of whole-bean coffee.

"Those are the emergency provisions?" Isaac asked.

"There's booze under the coffee."

"Who put her in charge of shopping?" Florence asked.

"I had some downtime before the full moon and made an executive decision. There's enough food and water for a month if we're frugal—more if we supplement with fresh food. There's enough coffee for six months, less if we use it in trade. And there's a decent amount of liquor. I also purchased plenty of ammunition. We won't need it, but it will be good in trade." The rest of the trunk was lined with strapped down gasoline cans and first aid kits. We were as prepared as I could make us.

"You are..." Isaac searched for a word.

"Amazing? Fantastic? Resourceful?" I suggested.

"I was going to say crazy, but those other words will work."

I smiled up at him. "You adore me."

"That I do, Princess. That I do."

I'd stuffed supplies in the storage spaces in the camper, too, but maybe now wasn't the time to show how much beer and wine I'd stockpiled. Priorities.

I went for a mid-afternoon run with Isaac, trying to burn off my nervous energy without expending the energy I'd need to get through the gate opening. By sunset, my stomach churned with anxious nausea. In twenty-four hours, I'd be opening my third gate.

RAYS OF SUNLIGHT hitting my face finally forced me out of bed. After coffee and breakfast, we packed up camp and drove to a state park 100 miles southeast of St. Louis. We set up camp in the abandoned campground and waited for our ride. At one o'clock, Christopher and Luis arrived. We drove back to St. Louis and convened at the pack's house before heading to Cahokia.

It was less than forty-five minutes until sunset when I walked into the center of the henge. Florence and I sat and built the magical weir that would slow the rush of gate magic into the world.

Florence took ownership of the weir and left me with nothing but nerves to hold on to. The pulse of power steadily increased. It was almost time. The wolves standing guard along the perimeter were a barely felt presence on the edges of my mind. Nervous energy steered me into a rapid, jerky pace in the center of the wood circle.

Raj, his eyes hidden by sunglasses to protect himself from the last rays of the setting sun, dropped into the circle, interrupting my pacing.

"Will you be okay?" I asked.

"This is fine. Are you okay?"

I nodded and then felt the first spike in magic.

"It's starting." I positioned myself in the center of the henge. Raj headed to a position along the perimeter to guard Florence's back. When I stepped into the unopened gate, the power snapped my limbs into an X and I hovered a couple of feet off the ground. Raw magic poured through me, overwhelming my senses. I fought to hold onto consciousness while I channeled the magic into the holding pond of the weir Florence maintained.

I tensed in preparation for the surge of power I'd feel when the gate opened. I dropped my shields in preparation, and was tackled to the ground. The energy coursed through me, burning my synapses when I couldn't control it anymore. I rolled over. Where were my bodyguards?

I looked around through the purpling dusk. The shifters, most of whom had gone furry, were fighting. It looked like there was a contingent attacking and one defending, but I couldn't tell which were on my side. Raj and Isaac were standing over Florence defending her from a small group of trees—Fae, then—and my attacker was…"Finn. What the fuck are you doing?"

"Stopping you."

"Too late." I pulled away from him and sent the last of the energy into the gate construct. The gate snapped into place and yawned open for a brief moment before slamming shut. It was closed now, but I'd done my job, and the magic was flowing out trying to find a balance between the two worlds.

"Not stopping you from opening the gate. Stopping you from noticing."

"Noticing what?"

He smiled and dread settled over me. I kicked him in the balls. While he was hunched over, I unsheathed my sword and cracked him on the head with the pommel. He slumped into unconsciousness. I ran over to Raj, Isaac, and Florence. They were okay, and the tree creatures were down for the count. It looked like the shifter battle was winding down, too, and Christopher and Luis were running over to us.

"Everyone okay?" I asked. Everyone nodded.

Luis asked, "Is it done?"

"It is."

"How long until she passes out?" Christopher asked.

"About twenty minutes, if prior experiences have any bearing," Isaac said. There was something wrong. I looked at him.

"What is it?"

"Not now."

"Later?"

He looked past me. I looked at Raj, and he shrugged. "I did not see what they showed him."

"Later," Isaac repeated.

"Fine. Let's get out of here." I turned and headed towards the getaway car, my friends flanking me. Between one step and the next, the world grayed out and I fell. Someone caught me, and the last thing I heard before the blackness overwhelmed my senses was, "That was not twenty minutes."

CHAPTER FOURTEEN

I WOKE UP gasping. Magic burned me as it looked for an escape. I flailed and realized I was tied down. I started screaming and Isaac was there.

"Shhh...you're okay," he whispered.

It took a few minutes to quell my panic and control my breathing. It was dark, but I could tell we were in the camper.

"Why am I tied up?"

"You're not." Isaac turned on the light. I looked down. I was in a sleeping bag that had twisted around my limbs. I wanted to laugh, but the panic was too near the surface.

"Help me out?"

Isaac set down the battery-operated lantern and unzipped the sleeping bag. I stretched out my limbs and sat up.

"How long?"

"One night this time. It's almost morning. How do you feel?"

"I have to pee."

"I'm not surprised. Let's get you up."

He helped me stand. We walked—okay, I shuffled—out of the camper and through the dark campground towards the bathrooms.

"I'd really like a shower. I feel über grungy."

"Go ahead and jump in. I'll run back to the camper and get your toiletries bag and some clothes. Now that you're awake, we can make some plans."

"Are Raj and Florence here?"

"Raj left before you woke up. He'll find us tonight and we can fill him in. Florence was in the camper and is probably up making coffee now."

I got in the shower, and true to his word, Isaac showed up a few minutes later with everything I needed to get clean, dry, and dressed. After I accomplished all of those things, we headed back to the camp site where there was fresh coffee waiting for me.

"Isaac, you are a god among men," I said, reaching up to kiss him.

"I made the coffee," Florence said.

"And you are a goddess among women," I assured her.

I drank my first cup in silence and then poured a second cup from the French press. "Okay, how bad is it?"

Florence and Isaac exchanged a glance. "You know I hate that bullshit."

"It's too early to know the full effects. Arduinna stopped by a couple hours ago and reported there's no power in most of the central United States, and all air traffic—really, all traffic—in the middle of the country has stopped. Most commercial flights have been cancelled regardless of origin or destination."

Florence said, "President Murphy and General Aldea have declared the first order of business is to send the National Guard to the dark zones to speed up rescue and evacuation before winter renders the upper midwest impenetrable. Somehow, they've managed to deflect any bad press regarding their failure to identify and destroy the terrorists responsible for this destruction. There has been an uptick in attacks against suspected terrorists, which in this country means brown people."

"This wasn't supposed to happen," I said.

"Humans are assholes," Isaac said.

"In all fairness, all sentient beings have an assortment of assholes," Florence said.

I waved at them, hoping they'd shut up for a moment. They did.

"How will the National Guard rescue and evacuate if technology doesn't work in the dark zones?"

"A combination of old enough cars, and horses. They've reinstated the Pony Express for news, and are bringing in food, medicine, and supplies via wagon. Evacuations are being limited to those who are at greatest risk. The leadership knows there's nowhere they can go that won't be feeling the effects of this within the year."

"How's Portland?"

Florence said, "It's a dark zone now. The gate energy has steadied and isn't pulsing anymore, but the city is dark and it's spreading. Arduinna requests we contact her as soon as you know where we're headed next. If the next gate is in or adjacent to a dark zone, they'll delay the announcement. But if you're going to destroy another section of the grid, the supernaturals will need to come out into the light."

"And the nuclear power plants?"

"No incidents at any in the dark zone and the rest in the US have been secured. This has affected the power in a lot of other places, but no one is complaining."

I looked at Isaac. He hadn't said anything in a while, and I remembered what Finn had said to me before I'd knocked him out.

"Isaac? What was going on at the gate Finn didn't want me to see? Raj said they showed you something?"

His face lost all expression and he looked away.

"You're not going to tell me?"

"I will. I can't right now."

"Can't or won't?"

"Won't. But soon. I promised. I'm still processing. I need to make a decision."

"If that decision will affect me in any way, I'd like to have a discussion before you do anything irrevocable."

He smiled, but stayed silent. *Dammit.*

"Fine. Let's head east. We're going to Savannah."

By mid-morning, we were back on the road. "I wish there was a pattern to these gates," I said. "It'd be cool if I was drawing a big picture over the country."

Florence laughed. "Like connect-the-dots?"

"Exactly." I marked gates one through four on my atlas and connected the dots. "This is a crappy picture."

Isaac leaned over from the back seat to study the map. "Maybe it's the beginning of a dragon?"

"If it's going to be a dragon, there are a lot more gates than I was led to believe."

"It'll be like the constellations. We'll have to use our imaginations."

"Savannah?" Florence said, changing the subject. "For some reason, I thought we'd be hitting the northeast. You know, destroying every section of the United States."

"That's what I thought, too. We know New Orleans is on the list, but maybe we'll go north next before heading south again?"

"We can get to Savannah in one long day of driving," Isaac said. "But it'd be better if we broke it up over a couple of days."

"What're the roads going to be like?" I asked. "Is it going to be like 'The Stand' with cars littering the freeways?"

"Probably not where we're headed. We're out of the range of the immediate magic blast, and headed into an area where the grid is still up."

I wrinkled my nose, trying to get my head around what was happening. "Each of the places in which I've opened a gate have a circular area, with the gate at the center, in which no technologies work?"

Isaac nodded.

"But if there were enough power stations in the blast zone, the magical blasts caused the grid to fail? And because the circular dark zones are growing, they can't get the grids back up?"

"Yes," Isaac said. "Essentially. The dark zones, as they're being called, start as rough circles approximately 100 miles in diameter, and everything within that circle—"

"Really more of a dome," Florence interjected.

"Right, everything within the dome that used technology newer than steam power failed."

"So radios, computers, cars, planes, anything with electricity or batteries?"

"Exactly. The entire country runs on a series of electrical grids. There are three main grids, the east, which covers basically everything from the Mountain Time zone marker east; the west, which goes from the same marker towards the Pacific Ocean, and Texas."

"Texas has its own grid?" I asked.

"Of course it does," Florence said.

"I've damaged the western grid by opening gates in Portland and South Dakota. The entire grid isn't down, but the magic bursts make it impossible for them to get the pieces of the damaged grid and the surrounding areas fixed. And now I've damaged a large swath of the eastern grid with my actions in St. Louis, which was powerful enough to affect more than the immediate area, and took down most of the power for everything between St. Louis and the western grid. Is all of that correct?"

"Basically," Isaac said.

"I am breaking the world."

"Yes, you are."

"And when I open the gate in Savannah, that will probably destroy all power in the Southeast, including New Orleans where we'd like to go and not be killed by a band of hungry, angry—"

"Hangry," Florence said.

I grinned. "*Hangry* vampires."

"Raj is going to have to do damage control. It's good he's with us," Florence said. "There may be a queen in New Orleans, but Savannah is another vampire hotspot."

"I hope he finds us okay," I said.

"He's had a taste of all three of us. He'll have no trouble locating us," Florence said.

"All of us?" I looked at Isaac. "I thought you were opposed to having him bite you for location purposes."

Isaac looked uncomfortable.

"Oh my god, it wasn't for location purposes, was it? You let him bite you for sexy-time purposes!"

"No," he said. "It was not that kind of bite. Florence was there."

"I was unconscious for one night, and my new mate is already going elsewhere for pleasure." I shook my head, trying to look sad while watching Isaac out of the corner of my eye. I'd forgotten about the bond we shared, though.

He grinned at me. "I can feel your amusement. Stop teasing me."

"Tell me about the biting."

"We agreed it would be a fantastic idea for Raj to be able to find each of us in case we were separated. You and I have a bond and can find each other, but it's hard for Raj to find you when you're near a gate. He did suggest another couple of bites from you would make you easier to find for him, but since you were unconscious when he proposed that, I told him maybe it would be wise to hold off until you were capable of making your own decisions about it."

"Thanks. I'll think about it. I'm more than a little worried about what more of my blood would do to him, since I've already given him a silver immunity and the ability to cross thresholds without invitation."

"Good point," Isaac said.

"If you don't want to get all the way to Savannah tonight, what's your plan for an overnight?" I asked.

"There's a State Park east of Nashville we should reach around sunset. We'll set up there."

We drove in silence for a while, and I fell asleep. You'd think I wouldn't be tired, but being magically unconscious did not count as rest. Every time I woke up, someone shoved food in my face. When I looked down at myself, I could see why. The last few weeks had taken a toll on me. I'd finally achieved a level of slimness that had eluded me in high school and college when I cared about such things. My jeans were baggy on me, and my fitted shirts were no longer fitted. I was still muscular, but if I lost much more weight, that would diminish, too.

I'd never had a fast metabolism no matter how much I'd wanted one. I managed to stay in decent shape by running, but keeping weight off was work. Not anymore—and it wasn't all I'd thought it would be.

"I need some weight gain 3000."

"You are always beautiful," Isaac said, "But if you're going to maintain your strength, you need to gain some weight back."

"The magic burns it off faster than I can keep it on. Between maintaining my shields and the constant physical activities, I can't eat enough."

"Well," Isaac said slowly, "I suppose I could help cut down on some of those physical activities."

I reached over and smacked him in the shoulder. "Not those activities, Wolf. The running, sparring, and shifting into a dragon on a regular basis."

"The sex is definitely the worst of the lot," Florence said. "You really should cut that out."

I turned around in my car seat and smiled at her. "If I get sexually frustrated, I can't be held responsible for the state of my mental shields."

She shuddered and smiled at me, "Excellent point. Keep on keeping your libido sated."

I smiled at her and finished off the bag of cheeseburgers we'd picked up in the last town we'd driven through. We drove through Nashville without stopping and left the interstate an hour later. We stopped for dinner in a small town in Tennessee. They had power, but everyone seemed nervous. They were close enough to the edge of the St. Louis dark zone and the threat of terrorism had everyone on edge. After restocking our perishables, we drove the remaining half hour to the State Park. It was closed for the season, but Florence magicked open the padlock barring access, and we headed in.

Raj stopped by and looked singularly disgruntled with the news we were headed to Savannah. He didn't even respond to my teasing him about biting Isaac while I was unconscious. After Isaac gave him our planned route, he took off without a word.

"That wasn't friendly," I said.

"Maybe he's hangry," Florence suggested.

We went to bed early, and I fell asleep almost immediately.

WE WERE on the road by the time the sun came up the next morning. We stopped in another small town for breakfast and coffee.

When we got back to the car, Isaac looked thoughtfully at our vehicle and said, "We'll need new plates."

"I don't follow," I said.

"License plates. We need plates from somewhere here in the South. It'll be easier if it looks like we belong."

"Is that why we're headed to Asheville?" The gates were getting easier and easier to find, and we already had the destination. Savannah was small enough that I'd be able to pinpoint the location quickly.

"I have an old friend there who is in the kind of business that will allow him to help us."

"Is it in the auto reclamation business?" Florence asked.

Isaac smirked. "He reclaims autos from people he doesn't believe should have them."

"As long as he doesn't try to reclaim mine. And as long as he doesn't pass on stolen plates."

"He wouldn't do that."

I bit my tongue to keep from saying anything about the last friend of his we'd relied on for help. I'd forgotten about our link, though.

Isaac looked at me out of the corner of his eyes. I could feel the annoyance surging from him. "I've apologized enough, don't you think?"

"You didn't need to apologize at all. Not your fault he was a dick. If I was truly still hung up on it, I would've said something out loud instead of squelching a thought that rose to the surface."

"Children," Florence said from the back seat. "I know your link is new, but you'll have to learn how to not react to every stray thought or feeling you get from each other. There are a lot stray thoughts and unconscious reactions you'll need to ignore. For instance, the first time you feel a surge of lust from Isaac when he's looking at another woman, you'll need to ignore that because he won't be planning on acting on it, and vice versa. The mind is a crazy place, and if you hold each other accountable for every passing thought or urge, you'll drive yourselves crazy."

Isaac drove in silence for a while. Then he said, "Sorry. I over-reacted."

"There really is no need to apologize. I was bitchy about Joseph when it first happened. I trust you."

He reached out and grabbed my hand and squeezed.

Time to change the subject. "Tell me about this car reclamation artist."

"He's the kind of fellow who defies description. You'll need to meet him to truly get a sense for who he is."

"Shifter?" I asked.

"Yep."

"What kind? Wolf?"

"Nope. After you meet him, see if you can guess."

I pestered Isaac about his friend for a while, and then fell asleep. I woke a couple of hours later as we were pulling into a RV park in Asheville. "Gah! Why am I so tired?"

"No idea, Princess," Isaac said. "You'd think you'd be all caught up on sleep."

"Seriously," I said, scrubbing my eyes with my knuckles trying to remove the grit.

"You've totally depleted yourself," Florence said. "Each time you open a gate and divert the magic into our weir to slow the flow into the world, you are drawing more on yourself than on the natural world and it's sapping your magical and physical strength. The gates need Fae magic to open and there isn't enough of it at any gate site—hence the reason for the gates in the first place. Since you're the biggest source of Fae magic in the vicinity of the newly opened gates, they pull it out of you to power themselves as they release their surplus of magic back into the world.

"It doesn't help that you don't have reserves to draw on. You're running on fumes. The gates are pulling on your magical energy to open, and you're letting them have whatever they need plus you're creating additional complicated magic immediately before the opening which leaves you with even less to work with. This is why you're exhausted and ravenous."

"Do you think it will get better as I get more experienced?"

"Not unless you're planning on using the next seven weeks to do nothing but eat and rest to top off your tank. If, instead, you're running around, fighting off attackers, working on your magical skills, and not eating enough—it's going to be the same, or maybe worse."

"The Portland gate was the hardest to find, but the easiest to open," I said.

"How long were you unconscious after Portland?"

"From mid-afternoon to the next morning," Isaac said.

"But only seven hours after the last two," I said.

"You're waking up long enough to eat your weight in food. You've been asleep more than you've been awake."

"We'll think about it," Florence said. "Maybe we can figure out a way to keep you conscious for longer. But in the meantime, you need to eat and sleep as much as you can. Your shields are weak right now."

WE STOPPED at another fast food place and then at a grocery store before looking for Isaac's friend. The shelves were barely stocked.

"It's starting already," I said.

"We knew it would. People are scared and with the majority of the country being inaccessible, people are preparing for shortages. Let's buy the minimum we need and leave the rest for the people who live here."

We picked up some fresh fruit and some canned goods and checked out. I pulled out my debit card and the clerk pointed to a sign above the register. "Cash Only."

We drove the car a ways out of town, and I couldn't stop gasping at the gorgeousness of the late fall scenery in the mountains. "This place is amazing," I said. "If I'd known about Asheville, I might've moved here instead of Portland."

"It snows," Isaac said.

"Snow is pretty," I replied. "It snows in Portland, too."

"It's cold, too."

"It is a bit chilly, but I can deal. This place is great. We should stay forever."

"Although I admire your spontaneity, it might be better to stay at least overnight before deciding to move."

"Fine. Whatever. Kill my dreams."

Isaac and Florence laughed. Isaac turned off the main road and onto a smaller dirt road. We wound through the trees for a few minutes before he turned onto something that could only be called— if we were being generous—a dirt path. Five minutes later we pulled up to a decrepit homestead. The clapboard house was grayed with years of weather and neglect. The porch sagged suspiciously in the middle, and one of the windows was plywood instead of glass. The garage had a variety of siding, and an even wider variety of cars and car parts in and around it.

Isaac turned off the car and got out.

"Hello!" he yelled. Florence and I got out of the car, too. "Hell-looooooo!" Isaac yelled again. His voice echoed around us.

"No need t' yell," someone said. "The holler will bring yer voice t' me."

I turned around. Behind me was a slight man with short-cropped hair and the biggest ears I'd ever seen on a person. He wore a blue chambry shirt under greasy overalls and worn, cracked work boots.

Isaac strode forward with his arm stretched out. They clasped hands, then forearms.

"Ike," he said. "I'm mighty pleased t' see you showing yer face 'round here again. Guess that warrant must've fin'ly expired."

"Ike? Warrant?" I asked.

"Tell you later," Isaac said. He grinned at me and winked at his friend. "Might I introduce you to my companions?"

"You'd better, or I'll think they're no accounts like me," the man said.

Isaac motioned Florence forward. "This here is Florence White Elk. She's a powerful mage, so don't you be messin' with her." The man was eying Florence with appreciation. She rolled her eyes and held out her hand. He shook it and then turned to look at me. I stepped forward.

"And this here is Eleanor Morgan." I held out my hand. The man reached for it as Isaac added, "My mate."

The man dropped his hand and took a leap backwards, stumbling over a large rusty…thing…that might have been part of an engine.

"Are you shittin' me, Ike? You got yerself a mate?"

Isaac ignored him. "Ladies, this is my old friend Extra Grady Wiggins."

"Pleased to meet you," I said.

"What the hell, Ike?" Extra said. "I didn't think you'd ever get hitched. Course I ain't seen you in so many years I've lost track, but hitched? To a human?" He turned to me. "No offense, ma'am."

"None taken." I was having trouble not laughing.

"She's not human," Isaac said.

"Not that it would matter," I said. Isaac grinned at me.

"Are you going to invite us in?"

"Yer not vamps, not out in the daylight like this," Extra said. "Invite yer own damn selves in."

Isaac looked at him until he relented. "Fine. Yer my friend, and the Indian witch seems nice enough. Y'all can come on in."

"Extra Grady, are you insulting my mate?"

Confusion crossed Extra's face. "No. I would never do something that stupid. I hope."

Isaac raised an eyebrow and stared. Extra wrinkled up his brow, perhaps replaying the conversation in his head. His forehead unwrinkled as it hit him. He bowed in my direction. "Ma'am, please forgive me. Out here in t' woods, I ain't had much time to polish my manners, and my social graces ain't what they should be. I would take it as a great kindness if one such as yerself would enter my home and partake of refreshments."

I smiled. "I would be delighted, Extra."

Isaac led the way into the decrepit house. I walked gingerly up the stairs, expecting them to collapse under our combined weight, but they were sturdier than they looked. I was a little uncomfortable with the idea of spending time in a dirty, falling down house that was, based on the number of holes I could see from the outside, likely crawling with vermin.

I was looking down at the floor, trying to avoid any sunken spots, loose boards, and random holes when we crossed the threshold. When I looked up, I couldn't contain my gasp of surprise.

"It's beautiful!" The house was gorgeous. The gleaming wood floors matched the gorgeously carved vaulted ceiling. All of the furniture looked hand-carved as well. "This is amazing. Why—" I stopped myself.

"Why don't it match the outside?" Extra asked.

I nodded. "Forgive my rudeness, but yes. Why not make the outside as beautiful as the inside?"

"This way, no one ever wants t' come in, and I'm spared havin' to offer hospital'ty to every jackass who wanders by."

"That makes sense." I was still in awe. "Did you do the carvings yourself?"

Extra nodded, and this time looked pleased rather than pissed. The bannister was comprised of intricate carvings. The spindles were cats, stretched up on their hind legs, and carved up the handle were a number of squirrels, running up the hand rail. "This is amazing."

"Might I offer y'all some refreshment?"

"I'd take a drop of some Mountain Dew, if you've got it," Isaac said.

"Now, Ike, you know that shit ain't legal."

I looked up, wondering what I'd missed that soda wasn't legal. "Moonshine," Isaac explained.

"How 'bout a Co-Cola for the ladies?"

"That sounds great. Extra brought out Cokes in dusty bottles for Florence and me. He pulled out a gallon-sized glass jar with clear liquid in it and poured out two shots. He handed one to Isaac, they clinked their glasses, and threw it back.

"Whew!" Extra said. "That's some good shit, there, ain't it?"

"It's been ages since I've had finer," Isaac replied.

Florence and I watched as they proceeded to throw back three more shots each. After that, the liquor became a sipping drink, and they were ready to get down to business.

CHAPTER FIFTEEN

"TELL ME WHY yer gracing my fine establishment for the first time in almost longer than I can 'member? And then mebbe tell me how you knew where I was to be found."

"I'll start with the second question, if that's alright, since the first will take some telling." At Extra's gracious nod, Isaac continued. "I'm sure you remember Rebecca Driver."

"Oh and I surely do. That was one fine bitch. Didn't she mate some asshole up in North Dakota? The day she mated, all the shifters in these here United States let out a mournful howl, they did."

"It was South Dakota, but the description of her former husband is spot on."

"Former, you say? How does that work? I thought you puppy dogs mated for life."

Isaac raised an eyebrow. Extra raised his glass in salute before downing the rest of the liquor in it and refilling both glasses. Isaac shook his head but accepted the shot anyway. "If a bonding takes place, it's difficult to end the mating while one partner is still alive, and that's as true for wolves as for any other shifter." Isaac took a sip of the moonshine and a shudder went through me. I almost laughed out loud when I realized that was Isaac's reaction. He wasn't enjoying the good ol' mountain dew as much as he was pretending. "However," Isaac said, returning to the thread of the story, "Rebecca and Greg never completed the bonding. I'm not sure how she managed to put him off, but she did. And it doesn't matter now anyway, because she killed Greg in a dominance fight and took over the Black Hills pack."

"Did she now? Mebbe I should be traveling west, then. She sounds like the kind of bitch I wouldn't mind getting to know better. I likes me a strong, powerful woman."

"Rebecca is a good friend of mine," Isaac said.

"That's not the stories I've heard," Extra interrupted.

"Really?" I asked.

Isaac shot a glare at me, but Extra answered. "I heard that this man o' yers and Miz Becky were more than good friends," Extra said. "But that was more than a few moons ago, now, weren't it?"

"It was more than a century ago, now, Extra," Isaac said. He tried to continue his story, but Extra interrupted again.

"Why did you ever end things with Miz Becky? I thought you two were going to get hitched."

"I met someone else," Isaac said. "So Rebecca's cousin..."

"Not this one, though. She ain't old enough to be your someone else, for all that ain't as human as I thought when we first met. She ain't no bitch, neither, though."

I worked through his last sentence trying to decide if the double negative of 'ain't no' was canceled out by the 'neither' and missed the first part of Isaac's reply.

"...settled in Portland for a spell. I reconnected with Rebecca this summer when we spent some time in the Black Hills. That's where we met Florence, too."

Florence bobbed her head in acknowledgment. She was expressionless except for the barest hint of a smile I didn't think anyone would see if they didn't know her. She was enjoying herself.

"Rebecca asked me to visit her cousin Christopher to carry the news of her victory to him, and we traveled down to St. Louis for a visit. While we were there, Christopher mentioned your name in passing. Since you and I are old friends, I made him tell me everything he knew about you so I could pay you a visit and relive some old times."

"Bullshit," Extra said. He belched loudly and for an uncomfortably long time. He looked over at Florence and me and said, "'Scuse me, ladies, fer my poor manners."

"No worries," I said, waving away his concerns. "Please continue."

"You didn't come down here to reminisce about the shenanigans we got up to during the Reconstruction."

"Not in front of my mate, anyway," Isaac said.

Extra downed another shot, refilled his glass and waved it towards Isaac. "You say you settled in Portland, then visited Miz Becky in the Black Hills before taking word of her down to her cousin in St. Louis? I don't s'pose you'd wanna give me your travel timeline, would you?" Before Isaac could answer, Extra continued, "I'd be mighty surprised if your visits di'n't coincide with these terr'rist events those guvmint idjits are always going on about on the teevee. Why would you think that'd be?"

"And now we come to the first part of your earlier question," Isaac said. "You're right. As much as I wanted to spend some time with an old and dear friend I hadn't seen in more years than is polite to count, that's not the only reason I perked up when your name was mentioned."

"'Afore you get started with this part o' the story, I find I need t' excuse myself a moment. I have a feeling this is going to be a long-winded tale, and I must go see a man about a horse."

Extra stood up and stumbled out of the room, presumably headed for a bathroom.

I looked at Isaac and tried to quirk an eyebrow. He shook his head slightly, asking me to stay quiet, and grimaced.

"You're drunk," I whispered. He started laughing. I rolled my eyes and leaned into the sofa, trying to make myself comfortable. I had a feeling this was going to take even longer than I'd thought.

When Extra returned, he refilled both glasses again and waved at Isaac. "Spin your tale, wolf."

Isaac told a grand story. He left large swaths of it out, but managed to cover the main points with alacrity. He didn't say much about me and my role in what was going on, kind of made it sound like I was along for the ride while Isaac and Florence were running about destroying the world.

Extra looked over at Florence and me when Isaac wound up his story. "You left out a few details," he said. "No way do I believe a wolf and a witch—pardon me for the term—are running around on Fae business. And the way Murphy is going on and on about 'no proof this is any kind of terrorist operations' leads me to believe this is Fae business. And since I know you ain't a Fae, and I can smell the witch—no offense, Miz White Elk—I'm going to have to go with the little lady as the Fae here. She didn't seem to have much to do with yer tale, but she don't seem like the kind of gal who sits on the sidelines, although if you don't start feeding her better, she'll be too weak to do anything else."

"I was afraid if I told you she was Fae, you'd kick her out."

"Why would I do that? I ain't afraid of no Fae."

"Not out of fear. It'd take a rabid grizzly shifter to scare some sense into you, Extra Grady. Out of anger—or self-preservation. It could be dangerous if it got out you knowingly harbored a Fae."

"Ain't nobody can tell me who I can and can't have in my house. You tell me what you need and I'll make sure you get it."

I was in awe of Isaac's manipulative prowess. I had a feeling if we'd started off with, 'Hi! I'm a Fae princess on a mission to break your world, might we have some new license plates?' we would've been shown to the door immediately. I resolved to reward Isaac for his cleverness later. Florence shot me a stern look.

"If you're of a mind to help us out, we could really use some new plates for the car and our camper. We've got Illinois plates on the car and Ohio plates on the camper, and we need something much more Southern to ease suspicion as we travel to our next destination."

"And where is that next destination? It ain't Asheville, is it? I'd rather you didn't break my city like you've broken them other ones. No offense, ma'am, but I like Asheville the way it is."

"We're headed to Savannah next, but the dark zones are going to keep spreading. The world is breaking, and this is only the beginning."

"So yer the one, are ye?" he said. For the first time, he gave me more than a cursory glance. "You don't seem too bad, for a Fae, that is. Good looking, anyway. I guess it's time to move on, then. I've enjoyed myself immensely in this line of work, but if you're going to make it impossible to take advantage of the technological wonders we have in this world, I'll need to find another way to keep myself busy. What kind of services do you think will be in demand when the gates are fully opened?"

During his last couple of sentences, Extra's accent shifted from backwoods to a more aristocratic Southern accent. I looked at him. "You'd do yourself a service if you didn't believe everything you hear, darlin'," he said. He went back to the original accent, "There ain't a one of us that don't hide who he truly is."

"Thank you for your aid, Mr. Wiggins," I said.

"Call me Extra, ma'am. No one has called me 'mister' in longer than I can remember, and I don't think I'd know to answer to it." He turned to Isaac. "I don't have any Georgia plates for a trailer, but I could do Alabama or Mississippi."

"We'll be heading into Louisiana at some point. Which would be best for evoking an air of belonging in both Savannah and New Orleans?"

"You'll be looked down on by the natives with either set. How 'bout I grab what's most handy?"

"That sounds great." Extra disappeared again. When he returned, he had Alabama license plates for a car and a trailer as well as the matching registration. "Will you all need new papers?"

"Wouldn't be a bad idea," Isaac said.

"Come on back to my portrait studio and I'll get you taken care of. You can pick up registration and title, as well as new drivers' licenses and passports day after tomorrow, if that'll fit with your timetable."

"That would be perfect."

We followed Extra back through a maze of rooms until we got to his 'portrait studio' which was a small room with good lighting and a blue backdrop on one wall. We sat for a few pics—we didn't want our driver's license pictures to match the passport pics—and then after some money changed hands, we were on our way. Florence drove this time.

After we were finally back on a paved road, I turned and looked back at Isaac. "Wow. He was interesting."

Isaac laughed. The odor of alcohol poured off of him and I felt the intoxication coursing its way through him. He was drunker than I'd seen him—at least since the night we'd met.

Florence dropped us off at the campsite, muttering about hormonal youngsters, and drove off.

Isaac wasted no time in pulling me close. "Now that we're alone, what do you think we ought to do?"

"We should talk."

He groaned, "I hate it when a woman says we should talk."

I glared at him. "Why? What's wrong with talking?"

"Nothing at all, darlin'," he said. "But we've been mated less than a month, the moon is shining, and you're beautiful. The last thing I want to do is talk."

"What did you have in mind?"

"Something involving considerably less clothing."

"We're alone until Florence deigns to fetch us. I suppose we wouldn't need to remain clothed to satisfy her modesty."

"Sure an' we're the only people in this part of the campground right now."

"It's chilly, though. I don't want to get cold."

"I could probably find a way or two to keep you warm."

"Before I commit to removing any articles of clothing, maybe you could fill me in on what you're planning?" I tried to widen my eyes into innocence and looked up at him. He leaned down, lips parted. I moved into him, anxious for the kiss. It didn't come—he grabbed my lower lip in his teeth and pulled gently, growling a bit.

Warmth rushed to my center. I might be a motherfucking dragon, but something about the wolf taking charge got my motor running.

Isaac abruptly let go of my lip and leaned back. The space between us felt cold and I leaned into him.

"Uh-uh, Princess. You're wearing altogether way too many clothes right now. I'll consider holding you close when you need me to warm you up."

I rolled my eyes again. "Whatever, wolf. Maybe I'll take myself to bed right now. I'm not sure I need you to get rid of this ache anyway." I strutted away, wiggling my ass much more than was called for—and probably more than was attractive.

I got a wolf-whistle for my pains. I pulled off my t-shirt, and returned to my lover. He eyed my exposed cleavage appreciatively and pulled me onto his lap when I got close enough. I leaned into him.

"Do you think what I'm doing is right?" I'd meant to flirt, but my mind was dwelling on more serious things.

Isaac's hand that'd been tracing circles on my back stilled. "Princess, I'm only going to tell you this once, so listen good. I love you. I've loved you from the day we met and you threw a knife at me, but it's been a long time since I've been blinded by love. I would've walked away from you if I'd thought you were the kind of woman to exult in the destruction of our world.

"Do I wish there was another way? Yes. Do I think there is another way? Nothing ethical. I support you and will be by your side as long as I can."

"You won't leave?" I asked, needing to hear the answer.

He looked at me, the gaze more piercing than I would've expected for a question designed to elicit simple assurance.

"Why would you ask?"

"That's not an answer." Icy fear crept into my heart.

"I don't want to leave you," he said.

"What happened in St. Louis?"

"I'll tell you, I promise."

"You're scaring the shit out of me."

"Listen, Princess. It's late. I'm tired and more than a little intoxicated. I'm not trying to hide anything from you, but I really, really need to tell you later. Please let it go."

I knew this was a terrible time to get into an argument. "How long is it going to take you to tell me this secret? I hope it doesn't come back to bite me on the ass." Just because it was a terrible idea didn't mean I wasn't going to do it.

Isaac pulled me into his arms. "Do you really want to fight? We're alone. Your shirt is missing." He cupped my backside. "Your jeans might go missing, too." He leaned in and bit the side of my neck lightly. I tried to stifle my moan, but couldn't stop the rush of warmth that washed over my body. Even if he didn't get the depth of my feeling through our bond, he'd smell my arousal, but I wasn't ready to let go of our argument yet.

"You're trying to distract me."

"Is it working?" His hands left my ass and cupped my breasts. He lifted them, rubbing his thumbs over my nipples. The roughness of his skin against the material of my bra caused my nipples to pucker up immediately. He leaned down and sucked first one and then the other into his mouth. When he backed away, I had two wet circles on my bra and the chilly November air caused my nipples to get even harder.

"You are beautiful," Isaac said.

"We should talk about this," I said. My voice was shaky now; it would take only one more sensual assault before I gave up. I tried to pull back, but didn't try hard. Isaac's hands were at my waist now.

"Tomorrow. I promise we'll talk tomorrow."

"Before you get any further, you should know you're not alone." Raj's voice floated to us out of the dark. "I'm not looking, and if you'd rather I come back later, I will. Of course, if you'd like me to watch— or join in—I can do that, too."

Isaac jumped away and I sat up. "Jesus Christ, Raj. How long have you been standing there?"

"Mere seconds. I wouldn't play the voyeur without your explicit permission."

Isaac's eyes were streaked with yellow and glowing in light of nearby street lights.

"It might not be a bad idea to take off right now."

"My apologies, Eleanor. I did not mean to startle your wolf."

"You can make your apologies later. At that time, we can talk about the wisdom of startling a werewolf who's standing over his nearly naked mate."

Raj bowed slightly and disappeared, but not without a parting message. *"You look mouth-watering, my sweet. I cannot wait until it's my turn to taste you."*

"Isaac," I said. "He's gone. Shall we continue?"

Isaac stepped between my legs. He lifted my hips and pulled off my jeans with one swift motion. He knelt, his mouth hovering above my center. When he made no move to touch me, I took matters into my own hands. I reached down and dipped my hand under the waistband of my panties, slowly brushing a finger back and forth across my clit. I gasped as that light touch sent shivers throughout my body. His breath tickled my skin as he sent a second finger to explore. I wasn't going slowly now. My hips churned with impatience as I stroked faster and faster.

"Stop," Isaac said. I was close to the edge now, and ignored him. He grabbed my wrist and moved my hand away. My hips rose up, trying to follow, but before I could complain, Isaac's mouth replaced my hand and I whimpered. He sucked on me through the wet material of my panties and my hands came down to hold his head. I tried not to push him into me, but control was not my strong suit at the moment.

He ripped off my panties and his tongue met my bare skin. My whimpers turned into moans as he licked and sucked. Only the weight of his head kept me on the picnic table. When he'd brought me to the edge over and over until the pleasure was nearly pain and my begging had turned into unintelligible gasping, he finally relented and thrust two fingers inside me and stroked. That was all it took and I came wildly beneath him.

Finally, the aftershocks of my orgasm ceased and he stood. "Up for another round?" he asked.

I sat up and reached for him. His cock strained against the denim. "That looks painful," I said. "I'd love to help you out."

Isaac grinned. "I was hoping you'd say that." He undid the button and pulled the zipper down. He was not wearing underwear and the minute he tugged his jeans lower on his hips, his erection sprang free. I reached for it, intent on returning the favor he'd granted me, but Isaac stepped out of my reach. "As much as I enjoy your mouth on me," he said, "I need to move right to the main event tonight."

I smiled up at him. "How do you want me?"

"Just like that, Princess." He drew close and thrust into me with one, long powerful stroke. He held still for a moment, then started moving against me. It didn't take many strokes to bring me to the edge again and only a few more before we fell over together.

A while later, after we were cleaned up and back in the camper, I turned to Isaac and said, "I'm holding you to that promise, you know."

"I wouldn't expect anything else. Are you warm enough?"

One of the benefits of sharing sleeping space with a shifter is you're almost always warm enough. It's like having your own personal electric blanket. I wasn't sure if I was cool in comparison, or something about being a dragon shifter made me run colder than usual, but I was thrilled I wouldn't have to spend the winter in the Northeast without power. The temperatures in Asheville were hovering around freezing, and this was about the limit for me. I slipped into a state of torpidity. It would be easy to hibernate, I thought as I slowly drifted off to sleep.

I WOKE the next morning starving and realized Isaac and I hadn't eaten the night before. I got up and pulled on several layers of clothes before leaving the toasty warm camper. Isaac had turned the heat on when he'd gotten up. I exited the camper and breathed in the scents of cold, fresh air and hot coffee. Perfect. I didn't see Isaac, but I knew he wouldn't have gone far. I grabbed my toiletries bag and headed to the little campground bathroom for my morning ablutions.

After a cursory wash with shockingly cold water, I was ready to face the world. Or at least face my coffee.

When I returned to our campsite, Isaac was frying bacon on the little camp stove.

"You are amazing," I said.

"Wait until you see the rest of your breakfast."

I finished my coffee and headed into the camper to dress for the day. Jeans, knee-high socks, and a t-shirt under a long-sleeved shirt, covered by a zip-up hoodie comprised the day's fashionable look.

When I went back outside, Isaac was plating my breakfast. Pancakes with melting butter and maple syrup and a side of bacon. "I am in awe."

"More coffee?"

"You spoil me."

"I'm buttering you up."

"I'm not going to like this, am I?"

"Eat."

After Isaac made me a second cup of coffee he sat down across from me and devoured his own breakfast. We ate in silence and I tried not to speculate on what he was going to tell me. All I knew is he didn't want to talk about it, Finn knew I'd have tried to stop whatever it was that happened, and I wasn't going to like it. Maybe we were twins, separated at birth and had some kind of Luke and Leia thing going on.

I compared Isaac's six-foot frame and dark brown skin to my five foot two height, reddish brown hair and tanned but definitely white skin. Maybe not twins separated at birth, then.

Isaac noticed my smile. "What?"

"I'm glad we're not twins."

"Me, too?"

I debated on whether or not to tell him my musings, and decided not to. A little mystery is good, right?

When we'd finished breakfast and washed up, I returned to the picnic table to nurse my third cup of coffee.

"Do you want to get in touch with Arduinna and see what's going on in the world?"

"Maybe later. Do you want to stop delaying and tell me what this is all about?"

Isaac sighed, but didn't start talking.

I tried to tamp down any impatience I was feeling. It wasn't easy. Maybe I should be the bigger person and give him more time. "If you're not ready to tell me, it's okay."

"Thank you, but it's not okay. I need to tell you. I'll never be ready. You'll need to tell Raj and Florence, because I won't be able to."

"Whatever you need, baby."

A smile ghosted across his face, and he looked down at his hands. "I promise I'm not delaying, but I need to ask you a question. Can you tell me what happened when you opened the gate?"

"Before I could finish opening the gate in a controlled fashion, Finn tackled me. It didn't matter. I'd already opened myself to the gate. Even if he'd knocked me out, it would've opened. My part was done. The only difference was there was less control. The gate magic burned me before I could spindle it and send it out. When I did manage to slough off the magic, the gate slammed shut. I don't know if that was something I did or if it would've happened anyway, but it didn't cease to exist. It made it…" I ran my tongue over my teeth, trying to find the right words to describe what had happened. I tried again. "The gates are unstable because of the difference in magic levels between the two worlds they connect. It's like opening a door on an airplane in midair or a submarine under water. It needs time to balance the atmospheric pressure on the two sides since there isn't an airlock. I don't know if that happened at the other two sites, but it must have because otherwise they would've been even more violent.

"Maybe the answer is to try not to open the gate, but rather to create it?" I was deep into my own thoughts now, and when I glanced up at Isaac, amusement and frustration were flitting across his face battling for supremacy.

"Anyway, Finn tackled me, and when I looked around to see what was going on since he shouldn't have gotten the jump on me, I saw a bunch of shifters had attacked, and you and Raj were protecting Florence from a group of marauding trees. I asked Finn what he was doing, and he said he was stopping me. When I informed him he was too late, he clarified that he wasn't there to stop me from opening the gate, but rather to stop me from noticing whatever the hell was going on with you. I kicked him in the balls, knocked him out with my sword, and came to help you."

Isaac grinned widely. "I love you, Princess."

I smiled back. "I ran over to you, but the fight was over, and whatever Finn didn't want me to see was gone. Now it's your turn."

Isaac's grin retreated. "After you levitated, we were attacked. The rogue shifters attacked first, but there weren't enough to be a challenge, merely a distraction. All of the shifters went after them. Then a few—maybe five—tree Fae attacked Florence. Raj and I went in to defend her. As I readied myself to deal the killing blow on the last Fae that was my allotment from Raj, it reached out and touched my arm and said, 'Look.' I looked up and above my head was a small…window. There was a bed, snowy white, like something out of a romance novel. Emma was chained to the bed."

I stared at Isaac for a couple of seconds before getting it. Holy shit. Emma was his girlfriend he'd thought Michelle had killed.

"Holy shit."

"Yeah."

"And then what?"

"Michelle appeared. She flirted with me. Suggested I come on over for a little bondage fun. When I refused, she laid it out for me."

I took a step forward, intending to pull Isaac into a hug, but he stepped back. "Not until I'm done."

I waited.

"I have until you open the gate on the winter solstice to make my decision. I can either walk through the gate and come to her, at which time she'll let Emma go, or I can watch her torture Emma with silver at every gate opening until the last one, when we'll get the main event —Emma's murder."

"Wait," I said. "The choices she offered you were to sacrifice yourself for her entertainment or watch Emma be tortured?"

"Yes."

"And she said she'd let Emma go?"

"Yes."

"What were her exact words?" I asked.

"If I walk through the gate, she will unchain Emma and push her through to this side."

I tapped my index finger on my lips. Something didn't seem right here. "She's not expecting you to walk through."

Isaac said, "I have to, Eleanor. Emma's been there too long; I can't leave her there any longer if I can help it."

"I'm ignoring the part where you've already made up your mind. I want to talk about Michelle. First and foremost, although she has the ability to lie, it sounds like she's gotten into the practice of telling truths that can be twisted—she'd have to if she's been among the Fae for this long. It's a defense mechanism when you're living among people who don't lie and can tell if someone is lying. But to make the condition that you *walk* through means that even if you go through the gate willingly, she's not expecting you to walk. She'll have someone positioned nearby to push you or break your legs. She's not going to let Emma go. She wants to torture you, and she knows torturing Emma is a sure way to torture you as well."

I fell silent, thinking. I tried to compartmentalize the part where Isaac had indicated he'd already decided to go; to leave me in an attempt to save his ex-girlfriend. He was willing to walk away from his mate to save some girl he'd dated for a few weeks and put himself back in the hands of a woman he'd been involved with for much longer than he'd even known me. It was illogical to feel jealous of Michelle. She was an evil, blood-sucking bitch queen from hell, but Isaac was going to trust her to keep her end of the bargain and go back to her. Away from me.

I started pacing. I was not compartmentalizing.

"Eleanor. Stop."

I paced faster. He grabbed me, hands on my shoulders. "Stop, please."

I looked up at him and my eyes filled with tears. "You've already made up your mind. Without talking to me first. Without trying to figure out another way."

"No, no I haven't. If I had, I wouldn't have…"

"What? Told me?" I wrenched out of his grip and resumed pacing.

"That's not what I meant."

"We're bonded. I know when you're lying."

"I don't want to leave you."

"Then don't! Don't leave. Let's talk it through. Let's find another way. Or we can go in guns blazing when we've opened the last gate and go rescue Emma together!"

"That's more than half a year away! That's months and months of torture."

"It's already been years, and it might not be months on that side. Time moves differently."

"Or it might be more years, and who says, 'let's not bother rescuing the torture victim now when it's inconvenient because she's already been tortured for a long time, what's a bit longer?'"

"Inconvenient? You think this upsets me because it's inconvenient?"

Isaac stared at me.

"Losing you to the woman who imprisoned and tortured you for decades is inconvenient? Having my mate willingly walk away from me to put himself into a situation that will likely result in his torture is upsetting merely because it's inconvenient? Isaac, you are being an ass."

I paced faster. My body temperature was rising with my temper and smoke rose from my body. I tossed some heat energy at the empty fire pit and the skeleton of the last fire flared and quickly burned out.

"Please build a fire, but don't light it."

Isaac didn't question me. He gathered some wood and laid out a fire. When it was done, I sent controlled bursts of heat into it, trying to individually light each piece of wood to burn off some of my temper.

When I was calm enough to yell again without lighting Isaac on fire, I turned back towards him.

"I can't lose you. I can't. This is not an option."

"Emma doesn't deserve this. I can stop it."

"You don't deserve it either, and I don't think she's going to let

Emma go. She'll keep her and use her to get you to do whatever she wants."

Isaac sat down. "You're right. She's not going to let Emma go."

"Let's talk it out. Let's find a solution."

I heard the faint rumble of the Hudson and knew Florence was approaching. "Can we talk it out with Florence and Raj?"

Isaac nodded. "Can we wait until tonight when Raj is here? I don't want to hear you explain it more than once."

"Of course."

He kissed me, and I smiled as pain pierced my heart. I was going to lose him. No matter what solution I came up with, I was going to lose him. I closed my eyes and leaned further into the kiss, trying to drown my despair before he felt it through our bond.

CHAPTER SIXTEEN

F LORENCE ARRIVED BEARING the gift of food. Cupcakes, to be precise. I didn't want to know how she knew I desperately needed comfort food. I dashed forward to relieve her of the dreadful cupcake burden when a stray thought hit me.

"Excuse me a moment," I said before dashing into the camper. I grabbed my small backpack and dug for my notebook. The notebook held the coordinates we'd used when looking for the gates in Portland and in the Black Hills, but I also used it to jot down important bits of information. I thumbed through it and froze when I saw what I'd been looking for. I found Isaac's cell phone and tapped the screen to get the time and date readout. Yep. Today was Florence's birthday. Shit, shit, shit.

I heard her laughing outside and hoped it was at something Isaac had said and not at me. I found my large duffle bag and started digging through it. I had a gift for her. I'd picked up a couple of things along the way that reminded me of her, but I hadn't purchased a card or anything. I laid the gifts out on the counter, found some clean bandanas, and wrapped them as carefully as I could.

Isaac and Florence sipped coffee at the picnic bench with the tray of cupcakes laid out in front of them when I went back outside.

"Happy birthday, Florence." I felt a little smug when I saw Isaac react and felt his surprise through our bond.

"Thank you, Eleanor," she said. "I was positive you and Isaac hadn't spent last night baking me a cake, and I do love cupcakes on my birthday."

"My skills in the kitchen are legendary," I said, elbowing Isaac when he snorted, "but even I can't whip up a cake in a camper." I thrust the package at her. "For you."

She untied the bandana and spread it open. Inside were three individually bandana-wrapped packages. She opened the smallest one first. It was a 100-carat spherical blue topaz. She gasped. "It's beautiful!"

"It's your birthstone and the website where I purchased it said it's a good focusing stone if you need to boost your psychic energy. Open the others."

Florence laid down the gem with reverence and picked up the second package. I grinned in anticipation. Inside was a bobble-headed dashboard mountable cowgirl with a stripper pole. I bit back my snickers, but Isaac, who'd not been prepared, could not.

Florence fixed me with a steely gaze. "She was not a stripper."

I lost the control I'd had on my laughter. It didn't take long before Florence's mouth was twitching, too, and soon she joined us. We laughed for a while, and every time one of us would start to get ourselves under control, Florence jiggled the little cowgirl stripper and we'd start all over again. Finally, we all regained control and Florence turned her eyes to the last package.

"I'm almost afraid to see what's in this one."

I held my breath.

Inside was a delicate bracelet. Florence pulled it out and covered her mouth. Tears ran silently down her face and her hands trembled. She handed me the bracelet and held out her arm. I fastened the clasp around her wrist and then she pulled me into a hug. "Thank you," she whispered. "This is perfect."

"What is it?" Isaac asked.

Florence held out her wrist. "It's Annette's name written in her own script."

"Wow, where did you get this?" Isaac asked.

"And where did you get the handwriting sample?" Florence asked.

"I saw the letter framed in your house. I scanned it and sent it to a jewelry maker I found on the internet."

"You had this made in September?" Florence asked.

"I knew you'd be coming with us and leaving a bunch of your stuff behind, and I wanted you to have this, not only as a small piece of what you were leaving behind, but as a reminder that I will hold to my promise to go Underhill with you when the gates are open to find your sister. We've had a lot of down time and I have to do something to let the internet know how much I'll going to miss it. Internet appreciation and a bottomless bank account are a heady combination. Just wait until the Solstice!"

Florence hugged me again. "These are spectacularly perfect."

"I did forget that today was your birthday. I was holding on to these as Solstice gifts. Now I only have six weeks to replenish my Florence stash."

"You know me well, child. Thank you."

"Do you have an Isaac stash in there?" Isaac asked, eyes narrowed.

"Nope. The gift of my body is all you need."

"Whatever," he said, standing up.

"Isaac Walker, you stay out of my things or so help me, you will never receive the gift of my body again."

He sat down. His glum look was belied by the twinkle in his eyes. "At least there's cake."

Florence handed out cupcakes and we munched in silence. My mood was much better than it had been before the birthday festivities and I wondered if Florence had decided to force the birthday issue to jolly me out of my funk. I looked at her. She was eating a pink champagne cupcake with a look of bliss on her face and I thought maybe this had nothing to do with me and she really, really liked cupcakes.

"What's on tap for the rest of the day," she asked, grabbing another cupcake—this one a red velvet cupcake with a cheesecake center.

"It's a waiting day," I said. "We can't pick up our new identities until tomorrow. Let's take Florence out for a fancy steak dinner after sunset. It'll be like the first time we all had dinner together."

"As long as Raj doesn't bite you again," Isaac said.

"Since 100% of the people at this picnic table have allowed Raj to take a sip, there is no room to criticize. You know I'm not interested in giving Raj more blood since we don't know what that will do to him."

Isaac grinned. "Sometimes you're so easy."

I punched him in the shoulder and he winced and rubbed it in mock pain.

"After dinner, we need to come back here and have a team summit, but until sunset, I've nothing planned. What would you like to do, Florence?"

"I saw a flier for hot air balloon rides."

"I'd love to do a balloon ride," Isaac said.

"That does sound like fun," I said. "I'll stay behind and make sure the car doesn't get stolen."

Two sets of eyes swiveled towards me and their heads tilted to one side. It was reminiscent of the bobble-headed stripper still jiggling away on the other end of the table and I giggled a little. "No ballooning for you?" Florence asked.

"I'm not exceptionally fond of heights. There's a reason I've never flown."

"You're a dragon," Isaac pointed out.

"In an airplane, smart ass."

"But still, you're a dragon. If something happened, as unlikely as that is, you could turn into a dragon and fly away."

"Hot air balloons are creepy. It's all gases and silk and trusting in science. Why don't I stay here and get in touch with Arduinna?"

"What if Finn comes back?" Isaac said. "I'm not sure you should be alone."

"I handled him last time he showed up. I'm strong enough again that my shields are at full power. I could stop him like a gnat in a spider web. And he still has a few body parts to lose."

"I don't want to leave you behind," Florence said. "It's not a fun birthday celebration if not everyone's included."

"We could go play paintball," I suggested.

Florence laughed. "I am serious, Eleanor. I'm not hung up on the idea of a hot air balloon ride."

I waved at them, "Go! Fly in the tiny basket held up with nothing but air and a giant pair of novelty boxers. Admire the fall foliage. Florence, I am counting on you to save my mate when it all goes terribly wrong."

She placed her hand on her heart. "My word of honor no harm shall come to him."

I smiled at her and then turned to Isaac. "Seriously, go. I need to talk to Arduinna. I can more than take care of myself against all comers." I flared fire into my fingertips until I looked like I was going for the Guinness Book of World Records fingernail length title. I shot the flames at the kindling I'd channeled my anger into earlier, and the wood in the fire pit burst into flames for a few seconds before the wood burned up. When there was nothing but ash, and the fire should have gone out, I held it there by force of will to make my point.

"If my shields don't stop an assault, and the fire doesn't ignite their desire to be far, far away from me, then I still have a few more things up my sleeves." I pushed up my sleeves and showed off my throwing knives. Each arm had a silver and a steel knife, and I had another set of each in thigh holsters.

"You've exceeded the legal limit for puns in your self-defense speech," Isaac said.

I grinned. "If I can't scare them off with magic or weapons, I'll make bad jokes. Or, I can turn into a giant motherfucking dragon and eat them."

"Save room for dinner," Florence said. "I wouldn't want you too full to enjoy your steak."

"I promise. Now go. I can take care of myself."

Florence gathered her gifts and the leftover cupcakes and took them to the car. Isaac pulled me into his arms. "Are you sure?"

"Absolutely. Florence should get her birthday wish, and it sounds like you'd enjoy it, too. Have fun. See you in a few hours."

"You're not pushing me away because you're angry?"

"I'm still angry, but that's not why I won't trust a fire and fancy bed sheet to keep me aloft."

"Control freak."

"You know it." I kissed him and pushed him away.

He strode to the car, and minutes later they were out of view.

I woke a few hours later feeling refreshed and ridiculously hungry. A nap had been exactly what I'd needed, and it was nice to have some time to myself. I made a sandwich using some of my legen—wait for it —dary kitchen skills and after devouring three sandwiches, was ready to call Arduinna.

I grabbed my rapier, double-checked my knives, and walked out. I really wasn't expecting an attack. We'd been here less than twenty-four hours and that seemed a little soon for the haters to get a bead on me. However, I wasn't an idiot, either, and certainly wasn't going anywhere unarmed.

Arduinna waited for me at the picnic table. She stood when I came into view.

I drew my sword. "How'd you find me?"

"You called earlier," she said.

"Not on purpose. I'd told the others I was going to call you. I must have put more intent behind that than I'd thought."

She bowed but her eyes never left my face. "What can I do for you, Highness?"

"Update on the state of the union. You know, the usual."

"May I sit?" she asked.

"Of course," I waved towards the picnic table. "May I get you something to drink?"

Arduinna made a short, harsh barking noise and it took a second for me to realize she was laughing. "What's so funny?" I asked.

"You offered to serve me. You are going to turn the courts upside down and sideways if you keep acting like this."

"I'm not ill-informed enough to let you get away with mocking me."

She sobered immediately, but the amused glint didn't leave her eyes. "You'll not harm me, Highness. I've taken your measure these last months."

"You know I won't harm you like Finn knew I wouldn't harm him?"

"I am safe as long as I don't physically harm you or yours, or put you in a position that would cause harm."

I resheathed my sword. "You're right, of course. But it's still not polite to make fun of the boss's daughter. And my question still stands. Would you like something to drink? The cooler is over there, and it's fully stocked with soda, bottled water, and all sorts of delightful booze. Help yourself."

"Thank you, Highness. Your hospitality is overwhelming. I will decline for now, and with your permission, get right into the report."

"Please do."

"President Murphy and General Aldea are planning on going public around Thanksgiving. From what I can tell, their plans include a retelling of your legend about pilgrims, American Indians, and ritual sacrifice."

I tilted my head to the side. "Ritual sacrifice? I don't remember that from my school pageants."

Arduinna was still for a moment and I had a feeling she was accessing some memories that weren't readily available at the surface.

"The killing of the large bird for a feast thanking your gods for a prosperous year?"

"When you put it that way, it does sound like ritual sacrifice, but most Americans won't think of it that way. They'll regard it as a turkey dinner."

"Noted," Arduinna said.

"We have the greater part of the month to get our shit together in Savannah and to prepare to potentially be outed. Do the country's

225

fearless leaders have a plan to keep all the supernaturals from getting lynched? I wouldn't want some neo-pagan teens at a Ren Faire to get burned at the stake."

"An appeal to your countrymen's fine moral fiber, I believe."

"Shit. We're doomed."

"I do not understand," Arduinna said. "You keep saying your fellow Americans will react poorly to finding out there really are vampires, witches, and shifters, but what makes you certain? Isn't it as likely they'll say, 'nothing has changed since yesterday except my knowledge of the world around me has grown'?"

"That'd be great, but it's more likely they'll look to all the unsolved murders, mysterious happenings, and terrible tragedies, and finally have someone to blame. Everyone wants a scapegoat, and now they'll know who caused the crib death, or the plane crash, or the heroin overdose, or the suicide. It was the monsters. The scary thing for me is some of them will be right. But for every vamp out there trolling the back alleys for a quick meal there are vampires who are creating families with those who desperately need a family. For every were-wolf who loses control at a full moon, there are a dozen in public service—the military, the police forces, the fire brigades—who take the jobs too dangerous for humans. And for every witch who causes a crop failure, there are several who work to ensure good weather for harvests, who protect our forests, and who work to repair the depredations visited on our earth."

I had gotten loud by the end of my speech, and if I didn't know better, I'd think Arduinna was laughing at me.

"So you feel strongly about this?" she asked.

I sat down with a thump. "A bit," I admitted.

"And nothing to say about the Fae?"

"Not a lot. I don't have a large sample size. I've met a lot of shifters and witches. I'm not as familiar with vampires, but the only Fae I know have fallen into two camps. Those who are being used and those who are using."

"What about the Brownie in Chicago?"

"I'm guessing he's being used. By you. I don't remember mentioning him to you."

Arduinna bowed from her seated position.

"I don't know what we get up to in the dark of the night, but I'm not sure there are any altruists among us. The others—the shifters, vamps, and witches—are at least human-based. We are other."

"And like anyone, we have our good folk, our middling folk, and the bad ones. Would you not consider yourself one of the good ones?"

I stared at her, "Are you kidding? I'm traveling around the country destroying the world. I sliced two fingers and an ear tip off of our favorite rogue elf. I am not exactly the good guy here."

"Then we have already lost."

"What's that supposed to mean?"

"If you do not believe in yourself, our people have no hope at successfully crossing the barrier and regaining our rightful status in this land."

"I'm not following. And for the record, I believe what I'm doing is right—or at least the most right decision I can make—but that doesn't mean I think it's good."

Arduinna sighed, startling me. She was beginning to be more unguarded around me, and I wasn't sure if I appreciated or was suspicious of her growing trust.

"Anything else I need to know?" I asked.

"The shields on the nuclear power plants are holding and the accelerated decommissioning seems to be going well. We cannot have oral reports due to the nature of the shields, but it looks like our test plants are managing to accelerate through at the rate of a month to every week. After the equivalent of one hundred years have passed, we will dismantle the plants and storage facilities and create magically enhanced concrete storage vessels for the waste material."

"One hundred years? What of the human workers inside? What will become of them?"

"They will die."

"But don't you need their knowledge?"

"No. By the time they die, the knowledge transfer will be complete, and the Fae at each site will be able to complete the final stages."

"Will the Fae be unchanged after being dosed with radiation?"

"I do not know. I hope they can leave a written report for us, but they will not survive to be studied. They will kill themselves after the final stage is complete to avoid contaminating the rest of us."

"Help me with the math, Arduinna. If the time is passing at the equivalent of one month for every week, and they are planning on staying for one hundred years, when, in our timeline, will this be finished?"

"It will take about twenty-three years."

"Wow. That is crazy."

"There's been no news of Finn on either plane," Arduinna said, done with the nuclear talk.

"He was there, you know, at Samhain."

"Was he? I didn't see him."

"Stop prevaricating with me, Arduinna. What do you know?"

"I'd heard he was there, it appeared he attempted to stop you from opening the gates."

"He said he wasn't trying to stop me, but rather to prevent me from noticing what was going on with Isaac."

"And what was going on with Isaac?"

"He was being given a choice. A choice to go Underhill and rescue someone to whom he feels responsible, or to stay with me and know his lack of action is resulting in her slow torture."

"So he will stay," Arduinna said.

"He says he hasn't made up his mind."

"You will not let him leave. You need his strength."

"Unfortunately—or not, actually—he doesn't regard me as his liege lord."

"He calls you Princess. Does he not recognize you as such?"

"Nope. It started out as a sarcastic thing, and now is a term of endearment."

"And you allow this?"

"I'm not the boss of him."

"You have lived too long among the humans. This will go poorly for you when you take the throne."

"I'll work on my royal manners, but a partnership of equals is preferable."

"I bow to your superior knowledge of the intricate workings of romantic unions."

I rolled my eyes. "Anything else, Arduinna? I'm a little nervous about the President's coming out party. Will she be coming out? What about the General?"

"I am not sure if their plans include revealing their own supernatural origins, or if they are planning on using exemplary poster children—who will not actually be children, if I understand correctly."

"If you find out anything else, let me know. We'll be here through tomorrow, and then we're headed down to Savannah, Georgia."

"That is the location of the fourth gate?"

"It is."

Arduinna stood and bowed, but didn't do anything else. I stared at her for a second before catching on.

"Dismissed."

AFTER ARDUINNA LEFT, I showered and got dressed. Florence and Isaac weren't back yet, but they should be soon. It was inefficient to get sweaty by practicing my blade-work so soon after a shower, and eating before we went out to dinner, even though I was hungry, was also impractical.

I was about three seconds of brooding away from hitting a major funk when there was a knock at the camper door. I looked at the door suspiciously for a second before drawing my sword and striding forward to answer it. Who would be knocking at my door?

"It is I," Raj said with a ridiculous amount of pomposity.

I grinned, opened the door, and resheathed the rapier. "Come in," I said.

"I'd rather you come out," he said.

I realized then he'd never been in the camper. I grabbed a pair of shoes and sat to put them on. "Why don't you want to come in?"

"Your scent is too strong in there. I would rather have the open air to disperse it."

"Are you saying I smell bad?"

"The opposite, actually. It is harder to remember why I shouldn't press you for another drink when I'm surrounded by your scent. The wolf's scent neutralizes it a bit—shifters don't smell as appetizing—but he hasn't been here for a while and you are overwhelming my senses."

I stood up, grabbed a jacket and my weapons, and made my way out of the camper. Raj waited for me by the picnic tables and I went and sat next to him.

"Where are the wolf and Florence?" he asked.

"I like that you call him 'the wolf' like learning his name is beneath your notice. You two are bros, now."

Raj grinned, and for a moment his fangs flashed at me. He was usually more careful with his smiles—several lifetimes of practice I assumed—but for some reason that glimpse didn't scare me. If I was honest with myself, the sight of his fangs caused some heat to pool low in my core. I tried to think of something else before he picked that thought from my mind. By the sudden intensity in his gaze, I guessed I was too late. I thought back to his actual question and answered, hoping to move on. "They went hot air ballooning to see the fall colors," I said. "It's Florence's birthday and that's what she wanted to do. I stayed here to guard our stuff."

"You're afraid of flying?" Raj asked.

"Flying is unnatural."

Raj stared at me for a moment, then hovered off the ground. "It comes naturally to me. And I've seen you in the air a time or two."

"That's different. If they'd asked me to go along and fly beside them, I would've. Although that might have been hard to explain. But airplanes? Balloons? And let's not even talk about helicopters." I shuddered, and it was only slightly exaggerated. "Flying not under your own power is an abomination unto the Lord. It's in Leviticus."

"No, it's not."

"It will be once I've made some much-needed edits. I have a few other ideas as well."

Raj smiled at me and there was another flash of fang. This time, I was sure he was doing it on purpose.

"Stop it."

His smiled broadened, and I crossed my legs in an attempt to tell my body to chill out. Why were his fangs hitting my mental g-spot?

I cast around for my train of thought. "Ummm...after they get back from their ballooning adventure, provided they survive it, we're all going out to dinner at a local steak house to celebrate Florence's birthday and recreate our first group meal."

Raj raised an eyebrow. "The entire night?"

"Isaac says we will not be recreating the bite."

"That was the best part."

"I'm concerned about what another sip of my blood would do to you."

"Concerned is not the word I'd use." He winked at me.

"One small taste made you immune to silver and removed the threshold prohibition. I don't know your other weaknesses, especially since sunlight isn't one anymore, but I'm not sure we need to find out."

"I don't have any other weaknesses."

I rolled my eyes. "Seriously?"

"I have a reflection, garlic isn't an issue, a holy water bath would get me clean, and a stake in my heart—unless it was laurel—would be uncomfortable, but not deadly. The only ways to kill me now are decapitation or getting me to hold still long enough to set me on fire."

"Raj, if you're drinking from a Fae who creates fire with her mind in human form and with her mouth in shifted form, how long would you stay vulnerable to fire?"

His eyes lit up with excitement and anticipation, and his fangs lengthened. Dammit, I was going to have to change my panties if he kept flashing his fangs at me.

"This would be a worthy experiment." For a moment, I thought he was going to see how many fang flashes it would take before I'd need a change of undergarments, but then I realized he was talking about increasing his immunity to fire.

"Or," I said, suddenly inspired, "It might be too much for you and you'd go up like a yule log after another sip of my blood because my blood is fire, and internalizing it would set you alight from the inside?"

"I didn't feel any heat last time I tasted you." His eyes began to glow, and I had trouble looking away. "Other than the heat in my loins I always feel when you are near."

I shifted and desperately sought for a way to change the subject. He reached for my wrist. "One taste, Eleanor. A drop. I can make it feel very good."

I slowly pulled my hand away and tried to pull my gaze away as well. My heart rate increased, which only fueled the intensity in his eyes. I couldn't break eye contact and a thin film of sweat broke out over my body. Heat pooled low in my center as my stomach knotted and I wasn't sure if Raj's blood lust was making me nauseated or aroused. I heard a car approaching and nearly did a dance of excitement that I wouldn't have to address my internal conflict.

Raj heard the car a moment after I did and the glow faded from his eyes. It was weird watching him wrench the control back. His eyes returned to their normal beautiful rich brown, and his fangs became less prominent. My fear faded at the same rate. Raj moved, putting space between us. "My apologies, Eleanor. I got carried away. Between the possibilities your blood offers and the smell of your arousal, I forgot myself. I'd like to say it will not happen again, but I try not to make promises I can't keep. I was unprepared for you."

"Apology accepted. There may be a day when I will allow you another taste, but not today. Keep your fangs covered and let's go have a wonderful birthday dinner with our favorite magic practitioner."

CHAPTER SEVENTEEN

AFTER DINNER, WE reconvened at the campsite for our strategic planning meeting. Raj flew ahead and was waiting with a glass of wine. It occurred to me that, except for when he drank the witch to convince her to give up information, I'd never seen him truly drink. I'd seen him take sips from Florence and me, but I was curious. Did his donors like it? Did he have to compel them? Was there a defense against being made into a juice box with legs? I eyed him contemplatively until I realized everyone was staring at me. Isaac did his best to look neutral and impassive, but a small twitch by his left eye gave him away. He was not looking forward to this. I reached out, squeezed his hand, and opened our mental connection. *"If you want, you can take a short walk while I explain the situation. I'll let you know when I'm done."*

I saw him consider it, and knew he was tempted. He said out loud, "Thank you, Princess. I will rely on you to relate this news that should rightly come from my mouth, but I will be strong enough to stand here and hear it."

I squeezed his hand again and then let go. "Okay, tough guy. A beer then?"

He strode to the cooler "Florence? Eleanor?"

I nodded in answer, but Florence said, "No, thank you. I'd rather have a glass of wine if Raj doesn't mind sharing."

"Of course not," he said. He grabbed the bottle and Isaac brought over a cup for Raj to fill for Florence. After everyone settled in with their beverages, I started the story.

I related what had happened to me as I finished opening the gate. "It was the easiest opening for me yet, but it was delayed somewhat when Finn tackled me, and a lot of the energy I was trying to channel out slowly slammed back through me burning out some of my synapses and magical channels until I was able to concentrate enough to push it back out to finalize the opening."

"The elf should die," Raj said. "It was unfortunate we left him alive after our last confrontation."

Florence shook her head. "He needs to live. Please trust me, but without him, the world will burn."

"I trust you, Florence," I said.

"You just don't want to kill your lover," Raj said.

"Ex-lover, and even that's too strong a word. But you're right, I don't want to kill him. Not because he briefly warmed my bed, but because he was once my closest friend. I can't believe he's irredeemable, but his latest cockfuckery makes me wonder if I'm wrong."

Isaac slammed shut the conduit between us and I felt dizzy for a second. This was the first time since we'd bonded that he'd completely closed the door. I didn't even know it was possible. It was weird being alone in my mind and it took me a moment to adjust. When I looked up again, Florence and Raj were looking at me expectantly and Isaac wasn't looking at me at all.

"A little warning next time you do that, Isaac," I said softly. He looked at me briefly, and then went back to regarding his toes with a clinical-like fascination.

I took a deep breath. "When Finn tackled me and I asked him what he was doing, he told me he was stopping me. I told him it was too late to stop me and opened the gate. He said he wasn't trying to stop the gate; he was trying to stop me from noticing what was going on with Isaac.

"You both know that Fae attacked Florence, but they were a distraction. The last one touched Isaac and commanded him to "see." He saw a bed, and on that bed was a woman—a shifter—chained. The shifter's name is Emma, and she was Isaac's girlfriend after he escaped Michelle the first time. He believed her to have been kidnapped and slowly dismembered until he agreed to trade himself back to Michelle for Emma's freedom. By the time the trade happened, Emma had been convinced the entire kidnapping and torture was an elaborate game designed by Isaac and Michelle for their own amusement. The trade happened on the full moon and when Emma's bonds were loosed, she attacked Isaac. He shifted, he fought—first to defend himself—then he killed her."

Raj looked like he wanted to interrupt, but I held up a finger. "Let me finish, Raj." He leaned back and nodded.

"After Isaac got a good look at Emma on the bed, Michelle appeared. She was flirtatious and offered a little BDSM fun. When Isaac refused, she revealed her agenda.

"Michelle said Isaac will have the next weeks to decide what he's going to do, but when I open the gate on the winter solstice, Isaac will need to have made a decision. She said, and I believe I am quoting, 'If Isaac walks through the gate, I will unchain Emma and push her through to this side.'"

"She is not expecting him to walk through the gate," Raj said.

"That is exactly what I thought."

Isaac pushed off the tree and strode forward. "You think she'll expect me to stay on this side?"

"We've been over that. She expects you to go through the gate. She knew you well and knows what buttons to push to get you to do what she wants. She's not expecting you to *walk* through the gate. She's been Underhill for a long time and has become skilled at lying with the truth." I turned towards Raj. "What did you want to say a while ago?"

Raj said, "First, I would like to renew my vow that I will help you find and destroy Michelle. She is a true monster in a species of abominations. I wish I'd killed her when I took over Portland, but she has gifts I do not. Might I ask a question, Isaac, about the night you believe you killed Emma?"

Isaac jerked his head down in a nod.

"Was Michelle present at the exchange, or did she send others to do her dirty work?"

Isaac raised his head and stared at Raj. "She sent lackeys. I didn't see her until they'd chained me."

"That doesn't sound like Michelle, does it? She'd want to be there to see her plans come to fruition, to watch you tormented."

"That's true," Isaac said slowly. "But I don't understand why you're asking."

"Michelle is almost as old as me. We all have gifts, some stronger than others. There are ancient vampires who will never be strong, because they were weak in life and there are vampires who are reborn incredibly strong—like Rasputin—because they were able to bring supernatural skills from their previous existence into this life.

"I'm not bragging when I say I was strong in life, and even stronger in this existence. Even before I drank the blood of a true-born Fae, I was strong. My gifts are psychic in nature. I can communicate with almost everyone, read their thoughts, and interject my thoughts into their minds. I am persuasive and can convince people they've forgotten me if I wish.

"Michelle, whose human origins are a mystery to me, has the ability to use glamour to appear as she is not, and not even I can penetrate it. It's my guess Michelle was present at the exchange she orchestrated, but playing the part of your Emma. Unless you removed her head and heart during your savagery, she would've healed, and quickly if she had a werewolf donor on standby. This is the reason I was unable to kill her when I came to Portland. The vampire queen wanted her head, and I was unable to deliver. It was the first time in over a thousand years —since I lost my kingdom—I'd failed to destroy my enemy. It's why I didn't know I was hosting a werewolf in my basement. She'd erected a psychic barrier between the sleeping quarters and the area she was using as a dungeon. I could feel something was off, but didn't know what. It was only when I started using some of Michelle's people as a food source that I realized something was wrong. I sent those who were able to ensure my guest was fed and looked after, but they were unable to release him from his bonds, and I was unable to penetrate the wall. It took fifteen years for the barrier to fall, and I think it only fell when she left this plane. Once the barrier fell, I was able to go into the dungeon and free my prisoner, which I did immediately."

Raj stopped talking but the tension did not disappear into the silence. Although the connection between Isaac and me was still shut down, he wasn't as in control as he'd been a few minutes ago, and anger, despair, and self-hatred leaked through. I looked at him and saw he was shaking. His eyes were streaked with yellow, and he was holding on to his control by the skin of his teeth.

"Isaac," I said, trying to put as much command as I could, "Change and sleep."

He looked at me, but before he could answer, he was shifting. His clothes ripped and then he padded over to me, curled up behind the table, and fell asleep.

I look across the table at Raj and Florence. They were both open-mouthed with astonishment.

"His wolf regards me as his Alpha," I said. "Don't tell anyone."

They nodded.

"He was about to lose control, and I didn't want to have an Underworld battle."

More silence.

"When he wakes, he might still be angry at you Raj. You should leave before that happens."

"Will he not be angry with you? You forced the change and put him to sleep."

"That makes it sound like I euthanized him," I protested. "I can't make him do anything he doesn't really want to do. He might be angry with you right now, but he likes you and doesn't want to kill you. When he wakes up and is calmer, he'll realize his ire is misplaced."

"What do you think he will choose to do?" Raj asked.

I looked at the sleeping wolf. "He's already decided to give

Michelle what she wants. He agreed with me that his sacrifice won't mean Emma's freedom, but I don't think I convinced him. He'll pretend to go along with whatever alternate plans we devise, but in the end, he'll leave me. He'll walk through the gate to save a woman he's thought was dead for thirty years, and he'll do it knowing it could mean his death, and it'll definitely mean leaving me. I won't be able to follow—I have a job to do."

Tears leaked from the corners of my eyes. What I'd said was true, but I hoped we'd find another way. Maybe if I could love him the way he needed me to love him, he'd stay for me.

Florence sat beside me, put an arm around me, and pulled me into her shoulder. I sobbed against her neck like a child. Raj reached out and held my hand until I cried myself out.

"We'll find a way to save him," Raj said.

I looked at Florence, hoping for comfort from my prescient friend. She met my eyes, but did not offer any assurances.

"We aren't going to find a way to save him, are we?" I whispered.

She smoothed back my hair. "There's always a chance."

"But?" I prodded.

"Will you not leave well enough alone, child?"

"You know I won't."

"In most of the futures I see, you enter New Orleans without him by your side."

"Most?"

"In some, you don't enter New Orleans at all and the world burns."

"Fuck."

Raj left and Florence drove back to town. I sat nursing the six-pack waiting for Isaac to wake up. I tried to work through every worst-case scenario, tried to get out all the tears, so when he woke I could be what he needed.

Maybe what I needed was a short flight. I stripped off my clothes, and called to my dragon. My body elongated and my face changed shape. My arms shortened, my legs lengthened, and those magnificent wings grew. Soon I was standing on all fours, my wings stretched out, catching the slight breeze. I leaned back on my haunches and sprung into the air. It was glorious; freeing. I glided around, staying away from the lights of the city.

After an hour of gliding in lazy circles in the general vicinity of the campground, I could feel my connection with Isaac stirring. I flew back and landed.

ISAAC WAS calmer when he woke up. "Are they gone for the night?" he asked.

"Yes. They left a little over an hour ago."

"What did they say after you sent me to sleep?"

"We talked prophecy, and they asked what I thought you'd do."

"What did you say?"

"The truth. I can say nothing else."

"You were crying."

I looked at him and mentally tugged at our bond. He was still blocking me. He wouldn't meet my eyes. I didn't know whether to continue being his rock or to reveal how much I was hurting. I went with the middle ground. "Florence sees me entering New Orleans without you, and if I'm reading between the lines of what she's said, if I try to stop you—or go with you—the world will basically end. I know you'll make the right decision, but I don't think I'm going to like it."

"Do you love me?" he asked then.

I hesitated. "I've never felt about anyone the way I feel about you."

Isaac reached out and touched my cheek. The sadness in his eyes felt like a stab to the heart.

"I wish I could say what you need to hear. I swear to you though, no matter what happens, I will find you. Never forget. As soon as I can, I. Will. Find. You." I emphasized the last four words with pointed jabs to his chest. When I finished speaking, Isaac pulled me into his arms. He was shaking, and I pulled his head into my shoulder as Florence had done for me earlier. When he stopped shaking, I let him pull away from me. He hadn't reopened the door that connected us, and it felt like he was already gone.

"May I approach?" Raj asked softly.

Isaac looked up and nodded, an almost imperceptible gesture in the gathering dark.

"I want to apologize. I know I opened old wounds, and it was not my intention to hurt you again. I did enough damage when I unwittingly kept you prisoner in my home. I will help you bring Michelle to justice. She has hurt you, you who are quickly becoming my friend. Through that hurt, she has hurt our Eleanor, who is dear to us both. Those hurts shall not go unanswered."

Isaac held out his hand and Raj did not hesitate before grasping it. There was a manly shake that got pulled into a bro-hug, and then a real hug. A moment later, I was pulled into the hug, too, and I had a brief moment's thrill when I realized I was the meat in an Underworld sandwich.

"You're leaning Team Vamp right now, aren't you?" Raj breathed into my ear, loud enough for Isaac to hear. It ruined the moment, which is probably exactly what he'd intended.

"I prefer blond vampires," I said, trying to sound serious.

Raj clasped his hands in front of his chest. "You wound me to the quick, my sweet!"

I rolled my eyes.

"And what of you, wolf? Are you going to go Team Edward?"

"Only in your dreams, vampire."

Raj laughed and even Isaac cracked a grin.

"Why'd you come back, Raj?" I asked.

"I wanted to make my apologies and see if I could spend the night with you."

I gave him a little side eye, and he smirked. "Not like that. I felt tonight would be a good night for you both to have additional protection. I promise I had no sexual designs on either of you."

"Now I know you're lying. You always have sexual designs on someone."

Isaac laughed, a little more freely this time. "She has you there, vampire. I've never known you to think about aught else."

"Careful, wolf. Your age is showing."

Isaac showed his teeth. "I am merely a pup in the face of your magnificent age, grandsire."

I left them to their manly banter and went to bed. Between the gate opening and discovering Isaac would only be mine for the next couple of months, I was physically and mentally exhausted. I knew Raj would keep Isaac busy with some manly bonding activity, and I needed some alone time to grieve. Isaac would need me to be strong. I couldn't let him know how much this was going to hurt me, because when he walked through the gate, he would need to focus on his own survival and not be distracted by my grief.

Our bond was still shut down on his end. I took the opportunity to live through all my worst fears. I imagined him dying in front of me while approaching the gate, feeling our bond break when he was Underhill, him realizing Emma was the wolf for him and requesting to dissolve our bond, and worst of all, him forgetting me.

I cried again, hoping Isaac and Raj wouldn't hear me. I wasn't quite successful, though.

"Do you need something?" Raj asked.

"No," I replied in the same way. *"Working through some shit. Does Isaac know I'm crying?"*

"I don't believe so. Would you have me keep him ignorant of that fact?"

"Please."

"As you wish, my sweet."

I rolled my eyes, knowing he'd get the gist of it.

I WOKE ALONE the next morning.

"Isaac?" I called.

"Out here," he replied.

I stretched, dressed, and went outside. It was chilly and a dusting of snow had fallen during the night. I shivered and went back inside to add another layer. I had a feeling cold was the enemy of the dragons. Maybe I wouldn't be moving to Asheville after all.

Isaac handed me my coffee and wrapped his arms around me.

I took a sip and had a sudden burst of grief. Isaac must have reopened our bond because he took half a step back and tilted my head up until I was looking him in the eye. "What?"

"I was thinking how much I was going to miss you making me coffee every morning."

"Is that all I am to you?" he asked. He was going for a teasing sound, but I knew my man well enough to hear the thread of hurt in his voice.

"Of course not! You're more to me than coffee. There's the cooking." I kissed him and smiled. After a moment, he smiled back, and we were okay.

"I can't wrap my mind around all the ways my life will be changed when you leave, but it's the little things that get me. I compartmentalize."

"I know that, and I'm sorry."

"It's okay, but I would like to institute a rule."

"I'm listening."

"You're leaving, right?"

"I don't have a choice."

"I disagree, but I will concede you feel you're choiceless, which is exactly the effect Michelle was going for. Yes or no—you're leaving?"

Isaac ran his hands through his hair, and then finally looked at me. "Yes."

"Okay. My rules."

"Rules, plural? I thought you said 'a' rule."

"I'm making it up as I go along. Now shut it."

Isaac sat, mimed zipping his lips, and leaned forward with an exaggerated look of concentration on his face. I rolled my eyes.

"Rule one: I will not try to talk you out of it or find a way for you to avoid this.

"Rule two: We will not pussy foot around the subject, and will in fact include the fact you are leaving in all of our long-term plans.

"Rule three: If someone comes up with an idea that might mitigate the situation—something that will ensure that you do walk through the gate instead of get dragged through, etc., you will listen and we will talk about it and determine how to best make that work."

Isaac nodded. "Are you finished?"

I thought about it for a second.

"Yes."

"Good. I have a rule, too. Rule four: you will not refuse companionship and love out of misplaced loyalty to me and you will accept the help offered to you by our friends."

I tilted my head at him, "I'm not sure I understand."

"If, when I'm gone, you want to begin a romantic relationship with someone else, do it. Don't worry about what I would think."

"Okay, I'll have mad, crazy sex with every hot guy that comes by—in your honor."

Isaac grinned. "You're selfless."

"I know."

He kissed me again and then let me finish my coffee.

"Isaac? I have one more rule."

"What is it?"

"Never, ever, ever forget I'm coming for you. It will take a while, and I don't know how I'll do it, but once the gates are opened, I'm coming for you."

"Raj said much the same thing."

"Raj said he's coming for you? Things went further between you two than I thought," I teased.

Isaac laughed. "He said I shouldn't forget you'd come for me. He did mention he'd be coming along for the ride, though. He hates Michelle almost as much as I do. There has to be more to that story than we know."

"There usually is. No one ever tells me the whole story. Speaking of, where is he?"

"He took off before dawn and said he'd meet us tonight in Savannah."

"I suppose we should pack up and get ready to go. Florence should be here soon, and then we can go get our documents. I'm looking forward to seeing your friend Extra again. We should invite him to come along."

"That is an interesting idea, but no."

"C'mon—you'll be leaving me soon, and I'll need someone to cater to my sexual fantasies."

Isaac snorted. "Okay, I'll ask him."

I grinned, and Isaac said, "No seriously, I'm going to ask him."

"Don't you dare, Isaac Walker."

"Watch me."

Further argument was interrupted by the sound of a car coming down the road. Isaac and I hastily cleaned up the camp site and were ready when Florence backed the car up to hitch up to the camper.

"Ready?" she asked.

Isaac and I climbed into the car. "Let's hit the road."

I'D EXPECTED to settle in for the long haul as Extra and Isaac traded stories and insults again, and really was looking forward to what Extra would say when Isaac asked him to accompany us as my companion.

When we got out to his house, there was a box on the front steps with Isaac's name on it. We got out and peered inside at four neatly stacked large envelopes. Isaac grabbed the envelopes and handed one to me and one to Florence. Inside were our papers. New birth certificates, social security cards, driver's licenses and passports, as well as some utility bills in our names from the addresses listed on our licenses. "Wow," I said. "He's good. I never would've even thought of half of this stuff."

"He changed my shirt," Florence said. I looked over at her stuff and she was looking between the passport and driver's license. It did appear she had on two different shirts—and the color wasn't the only difference—the neckline and style were different, too.

"Impressive. My name is Libby DeWitt and I'm from Birmingham. What are your names?"

"Margaret Hayden," Florence said. "But it looks like you should call me Peggy. I'm from Duck Pond, Mississippi, but I was born in Pearl River. They both sound like lovely, damp places."

"Okay, Peggy. I hope we get a chance to visit your birth place."

"I'm Joseph DeWitt," Isaac said. "Apparently we're married."

"And apparently Extra Grady is a traditionalist who thinks the woman should take the man's last name," I grumbled when I looked at my birth certificate. "My maiden name is Duvall."

"If it makes you feel better, if you'd been the shifter and not me, I would've been the one to change my name. Or if we were both shifters, whichever one of us was more dominant would keep their name."

I was mildly mollified, "Okay then. Is the bigger envelope our plates?"

"Yes. There are plates and registrations for both Alabama and Mississippi in here; we can switch out later if we need to. It's our rig if we're from Alabama, and Florence's if we're from Mississippi."

"I wonder how necessary this all is," I wave my hand trying to encompass all of our falsified documents. "Soon enough, we won't be trackable by computers anymore. Does it really matter if we use our real names? Will anyone even ask for ID or care what it says?"

"I haven't lived for the better part of three centuries by hoping everything will work out for the best. Paranoia and extreme caution are always the way to go."

I rolled my eyes. "Whatever, oh wise one. Maybe you should get a little hut on top of a mountain where people can hike to you for your special brand of wisdom."

Isaac bopped me over the head with the lighter envelope.

"We didn't get false documents for Raj."

"He won't be traveling with us during the day, and he can glamour anyone he wants into believing whatever he wants them to believe."

"So handy," I said.

Extra had thoughtfully left a tool box for us, and we each grabbed a screwdriver and went to work. A few minutes later Libby and Joseph from Birmingham were traveling with their friend Peggy from Duck Pond, Mississippi on an extended tour of the southeastern United States.

We got back into the car with Florence in the driver's seat. I hopped in back and spread out the map to serve as navigator. We got on I-26 and Florence drove all the way to Savannah. We arrived in mid-afternoon and pulled into the first motel we found. Isaac went in and got us two adjacent rooms under our new names, and then we went out to stock up on supplies. I could feel the gate's presence, but it didn't have the same urgency I'd felt previously. The solstice was several weeks away and the gate was barely vibrating against my mind. It would be easy to find, though, and I was looking forward to locating it the next day.

I wasn't sure what we were going to do for the next six weeks. There would be a couple of full moons to deal with, general announcements about the coming destruction of the United States, and probably a run on the grocery stores and banks. Riots in the streets. The attempts on my life would probably continue, if not escalate.

Now that I thought about it, it seemed likely we'd be busy for the next few weeks. In the middle of it all, I needed to get the most out of my time with Isaac, since that time was coming to an end.

CHAPTER EIGHTEEN

S AVANNAH WAS PERFECT in November. The humidity tinged the air in the southern coastal town, but it was enough to keep me warm without making me sweat my skin off. The potential for hotter and wetter hung in the air, but waking up to temperatures in the low sixties was perfect. The longer I went around with a dragon in my skin, the harder it was to stay warm.

We spent our first morning in Savannah perambulating around the city. People were out and about, but they were nervous and jumpy. No one actually looked at us twice, for which I was grateful, but people definitely noticed us. I wasn't sure if it was because we were a walking diversity poster or because there were supernaturals specifically looking for us. I did my best to ignore them as much as I could. Instead, I concentrated on feeling the gate energy.

Eventually we ended up in Bonaventure Cemetery, where I fully expected to find the gate, even if the energy was now pulsing behind me. The cemetery was as beautiful as expected, and I felt like I could spend the rest of the day there, meandering through the headstones. I'd never seen the movie set here, but I'd still had expectations based on the previews and still shots, and the cemetery did not disappoint. Everything was weeping trees, trailing moss, and creepy little statues that probably moved the moment my back was turned. It was hard to not go full Whovian and attempt to stop blinking.

We wandered the cemetery for a good hour before I gave up and admitted there was a significant lack of gate in the area. I promised myself I'd come back at least once in the next weeks, and we left. The closer we got to our lunch destination on the banks of the Savannah River, the stronger the gate energy was. Soon it pressed in on all sides like a vise tightening on my chest. I tapped Isaac on the shoulder—he was driving—and when he looked at me, motioned for him to pull over. He did, and I stumbled out of the car and looked around. After doing a full three-sixty, I headed to the cemetery across the street. A sign informed me I was entering Colonial Park cemetery, the oldest in Savannah. The entrance was full-on creepy cemetery. A big stone and wrought-iron gate topped with a bronze eagle framed more of the weeping trees. Weather-stained head-stones presided over the closely shorn and browning grass. I followed the pull of the energy through the gate and stepped into a crossroads in the center of the cemetery. Energy flowed around and into me.

I hadn't realized how depleted I still was from the last gate opening a week ago until that moment. Whatever Finn had done had more than sapped me, it'd damaged me. The gate—even at barely a fraction of its power—restored what was missing. I instantly felt taller and stronger and more alive. The exhaustion that had been plaguing me since I'd woken up four days ago receded in the face of the pure, raw, magical energy my body took in. I threw my arms out, looked up at the sky, and laughed.

"Eleanor," the man next to me said softly. "You're scaring the humans and drawing attention to yourself."

I laughed again. Of course they were scared. Who wouldn't be in the face of such awesome power? The dragon queen didn't hide in the shadows.

"Snap out of it, Libby," he said. He reached out and touched me. My instinctive reaction slightly outpaced my rational mind, and I sent a burst of flames towards the one who dared lay hands on me just as his name came to me. I managed to pull my magical punch enough that he only got singed and not immolated.

I stepped out of the crossroads and under the nearest tree. I noticed that the tree itself wasn't weeping; it was draped in a green-tinged mourning cloth. "What's the stuff hanging from the tree?" I asked. My voice had a timbre in it that wasn't usually there. It was almost as if I had two voices, speaking simultaneously and in stereo.

"Spanish moss," Florence answered.

"I didn't mean to hurt you." Isaac and I stared at the almost vine-like burn patterns up his arm.

"They're not healing," he said.

"I don't know what happened." I felt hollow. Logically, I knew I should be freaking out. The fact that I was so calm was also freaky. I tried to push some emotion through, but it was too much work, so I went back to staring in fascination at what my magic had done.

"Thanks for pulling your punch at the last minute."

"Least I could do. Is anyone still watching?" I winced at the lack of concern in my own voice.

"Everyone is still staring," Florence said. "Half of them are considering intervening between you two, but they can't decide which of you needs assistance. The other half are working really hard to forget what they saw but haven't gotten there yet. There are a couple minds, though, that aren't merely curious, but intrigued. I can't get a lock on their thoughts, but they're bordering on smug. We should probably find those two and see what's making them this happy." Florence turned around, looking for the source of the troublesome thoughts, and then swore softly under her breath. "Dammit. They must have sensed me searching. They've locked themselves down. I wish Raj were here."

LATER, after I'd eaten and the vibrations of gate energy had calmed down, I made an announcement. "I found the gate."

Isaac and Florence burst out laughing.

"No shit, Sherlock," Isaac said after a couple of minutes, drying his tears on a napkin.

After lunch, we headed back to our cheap motel after making a brief stop at a drugstore. Isaac's burn patterns were fading, but not as quickly as he usually healed from injury. I rubbed aloe into his arm, ignoring the hissing sounds he made as the cool gel touched the worst of the burns.

"Magical injuries must not heal as quickly as mundane injuries," I said, trying for nonchalant.

"Guess not," he said through clenched teeth.

Florence sat on one of the rickety chairs, observing in silence.

"For a second, I lost myself to the power."

"I figured."

"I didn't think werewolves could be injured by magic."

"Generally we're immune."

"Are you becoming less immune? Or are you not immune to Fae magic?"

"Not sure."

I continued to massage the aloe into his burns, which were kind of attractive when you tilted your head and looked through squinted eyes.

"Are you admiring them?" Isaac asked.

"They're pretty. Like flower vines."

"They're burn scars."

"But decorative ones."

"Are you out of your mind?"

I stopped to think about the question for a moment. I didn't feel the way I'd felt when I stood at the crossroads in the cemetery, but I didn't feel quite myself. It was if I was observing a grand drama. I knew I should feel a little more concerned about his impossible injury and my lack of concern about said injury, but I couldn't quite muster up any more feelings.

"It's possible," I conceded. "I'm missing some emotions right now."

Isaac pulled his arm slowly out of my grasp. I looked at him. "Are you upset?" I asked. I tried to feel his emotions through our bond, but couldn't grab on to them.

"Do you think I should be?"

"Did you shut down our bond?"

"No. Why do you think I did?"

"Will you both stop asking questions?" Florence interrupted. Then, she laughed as she realized her inquiry fit the pattern of the conversation.

"What's going on with her?" Isaac demanded.

"If I had to guess, I'd say she's still high on gate energy, and her spirit wasn't quite ready to accept that much Fae magic without an outlet."

"And that means?"

"When she opens the gates and gets an infusion of the gate magic, it has an outlet. It goes into the gate opening, and then pools in the magical weirs before spreading over the region. When Finn interrupted last week, he left an open wound on her psyche. The gate magic didn't finish channeling through her, and it left her not quite herself. When she stood at the gate site today, even though it wasn't time to open it, the gate filled her back up. But since she's not used to keeping the gate energy while conscious, it overwhelmed her. Usually her energy stores are drawn from earth magic, not Fae magic—every time she opens a gate, she gets a little more Fae magic, which is why her own talents are manifesting and strengthening. It gives her a chance to adjust, usually while unconscious. This was a huge infusion, but without the time for her body to adjust."

"Once more in five words or less," Isaac said.

"She's becoming more Fae. Asshole," Florence said, counting the words out on her fingers.

"You watched Buffy, too?" I asked.

Isaac laughed.

"Of course," Florence said. "You should know by now I couldn't resist a hot, lesbian witch."

I was getting tired, and was beginning to feel a little sheepish. "I need a nap."

"Not surprised," Florence replied. "You'll probably sleep for quite a while. The magic needs to settle in. Try to remember who we are when you wake up. I'm even less immune to Fae fire than your wolf."

My eyes were growing heavy and it felt like someone had thrown a handful of sand into my eyes.

"I'm going to lie down," I said, heading towards the bed. I tripped and everything went black.

I woke refreshed and a little hungover—like you do when you've slept too long. I rolled over and looked at the clock. Six. The curtains were drawn and I couldn't tell if it was getting dark or getting light. I looked around. I was alone in the room, but I had to believe my friends wouldn't have left me alone for too long while unconscious and unable to defend myself. I sat up and realized I'd been stripped down to my panties. I shivered. It was cool in the room. I became aware of an increasingly uncomfortable pressure on my bladder and got up to shuffle my way awkwardly to the bathroom. I flipped on the light and blinked several times before dropping my drawers and sitting on the toilet.

After I finished doing my business, I heard the door open.

"Shit," someone said. "She's gone."

I was about to announce my presence, but realized I didn't recognize the voice.

"She's in the bathroom," another unfamiliar voice said. "There's light under the door."

"Where're the bodyguards?"

"Out grabbing coffee."

"If she's in the bathroom," first voice said, "that means she's awake."

"Yeah," the other guy agreed.

"That means she can hear us," he said. Score one for the Mensa member.

"Shit," second guy said.

"We'd better do this now, then. Before she escapes."

I heard them rush towards the door and I prepared myself. One of the bodies hit the door hard like he thought he was going to break it down. It took three more crashes before the door collapsed under his considerable weight and he stumbled into the tiny bathroom. He pulled himself upright and then they both stared up at me.

I was standing on the toilet tank in nothing but a pair of silk, thong panties, my hands glowing red with fire.

"That shit won't hurt us," the second guy—clearly a shifter of some kind—said, sneering.

"I don't know," Smartie Pants said. "Her magic doesn't come from here."

"We're immune to magic," the other said. "And now that I've seen her, I think she won't be nearly as hard to kill as the bounty suggests."

He started forward and I threw my first fireball at him. He laughed for a brief second before he started to burn. I threw the second fireball and the smarter one, who'd already begun a strategic retreat, went up in flames. Neither of them had ever heard of stop, drop, and roll, because they both ran around like decapitated chickens fanning the flames into a frenzy. I wrapped them in shields to contain the flames and their screams and watched them burn. I felt more human than before, but still more detached than I should. I called the flames back into myself when they collapsed, but left my hands glowing in case they weren't dead yet.

And that's when the rest of the team came back. I must have been quite the sight—mostly naked, glowing with fire, and standing over two charred corpses.

"Hey guys," I said, extinguishing my hands. "I hope you brought coffee."

Raj handed me a cup. He didn't say a word, but eyed me appreciatively. "Isaac felt you wake up," he said.

"What happened?" Isaac asked. I took a long drink of the delightfully sweet and nutty latte.

"I'm guessing these two woke me up when they hit the edge of my flypaper shields, but I didn't realize right away what'd happened. They surprised me in the bathroom—hence my state of undress—and I burned them up. They were cocky because they thought magic wouldn't hurt them. I'm glad we found out my magic does, in fact, damage shifters. Otherwise I might have tried to fight my way past them to my knives."

"You weren't wearing your knives?" Isaac asked. "We've talked about this."

"You're the one who stripped me and put me to bed without them. I was groggy when I woke up."

"Which makes sense if you didn't wake up on your own, but only because someone breached your defenses," Florence said, obviously trying to head off an argument.

I smiled at her gratefully, and continued, "I lit them on fire and they died. And then, I was rewarded with coffee." I took another long sip and couldn't stop the look of bliss that washed over my face.

"Maybe you should get dressed," Isaac suggested.

"Don't hurry on my account," Raj said.

I rolled my eyes at both of them and grabbed my backpack. "I'll be right back." I went back into the bathroom and gingerly leaned the broken door in the doorway. I set my coffee down and stripped off my panties. I took a quick shower, got dressed, and headed back into the bedroom. "Where's Raj?" I asked.

"Disposing of corpses before he hits the sack," Isaac said.

I laughed.

"How long was I out?"

"Two nights," Isaac said. "It's Saturday."

"Hmm, I feel good. Really, really good. Well rested, back to myself, and all-around awesome."

"Do you feel our bond?" Isaac asked.

"Yes, of course. Why wouldn't I?"

"Before you fell asleep, you asked if I'd shut it down and I hadn't. Florence thought your inability to sense my emotions was a product of your own being on the blink."

I contemplated that and reached down our bond and felt his concern radiating out at me.

"I feel it now." I said. I sent a pulse of affection—and a little lust—

back down the bond towards him. His eyes immediately yellowed in response and Florence sighed.

"I'll leave," she said in her most long-suffering voice.

"Don't you want to stay and help clean up?" I asked, looking at the charred spots on the floor.

"I'll pass. You made the mess; you should clean it up." She waved her hand toward the small table in the corner. "I brought you a half dozen disgusting fast food breakfast sandwiches. Enjoy them while you can. Supplies are rapidly running out, and I don't know how much longer the southeast will be functioning like normal. Already places are starting to close down."

That was a sobering thought. I grimaced, felt my stomach try to wrap itself around my backbone, and went to retrieve the sandwiches. "Thank you," I said. "For everything. The sandwiches, the updates, watching my back, being my friend." Tears welled up in my eyes, and I blinked them back.

"It looks like she's back to her regular self," Florence said as she opened the door.

"This is not regular. I never cry, certainly not over friendships."

"Maybe you're finally catching up." She walked out and pulled the door closed behind her.

I sniffled a couple of times and then opened the first sandwich. It was hot, greasy, disgusting, and delicious. I gulped it down in record time, chasing each bite with coffee. In fifteen minutes, I'd ploughed through half of the sandwiches and was still hungry, although I was at least slowing down. Amusement and horror warred for space on Isaac's face as he watched me eat.

"More coffee?" He extended another cup towards me.

"Yes, thank you." It took me another thirty minutes to finish the last three sandwiches and my coffee, and when I wiped the last greasy crumbs from my face, I patted my new food baby in satisfaction.

"I feel good," I said. I drained the last drops of my coffee, threw away all the garbage, and started towards Isaac. I had a specific idea of what would come next in the quest to assuage my appetites. Then I slipped on a stray piece of burnt flesh. "Dammit!"

Isaac laughed. "We should take care of these," he said, nudging one with his foot. A limb detached from the corpse and dusted into the carpet. I wrinkled my nose at it.

Isaac grabbed some industrial-strength garbage bags and some rubber gloves from his backpack and tossed them to me. He geared up in the same way, and we went to work. After gingerly pulling the pieces off my assigned corpse and stowing them in the bag, I closed it up and headed to the door.

"Where are you going?"

"The front desk to borrow a vacuum and book a new room. I can't sleep here," I said.

"Good thinking," he said.

I was back in fifteen minutes with a vacuum and the key to another room. A few minutes later, the carpet was looking as good as...well, not new, but at least as good as it had before I burned up a couple shifters. Maybe better, even. There were a few scorch marks on the wall I couldn't get out, but considering the state of the rest of the room, I doubted anyone would notice.

"We should talk," Isaac said after we moved our stuff into the less stinky room.

"That sounds serious."

"I'm concerned about your propensity to fight all your battles basically nude."

"That concerns me a little, too. Although the first time you and I fought, I wasn't the naked one."

"I wasn't sure you'd noticed," Isaac grinned at me.

"Are you kidding? You may have been filthy and stinking, but your true...qualities...shone through the dirt."

"My true qualities?"

"Speaking of those qualities, we should probably examine them in detail now."

"My sparkling wit, my blinding intellect, or my great wisdom?"

"How about your huge—" Isaac quirked an eyebrow at me, "—ego?"

He laughed, then grabbed me, threw me down on to the bed, and pinned me spread-eagle. "Tell me more about my huge...ego," he demanded.

I wriggled under him, but couldn't free myself. Isaac pulled my arms up above my head and held both wrists with one hand. The other hand he trailed down my cheek, brushing his thumb over my lips. My lips parted, and I darted my tongue out to moisten them. His eyes followed the movement, so I did it again, more slowly this time. He leaned forward and lightly kissed me. I jerked my face upwards, trying to claim more of his lips, but he laughed and moved away.

"Patience, princess," he said.

His hand resumed its journey, trailing down the side of my neck, and his lips followed. When he'd gone as far as he could while still holding my arms overhead, he released me and said, "Grab the headboard and don't let go."

"Make me," I said.

"Do it or I'll stop."

I grabbed the headboard.

He brushed his hands over my breasts, cupping them and raising them towards his mouth. He sucked through the material of my shirt and bra, and the roughness of the material combined with the wet heat of his mouth sent bolts of electricity through my body and into my groin. I moaned.

Isaac pushed my shirt up and slid his hands under my back. I arched my back, and he unhooked my bra.

"Arms," he said.

I let go of the headboard and he pulled my shirt and bra off.

"Headboard."

"Bossy."

"Now."

I grabbed the headboard again, and he resumed his actions. He repeated his earlier actions with my breasts, and pulled another soft moan from me. He sucked and bit at my nipples until I was writhing against him. Then he unloosed his secret weapon. He ran his calloused, rough fingers along the soft skin on the underside of my breasts. How he'd ever found that this was even more sensitive than my nipples, I don't know, but I wasn't about to look a gift horse—or gift wolf, rather—in the mouth. In seconds, I was on the verge of orgasm, and he hadn't even touched me below the waist yet.

"Isaac," I moaned. "Need."

"Tell me," he commanded.

"You. Inside me. Now."

"Now who's being bossy?"

I arched my hips against him and felt the hard length of him straining against his jeans. I rubbed back and forth and the friction sent me over the edge quickly. "Cheater," Isaac accused.

"Just doing what needs to be done."

"You're okay with stopping now?"

"Sure," I said, calling his bluff. "If you are."

He grinned and unbuttoned his pants. "Maybe we can play a little bit longer." I watched him shimmy his jeans off and licked my lips involuntarily when I saw his magnificent erection straining against his boxer briefs. "Are you sure you want to stop now?"

"Maybe a little longer." I licked my lips again.

"And what would you like next?" he asked as he slowly removed his underwear.

"You in my mouth." My voice was hoarse with desire.

"Let go of the headboard." I hadn't even realized I was still holding on. I let go and rolled over onto my hands and knees. I crawled towards him and without ceremony took as much of his length as I could into my mouth. He gasped and grabbed my shoulders. "Christ, Eleanor. A little warning next time."

I didn't answer, but instead started to move up and down, going a little further down each time. I wouldn't ever be able to take his full length, but I was determined to do my best to get as close as possible. Soon, he was bucking against my mouth. "Stop. I'm going to come."

I didn't stop, but instead increased my rhythm and reached down to grasp his balls and gave them one gentle squeeze. He swore loudly in an unfamiliar language and came. I swallowed him down and then slowly withdrew, cleaning him as I retreated. I leaned back on my knees and gazed at him in satisfaction. I was still aching with desire, and knew we weren't quite finished yet.

"You'll pay for that," he growled at me.

"I'm counting on it."

He pushed me back into the bed and plundered my mouth with his tongue. His hands fumbled with the button on my jeans and I lifted my hips to help him remove them.

"You're not wearing panties," he said.

"I know."

"Taking them off is my favorite part."

"Your favorite part? Really?"

"Maybe not my favorite part." That was all the warning I got before he buried his face between my thighs. One long lick and I was quivering and then he really went to town.

Isaac brought me to the edge over and over until I was begging him for release. My legs trembled and I was hoarse by the time he finally helped me with the thrust of three well-placed fingers. I rode his hand to completion and lay gasping and sweating while he crawled his way up my body.

"Are you ready to beg for mercy yet?"

I reached down between his legs and found he was hard and ready to go again. "Never."

That was all the invitation he needed before spearing me with his entire length. It didn't take much to send me spiraling into the abyss of pleasure again, and Isaac quickly followed me over the edge. We lay gasping in each other's arms for a long time and eventually I drifted off again.

WHEN I AWOKE, it was early afternoon based on the angle of the sun through the cheap blinds. Isaac was nowhere in sight, and I began to feel a little frustrated by the number of times people were willing to leave me alone while unconscious. I may have insisted I didn't need taking care of, and I had woken up and defended myself every time someone had tried to sneak up on me in my sleep, but I kind of thought a lot of my naked battles could be avoided if someone would hang out and keep an eye on me.

"I'm in the bathroom. I haven't abandoned you."

I blushed. I was broadcasting a little bit more than I'd thought.

"Florence warded the door this morning before we went for coffee."

"It didn't really take all three of you to go get coffee, did it? Someone could've stayed. It's weird you'd all take off when I was practically comatose."

Isaac walked back into the bedroom. "You were bait."

"Excuse me?"

"Do you remember Florence saying there were a couple of minds in the cemetery on Thursday that were intrigued but when they sensed her they shut down?"

I thought back and answered slowly, "Maybe?"

"Those minds had been popping up in the perimeter of her abilities for the last couple of days, but the minute they sensed any of us, they retreated. Since they kept coming back, even though you were well guarded, we decided they would pounce the second they saw an opportunity."

"So you used me as bait. While I was unconscious and unable to agree to this plan?"

Isaac had the grace to squirm uncomfortably.

"Whose idea was it?"

Isaac didn't answer.

"C'mon, Isaac. Was it yours?" I heard his answer emphatically through our bond before he even opened his mouth. "Raj. That's what I thought. How'd he get you to go along with it?"

Isaac decided to turn state's evidence. "By pointing out, and rightfully so, that the wards would alert us to their presence and my bond with you, not to mention Raj's ability to track your thoughts, would alert us to your consciousness level."

"And how'd that work out?" I snapped the instant before I realized I already knew the answer.

"Quite well, actually. Raj and I knew you'd woken up before the wards signaled the suspects had breached the room. We were already on our way back to lend a hand when you killed them both. You got a victory, we killed two more enemies, and you got a hot coffee reward immediately after."

I looked through the plan, rolling it over in my mind, but couldn't find any strategic holes. "Fine. You're right. It did work out perfectly, but I would appreciate being made aware of any future plans to use me as bait. If you ever use my unconscious body as bait again, at least make sure it's properly armed."

"I promise."

I planted a kiss on Isaac's mouth. I'd meant it to be soft and forgiving, but I couldn't lie with my body any more than with my words. Angry kisses were even better at stirring up physical cravings than forgiving kisses, and I crawled out of bed and went to clean up before I talked myself into make-up sex.

CHAPTER NINETEEN

T HE NEXT FEW weeks hopped and skipped by lazily. Some days took forever to get through and then I'd blink and four had passed in blurry, rapid succession. The situation in the United States deteriorated rapidly. Food riots had been reported along the eastern seaboard, and little news was coming from the rest of the country.

Martial law had been declared on much of the west coast, and although there had been no official announcement, the rumor on the streets was the west coast had seceded from the rest of the country. There was no air travel at all in the United States, and although most of Canada and all of Mexico were still immune from the effects of the spreading gate energy, they were limiting flights as well.

Things in Savannah were slowly worsening. Restaurants and grocery stores closed as regular food shipments stopped. The government hadn't announced what was going on, and the National Guard mobilized to keep the peace. A curfew was declared and those who broke curfew were summarily thrown in jail.

I spent my time torn between worrying about the decay of my country and the increasingly ubiquitous violence, training my combat and magical skills, and spending as much time with Isaac as possible.

The tighter I tried to hold on, the more rapidly he slipped through my grasp.

Despite agreeing to our rules, he refused to talk about any alternative possibilities. He always found somewhere else to be and something else to do every time anyone brought it up.

I tried not to let my growing frustration with his unwillingness to talk about any possible options color the time we spent together, but it was difficult not to seethe and yell and throw hurtful words like, "I thought we were in this together," and "Why are you leaving me without a fight?" But I didn't. I'm sure he knew how I was feeling—I couldn't hide my true emotions from flowing through our bond—but he was willing to overlook it for the sake of never ever fucking talking about anything that might help.

He disappeared for the three days of the full moon, refusing my aid in maintaining his control. There wasn't a pack in the area, so he was going to go it alone; something I pointed out didn't have to do since his wolf treated me like an Alpha. He left anyway.

By the end of the month, he'd perfected his avoidance technique, and I'd perfected my hurt, snippy tone. Florence avoided us as much as possible. Ostensibly to give us as much alone time as possible, but I think it was mostly to avoid the near-constant bickering that erupted whenever Isaac and I were alone but not naked. Even Raj started showing up more infrequently, and only when there was a new juicy rumor to share.

I hadn't seen Arduinna since I arrived in Savannah and I was growing impatient. I'd thought that President Murphy and General Aldea were planning the big coming out for Thanksgiving, but I wanted confirmation of what to expect before it happened. When I said as much to Isaac, he pointed out the rest of the supernatural population wouldn't have that luxury. That led to another spectacular bicker. I refused to call them fights.

The day before Thanksgiving, Florence requested we set up the camper in the parking lot of the cheap motel we were still staying at. We hadn't bothered to move around every couple of days. A few more idiot shifters had come after me, but no one else had even managed to catch me by surprise, much less inflict any damage.

Thanksgiving morning, I flipped on the television to see what was going on in the big, wide world and to see if there was going to be a parade. There was. It was kind of pathetic, but as the announcers stated, not having the Macy's Thanksgiving Day parade would be akin to letting the terrorists declare victory, and by gosh and by golly, we weren't going to do that. And by the way, don't forget about Black Friday tomorrow.

At the conclusion of the tiny parade, the station moved to a DC location for a "Thanksgiving Day Address" by the President. I didn't know if this was an annual tradition or not, but when I saw Aldea standing beside her, I knew it was happening. I opened the door and hollered across the parking lot. "Florence, Isaac, come in here! The President is making an announcement."

I heard muffled swearing from the camper, then both Florence and Isaac strolled over as the President began speaking.

"My fellow Americans, I come to you on a day of Thanksgiving. This tradition goes back before the founding of our country to a time when two peoples met and broke bread together in the spirit of sharing and brotherhood. The United States of America has continued to celebrate Thanksgiving not only on the fourth Thursday of every November but in our everyday lives. We have led this world; a shining example of what peace and democracy should be."

I had a lot of trouble not laughing. For someone who couldn't lie, she sure was laying it on thick.

She continued, "The past weeks have brought new challenges and troubled times to our once peaceful country."

"Peaceful?" Florence snorted. "That sounds like a lie."

"It was peaceful once," I replied. "December 15, 1832, I think."

We'd missed a few lines, but my guess was she was rehashing the events of the past few months.

"And now we are a nation broken. Divided by an expanse of land that was once easily traversable, but now as forbidding as it was to Lewis and Clark. But like those great men, we will rebuild the routes west. If the Civil War couldn't divide this country permanently, then neither will these events." She paused, then, and looked directly at the camera, no longer reading from the teleprompter.

"Many believe the events in Portland, in Rapid City, South Dakota, and in St. Louis were the work of terrorists. However, after nearly four months of exhaustive research, we have found there are no terrorists. This is not an attempt to destroy our country and way of life. It is a series of...natural disasters."

There was a murmur from the press corps, but she pressed on. "A better term might be supernatural disasters." She took a deep breath, glanced back at Aldea, and continued, "What I am going to say next is going to sound like something out of a fairy tale or a Hollywood movie, but it is nothing less than the truth. I cannot lie to you, but I did not wish to share the truth until we were sure.

"There is more to this world than you've seen. Living among us are the creatures we've read about in tales and seen celebrated on the big screen. There are vampires and werewolves and witches. Once, long ago, they were stronger, but the industrial revolution and the advent of technology began to slow the magic in our world to a mere trickle, and their numbers dwindled.

"Now, the magic is returning. There are eight gates opening throughout the United States. Three have opened, and there are five more to go. Once the eighth gate opens, the pendulum of industry will have swung back in the other direction and magic will once more rule the world. At this time, the supernatural creatures that have hidden in the shadows are growing in strength and will soon grow in number. Like human beings, there are good and middling and bad supernaturals. It would not be wise to assume the vampire next door is benign and sparkling, but he is unlikely to be Nosferatu. The witches, for the most part, are bound to earth and would do nothing to harm either the earth or her human children. Werewolves are bound to the full moon but are not mindless beasts savaging your livestock and stray wanderers. They have lived among you for centuries. Have sat next to you in church, have taught your children, have treated your wounds, and have served in our armies.

"I am working with a team of supernaturals as well as engineers to determine what steps we need to take to restore communication in the dark zones and to prepare for the eventual cessation of modern technology. I've met with other world leaders to warn them this effect will not be limited to the United States and to help them plan accordingly.

"Our country has survived for two hundred and thirty-seven years, has weathered wars and economic hardships, and it will survive this. I will do everything in my power to keep this country together and thriving. Starting next week, I will do weekly radio broadcasts to update everyone who can hear on our progress in restoring communication to the rest of the country.

"These United States will continue to spread a message of peace and democracy for another two hundred years, and we will continue to be a beacon of hope for the rest of the world. This is not our last Thanksgiving, but our first as an awakened people.

"Gods bless you, and Gods bless the United States of America."

She bowed her head briefly and left the podium.

"Holy shit," I said.

General Aldea and another man took her place at the podium. The press was about wetting themselves trying to get their questions in.

"Wait," I said. "Is that Arduinna?"

The man standing next to Aldea didn't have green hair or green skin—and was a man—but he bore a striking resemblance to my father's enforcer.

"Do you want to hear the press questions?" Isaac asked, hand on the remote.

"Not really, but I should listen."

"I need to get back to the meal," Florence said. "Let me know if anything earth-shattering happens."

"I'm the only earth-shattering thing happening around here."

The questions posed by the press to General Aldea and almost-Arduinna were exactly as I would've guessed had someone told me I'd be watching a press conference where the existence of supernatural entities had been outed, and a new eschatology announced. There was little substance to the questions. Most concerned the nature of vampires and werewolves and how to kill them. The General neatly deflected these questions without giving any concrete answers that would endanger the supernatural communities then deftly returned to the important matter of preparing the world for the continued magical disruptions.

One reporter seemed not to be giving in to panic. "Where will the next gate open?"

The general stepped forward to answer. "I don't know. No one does."

"But you evacuated St. Louis ahead of the disaster there."

"There were signs ahead of time, but all we currently know is when, not where."

"Will you announce the next location ahead of time as well?"

"Once we know where it will happen, we will make that information available to the public."

"Did you know before the Black Hills disaster?"

"We had enough warning to divert most air traffic. I expect we'll nail down the location about a week before the disaster—or gate opening—rather."

The reporter wrote this down, and then noticing no one else had their hands up anymore, she asked another question. "You have called these events 'gate openings.' If gates are opening, what's coming through? And where do the gates go?"

The man I thought was Arduinna stepped forward. "That is an excellent question. The short answer is that as far as I have seen, nothing has come through any of the gates."

"But where do they go?" the reporter persisted.

"Since we know of no one coming through and I haven't been through one of those gates, how could I know?"

If this was Arduinna, she must be nervous. She was usually better at not-lying.

The reporter was not blown away by her not-so-subtle prevarication. "You haven't answered the question."

Aldea stepped forward again. "I believe the gentleman said he didn't know—that no one knows."

"Actually, he didn't." I couldn't see the woman's face, but I saw the set of her shoulders and watched her straighten her spine. She knew she was on to something and wasn't going to let it go. "I would like to ask again. Where do the gates go?"

Aldea and his companion exchanged a glance before Arduinna— for lack of a better name—nodded slightly. I wondered if the general —a powerful old vampire—was taking orders from my father or if they were following a previously planned course of action.

Arduinna leaned forward, "It is the belief that the gates go to a different plane inhabited by other supernatural creatures who are linked to, but not of, this world."

The reporter leaned back and scribbled something in her note-book. She looked up again. Everyone stared at her, waiting for her to say something else. She glanced around the now-silent room.

"Mr. Greenwood," she said, addressing Arduinna, "Is it your belief that this country, this world, this plane of existence, will be destroyed as these gates are opening? Is this step one in an upcoming genocide of the human race?"

I saw Arduinna's shoulders relax infinitesimally. This line of ques-tioning was one she was comfortable with. "I can assure you with 100% confidence, there is no intention by any large group of beings, whether of this plane or another, to annihilate the human race and destroy this world. I cannot speak for every creature that exists, but there are no plans that I, or the President, or General Aldea are aware of that would result in the end of this world. Things are changing— and changing rapidly—but I believe the end result will be humans, and earth-based supernaturals, and other-worldly beings living side by side in relative harmony. The other beings may be different biolog-ically, but they still carry the spark of what you would call humanity. There will be no war for supremacy on this plane."

I almost applauded. That was well done. It almost made up for her awkward missteps earlier.

The press conference wound down quickly after that, and I clicked off the television a few minutes later.

"Well?" I asked Isaac.

He shrugged. "They did a decent job. I'm glad Aldea was there to tell the lies. It would have been awkward if Arduinna had announced Savannah was the next site. I'm surprised there haven't been more attacks on you."

"Me, too, but I'm trying not to look a gift horse in the mouth." I thought about that for a minute. "Why would you look a gift horse in the mouth? And what purpose does it serve not to do that?"

Isaac laughed, "I have no idea, Princess."

"Do you know what time Florence is planning on serving us Thanksgiving Dinner?"

"As soon as the sun goes down."

"Oh my god, I am going to starve to death before then." I clasped my arms over my aching midsection and moaned theatrically.

"Fortunately for all of us, there are snacks. I'll be right back."

Isaac was gone for less than ten minutes and returned bearing a plate of sandwiches. I ate several and drank about a gallon of water before I felt sated.

"I'm going to go help Florence," Isaac said. "Do you need anything else before I go?"

"The service is fantastic, but I'll survive a few hours on my own. Does Florence need me to do anything?"

"She requested you stay as far away from the kitchen as possible."

I pouted. "I am not that bad!"

Isaac kissed the top of my head. "You are magnificent."

I grabbed the remote and turned the television back on. There were only two channels, and they were both replaying the President's announcement. I turned off the TV again. I was bored. Which was ridiculous. I wondered where Raj was and whether he was awake. Maybe he'd come hang out with me, and we could talk, and he could flirt with me. I grabbed Isaac's cell phone and texted Raj. "Are you awake? Come over. I'm bored. EM."

I waited a few minutes before giving up. Noon was not the best time to ask a vampire over for a playdate, whether or not he was immune to the sun. Maybe I would read a book. Or take a bath. Or both.

I started the bath water and dumped in a generous amount of lavender bath salts. Then I rifled through the short stack of books that had begun to accumulate in our room. Isaac, Raj, and Florence were all voracious readers, and the longer we stayed in one place, the more books appeared. I enjoyed a good book as much as the next normal person, but didn't feel quite as passionate about the whole endeavor as my companions. I settled on "The Handmaid's Tale," as a comfort read. I was fairly certain no matter what happened, our new future would not be quite that dystopian. I stripped and slipped into the bathtub. I read for a while until my eyes grew heavy. Then I placed the book carefully on the floor, slid down into the water, and closed my eyes.

I WOKE with a jolt some time later. The bathwater had left tepid behind a long time ago, I was covered in gooseflesh and was shivering. I pulled the plug with my toes and stood up just as the door opened. I'd flamed my hands before I even had a chance to see who'd surprised me in my bath. My throwing knives were lined up along the tub, and my sword was unsheathed and leaning against the toilet. I would not be caught unarmed again. The intruder cleared the bathroom door, and when I saw who it was, I let the fire in my hands die and grabbed a towel.

"What the hell, Raj?"

"You asked me to come over, but then didn't answer the door when I knocked. I let myself in."

"That explains you being in the motel room, but not in the bathroom." I wrapped the towel around myself and stepped out of the tub. I was shivering violently now. Getting cold was a really, really bad idea.

"My apologies, my sweet. I did knock, and when you didn't answer, I grew concerned."

"I need to dry off and dress. Can you..." I flapped my hand at him, and he stared at me until I said, "Raj, leave. Now."

He smiled at me, flashing a bit of fang, and said. "I could leave, but maybe you should have someone stay to guard you."

I rolled my eyes. "Raj."

He pursed his lips in a pout that stirred things low in my belly. "Fine. But there will come a time soon when you will be begging me to stay." He left me alone. I dried off, put on a bra and panties, and then re-armed myself. I walked out into the motel room to finish dressing.

"Now you're teasing me," Raj said.

I grinned. "You're the one who stayed. I'm sure you saw what clothes I had in the bathroom."

He smiled, and this time I was positive the fang flash was deliberate. "That is true."

I put on thick socks, jeans, a tank top, and a heavy sweater. I was still shivering a bit. "I need something hot," I said.

Raj was by my side before I could blink. "I could heat you up," he said, his warm breath tickling my ear. I stood, frozen, and he leaned in and breathed along the line of my neck. He didn't touch me, but I felt his heat a hair's breadth away from my skin.

"How about coffee?" Isaac said from the doorway.

I took a deep breath and stepped away from Raj who looked completely unrepentant.

"Thanks," I said taking the steaming cup from Isaac's hands.

"Spoilsport," Raj said.

"What time is it?" I asked.

"About 4:30," Isaac replied.

"You're here early," I said to Raj.

"You called me. If it is in my power, I will always come when you call."

Jealousy surged through the bond Isaac and I shared. "You called him?" he asked.

"I texted him. I was bored, and it was four hours ago. I thought we'd play cards or something."

"Or something?" Isaac asked, looking at Raj who was still standing too close to me.

"He didn't show; I took a bath and fell asleep in the tub. I got cold as the water chilled. The cold isn't agreeing with me lately." My shivering had lessened, but I was still colder than I should be. The dragon's metabolism was beginning to affect me more and more.

I thought soothing thoughts at Isaac along with the images of what had transpired between Raj and me.

He straightened his spine and focused on a point above my head. "Once I'm gone, I won't hold it against either of you if you find comfort in each other's arms."

This isn't where I wanted this to go. I opened my mouth to say something to that effect, but Raj beat me to it, "Wolf, you know I harbor…feelings…for your sweet princess, but I'd never take advantage of her grief."

"I know you'd never take advantage of her, but I know you want her, and I want you to have her if I'm not here."

This was going too far. "Isaac, are you attempting to leave me to Raj in your will?"

He looked startled. "Nooo…"

"Then why on earth would you say, and I quote, 'I want you to have her?'"

He hemmed and hawed for a few amusing moments before he finally said, "I don't know. Would you take my possessive alpha wolf and super old patriarchal upbringing as an excuse?"

"You know that's never an excuse with me. I won't beat you up over it this time, but if you ever say anything like that again, I will light you on fire with my brain."

He bowed slightly, "I beg your forgiveness, Princess."

"Forgiven. This time." I nodded regally.

"I must excuse myself," Raj said. "I find myself suddenly ravenous," Raj said.

Isaac held out his arm. "Feed from me."

273

Raj and I stared at him with astonishment. "Are you serious?" I asked as Raj said, "Do not tempt me, my friend."

"Would you rather drink from here?" Isaac asked, tilting his neck.

Now I didn't even have words for my astonishment. I shared a confused glance with Raj before the vampire answered carefully, "There is only one spot more tempting. What has prompted you to make such a generous offer?"

Isaac rubbed his hand across his face. "Is it true the more you've fed from someone, the easier they are to find?"

Raj nodded, "It is true, although it takes a minimum of three feedings for me to have an unbreakable connection with someone. Fewer than that and another vampire could negate my connection. Once I've fed three times, no other vampire can supersede my claim."

"Then I need you to feed from me two more times before the winter solstice. I need you to find me in case Michelle breaks my bond with Eleanor."

"How could that happen? I thought our bond would hold until one of us died?"

"That should be the case, but I haven't made it this far in life without planning for every contingency. It's another safety measure."

It made sense, and I didn't mind Raj feeding from Isaac, but the reality of Isaac leaving was approaching too quickly.

"If I feed from you," Raj said, "it will be more than the taste I took before. I'm hungry."

"I'm ready."

I backed away from the bed with my coffee and settled carefully on one of the extremely uncomfortable motel chairs, trying to stay as unobtrusive as possible. Raj was staring covetously at Isaac, his eyes flashing red. Isaac's were answering with a yellow glint.

"Isaac, once I start, it will be difficult for me to stop until I am full. It won't harm you. Not only do you heal preternaturally fast, but I do not need as much blood as a younger vampire. I'll be gentle, but if you've ever been fed from violently before, this may still be…upsetting. I will stop if you ask me to, but it will be difficult."

"I understand. For the record, my safe word is pineapple."

Raj laughed, and I grinned at them both.

Isaac continued, "As for the potential for an uncomfortable flash-back, there's a reason I offered my neck and not somewhere else."

Raj smiled, flashing his fangs. I looked between the two of them, not getting it at first. And then it hit me. "Oh," I said. "Huh."

The men barely acknowledged me.

"How would you prefer to do this?" Raj asked.

"Sitting here?" Isaac waved at the bed behind him and then sat.

Raj sat next to him, put his arm around Isaac, which was a little awkward due to their size discrepancies, and said, "Now?"

Isaac nodded. Raj opened his mouth, fully showing his fangs, and then licked Isaac's neck. Not gonna lie. It was hot.

"*The saliva acts as a topical analgesic*," Raj's voice whispered in my mind. "*I can choose to release it in great enough quantities to have a pleasant hallucinatory effect when it hits the bloodstream.*"

"How pleasant?" I asked out loud.

He grinned and sank his fangs into Isaac's neck. "*Watch.*"

Isaac jumped. His eyes were closed and although he didn't look like he was in pain, he didn't look as though he were having the best time ever, either. That changed quickly. His eyes opened half way and took on the heavy-lidded stare I recognized as supreme arousal. I glanced down at his lap—yep, supremely aroused. He moaned softly. I wanted to go to him—to touch him—but I held myself still. Raj's drinking slowed down and soon he stopped. He pulled away from Isaac's neck, and licked the stray drops of blood, healing the entry wounds.

Isaac stood up and swayed for a minute. I was by his side and wrapped around him for support in a second. "Are you okay?"

"Yes, give me a second." He stood with his eyes closed until he regained his balance and then let go of my arm. "I need a couple of moments."

"Eleanor and I will go check on Florence."

I started to protest, but Raj grabbed my arm and started directing me towards the door. "*Give him a moment, my sweet. He wouldn't ask if he didn't need it.*"

I knew Raj was right, but I glanced back at Isaac to be sure. His attention was elsewhere, so I followed Raj out the door.

"What's going on?" I asked.

"I believe he is going to relieve some of the discomfort my bite caused him," Raj said, not bothering to suppress his mirth.

"What do you mean?"

Raj looked at me. "You saw the physical manifestation of his discomfort."

"It looked like he was enjoying himself," I said.

"He's going to jack off," Raj said bluntly.

"Ah. I'm missing all the dirty jokes today. That's not like me." I squelched the note of hurt that Isaac hadn't wanted me to help him with that particular problem.

We went into the camper where Florence was finishing up the food preparation for dinner. "How can I help?" I asked. She looked at Raj and me and pursed her lips for a moment before answering. "Set up a card table in the motel room, and then we'll start bringing the food in there."

"Is there anything we can do here first? Isaac is having some alone time."

"For how long?" she asked, sounding exasperated.

Raj tilted his head, "Not much longer. Please tell us what, besides the table, needs to be carried in. We will gather the items, and by then we should be fine to start working."

Florence pointed out everything that was ready, found plates and utensils and serving spoons, and we started the multiple trips to take all the food to our motel room.

I don't know how Florence managed to create a full Thanksgiving dinner in a camper, but she did. Turkey, mashed potatoes, dressing, gravy, candied yams, dinner rolls, corn, and cranberry sauce weighed down the flimsy card table. There was enough for an entire army, and since only three of us ate food, I was sure there were going to be leftovers. We uncorked a few bottles of wine, sat down, and dug in. This was easily the best time I'd had in months. The conversation and the wine flowed easily, and before I knew it, most of the food had disappeared. The amount of food needed to feed a couple hungry shifters was a lot more than I would've guessed.

Isaac and I both had fourths (Florence stopped after seconds), and I leaned back from the table groaning in satisfaction. When Florence stood to begin clearing the table, we all jumped up to help. An hour and a soapy sponge fight later, everything was clean and the meager leftovers put away. There was an aura of contentedness. Isaac was sitting on the bed, and I was reclined between his legs. Raj sat near us on a chair, one leg casually swung over the other as he sipped his wine. Florence was in the other chair and had tipped it back to lean against the wall.

"This is the good life," I said.

Florence tilted her head and gave me a look.

"I mean it. Delicious food and wonderful wine with the most important people in my life." I sniffled a little. "It almost makes a girl feel emotional."

"She's faking," Isaac announced.

"Hey! I have feelings."

"All it takes is a good meal and some wine, and you let go of all the self-doubt and recriminations that have been plaguing you since August?" Florence asked.

"Pretty much." I settled back against Isaac's chest again.

"I'll keep that in mind."

"A feast a month would keep me cheerful. If you could arrange that, I promise to stay happy all the time."

"I don't know about a feast a month, but I promise whenever I do make a meal like this, it will be worth your while." She stood up and headed to the door. "I'll be right back."

She left and I looked at Raj. "Where's she going?"

"Must you always know where people are and what they're doing? Some people need privacy from time to time."

"I doubt she left in the middle of my 'I love everyone' speech to jack off," I said.

"I missed something," Isaac said. I twisted around to look at him and tried to raise one eyebrow. He looked confused. I probably did, too, since I still hadn't managed to perfect that particular expression.

"I know what you were doing after Raj finished his Thanksgiving Dinner."

"Thanks for sharing with the group."

"Raj is the one who gave me the heads up."

Raj snorted in suppressed laughter.

"Not everything is a dirty joke, Raj," I said, trying to sound stern. Before he could answer, there was a tapping on the door. I jumped off the bed and had knives in my hands almost before my feet hit the floor.

Raj and Isaac stared at me. "It's Florence," Isaac said.

"Why would she knock?" I countered.

"Because my hands are full. Open the door." Florence said.

I resheathed my knives and, after a glance through the peephole to confirm her identity, opened the door. Florence came in with a pie balanced in each hand and a shopping bag with bowls, clean cutlery, and ice cream hanging from one arm.

"Let me help you," I said, grabbing the pies.

"Those are for everyone to share," Florence said.

"How on earth did you make pie? This is insane!"

"I've got mad skills." She cracked a grin.

One pie was heaped high with beautifully browned meringue peaks. The other had a cross-hatched top crust through which golden peaches and bright purplish red berries were peeking through.

"What kind of pies?" I asked.

"Lemon meringue and blackberry peach."

"Those are my favorite."

"I know."

I cut the pies and served them up. I had a piece of lemon meringue first, and it was glorious. Then, because it was there, I had a generous slice of the blackberry peach—still warm from the oven—and a scoop of vanilla bean ice cream.

"I've died and gone to heaven," I moaned through a mouthful of delicious flavor.

"You're easy to please," Florence said.

"This is not easy. I'm picky about my pie, and this is the most amazing pie ever."

"Thank you," Florence said.

After the three of us—okay, mostly me and Isaac—polished off both pies, I ran the ice cream back to the little freezer in our camper. Then I returned to the room, unbuttoned my pants, and laid down on the bed.

CHAPTER TWENTY

I T FELT LIKE Thanksgiving had been a bubble in the time lapse of our sojourn in Savannah. We hit it, and it stretched out the day before popping and sending us hurtling much too fast towards the inevitability of Yule. There was so much going on it seemed impossible to contain it all in a few weeks. Cell phone service was hit or miss, even though we still had power in this area of the country. There were emergency bulletins every other day. There were food riots in all parts of the still-lit United States. And although the government hadn't yet confirmed the rumor that California and now Texas had both seceded, the word on the street was that in Texas, bands of armed vigilantes had given up patrolling the border and were now patrolling for supernaturals.

It wasn't as bad anywhere else—or at least not as organized. Most supernaturals had the sense to stay under wraps, no matter what the President had said. I wished either Murphy or Aldea—or both!—had outed their own extra-special status. Of course, if the Fae weren't part of the announcement, the President really couldn't say she was of the supernatural class of characters she hadn't told anyone about. I wondered if she was on my side.

Most likely, she was on her own side, and I was a means to an end.

That supposition was proven correct the day after Hanukkah ended when the President made another special announcement declaring martial law and temporarily dissolving the other two branches of government. She designated Aldea General of the Armies and Admiral of the Navies, which made him the highest ranked military officer, like ever, and meant he not only directly reported to her but the leaders of the individual military branches now all reported directly to him. Since his position was purely symbolic before, this was an enormous change. And with Aldea and the highest ranked officers in each the various branches of the military present to back up her announcement, it seemed strikingly ominous for a woman who'd lived in the land of the free, home of the brave, et cetera, et cetera, for her whole life.

"Those people aren't people," Florence said.

I peered more closely at the television screen. "Which people?"

"The generals and admirals, all the military leaders there—none of them are human."

"What are they?" I asked.

"A mix of Fae and vampires, mostly."

"No shifters?" I asked.

"No, but there may be a practitioner or two in there."

"Is Murphy seizing power?" I asked.

"Looks like it to me."

"I wonder what her end game is."

"Maybe it's time to have another conversation with Arduinna," Florence suggested. "She's there again."

"Where?" Either Florence's eyesight was exponentially better than mine, which seemed hard to believe, or she was able to see or sense auras even through the television.

"She's towards the back of the room, near the curtained doorway. She's still disguised as the President's Chief of Staff, Seth Greenwood."

"Disguised? Or has she always been Seth Greenwood? And how can you tell?"

"Her aura is a specific shade of red-laced green."

I was right about her seeing auras through the medium of television.

"Do certain types of supernaturals have specific aura colors?" I asked.

Florence glanced at me in surprise and then muted the television. "Haven't you noticed?"

"I can't see auras at all unless I concentrate really hard."

"Really?"

"Really. Do they?"

"Yes. Kind of. Vampires, being dead and all, don't really have an aura. They do, however, have a reddish black glow in both their chests and their heads, which I believe signifies the fact their 'life' is centered in those two areas. If they've recently fed deeply, vamps temporarily have a weak aura that matches that of the person they drank from."

"Nice use of air quotes," I congratulated her.

"Thank you. Shifter auras come in a variety of colors, but the primary color is always a deep, verdant green. Then, depending on the animal they shift into, there is another color spiking it. Isaac's is green and silver, like all wolves. Of course, they're not all the same. For living creatures, an aura is like a fingerprint, but if you see a rich green aura laced with silver, you've got a werewolf on your hands. Green and gold mean a type of cat shifter."

"What about mages and the Fae?" I asked.

"Mages all have a primary color of blue, and the secondary color depends on how they get their power. Earth mages, like me, are shot through with green. Those that get their power through religious belief or ceremony have silvery-white accents to theirs. Witches who practice blood or death magic have red or black streaks in their auras.

"Fae are the most difficult for me to identify. There isn't one color specific to all Fae. If I had to guess, I'd say the main color depends on the classification the Fae identifies with. Arduinna is a tree Fae, correct?"

"I believe she's *the* Green Man, or Woman, rather."

"So she, and all other tree Fae we've seen have a woodsy green aura, but hers is laced with the deep red of power. She's more powerful than she's let on, and I wouldn't be surprised if Murphy, who has a similar green in her aura but much less red, is answering to Arduinna and not the other way around."

That gave me something to mull over for a bit. "Interesting. Maybe she is on our side, after all."

"Or on Arduinna's side."

"I'm beginning to wonder if her side is my father's side," I said.

"Didn't she say it was?"

"I can't remember exactly what she said. And without an exact wording, who knows? That woman is really, really good at verbal misdirection."

"And are you sure your father's side is your side?"

"I'm absolutely sure it's not, but I do think we're currently aligned, as long as I don't make too many waves."

"And how long is that likely to keep up?" Florence grinned at me.

I stuck my tongue out. "Probably only until I get these gates opened. Once I can cross over myself, I'll be making all kinds of waves. I'll have missions! And things to do! Mates to find!" I glanced over at Isaac who hadn't said a thing for our entire conversation. He hadn't said much of anything for the last week. He still refused to talk about anything having to do with his plans to take the bait Michelle was dangling. I'd tried serious conversations, waiting for him to come to me, and now, light-hearted jokes about the inevitability I'd be coming Underhill, metaphorical guns blazing, to save his idiotic ass.

He looked up then, "Idiotic?" he asked.

I rolled my eyes. Sure and that was the one thing that'd get him to talk. Him catching a stray thought through our bond.

He smiled at me, but the smile didn't reach his eyes. He always looked at me that way now. Love, tinged with sadness and regret, and with an intensity that made me believe he was trying to drink me in, memorize me. It gave me the creeps and pissed me off. It was like he believed this was it but yet refused to do anything about it.

It wasn't quite the time for this to come to a head, but we didn't have too much time left. Soon, I'd need to push him hard enough to make him understand. He might get to make this sacrifice of his own free will. It's possible I could stop him, although since I'd have a gate opening to worry about, I'm not sure I could do that on my own, but he was not going to be able to stop me from coming to his rescue when I had the chance.

"Idiotic ass."

IT WAS two weeks until the solstice. Two weeks until the next gate opening. Two weeks until Isaac walked away from me.

It wasn't enough time. I wanted to nail down the calendar pages. I wanted to revel in the days we had left, to spend them laughing and frolicking and taking comfort in each other's arms. The more I tried to pin time down, to force it to go slowly enough that I could wring every last drop of pleasure from it, the faster it sped along.

Fucking time.

There weren't any distractions. I'd almost welcome the interruption of a band of hostile supernaturals, determined to take me down, but no one had shown their faces since the President's announcement on Thanksgiving. We still hadn't found out who'd set the bounty, and since no one seemed to be in a hurry to try to collect it, it didn't seem likely we'd find out any time soon.

Fucking cowards.

I was trying to stay positive and upbeat and glass half fucking full, but it was difficult when I knew that in two weeks, I was losing the man I cared about—the idiot wolf I'd only known for less than half a year.

Fucking noble werewolves.

For some reason, Florence started avoiding me. I told myself it was because she didn't want to interrupt any of my planned frolicking, but it might have been because my mood was darker than my dragon skin. Isaac didn't avoid me, but he wasn't participating in my plans to laugh and frolic and take comfort, either. He barely spoke, and his mood was even blacker than my own.

In other words, we were a joy to be around.

Raj hadn't done more than pop by for brief news exchanges since Thanksgiving, and I had begun to wonder if that was my fault as well. This had to stop.

"This has to stop," I said out loud. Isaac and I were, once again, holed up in our motel room watching spotty television.

"What has to stop?" Isaac asked. He didn't take the trouble to add any inflection, and the depressed monotone was pissing me off.

I waved my arms around to encompass him, and me, and the motel room, and everything. "*This*. This grumping around on both of our parts. We have two weeks minus three days left until you desert me, and we're spending it inside a cheap motel room, barely talking and fully clothed. This is not okay."

"Deserting you? I am not deserting you." His voice rose in both pitch and volume, and I felt a little relieved. Finally, the man was showing some emotion.

"What would you call it? You're leaving me to save your former lover at the request of the woman who had you tortured for decades. How else should I look at it?"

There was a brief flash of yellow in his eyes, and I felt a stab of hope that we were finally going to have it out. Then it was gone. His voice returned to the same monotone I'd heard for the past week.

"Call it whatever you want."

"What the everlasting fuck is wrong with you?" I yelled. I'd always been an incredibly even tempered person. Sure, I had my moments, but overall, I was cool, calm, and collected. This man knew how to push my buttons, though. "We have two weeks left before you willingly sacrifice yourself with the slim hope you'll be able to save a woman you didn't even know was alive for the last however many fucking years. *And* you're basically ignoring me! We've only been mated for seven weeks, will only be together for two more, and you're sitting over there sulking like a toddler who's two hours past nap time.

"We should be fucking like bunnies at this point, trying to grab every last second of pleasure and companionship we can from each other before you give yourself over to something you may or may not survive long enough for me to pull you out of! You look at me when you think I can't see you, but the moment my attention returns to you, you glance away, like eye contact will burn you. I know you're not tired of me. I know you still care about me. I know you aren't looking forward to leaving me. And I know you don't want to be Michelle's prisoner again. I know these things because of our bond, but dammit, Isaac Walker, if you don't start fucking acting like this is as hard for you as it is for me, you can spend the next two weeks without me by your side to warm your bed. Tell me what's going on in your head. Why are you making this harder than it needs to be? Talk to me. Please."

He closed his eyes and tilted his head down to the floor. When he started talking, his voice was so quiet, I had to lean forward to hear him.

"How can I be the kind of man worthy of you if I don't try to save someone who's in trouble because of me? I've spent so much time under the control of others. I don't deserve respect—from you or from myself—if I don't do something now."

I took a deep breath, framing my reply. "I can't say I completely understand, but the one thing I do know is that this is a trap."

"I know it's a trap, but I think I've got a shot at the Death Star, Admiral. Knowing what I'm walking into is the best way to mitigate the effects."

"I hate this so much." I stifled a sob. "Please don't."

He pulled me into a hug, and I buried my face in his shoulder. "I love you."

The left side of my mouth quirked up. I was certain my poor attempt at a grin wasn't hiding my grief. "I know."

"Nerd." He kissed me, but with none of the heat I was hoping for. A moment later, he turned back towards the television and started channel surfing again.

I left.

It was nearly dusk. It didn't feel like December to me. It was disgustingly hot and humid. The temperature had been in the eighties for the past few days, and I was about done with the south. I decided it was called the Dirty South because any amount of time outside, no matter the time of year, left a body sticky and sweaty and gross and in desperate need of a shower.

Ack! I couldn't even enjoy the nicest winter weather I'd ever experienced because of that idiot shifter and my terrible, fucking mood. I decided to go for a walk to sweat the bitchiness out.

I'd spent a fair amount of time over the last month familiarizing myself with Savannah, and I was comfortable I could wander without getting lost. I was dressed in jeans and a tank top. I considered finding a light shirt to put on over my tank to conceal my throwing knives and rapier, but the world had changed enough in the past weeks that no one would likely even notice I was armed, much less look twice.

I headed towards the cemetery that housed the gate. I chose a bench as far away from the pulsing energy as possible. Even this far away, the tendrils of power reached out to me. It fed me, but fed from me, making me believe that if I lost control, I'd be trapped until it opened and spit me back out.

Someone was watching me. Without turning, I patted the bench next to me and said, "You might as well sit down."

There was a whisper in the air, and Raj sat down next to me.

"You disappeared."

"I went for a walk," I countered.

"Without telling anyone."

"I'm an adult. Also a dragon."

"There are other concerned parties who worry when you wander off."

"Were any of those concerned parties Isaac?"

His silence spoke louder than words would have.

"That's what I thought."

"He loves you, you know."

"That doesn't excuse him acting like a jackass."

"He believes that if he shuts himself down, it will hurt less when the time comes."

"Will it?"

THE WANING MOON

"No. It'll hurt as badly then and more in the interim. He is acting like an idiot."

"You should tell him."

"I did."

"What did he say?"

"He said, and I quote, 'Mind your own business, you stupid, fucking bloodsucker.'" Raj did a credible imitation of Isaac's voice.

"Rude."

"It was."

"Do you think he'll snap out of his funk before Solstice?"

"I don't know."

"Raj, I'm afraid losing him will break me."

"You're unbreakable."

"I don't think I am. This is the first time I've ever allowed myself to feel this deeply about anyone. And not only is it ending too soon, and not by my choice, but he's not giving me—giving us—the chance to part with happy memories. Whenever I look back at this time, I'll have these weeks of sullen hell in my memory bank."

"I know, my sweet." He wrapped an arm around me, and I leaned into him.

"Why can't he leave me with something better?"

Raj pressed a kiss into my hair and pulled me tight against him. We sat like that until the last of the light faded from the sky and the air cooled. "We should head back," I said.

"If you'd like."

Raj and I didn't speak for the forty-five minutes it took to walk to the motel. My stomach growled and I hoped there was food prepared. I was getting tired of our standard fare of heated-up tinned food and sandwiches. Most of the restaurants and fast-food joints were closed now. Other than the curfew that started at ten every night, I hadn't paid much attention to what was going on in the city. I had noticed a significant lack of fresh food options.

"At least you always have fresh food available," I griped to Raj. "I'm sick of canned soup and canned beans and canned meat products."

"It won't be long before there are more options again," Raj said.

289

"What do you mean? Without refrigeration and transportation, how will we get this magical food of which you speak?"

"Key phrase is magical, of course. In a few years, there will be transportation and refrigeration again. The ley lines will open for travel as soon as the magic spreads far enough across the country, and there are ways of keeping food preserved that don't require modern technology. Some of what will happen will be magic, some will be a return to an earlier way of doing things, and some will be a combination of the two. You may not have Taco Bell any more, but there will be restaurants. Farming will continue, possibly even spread as the infrastructure of the cities begins to crumble without maintenance, and there will eventually be a way to preserve and transport food to market."

I felt better. I wasn't dooming the world to a pre-stone age existence.

"You really didn't think of that?" Raj asked.

"I hadn't."

"Huh."

"What's that supposed to mean?"

"Nothing."

He was teasing me now, and I stuck my tongue out at him. "Watch where you point that thing. A less gentlemanly creature might take advantage of such a blatant invitation."

I laughed and started to answer in kind when he stopped. I had knives in my hands in a moment and looked around for the source of the attack. Nothing jumped out at me—literally or figuratively. We were on the edge of the parking lot directly across from my hotel room. The door to my room was open a crack and a sick feeling crept into my gut and built a nest.

"What is it?" I whispered to Raj.

"You can put your knives away," he answered in a normal tone of voice. "No one here will attack."

I resheathed my knives and looked up at him and then over at the open door.

"Raj, what's going on?"

He didn't answer, but grabbed my hand before he started moving again. Whatever large bird had moved into my gut was now laying eggs and making a general nuisance of itself. This couldn't be right.

"Raj. Please." I tried to tug my hand out of his, but he wouldn't let go, and unless I wanted to be down a hand, I had to cede to his iron grip.

Time—and Raj and me—marched inexorably on. We were far too close to the door for my comfort, and I kept trying to slow down. I didn't know what was on the other side, but I knew it wasn't good. I couldn't even speculate because I couldn't come up with a possibility that would leave me sane. I decided clinging to Raj's hand was the far better option than trying to get away again, and I hung on for dear life.

We crossed the threshold of the room and I saw Florence sitting there. There was no blood or viscera anywhere, and for a second, I felt a great whoosh of relief. No one had died. As long as everyone was still alive, we would get through this. Florence held out a piece of paper. I took it in suddenly numb fingers. The eggs that had been laid in my stomach started hatching, and I was host to a flock of large seabirds, all clamoring for space and food and attention. I looked around for Isaac. I hadn't missed him on the first pass. He wasn't here.

I looked at the folded piece of paper in my hands. Raj guided me to the bed and helped me sit down. The numbness in my fingers was spreading, but unfortunately, it wasn't spreading to my stomach. Things there were still in an uproar.

I stared at the piece of paper again, trying to divine its purpose.

"I should probably read this." My voice was as free from inflection as Isaac's had been earlier.

Raj sat next to me and put an arm around me. This was going to be bad.

I opened the piece of paper. There weren't a lot of words on it. It couldn't possibly be enough words to break my heart. Heart-breaking should require reams of paper, or at least something legal sized, crammed full of script front and back. This was barely enough to qualify as a paragraph.

I tried to focus on the words, but they swam in front of my eyes. I shook myself. This was ridiculous. Regardless of what I'd told Raj earlier, I was not going to break, no matter what happened. I was strong; I was independent; I didn't need a man to complete me. And I was a motherfucking dragon in my spare time. I was unbreakable.

"Eleanor," Florence said. Her voice sounded like it was coming from a long way away. "You should read it before you burn it."

I looked down and saw smoke rising in delicate tendrils from the corners of the note. I gathered my will and tamped down the angry heat flaring through my body.

I focused and stared at the writing until the letters came to attention and formed orderly ranks and files of words.

"Princess,

"I'm sorry I've been difficult to be around for the last few weeks. I know it's making it harder for you. I'm taking off until Solstice to give you the space you need to concentrate on the next task. I'll come say goodbye before the gate opens. In the meantime, I will not be in the city, and I will be closing down our bond as much as I can. Please don't try to find me. I love you.

"Isaac."

I released my hold on the fire and the note flared up and turned the paper to ash in seconds.

"Fucking asshole." I reached through our bond and felt him to the north. He was moving rapidly away from me. I could feel the pain and regret and the absolute confidence he was doing the right thing. "I can't believe he did this. What an inconsiderate jackass."

I was suddenly calm and focused. This would not do. He did not get to make arbitrary decisions that would affect both of our lives without at least having a civil conversation about it. I yanked open our bond as wide as I could without his cooperation and sent a message. "Ishaq ben Ekkileb, you can run for now, but if your furry ass isn't back in range by the full moon, I will come after you. I am your Alpha, and as such, I do not give you permission to leave our pack."

I spoke out loud as well. I wanted Raj and Florence to know what I was saying. They both looked shocked, although Raj's shock was tempered with amusement.

I received an impression of anger from Isaac, but he didn't slow down.

"Your ass is mine, Walker, until the day I choose to release it."

I slammed shut our bond and looked up at my friends. Florence looked pissed and sympathetic, which was exactly how I wanted her to feel. Raj looked faintly amused. He held a full shot glass and an open beer. He handed me the shot and I threw it back. The whiskey burned on the way down, but the beer he handed me in exchange for the empty glass cooled it immediately.

"Thanks, Raj."

"It was Florence's idea," he said.

"Thank you, Florence."

"Are you okay?" she asked.

"Not in the least. But I will be. Either that ass will be back for the moon, which would show a distinct increase in common sense, and is therefore unlikely, or he won't show up until the solstice. If he does get his head out of his ass to realize he's throwing away the best thing that ever happened to him and is out of range of the only Alpha who can help him control his wolf during the full moon, then our relationship is salvageable. If he doesn't show up until solstice, then it really will be goodbye."

"You won't go after him Underhill?" Raj asked.

"Of course I will," I said. "I'm not going to abandon him to the vampire who tortured him. But after the rescue, we will break our bond and go our separate ways."

"Would you do that? Not give him a second chance?"

"I can't think of a reason why I would. I might, however, let him grovel a bit before kicking him to the curb."

"Can I get you anything more?" Florence asked.

"How about another one of those delightful tiny cups of whiskey?"

CHAPTER TWENTY-ONE

W HEN I WOKE up the next—I opened one eye cautiously and peeked at the clock—morning, my head was pounding and my mouth tasted like something foul had crawled inside and died. It took me a second to realize I was profoundly hung-over.

I rolled over and sat up gingerly, trying not to move my head too much. There was a large glass of water and a small bottle of aspirin on the nightstand next to me. I loved it when Florence used her precognition for good.

I swallowed three aspirin and downed the entire glass of water before attempting to get out of bed. I shuffled slowly to the bathroom to take care of necessities and drank two more glasses of water, and then hopped in the shower to try to scrub the hangover away. By the time I was clean and dressed, I felt almost human again. It would've been the perfect morning for Taco Bell. Taco Bell was like magic for hangovers.

Oooh, magic. I should be able to magic my hangover away. If I could burn up the alcohol in my blood with magic, rendering me sober, I should be able to burn away a hangover.

I concentrated for a little bit, but all I managed to do was to give myself a tension headache on top of my hangover headache.

I left my room and knocked on Florence's door. She opened the door and on the table was a large breakfast burrito and a hazelnut latte. My mouth dropped open. "For me?"

Florence nodded. "You may have twenty-four hours of self-indulgence, and I'll help out as much as possible."

I sat down at the table, but didn't know where to start. I compromised by holding the burrito in one hand and the coffee in the other and alternating hands.

"You are the best, ever," I said through a mouth full of food. I took a swig of coffee. "This is way more awesome than ice cream for a broken heart."

Florence winced, but didn't comment on my atrocious table manners. Best friend ever.

After I finished, I didn't know what to do. Hurt and anger warred for supremacy, and both were paralyzing.

"Tamp it down," Florence said.

"What?"

"You're smoking. Please don't light my motel room on fire."

Anger was winning the battle. Good. Anger could yield productivity. Hurt could not.

"Now what? I need a to-do list. Something to channel my anger into."

"You should talk to Arduinna."

"That's a good idea."

"Tonight we should see what's going on with Raj. He's been mostly absent lately."

"He was here last night."

"Yes, but that was the first time, barring Thanksgiving, he'd spent any measurable amount of time with us since we got to Savannah. Something's up with him. He didn't even hit on you last night."

"I was grieving."

"When has he ever had a sense of propriety where flirting is concerned? He flirts as naturally as he breathes."

"Good point." I sat and stared at Florence. She stared back. "What do we do now?"

"Eleanor, if you're not up to anything today, that's okay. We can sit and watch bad movies and throw popcorn at the television screen."

"No, I'm..." I tried to tack the word 'okay' onto the end of the sentence but was unable to. Stupid inability to lie. "I'm anxious to not spend the rest of the day trapped in my own neuroses, of which I have only a few."

I was pleased it was true that I didn't have many neuroses. Or maybe it was true that I thought it was true, and I really was incredibly neurotic and my belief that I wasn't was further proof. I blinked rapidly. That line of thinking was not productive and was more likely to increase the headache pain.

"Let's call Arduinna."

We were in a not-so-nice area of town, and there was a small park a couple of blocks away I'd been avoiding. It wasn't much of a park, regardless of what the rusty sign riddled with bullet holes would have us believe. It was one city block of brown grass and greenish weeds, a rusty chain link fence with more holes than a doughnut shop, and a pot-hole ridden asphalt path meandering through trees that had definitely seen better decades. I took off my sandals and stepped out onto the earth. The sharp, dying grass felt like broken glass under my feet. I jogged to a small thicket of trees and bushes where everything looked alive. Ish. The grass was even green-adjacent.

I sank to the ground and crossed my legs. Florence found a bench that looked like it would hold an adult human and sat down with a book. I closed my eyes, touched the bark of the nearest tree, and formed a picture of Arduinna in my mind. I called her and sat back to wait. It was less than ten minutes before she appeared. If I hadn't been staring at the right tree at the right time, I wouldn't have seen anything. The trunk bulged slightly and Arduinna's form detached itself from the tree. She turned around and looked at the tree in distaste before turning back to me and bowing.

"If it pleases your Highness, I would appreciate it if you would find healthier and larger trees to call me from in the future. That was unpleasant."

"My apologies, Arduinna. I didn't know exactly how you traveled and didn't realize the health and size of the tree would make a difference. I'll keep that in mind in the future."

Arduinna looked uncomfortable, but I couldn't figure out what exactly the problem was. "Is something bothering you?"

She hesitated, and then said, "May I speak freely?"

"Of course." I bowed my head in what I imagined was a regal fashion.

"It is awkward for me to have my head higher than yours, but sitting in your presence without invitation would be a faux pas. I was trying to decide the best course of action."

"Why is it awkward for your head to be higher than mine?"

"There is a reason thrones are on a dais—royalty likes to look down on the little people."

"I don't want you to be uncomfortable. Would it be better if I stood or if you sat?"

"I would prefer to sit, Highness, if it would be okay with you."

"Please, sit. In fact, I would like to issue a standing invitation—heh —for you to sit in my presence without prior permission unless there are other Fae around."

"You are gracious."

"I know. You, however, didn't even crack a smile at my pun, and that hurts my feelings."

Arduinna stopped halfway into a seated position and glanced at my face. "Highness?"

"Sit. What happened to your sense of humor? I swear it was more developed last time I saw you. Is the President getting you down?"

"The President?"

"Don't dissemble. I've seen you on TV. Florence believes Murphy reports to you. Is that true?"

"She is a member of your father's court," Arduinna said.

"Stop. One word answers, only. Does President Murphy report to you?"

"Yes."

"You have more control over the outing of the supernaturals than you led me to believe?"

Pause. "Yes." I could practically hear her teeth grinding. She hated when I forced her to answer in absolutes.

"Is Arduinna or Seth your true form?"

The pause was longer this time. "Both," she finally admitted through clenched teeth.

"Explain, please."

She stared at me, frustration apparent on her face. I couldn't figure out what was wrong.

"You commanded her to give one word answers only," Florence said. "She can't explain in one word."

Oops. "You are no longer bound by the one-word thing. Instead, give the simplest, most direct answer possible."

Arduinna's shoulders relaxed. "I am not bound to either form permanently. I am either. Or both. I took the female form to talk to Finn because he is intimidated by strong women. Because that's how you met me, I thought it simpler to keep that form in our interactions."

"And you didn't think I'd recognize you with the President."

"That is true."

"Was it your idea or my father's to not out the Fae?"

"Mine."

"Please explain your reasoning."

"I thought it would be easier to start with supernaturals who are— or were—mostly human before talking about a different race of beings who will come through the magical gates you're opening."

"Don't you think it'll breed resentment among the supernaturals you did out or spur them to out the Fae in retaliation?"

"That is a possibility, but it will take time."

"When will you announce Savannah is the next gate site?"

"December ninth."

"That's tomorrow."

"I have an excellent grasp of the passage of time."

"Careful, Arduinna. That sounded like sarcasm, and that's the beginning of a sense of humor."

"I would appreciate it if you would keep that information to yourself." Arduinna almost looked like she was fighting a smile. Almost.

"The solstice is at noon. Raj will not be able to guard me. It's me and Florence, and she'll have her hands full spindling the magical threads into the weir. I'm afraid to ask for help from the Fae, but I haven't been attacked in so long I'm afraid someone is saving up."

"I will send a dozen of my most trusted agents to you."

"They'll watch, guard me against supernatural attacks, but not interfere?"

"What if the half-breed shows up?"

I glanced back at Florence. "Do we still need Finn alive?"

She looked up over the top of her reading glasses. "Yes. I promise to let you know when he's outlived his usefulness."

"Are they allowed to kill?" Arduinna asked.

"Any supernaturals that aren't me, Raj, Florence, Finn, or Isaac."

"What about Renfields?"

My moral compass was on the fritz. I tapped my head a couple of times, hoping to get the needle spinning again, to no avail. "Florence, can we kill Renfields?"

"As long as it's self-defense."

"There you go," I said to Arduinna.

"You should make those kinds of decisions and not defer to someone else."

"I have advisers. They advise me."

"I would kill them."

"Me, too. That's why I have advisers."

From the look she gave me, I didn't think Arduinna approved.

"Anything else, Your Highness?"

I thought about it for a second, and then remembered yesterday's press conference. "Three more yes or no questions. Are any of the military leaders human?"

"No."

"What about the President's chief advisers?"

"No."

"Last question: does the president have any intention of restoring the other two branches of the government or is she trying to set herself up as head of a new monarchy?"

Arduinna grinned this time, and her teeth, which were faintly green and mildly pointy showed, turning my stomach a little. "No."

Dammit. I rolled my eyes at her. I rose to my feet and held my hands out to her to help her up. She looked at my hands, shook her head, stood in one smooth motion, and bowed.

"You're dismissed, Arduinna."

She turned back to the tree she'd arrived through, looked at the other offerings in the "park." She sighed audibly, braced her shoulders, and walked into the tree, dissolving from view.

I returned to Florence. She closed her book and put away her glasses. "Learn anything interesting?"

"Nothing we didn't already suspect. I'm glad I asked for the Fae guard. I doubt Raj can help."

THE SUN SANK below the horizon as street lights flared to life. I dropped the motel room curtain and looked back at the room. Florence was reading and pointedly ignoring my restless pacing. A knock echoed through the room. "Come in, Raj."

I gasped when he entered. He usually looked perfect—never a hair out of place and always immaculately dressed. Now, however, he was bruised, bloody, and his hair was anything but the beautiful tousled curls I almost never fantasized about running my fingers through. His clothes were torn and blood-stained, and he was limping. The physical damage was already healing. The real question is who or what could've done this to an eleven-hundred-year-old vampire.

"Do you still have that casket? I might need to borrow it."

"What happened?"

"Blake—the leader of the Savannah vampires objected to my extended visit."

"Blake? Seriously?"

"It wasn't even his real name. He renamed himself when he took the city."

I couldn't hold back my laughter anymore. "I can't believe he wanted people to call him Blake. How's he look?"

"Dusty." His eyes glinted red and the faintest hint of ruthless satisfaction curled itself into a smile on his face. Alarm bells sounded in my head as my limbic system kicked in and I had to quell the urge to back away. I took a deep, steadying breath and reminded myself that Raj was my friend.

"How did this—"I waved my hand to encompass the damage done to his face—"happen?"

"Blake was strong—he'd have to be, as Savannah is a highly-valued territory—but not as intelligent as one would hope. He refused to regard my presence here as anything but a challenge. He was within his rights to refuse to let me stay in the city and to challenge me if I defied him. But most would've accepted my word that I'd leave the city untouched just to avoid fighting the second most powerful vampire in the country.

"Instead, he strung me along, refused to meet with me to finalize our arrangements, and when I ran out of patience and pointed out that he was both undiplomatic and idiotic, he sent humans bearing blow-torches to surprise me in my sleep this morning. Fortunately for me, I wasn't sleeping."

"This happened this morning?" He should've healed a lot more by now.

"Some of it. The rest happened about thirty minutes ago when I found him rising for the evening. He had a large contingent of body guards."

"All vampires?"

"Mostly. Those he sent this morning were human. He didn't believe older vampires are more resistant to sunlight and thought to catch me unawares."

"How did they find you?"

"I was careless. When I discovered how short-sighted Blake was..."

his lip curled in derision, "I stopped taking pains to cover my tracks. He must have had someone follow me home."

"You don't sound too sure about that."

He shook his head. "I'm not. I didn't reach this age without developing a highly-trained sense of paranoia. I didn't even share my daytime resting spot with you, so I couldn't have been betrayed."

"Hey!"

He waved away my objection. "Even if I'd shared it with you, I wouldn't be accusing you of betrayal. I would just assume someone had overheard us or plucked it from my mind. I trust you implicitly."

"Okay, then. I guess. So what do you think happened?"

"I don't know—a phrase I seldom have occasion to utter. Alas, I am unlikely to ever find out. Blake—" he paused until my giggles faded into indelicate snorts. "As I was saying, the former master of Savannah and most of his inner circle are dead. It's shocking how much mess one leaves behind when defending themselves against a few dozen vampires and their Renfields."

"A few dozen?"

"Give or take. It was rather a lot, even for me."

"And you're sure you're okay?"

"I'm irritated and hungry, but no lasting damage was done."

"Can I get you anything?"

"I hate to ask, but I lost a lot of blood…"

"I'll do it," Florence said.

"You don't have to," I said.

"Yes, I do." She rolled up her sleeve and held her wrist out to Raj.

"You honor me," he said, before biting down. He fed deeply but quickly, and before much time had passed, he was healing the puncture wounds. I held out a cold, wet washcloth.

"May I clean you up?"

He submitted to my ministrations, and I was pleased to see all of his wounds were closed, and once the blood was washed off, it looked as though he'd been healing for weeks instead of an hour. By morning, he'd look good as new. I opened my mouth to ask more questions about Savannah, Blake (heh), and how one goes about slaughtering a few dozen supernaturals and emerging relatively unscathed, all things considered.

"What have I missed?" Raj asked, clearly heading off my questions at the pass.

After we filled Raj in on the not-so-informative conversation I'd had with Arduinna, I decided to grill him a bit.

"Is this what you've been up to since we arrived? Fending off local vamps? I noticed you haven't been around much, except last night and Thanksgiving, and your flirting has been sub-par."

"*You've* noticed?" Florence asked.

"I'm royalty. Isn't it my job to take credit for other people's thoughts?"

She shook her head and smiled at me.

"What do you mean my flirting has been sub-par?" Raj looked offended.

"You didn't even try to hit on me last night."

"You were grieving."

I couldn't help it, I started laughing.

"How is that funny?"

"Florence and I had this exact same conversation this morning."

"Which of you threw out the grieving line?"

"Me. Florence knows us all better than we know ourselves."

"I'm not going to take advantage of you when you're emotionally compromised."

"You didn't even flirt a little at the cemetery. You were comforting, which was nice, but it was devoid of sexual innuendo."

"I apologize that my preoccupation with Blake of Savannah kept me from your side."

I rolled my eyes. "Is Savannah yours now?"

"Yes." He didn't sound thrilled.

"Are you going to stay?"

"Definitely not. If I'd wanted the city, I would've taken it when we arrived."

"You could've just done that?"

Raj grinned and a shiver ran up and down my spine. It was easy to forget this man—this vampire—was a thousand years old.

"All by design, my sweet."

"Between the Pacific Northwest and Savannah, you have a great deal of territory and power."

"I'll show you how powerful I am."

"Much better!" I treated him to a polite golf clap. "But seriously, what're you going to do about Savannah?"

"I'll appoint a lieutenant, much as I have in Portland and Seattle. Then, if we need to incentivize the Queen to grant us safe passage, I'll offer her Savannah. With a competent lieutenant in place, she can add the city to her territory without needing additional administrative staff. More taxes, not more work."

"You're a generous man."

"Something else I'd be delighted to demonstrate. We'll add that to the list."

"There's a list now?"

"Of course. Power, generosity, what else?"

"Stamina?" I suggested.

"Would you walk me back to my motel room?" Florence asked. I gave her side-eyes, but complied with her request. She asked me in. "Do not sleep with the vampire out of pique or hurt feelings."

"I have no intention of sleeping with Raj."

She tapped the side of her head. "I'm psychic. I know what you were thinking."

"Idle speculation and desire do not equal intention."

"You'd feel badly about it tomorrow."

"I'm not having sex with Raj."

"A word of advice: no matter what happens, don't go to bed with him until we leave New Orleans. What happens there will change you, change him, and might change your mind."

Florence did not often offer advice; I couldn't afford to ignore it. "I'll go say good night to Raj."

"You don't have to kick him out of your life. Just don't let him into your pants."

I hugged her, which surprised us both, and said good night.

Raj was waiting in my room. "I can stay if you'd like," he said.

"I'd like, but you have to keep your hands and all other body parts to yourself."

"Deal."

THE CLOSER WE got to the full moon, the antsier I got. I tried to convince myself Isaac wouldn't do the sensible thing, wouldn't come back for the full moon, but no matter how many times I tried to dash my own hopes, they kept springing eternal.

Raj was around more now than he had been before, but not a lot more. He was trying to figure out which of the remaining vamps would be best suited for leadership and least likely to betray him. He was interviewing everyone who was left, and although I was, for some reason, not allowed at those proceedings, it amused me to imagine the vampires showing up to Raj's corporate office in ill-fitting and uncomfortable suits, to try to convince Raj why they were the right ones for the job. In addition to being amusing, it gave me a chance to imagine Raj in a suit and tie, which was kind of nice.

Still, he carved time out of his busy VR (vampire relations) work to spend the early part of each evening with me. He flirted outrageously, turned every other sentence out of my mouth into sexual innuendo, but never once tried to push past the boundaries I'd established between us. He was waiting for me to come to him. It's a good thing he was patient, because I had no intention of crossing that line.

If I did it now, even without Florence's warning, I'd regret it because there was still a chance Isaac would pull his head out of his ass and try to salvage our relationship. And even if we were 'on a break,' it would still hurt Isaac that I'd slept with Raj.

If I slept with Raj after the full moon, it would be out of hurt and anger, and although that wasn't the worst reason in the world to have sex, it wasn't a good enough reason to cross a previously established relationship line, at least not when I planned on remaining friends with said someone.

I was less clear on the reasons to stay out of Raj's pants between opening the fourth gate and whenever New Orleans was, but Florence said to keep my libido in check, and I would listen.

I heard a quiet knock at the door and smiled. "Come in." Raj walked in, and for some reason was wearing a gorgeous, obviously insanely expensive, suit. I gasped.

He held out his arms a bit and spun. "Good?"

I tried to restart my brain and list all the reasons why sleeping with him now was a bad idea. "Why?" I sputtered out.

"I enjoyed your fantasies about my interviewing practices."

We were headed down a dangerous path and I needed to rein it back in.

"I thought you were going to stay out of my head?"

"When did I ever agree to that? I certainly won't now that I know what lovely things are happening in there." He loosened his tie and unbuttoned the top button. I tried not to stare.

"You're not playing fair."

"Why would I? You've known my objective since day one."

"The objective to capture and imprison me?"

He chuckled. "That is still my objective, although figuratively rather than literally. I want to capture your affections."

"I have great affection for you, Raj."

"I don't know why you hesitate. Your only objection before was the presence of Isaac. He is no longer in a position to object. Why aren't we spending our nights in sensual discovery?"

"You're busy with your VR duties."

"I wish you wouldn't call it that. Unless you're going to put on a power suit—and skip the blouse."

"And secondly, Isaac is not out of the picture. He has until the moon rises tomorrow to show up and try to make amends."

"And when he doesn't?"

"If."

"My apologies, my sweet, and if he doesn't? Will you then seek comfort in my bed?"

"No." My thoughts flicked to what Florence had told me and Raj picked it up immediately.

"You won't sleep with me because the witch told you not to?"

"I do everything she tells me to do. She's very wise."

"And it all comes down to New Orleans?"

"That's what she said."

"I hope we go there next. I am eager to get that barrier out of the way." He stared at me, and my resolve tried to flee.

"Stop."

"Stop looking? At such a one as yourself? Don't ask for impossibilities." He was back to being outrageous, which meant he was letting it go.

"For now."

Moonrise of the first night of the full moon was late afternoon. When Isaac hadn't shown up by noon, I opened up our bond as wide as I could without cooperation and searched for him. He was almost due east, and I got the impression he was surrounded by swamp lands and small animals. Before he shut me down, I got a name. Turtle Island.

"He's on Turtle Island," I told Florence. "I don't know where that is, but it's not too far and it's almost due east. He has no intention of coming back and asking for my help."

"Do you want to go to him, or leave him to it?" she asked.

"I don't know. He seems to have found an uninhabited island which should minimize the potential to cause damage. Maybe I should let him be."

"What do you want to do?"

"I want to go over there, turn into a dragon, and sit on him until he admits he's a giant idiot."

"How long do you think that's likely to take?"

"Probably longer than we have. What is wrong with the men in my life? Why are they all stupid?"

"It is the way of men to be stupid," Florence intoned solemnly.

I laughed, as she meant me to do.

"Well?" she prompted.

"He needs to make his own choices, and if he's going to continue to think I need protecting, it will never work out between us. By that same token, I suppose I should stop treating him as someone who needs protection. A partnership of anything less than equals was doomed from the start. I'll assume he's made a logical, rational decision that will not result in any unfortunate human casualties."

"That's it?"

"You don't need to sound skeptical."

She raised an eyebrow at me.

"Fine. And after dark, I'm going to turn into a dragon and do some stealthy, dragon recon."

"That sounds more like you."

"It's not that I don't trust him."

"You don't. You care about him, and you know he cares about you, but you don't trust him to make the right choices or to be strong enough and wise enough to handle his change. That's why you won't consciously let yourself love him—it's not because you're incapable of love."

I wanted to argue, but I couldn't. She was right. The hollow ache in the center of my being that had shown up when Isaac told me what he'd learned at the last opening grew and I fought back tears.

Florence didn't relent. "You don't trust anyone."

"You're my posse."

"I'm not part of anything that's labeled a posse." Florence said, cutting me a little slack.

"My sidekicks, my Scooby gang."

Florence ignored my witty repartee.

"If you can't convince yourself you trust him, you'll never convince Isaac."

"He doesn't trust me either."

"He doesn't. I'm not exonerating his idiocy. You came together quickly and passionately, but didn't have time to build a foundation. You trusted each other with some of your secrets, you had heat and passion and affection, but you never developed trust."

I blinked, trying to dash away the tears from the corners of my eyes. "It's a shitty situation." Tears streaked slowly down my face.

"It is, but it's not hopeless."

"I said if he didn't come back for the full moon, I didn't want him back at all."

"You said that to me and Raj, not to Isaac. And it's okay if you change your mind, and it's okay if you don't. Get through the next few days, open the gate, keep going. This doesn't have to be the end."

I cried until my throat hurt and my head throbbed and I'd used the world's supply of tears. Florence held me until my tears subsided, tucked me into my bed and kissed the top of my head before leaving me alone. It was still early afternoon. I was asleep by moonrise.

CHAPTER TWENTY-TWO

I MADE IT through the three nights of the full moon fairly well, if I do say so myself. I did fly-overs the first couple of nights. Yes, multiple. Yes, after saying I wasn't going to. Yes, I have issues.

I had a couple of tense moments when Isaac's wolf tried to pick a fight with an alligator, but the alligator—the wiser of the two—took one look at the enormous wolf and declined to engage. I don't know what Isaac did during the day, but at night he roamed the island generally not being a danger to anyone but the local waterfowl. I stayed in the motel the third night to pretend I trusted him.

I woke up Wednesday morning feeling both self-satisfied and a little panicked. I'd stayed away from the island for the entire previous night. However, now we were only three nights away from the winter solstice. I was having a little trouble wrapping my head around all the ways my life—not to mention the world—had changed since the last solstice. I decided to stop trying to wrap my head around it and to keep moving forward. Gazing too intently into one's navel is a good way to run into a wall.

Because solstice was likely to be a bit busy, what with the gate and me probably being unconscious, I convinced Raj and Florence to have a small celebration the night before. We didn't go all out like we had at Thanksgiving, mostly because I couldn't convince Florence it was necessary, but we had a miniature feast.

After dinner, we sat in the motel parking lot and tried to catch a breeze. I excused myself after a few minutes and went back to the room to get the gifts. I'd blown my wad on Florence's birthday gift, and her solstice gift wasn't nearly as personal and thoughtful, but I hoped she'd like it anyway.

I'd gotten Raj a few small items, a mixture of funny and sweet, and one thing I'd run across in a weird antique store in downtown Savannah. Isaac's gifts were wrapped and waiting by the bed, in case he showed up. When I got back outside, Raj and Florence were sitting exactly where I'd left them, only now they had gifts on their laps. I grinned. This was going to be awesome. I loved getting presents.

I sat down, dropped my pile of gifts on the ground, and held out my empty hands. "Gimme!"

"So gracious," Florence said.

I folded my hands demurely in my lap and looked up at her through my lashes. "Thank you in advance for my presents, although your friendship is gift enough."

She and Raj both laughed, and Florence started to hand me something.

"No, wait! Me first," I said.

I handed Florence her gift—not wrapped in bandanas this time. She started to open it, and I interrupted. "It's not as awesome as what I gave you for your birthday. You should probably lower your expectations."

"Lower than a pole-dancing cowgirl dashboard doll?"

I rolled my eyes but conceded the point. "Maybe not quite that low."

She laughed and finished unwrapping the present. It was a framed photo of us Isaac had taken at the Arch in St. Louis.

"Thank you. This means a lot to me."

"Now you, Raj," I said, handing him three gifts.

He opened the first one and glared at me a little before turning the box to show Florence. It was a gift box containing Twilight branded body glitter, a crucifix tie tack, and a Spike action figure. I clapped my hands in unsuppressed glee.

"How much do you love it?" I asked.

"On a scale of one to ten? Are negative numbers allowed?"

I stuck my tongue out at him. "Please, please tell me you'll wear the body glitter at some point."

"Is it edible?"

I shivered. "Stop. You promised."

"No, I didn't."

"Open the next one."

"I hope it's a signed, first edition of Breaking Dawn."

"Better."

He tore off the paper and held up a miniature coffin.

"Open it!" I said.

He opened the coffin, and nestled in the white satin lining was a bottle of his favorite wine. "Perfect! Let's drink this now." He opened the wine and poured us each a glass.

"Last one." I held my breath.

He opened it slowly and then turned the full force of his grin on me. "Eleanor, this is magnificent."

"I want to see," Florence said.

Raj lifted his gift out of the expanse of wrapping and tissue paper on his lap and showed Florence. It was an antique sword in a similar style to his current sword but inlaid with rubies on the hilt.

"Matches your eyes," I said.

"Ha," he replied, rather absently. He was caressing the scabbard, and his gaze was a little unfocused. "This is a magnificent gift."

He knelt in front of me and handed me the sword. I wasn't quite sure what to do with this. "I pledge my sword to you and promise to always be faithful, to never cause you harm, and to go forth in all dealings with you in good faith. My sword and my life are yours."

"Your pledge is accepted, and I give you one in return. I will provide for you as much as you need and will return your faithful service with the promise of my own." Someday I was going to figure out how the right words came to me when I needed them.

Raj kissed my hand and rose, taking back his sword. Something important had happened. A look at Florence confirmed this. She looked pleased.

"Things progressing how you want them to?" I asked.

"They usually do."

I took a long sip of my wine and waited. No one said anything further. "Okay! My turn!"

Florence laughed and handed packages to Raj and me. Raj went first. He received another bottle of wine, this one a 'Dracula' Cabernet, as well as a pair of ruby cufflinks.

"Thank you," he said, kissing her hand. I tore into my gift. Custom leather sheaths for my throwing knives, each decorated with a beautiful quill and beadwork dragon in a different position. "This is amazing!" I immediately removed the old sheaths, but before I could move my knives to the new ones, Raj laid a gift on my lap.

"Open this first," he said. I did.

Inside were a dozen perfectly balanced throwing knives. Six were silver with a laurel wood inlay, and six were steel. I'd never seen anything that gorgeous. I sheathed them and strapped them on to my arms and legs. I'd leveled up to a new weapons set. "You guys are the best."

"One more gift," Raj said, handing Florence a small package. Inside was a sapphire and diamond cuff.

She slipped it on. "Thank you."

Raj refilled our glasses, and we toasted. I tried to ignore the ache in my center that said someone was missing and enjoy the moment.

I raised my glass again, "To us," I said. Raj and Florence clinked with me, and we drank deeply. We finished the bottle and then separated for the evening. Raj promised to find us as soon as he was able to move comfortably around in the daylight.

"Good luck, my sweet. My thoughts are with you, and if we're lucky with the weather and it's cloudy, my body will be with you, too."

"I'll see you tomorrow."

THE NEXT MORNING I woke when the door opened. I peeked through bleary eyes at the bedside alarm clock. Six-oh-seven. This had better be good. I rolled over and looked at the door. Isaac stood there with an absurdly large package in his hands.

"Happy solstice." He thrust the gift towards me.

"I'm mad at you."

"I know." I glared at him for at least a minute before sitting up with the covers still wrapped around me, grabbing the gift, and ripping off the paper. It was a back scabbard, done in the same ornamental bead and quill pattern as my throwing knife sheaths, and containing a new sword.

"This is beautiful," I said.

"Florence made it," he said.

I gestured towards my throwing knives on the bedside table. "I figured." I stood up, forgetting for a moment I was mad at him—and that I was nude. I heard the sharp intake of breath as I came out from under the covers. I pulled the sheet around me, pissed that whatever was going on made me want to be modest.

"I got something for you, too." I handed him a small pile of gifts. There was another framed photo, this one of us in the Black Hills, touched up in sepia tones since I'd never convinced him to get an olde-timey photo done in Deadwood, moonstone cufflinks, and a geode that looked like a dragon egg. I'd wanted something that would signify our connection or something that would delight him as much as Florence's topaz or Raj's khanda. Instead, everything was nice and superficial.

"Happy solstice."

"Eleanor…"

"Give me a minute." I walked into the bathroom and closed the door. I finally felt ready to deal with my mate after I was cleaned and dressed. I returned to the main room.

"What do you want, Isaac?"

"I saw you at the full moon."

"I saw you, too."

"You didn't trust me to find a safe space."

"You spent our first few full moons together telling me you couldn't be trusted. You spent no time telling me you could. What was I supposed to think?"

He didn't answer.

"What do you want? Why are you here?"

"I wanted to say goodbye."

"You could've left a note. Again." That was maybe a little bitchier than I needed to be.

Isaac whumped down on the bed. "I thought it would be easier if I left instead of moping around."

"Easier for whom?"

"You, of course."

"You thought it would be easier for me if my boyfriend—my *mate* —disappeared while I was out on a walk, leaving nothing but a note? Do you know what would've actually been easier? If you'd gotten over yourself and talked to me about what was going on."

"I tried..."

"You tried to talk? To whom? When? As I recall, you barely said two words about anything important."

"I'm not used to having a partner."

"Neither am I, but disappearing for the last two weeks we might ever have together was not the way to get used to it. Isaac, this could be it. This could be the last time we're ever together. Ever. And you disappeared for two weeks. We've had too little time together, and it's not fair. It's not fair you were forced into making this choice. But it's especially not fair you took away the last days we should've spent together. Instead of making good memories of our time together, you gave me two weeks of anguish, of heartbreak, and anxiety.

"I care about you, Isaac, but I'm pretty fucking mad right now."

He bowed his head and didn't meet my eyes. I opened the bond between us as wide as I could. His heartache was palpable, and perversely that made me feel a wee tiny bit better.

"I love you, Eleanor."

"I know."

"I'm sorry."

"Me, too." He pulled me into his arms. "I will find you."

"I'll be waiting."

"Arduinna is sending a dozen guards to the cemetery to protect me and Florence while we do our magic thing. Unless it's cloudy, Raj won't be able to make it. At least we won't have to worry about being attacked by an organized contingent from the Savannah vamps."

"Why not?" I'd forgotten he hadn't been here.

"Raj took the city."

"Seriously?"

"He's going to give it to the queen when we get to New Orleans."

"Wow, you disappear for a couple of weeks and miss all sorts of news."

"Did Raj feed from you the third time?" I asked.

"Yes." He didn't elaborate the whens and hows, and I ignored the sudden stab of jealousy. There was no way I was analyzing that right now.

"Are you going to wait and go with us to the cemetery? You should at least say goodbye to Florence."

"I'll wait."

"She'll be here soon with breakfast. I don't know if she'll have anything for you."

"She knows I'm here. I stopped at her room first."

I cocked my head. "Why?"

"To make sure you hadn't set any Isaac-themed booby traps for me."

"I'm not petty."

"I would've deserved it."

"True."

I was having trouble thinking of things to say. All the big things, the things I'd planned on saying before he left were wiped away in the last two weeks of misery, and I didn't have time to recreate them.

There was a knock on the door.

"Come in, Florence," I said. I felt a rush of relief we wouldn't have to figure out what to say to each other anymore, and Isaac looked at me, hurt because of my relief.

Florence came in with a tray of coffee and a box of Pop Tarts.

"This is how we're fortifying ourselves for the big day?" I asked.

"Could you really choke down anything more?"

I thought about it and gagged at the thought. Too many nerves.

"That's what I thought. Eat at least one."

I ate two Pop Tarts and drank my coffee. It was hours until go time, but I was already feeling nervy and antsy. How was it possible the last few weeks had gone so quickly I could barely catch my breath, but now that we were at the finish line, time had slowed to a crawl?

By nine, I was pacing the motel room. We weren't bothering to pack. Raj had driven the car out of the city the night before, and everything that was truly valuable was in a backpack we'd carry with us.

We were going to walk to the cemetery, but it was only about forty-five minutes away, and solstice wasn't until noon. Isaac and Florence were engaged in a quiet conversation, and I could tell it was meant to exclude me. I did my best to keep pacing and not to eavesdrop.

"...take care of her," Isaac said.

He'd better not be asking anyone to take care of me. I decided he was talking about taking care of business, aka her, aka Michelle, in a fatal fashion. I worked even harder at not listening.

At 9:30, I stopped. "Let's go to the cemetery."

"It's early yet," Florence said.

"I can pace there as well as here, and then we can scout the area to make sure there are no marauding bands of shifters or Renfields or rogue, evil witches."

"We haven't seen anyone since you killed the first waves of shifters."

"That's what worries me."

"Maybe everyone has accepted the inevitability of it all," Isaac suggested. "At this point, everyone will be better off if the rest of the gates open, rather than stopping in this in-between stage."

"Logically and rationally that makes complete sense. But some of these groups—like the witches we ran into at the caves—are not operating in a world of logic and rational thinking."

"Okay, let's go," Florence said.

Isaac grabbed his backpack, and I grabbed mine. Florence came and took it from me, though. "If anyone is waiting for us, it makes sense for you to be able to easily access your sword, something you cannot do with a backpack over it. My weapons"—she waggled her fingers in what I can only assume was meant to be a menacing fashion —"won't be hampered by the pack."

I handed it over, took a deep breath, and walked out of the room.

THE CEMETERY WAS PULSING with power, and I couldn't spot a single human wandering through. There were several non-humans in a rough perimeter around the graveyard, though. I looked at Florence and pointed, none-too-subtly, "Twelve?"

She nodded, and I relaxed infinitesimally. It was most likely the Fae that Arduinna had promised. One of the twelve came forward and knelt before me. "Your Highness, I am here to pledge myself and my brothers and sisters in arms to your protection this day. Tell me what you require of us."

"Rise." I took a long look at him. He was tree-like and bore a superficial resemblance to Arduinna. His skin resembled bark, and his hair gave the impression of branches and leaves. "Protect me and my companions," I gestured at Florence and Isaac. "There is possibly one more. If you see a dark-skinned, dark-haired vampire, he is ours, too. It's unlikely he'll show up since it's noon, but I don't want any mistakes."

"Remind them about Finn," Florence said.

Right. "Do you know the elf who goes by Finn?"

The tree-Fae nodded without comment or expression.

"Don't kill him. He's still useful. And don't kill any humans unless they attack first. Everyone else is fair game."

"As Your Highness wishes."

"Do you know what to expect?"

"Only that you will open a gate."

"I'll be funneling a great deal of magic and Florence will ensure it doesn't enter the world in an uncontrolled blast. I'm going to glow and levitate; that might look alarming. Once the gate opens, Isaac will be going through. There may be an escort provided for him. Kill anyone who isn't Finn if they even look like they're even thinking about being trouble. If there's a small, blond werewolf, let her go and offer your protection. She's been used harshly by the Dark Queen and her vampire pet."

The man nodded and opened his mouth, then hesitated.

"Say what you wish with no fear of reprisal from me."

"How long until these events of which you speak will begin?"

I looked at Florence. "Time?"

"10:30."

"About ninety minutes. The magic will start pulsing before that."

I stared at him, and he determinedly did not stare at me. Then I remembered. "If you have no more questions or information for me, you can return to your post."

He started to back away from me.

"You may turn your back to walk away. I appreciate your service."

He looked surprised, but whether by my gratitude or my lax attitude, I didn't know.

"Now what?" Florence asked.

"Now I pace."

I stalked the length of the cemetery nervously, and occasionally sat on a bench and tried deep-breathing exercises to promote calm. They weren't helping. I wanted to cling to Isaac, but he seemed cling-resistant at the moment. Perhaps he'd rubbed himself all over with a dryer sheet. I snorted at my ridiculous silent joke. I finally decided I didn't care if he was avoiding my cling. He was my mate, and this was goodbye.

I went over and slipped my hand into his. He looked down at me. "This is about it."

"I know."

"I feel like we should have grand speeches, flowery exchanges of words and promises and feelings."

"I love you."

I closed my eyes and tried to will away the tears threatening to well up.

"I'm sorry," he said.

"The only thing you need to be sorry for is the last two weeks."

Isaac smiled and caressed my face. "You're amazing, Eleanor."

"Don't forget I'm coming for you."

"I won't."

"I want you to know my true name."

"Don't tell me. It's no coincidence Michelle is coming after me now. Don't give me anything that could be used as leverage."

I opened wide the bond between us. *My name is Ciara nic Mata.*

"Dammit. I didn't want to know."

I smiled at him. "I trust you." I stood on tiptoe and brushed my lips lightly across his.

He grabbed me and kissed me back, deeply and passionately, until I was panting and weak-kneed. "Goodbye." He let go of me and walked away.

I looked up, steeled myself, and said softly, "Goodbye."

I stepped into the crossroads and looked towards Florence. "Ready?"

"Ready," she called back.

It was time.

CHAPTER TWENTY-THREE

I FORCED MYSELF not to look back at Isaac. The gate already pulsed with magic, and I started spinning the magic thinner and thinner, like cotton candy, and sending the magical wisps to the weir Florence had constructed. Once I was in the crossroads, magic rushed into my body. I was filled to capacity in seconds and couldn't spin it off fast enough. This was going much faster than it had the last three times. I looked up and saw Isaac. He was staring at me, and my heart broke a little bit more.

Before I could say anything, the gate energy did its thing. My limbs snapped wide, and I was pulled off the ground. I channeled the energy out in as controlled a fashion as possible, but couldn't keep up. The gate widened behind me and around me until I appeared to be floating in a portal-like void.

Isaac appeared in front of me, and I heard voices behind me.

"Are you coming?" A woman's voice asked.

"Yes. As agreed, you will release Emma if I walk through the gate." I couldn't see what was going on behind me, but whatever it was caused Isaac to pale to an ashy, gray color, not an easy feat for a man as dark-skinned as he was.

Two shots rang out, and I watched in horror as red bloomed on each of Isaac's knees. Pain ripped through his body as he lost control over our bond. I cried out in anguish in concert with his voice. Only the gate energy kept me upright. I don't know what was holding Isaac up. From the burning I was getting along with the pain, he must have been shot with silver bullets. They really weren't intending him to walk through that gate.

Isaac moved forward, and I felt a whoosh of air behind me and a hissed command, "Knock him down!"

Two Fae rushed forwards, but before they could get to Isaac, they were knocked out of the way, one on either side. They weren't knocked into my field of vision, though, and the magic was burning hotter and brighter and making it much harder to concentrate.

"I'm here, Eleanor." Raj's voice rang through my mind. *"Thanks for inviting me to lunch."*

"Stop!" I heard the woman yell behind me. "I command you to stop!"

"You can't command me," Raj said. "But if you'd like to come forward and force me to stop, you're welcome to try. It's overcast; I'm sure you'll be okay."

She didn't answer, and Raj laughed. "Not sure that your power is enough to match mine after all?"

Isaac had, by this point, hobbled past me. He didn't look at me and didn't touch me—which was just as well since anyone touching me while I was suspended in mid-air was a terrible idea.

"The girl," he said.

"You've not yet walked through the gate," the woman said in calmer tones than she'd used with Raj.

Isaac repeated, "The girl."

"You thought I would honor my bargain?" the woman who must be Michelle asked. "You are still so naive."

"You must honor your word," another voice said. "You dwell here now, and if you wish to continue to do so, you will follow our laws."

Motherfucker. Finn.

"Motherfucker," Isaac said.

"Your Queen will hear of your insubordination," Michelle said.

I heard a cry and heard someone fall.

"Help her!" Isaac yelled.

And then everything went crazy. A huge burst of energy shot from the gate straight up into the sky and burst like the grand finale of an expensive fireworks show, made even more impressive by how bright the show of colors appeared at noon.

A last rush of energy flowed through me to close the gate, making it inaccessible again until all the gates were opened. The force holding me aloft let go, and I tumbled gracelessly to the ground. Every muscle hurt, but none more than my heart.

I climbed to my feet.

"Freeze! Hands up!"

I turned around. A SWAT team stood in front of me with every one of their big, scary guns pointed directly at my person. Of all the things I'd tried to anticipate going wrong, getting shot up by the cops hadn't made the list.

I raised my hands slowly.

"Drop your weapons."

"I cannot drop my weapons if my hands are up. May I lower them?"

"Don't be a smart ass, just do it!" someone barked at me.

I lowered my hands and pulled the scabbard over my head. The Fae melted quietly into the trees, apparently deciding they weren't there to guard me from humans. Once I'd set down my sword, I removed my knife sheaths from my arms and thighs. As I dropped the last one to the ground, I heard a cry behind me. Without thinking, I turned to see what was making the noise. Before I located the source of the noise, I heard a gun discharge, and a bullet tore through my body.

"Fuck," I said, and then I collapsed.

MY AWARENESS RETURNED, and with it came burning pain in my left shoulder. I tried to open my eyes, but it was a few moments before that endeavor was successful. Fluorescent lights, industrial yellow paint on plaster walls, and an IV line leading from my left arm. I used my superior powers of deduction to determine I was in a hospital. I tried to move, and a sharp pain shot through my shoulder. I wiggled my right arm experimentally, as that was the one that hadn't been shot. I was handcuffed to the hospital bed.

"She's awake."

The first person through the room was a medical assistant. He took my vitals and checked my bandage. Before he finished, the room started filling up. A doctor, a nurse, and more police officers than seemed necessary for a gunshot victim who was handcuffed to a hospital bed. Of course, since I was a victim of a police shooting, and had been shot in the back after disarming, I supposed they might want to make sure I wasn't dead. Or maybe they wanted to finish the job.

"Water?" I croaked.

"Ice chips?" The MA handed me a cup.

The doctor checked me out while asking questions about mobility.

"What happened?" I asked once my throat was sufficiently moistened to produce intelligible speech.

The doctor answered, "The bullet lodged in your shoulder, and we had to remove it. Fortunately, it didn't hit any major arteries and other than the hole in your shoulder didn't do any significant damage. I thought you'd be healing by now. Don't your people heal faster than this?"

"My people?"

"Werewolves."

"I'm not a werewolf."

"She can't be a vampire," one of the detectives said. "She was shot outside in the middle of the day."

"I'm not a vampire."

"Witch, then," someone said.

"I am not a witch." I hoped they wouldn't ask me what I was.

"Maybe she's human." Every eye in the room focused on me, and a ripple of apprehension went through the police officers. And then I understood. If I were other, they wouldn't be in trouble for shooting me because my body was a deadly weapon, whether I could turn into a wolf or cast spells. However, if I were a human, once I'd divested myself of my weapons, I was less of a threat.

I decided to misdirect before anyone asked me the wrong question. "I'm the companion of a vampire." I was hoping they would assume that meant I was a Renfield.

"I don't see any marks," the nurse said. I looked up at her quizzically, and she crooked her first two fingers and made a stabbing motion. Heh. Sharp, pointy teeth.

"Older vampires don't often leave marks."

"Your companion is old?" the detective asked.

"Old enough to not leave marks on my body if he doesn't want to."

"Will he come for you?"

"I don't know. Did you bring in anyone else after you shot me?"

"We have two women in jail: a witch and a werewolf."

"Are they okay?"

"They're in jail, which means they weren't shot," the MA said.

I really looked at him for the first time. He wasn't human but wasn't advertising that fact. He must be a practitioner. His aura felt young, and young shifters and vamps wouldn't do well in a hospital.

"Are my friends okay? What are we being charged with?"

The officers looked at each other.

"Don't we have to be charged with something if you're going to hold us?"

"You can be held for three days without being charged," the detective said.

"But shouldn't you tell me what you're considering charging me with? You don't arrest people in cemeteries and hold them for three days on a regular basis, do you?"

"A better question," the MA said, "is whether they think those laws apply to non-humans and if they believe being supernatural is a crime in and of itself."

I looked over at the police officers. They were all carefully not meeting my eyes.

"How long have I been here?" I asked. I didn't feel about to collapse into unconsciousness like I usually did shortly after a gate opening.

"Almost two days," the MA said.

"I was unconscious for two days for a bullet wound in my shoulder? Is that normal?"

"Not if you were human," the doctor stepped into the conversation, on less shaky ground now. "We surmised you were in a healing sleep or something. We haven't had much chance to treat supernaturals. But you aren't healing any faster than a human."

"Now what?" I asked.

"You'll probably get transferred to the jail infirmary and then charged and arraigned if they're going to follow the rules," the MA said.

"What's your name?" I asked.

"Ralph, but everyone calls me Ralphie."

"Ralph, you are awesome."

He blushed.

I looked over at the officers. "Is that what's going to happen?"

"We could charge you with illegal concealed weapons," one of them said.

"And illegal discharge of fireworks, disturbing the peace, and public intoxication," the detective added.

"Half of Savannah is armed to the teeth, I wasn't drunk, and I didn't set off any fireworks—facts I'm sure will be supported by any forensic investigation."

"There wasn't one," the detective said. "We don't waste our limited resources on supernatural crimes."

So that was the way of it, now. I was exhausted. "What time is it?"

"Seven in the morning."

"I need a nap."

JUDGING BY THE SHADOWS, it was late afternoon when I woke up again.

I was alone in the room but could see an officer outside the door. This was ridiculous.

"*Hello, my sweet,*" a voice whispered through my head.

"*Raj! Are you okay? They didn't mention you at all.*"

"*They were unable to arrest me. I have a confession: I gave you some of my blood when you were shot.*"

"*Why would you do that?*"

"*To stop the bleeding and help you heal faster.*"

"*The doctor says I'm not healing any faster than a human.*"

"*The doctor is lying.*"

I moved experimentally and felt the stabbing pain through my shoulder again. "*My shoulder really hurts.*"

"*We wanted you to appear human until I could arrange your rescue. It was safer. The cops are a little trigger happy. Now that you're awake, I'll have the doctor finish healing your shoulder and get you out of there.*"

"*What about Florence and the wolf?*"

"*They're being held in solitary confinement and aren't allowed visitors or a lawyer.*"

"*Can you break them out?*"

"*Of course. I was waiting until we could all disappear at once. Where are we headed?*"

I concentrated. "*Dammit. North.*"

"*Anything more specific?*"

"*Somewhere with lots and lots of rocks. Mystical rocks.*"

Raj's mental voice sounded mildly amused. "*We're going north to find magic rocks?*"

"*Yep.*"

I MUST HAVE DOZED off because the next thing that registered was someone pulling out the IV line. "Raj?" I asked.

"No. It's Doctor Robinson."

"Doctor who?"

"No, although bow ties are cool."

I giggled. "You're funny."

The doctor, whom I now recognized as both the doctor who'd attended me earlier and a vampire said, "And you're more susceptible to the drugs than I thought you'd be. I'm going to remove the iron filament in your shoulder. It's thin enough and short enough not to have done permanent damage, but it will hurt coming out."

"Do it." I braced myself but still gasped when she pulled out the wire. "Fuck."

"It's out, and you'll be healed soon."

"What's next?"

"The Master of Savannah is breaking your compatriots out of jail and should be here within the hour."

"What about the cops?" I gestured towards the door where I sensed the life energies of two humans standing outside.

"Provided they don't get a call regarding any escaped prisoners, they'll stay there quietly until I get a text from the Master."

"And if they do get a call?"

"Then they'll fall asleep a little sooner and with more dramatic outcome."

"Are you going to kill them?"

"I was instructed not to."

"So you're a giver of life and death?" For some reason, the doctor's cavalier attitude towards murder bothered me.

"I cannot give life, only prolong it. Taking it, however, is easy."

"Easy is seldom right," Raj said from the shadows.

"Master," Dr. Robinson said, genuflecting. I watched her eyes instead of her bow. She didn't look subservient.

She's not as compliant as she'd like to appear," I said.

"But she's useful, both for her medical skills and her psychic skills," Raj said. I tilted my head in question. "She's skilled at glamour and can read minds almost as well as I can." There was a note of warning in Raj's voice, and I looked over at the doctor. She looked smug.

"Fortunately, we don't need her to be compliant. All she needs to do is to put the guards to sleep before they are notified Florence and the baby wolf have escaped and then cover your tracks."

"Remind me again what I'll get out of this?" Dr. Robinson asked.

"You'll be the de facto leader in Savannah after I leave town and will retain that position once the Queen has claimed this territory. But most importantly—to you, at least—you'll live through this."

I seldom saw Raj being his vampire self—the vampire who had lived for a millennium, who had been a prince and a commander of armies, and who was still a commander of a different type of troops. It was scary, and if I was honest with myself, a little arousing.

Raj flashed a grin at me.

"Are the terms still acceptable?" he asked, the silk of his voice hiding the violence that was lurking below the surface.

The doctor gulped noticeably. "Yes."

"Then do it."

Dr. Robinson bowed slightly and awkwardly, revealing she hadn't grown up bowing to anyone.

The doctor moved to the doorway while Raj helped me out of bed. I was as wobbly as a newborn calf and Raj had to steady me until I found my balance. I looked towards the door and saw the men on the other side slump in unison.

"It is done," Dr. Robinson said.

"And the cameras?" Raj asked.

"On the fritz tonight."

"Your aid is appreciated," I said.

"Does this mean you're in my debt?" the doctor asked.

"No," Raj said. He grabbed my arm and led me out of the room. When we got to the end of the hall, he scooped me up and carried me into the stairwell. We went from the fifth to the first floor in seconds and then we were outside. I tilted my head up to catch the fresh air.

"Put me down?"

Raj complied immediately and when my bare feet hit the ground, I felt whole for the first time since I'd woken up in the hospital. Between the gate opening, being shot, the iron embedded in my shoulder, and spending almost three days out of touch with the earth —I was drained.

"We don't have much time," Raj said.

"I'm ready now, as long as we'll be somewhere green and growing soon."

"Nature is bad for you. I'm going to miss the cities and smog when this is done. The industrial and technological revolutions were the two best things that have happened in the past thousand years."

I held my arms up to him. "I'm ready."

EPILOGUE

FINN PACED BACK and forth in front of Isaac. The shifter was naked and chained to the wall with silver. The stripes of his last lashing hadn't yet healed. Isaac's eyes were closed, but he was not unconscious.

Finn tried to keep silent, but when Isaac opened his eyes, he couldn't stop himself. "Guess you're not so strong after all."

Isaac focused on Finn. It was obvious to Finn that Isaac was dazed from the combination of being injected with a score of different types of drugs to see which would keep him compliant and the constant physical torment.

"What do you want?" Isaac asked. His words were slurred and hard to distinguish.

"I came to see the beast laid low."

"I thought you loved Eleanor," Isaac rasped.

"All of this is for her."

"This isn't love."

"What do you know? You're nothing but a fucking animal."

"I'm her mate."

"It's not real. She's a Fae princess. She wouldn't mate with an animal."

"You know her, Finn. You know she doesn't lie." The more he talked, the stronger his voice got.

"Not to me, maybe. But who knows what she'd say to you to get what she wanted."

"She cannot lie, you idiot," Michelle said. Finn started at her voice. "I know enough to know she is a full-blooded Fae and is bound by their magic." She strode all the way into the room. She resembled a Nordic princess. Tall and willowy with blond hair cascading down her back and over her shoulder. Her eyes were blue ice chips in her fair complexion, and her lips—pursed now in displeasure—were a pink, perfect cupid's bow. "Why are you here?"

"I got him for you. I engineered everything."

"And our deal was I would have him, and you would be content."

"I wanted to see."

"You whine. You call him an animal, but you are the sniveling beast. How one this pathetic ever gained the attention of two monarchs and entered the bed of the catalyst is beyond my ken. Go report to your master and get out of my sight."

Finn drew up to his full height. "You cannot order me around. I am a trusted servant of the Dark Queen."

"You are a cur not fit to fight for scraps under her majesty's table." A new voice joined them.

Finn paled. "My lord."

"Her majesty will hear of this."

"My apologies. In my zeal to see this animal punished, I went too far."

"Yes. You did. Now get out."

"You are watching her?" Finn asked, his voice pleading. "You are protecting her?"

"I do my duty. Do not make me tell you to leave again."

Finn bowed and backed out of the room with the grace of someone who was used to such an awkward stance.

Isaac was staring at the newcomer. "You? But, why?"

Michelle laughed. "You did not suspect him? How blind you are."

"She trusted you," Isaac said.

"She doesn't trust anyone, not even you." He turned towards Michelle. "Her majesty is pleased and grants you leave to play with this one for as long as you wish, but requests you leave him alive in case he is needed for leverage in the future."

"Requests or demands?" Michelle asks.

"You learn quickly. It is a request, but one I would adhere to if I were you."

"Her wish is my command, then." Michelle picked up a silver-tipped whip from a table of various leather and silver instruments coated in blood. She hefted it once and brought it down across Isaac's stomach. He was silent, as he always was at the beginning. Soon, though, he was crying out in pain.

She laughed softly. "I'm glad I haven't lost my touch." She turned around, "You may watch if you like."

"Your offer is generous, but I must return to the Midworld before my absence is noticed."

Michelle nodded, but her attention was already back on Isaac. "Later, then."

THE RUBY BLADE

ELEANOR MORGAN BOOK THREE

I T WAS COLD. I hated the cold. I hated just about everything about winter. Snow, slush, ice, the dearth of daylight hours. But mostly, I hated the cold. I burrowed down into the blankets piled on top of me trying to extract a bit more warmth from them, but couldn't stop my shivering.

"I'd add my body heat to yours if I thought it would help, but alas! I have none." Raj's voice came from somewhere outside my blanket burrow.

"Why is it so cold?" I asked, nearly biting my tongue with my chattering teeth.

"It isn't that cold," Florence said. "It's above zero."

"Well, now that I know the temperature, I'm much, much warmer."

"Where's the girl?" Raj asked Florence.

"She has a name," Florence replied.

Raj growled.

"You can't intimidate me," she said.

"I could exsanguinate you before Eleanor could get out from under those blankets."

"But you won't."

"Don't push me, witch."

"Oh, I'll push. And right now, I'm going to push you to remember our young guest's name."

Raj sighed in defeat. "Where's Emma?"

"Hiding in the bathroom, which you must already know. She's scared of us. Why?"

"She's a werewolf. She could help raise Eleanor's core temperature."

"She's even more afraid of Eleanor than of you. I'm not sure she'd agree to do that."

"She doesn't have to agree to it," Raj said.

"Yes she does," I interrupted. "I'm not cuddling with a strange wolf who's being forced into it. A strange wolf who happens to be my mate's ex-girlfriend. If she's afraid of me and has issues with my relationship with Isaac, she's not the person I want under these blankets with me."

"You and Isaac are mates?" a soft voice floated over us. It was high and musical and sounded very young.

I poked my head out from under the blankets. Emma was peering around the corner of the bathroom door.

"Yes."

"Do you mean…sex?" she whispered the last word as if it would somehow sully her to say it aloud.

"We did the ceremony during the Hunter's Moon with an entire Pack serving as witnesses." Yeah, I was staking my claim. It wasn't a jealousy thing. Not even a tiny bit. It was following pack protocol. This is what any wolf would do regarding their mate. I was absolutely one hundred percent not threatened by Isaac's ex-girlfriend. Not even if she looked and sounded like a fairy princess. Which she wasn't. I was the only fairy princess in this room.

Raj made a weird noise and I glanced over at him and realized that he was laughing. Probably at me.

"Shut it," I said to him. "Help me sit up?" I asked Florence.

Florence helped me struggle to a sitting position and readjusted the blanket burrito around my shivering body.

"Why am I so fucking cold?" I muttered. No one else looked like they were freezing to death. There was no heat in the motel room due to that whole "no electricity" problem I'd created, but everyone else looked comfortable. True, everyone else was a fully clothed werewolf, a vampire who didn't really feel the cold, and a mage who probably had some kind of magical warming spell.

"You're cold blooded," Florence said.

"I am not. I mean, I'm not the most touchy-feely person around, but I wouldn't go with cold blooded."

"You're a dragon," she said. "The more you accept your dragon half, the more you'll take on the strengths and weaknesses of a dragon. There aren't a lot of weaknesses, but as a reptile, an inability to regulate body temperature is probably the big one."

"So, what do we do? We're still headed north. There's no heat anywhere. I need to function."

"Maybe we can find an outdoor store and get some cold weather gear for you. With insulated underthings and wool clothes and a sleeping bag, maybe you can stay warm enough to stay awake."

"Or maybe I can just hibernate while you all go find the gate and then you can wake me up when it's time for my part?"

"That's a brilliant idea," Florence said. "There is nothing I'd like more than to wander around looking for some magic rocks—that's still our goal, right?—in the snow, hope that we've found the right ones, and then wake a sleeping dragon who'll probably be hungry after six weeks of hibernation. Best adventure ever."

"Florence, at this point, you're abusing sarcasm." She grinned at me and I smiled back. "Besties for life," I said. She rolled her eyes.

I turned back towards Emma. She hadn't moved any further into the room and didn't appear reassured by our witty banter. She was trying to keep an eye on both me and Raj at the same time, and it made her look more than a little absurd.

"Emma," I said, trying to sound soothing. "We're not going to hurt you."

She snorted, and I was relieved she had a bit of spirit. "I'm in a room with a day-walking vampire who's older than dirt..." there was a sound of protest from Raj, "the most powerful mage I've ever seen, and some kind of bizarre dragon Fae and you think I should feel safe?"

"Bizarre?" I asked.

She ignored my indignant query. "I spent six years chained up in a dungeon full of Fae and the craziest vampire of all time. I've been beaten. Starved. Tortured with silver and prevented from changing. And now, I'm locked in a motel room with more Fae and vampires."

"Six years passed Underhill?" I asked. Crap. Just what she needed.

Emma nodded, and then her eyes widened. "How much time passed here?" Apparently she'd picked up the implication in the word 'Underhill.'

"What year were you taken?" I didn't know exactly, although I had a pretty decent idea. Isaac's Vantage was a 1962. He'd escaped Michelle in the fifties and was out for less than ten years. That meant that Emma had been taken sometime in the early sixties.

"Nineteen sixty-four. It was spring. April."

"Emma, I hate to tell you, but it's December 2013. It's been almost fifty years here."

She folded in on herself in a slow collapse. Florence rushed over to her and caught her before she hit the ground. She was sobbing and I felt like an ass. There had to have been a better way to break the news to her. She'd been a young wolf when Isaac had met her, which meant she probably still had family alive at that time.

Florence held her and patted her hair like a child. She looked at Raj over Emma's head.

"She wants to move Emma to the next room. She thinks our presence won't help her calm down." Raj said to me.

I nodded and projected towards Florence, *"We'll be okay. Raj will stay with me. Let's take the next day to calm down and regroup. Maybe I can figure out a more specific destination."*

Florence helped Emma to her feet.

"Emma, we're going to get another room. Are you hungry? Do you want food?"

I didn't hear her reply, but they walked out of the room, Florence's arm protectively tented around Emma's shoulder.

"What about you?" Raj asked aloud. "Do you want food?"

My stomach growled loud enough to be heard through the layers of blanket and Raj laughed. "I'll see what Florence left us."

I shivered again. "Could find me more socks? Do we still have Isaac's stuff? Maybe he has a pair big enough to fit over the three pairs that I'm already wearing."

"I'll see what I can do."

I huddled into the blankets and watched Raj move around the room. He found a pair of large men's socks and helped me put them on. He handed me a granola bar and I looked at it in disgust before removing the wrapper and taking a bite.

"I miss Taco Bell," I said.

"I miss the internet," Raj replied. "Finding magic rocks would be much easier with Google."

"Do we have maps?" I finished my granola bar and wondered if I could use my magical powers to heat a cup of water and make ramen.

"In the car." Raj gave me a large ceramic mug, filled it with bottled water, and handed me some beef ramen. I concentrated on heating my hands without starting fires, and soon the water was simmering. I dropped the noodles in and stared at the cup, willing them to cook faster. By the time I'd decided they were done enough and had stirred in the seasoning packet, Raj was back with a US atlas and some detailed area maps.

"Where are we now?" I asked around a mouthful of too-hot noodles.

"Charlotte, North Carolina."

I looked at the US map and tried to get a feel for where we needed to go. I wasn't having much luck, which was pissing me off. The last time I'd *known* it was Savannah. Just like I'd known we were headed to the Black Hills. I didn't want to drive all over the snow-covered and freezing northeastern United States looking for some fucking mystical rocks. I closed my eyes and tried to intuit the location of the next gate. All I got was north.

"Dammit," I said. "I guess we keep driving north. Hopefully soon I'll get something more. I hate not knowing almost as much as I hate being cold."

"I wish I could warm you up," Raj said.

"Maybe I can figure out how to just heat my whole body the way I heated my hands to boil the water." I wasn't ready for any other types of heated discussions.

Raj bowed slightly and returned his attention to the maps. "We'll stay on I-77 tomorrow until we get to I-81, and then start heading northeast. It's December 25th today and we have until February 2nd to find the gate, right?"

"It's Christmas?" I exclaimed. "Shit. I can't believe I didn't even notice."

"Merry Christmas, my sweet," Raj said. He kissed my forehead and handed me a glass of wine that I hadn't seen him pour. His cold lips triggered another full body shiver. He held his glass towards me. "Cheers." We clinked glasses and I drank deeply, hoping the wine would make me feel warmer. It helped a bit. The second and third glasses helped even more. After we'd emptied the bottle, Raj helped me lay down again in my cocoon and I felt myself drift off. Hibernation sounded like a really good idea.

WE DROVE TO ROANOKE, Virginia the next evening. Florence took the entire driving shift because I was too cold to drive, Raj claimed not to know how, and Emma was still too...whatever she was. I was almost positive Raj was lying, but didn't call him on it because it wasn't too long of a drive—or at least it shouldn't have been. The detours around stalled cars and closed sections of the freeway extended our three-hour drive into a five-hour journey.

"Someone else needs to take a turn tomorrow," Florence announced. "I am too old for this shit."

Everyone turned and looked at me. "Hey! Emma's probably the youngest, even if she was born before me." Florence gave me a frigid look and I was glad she hadn't put any magic punch behind it. I was cold enough as it was.

"If you don't mind the heater going full blast and a limited range of movement from the piles of blankets I require, I'll take my turn." I tried not to sulk. I didn't want anyone else to make a comment about my age. Hanging out with the all-but-immortal definitely had its downsides.

"I can drive," Emma said quietly. "It doesn't feel like it's been that long since I've done it and your car doesn't look too different from what I'm used to."

"You don't need to take a turn until you're feeling back to yourself," Florence said.

"I might as well make myself useful. I don't understand why we're here and what we're doing, but I don't know what else to do at this point but stay with you. Isaac's scent is all over that Fae," I suppressed my desire to punch Werewolf Barbie in the face and settled for smiling. Based on the increasingly chilly air around me, Florence didn't think my smile was as friendly as I'd meant it to be.

Emma continued speaking, either ignorant of or ignoring the unspoken communication between Florence and me. "If Isaac was with you and that Fae," I couldn't smother the growl that time, but Emma soldiered on, "then he must have trusted you. Until I figure something else out, I guess I'll stick around."

I was starting to feel truly warm for the first time since we'd left Savannah, and noticed Raj eying me warily. Florence was giving me some side-eye, too, but her expression wasn't wary, it was pissed. Something in Emma had triggered her protective instinct and apparently our pre-existing friendship wasn't trumping that.

I tried to tamp down my anger enough that I wouldn't start any fires but not so much that I started shivering again. "Let's find a place to crash for the rest of the night. We can start driving north again in the evening. I need food and sleep."

"You've been sleeping a lot these last few days," Florence noted.

"Byproduct of the gate opening, being shot, and the cold."

"And mourning, too, I suspect," Raj said. He was glaring at

Florence, although I had no idea why. "Eleanor's had a rough go of it these last couple of weeks. She's probably hitting another magical level, too, which will be burning through her resources. We need to get her some protein."

"And beer," I added. "Eleanor definitely needs beer. It's possible that it's a Fae remedy for power surges." Sometimes I hated my inability to say random made-up shit to be funny. Phrasing was key, but it made my jokes much less amusing. At least I'm assuming it was the phrasing that made it unfunny, since no one in the car looked amused.

Florence sighed. "I'll find a motel. Do we want something operational, or do you want to find something vacant and squat?"

"If it's up to me, I'd like something with a fireplace." Now that my anger was simmering down, I was back to shivering. I really needed to find the balance if I was going to survive this winter road trip.

"I'll see what I can do."

We drove into town and found a restaurant that'd specialized in wood-fired pizza before the surge. It was the only restaurant in the area that seemed operational, so we stopped there. Places were still taking cash—no credit or debit cards, of course—but I felt guilty paying in a currency that might soon have no value. We did it anyway, picking up four large pizzas. We also got directions to some romantic honeymoon cabins outside of town that had fireplaces and spring-fed hot tubs. We were the only customers and spent our soon-to-be-worthless cash on four cabins, each with its own fireplace and hot tub.

I raided my stash for a couple of bottles of wine and invited everyone to my cabin for dinner. We ate pizza until we were stuffed and then sat in front of the large roaring fireplace with our wine until Emma's eyes drooped. Our conversation was mainly about the next day's driving plans, and although Emma listened attentively, she asked no questions. Florence roused her and led her off to her own cabin, adjacent to Florence's.

"Turn around," I commanded Raj.

He slowly turned a full 360, and I rolled my eyes at him.

"I'm going to strip. Turn around."

"I've seen you naked before," he said.

"By all the gods, Raj, please just turn around."

He did and I stood, sloughing off my blankets, then quickly removing my coat, a hooded sweatshirt, a long-sleeved t-shirt, a t-shirt, a tank top, and a sports bra. Once my top was bared, I moved closer to the fire and started on my lower half. Jeans, long underwear, four pairs of socks, and a pair of panties later, I was nude.

"Okay, you can turn around again," I said after I slid into the natural hot spring.

His eyes flashed red as he raked them down my newly naked body.

"Are you going to invite me to join you?"

"Only if you're going to promise to keep your parts to yourself."

"I think you misunderstand the purpose of an ensuite hot tub."

"I think you forget how recently I lost my mate."

Raj stripped quickly and efficiently. I averted my eyes so I wouldn't see him nude up.

"You can stop pretending not to watch now," he said.

I couldn't deny it, since I couldn't lie, so I stayed silent.

He grabbed our wine glasses and the half-full bottle and stepped into the hot tub. I gave up pretending to look away and eyed his naked body appreciatively. He was a pretty man and his dark skin glowed with golden-brown undertones. He handed me another glass of wine and then took a seat as far away from me as possible.

After sipping our wine in silence for a few minutes, he looked directly at me. "We'll find Isaac," he said. "I promise. We will find him and we will punish those responsible for this."

Then, for the first time since Yule when I said my last good-byes, I cried. Raj set down his wine and slid over to me. He put an arm around me and let me sob into his shoulder for what seemed like eons. Finally, I was cried out. My eyes felt red and swollen, and I knew that I was the very picture of beauty.

"You are always beautiful to me," Raj's voice caressed my mind.

"I need a tissue," I said.

Raj reached behind him to his pile of clothes and whisked out a handkerchief for me. I blew my noise, wincing at the picture I must be presenting.

"Thank you."

Raj looked at me but didn't say anything. He scooted back across the hot tub. I squelched the pang of disappointment I felt when our bodies lost contact. It'd been five days since Isaac had disappeared from this plane, five days since I'd been in his arms. Five days was a little too soon to be lusting after someone new, even if that lust was a pre-existing condition.

"Pre-existing condition?" Raj asked.

"Stay out of my head."

"Why?"

"It's private."

"Eleanor, my sweet, I will not push you. I am patient. I know the witch said to stay out of my bed until after New Orleans, and that you intend to listen to her. I will not stop trying to seduce you—that's been my goal since we met—but I won't push too far past your limits."

"Not too far?" Now I was trying not to be amused.

"I have to push a little. But I am old and I am patient. You will come to my bed sooner or later. I prefer sooner, so I push."

"So confident."

"Of course."

I laughed. I was finally warm and the combination of the heat and the wine was making me a little sleepy and a little reckless. I wanted to know what it was like to kiss the vampire—really kiss him, not the kisses he'd stolen in the past. And then, I wanted to know what it would be like to have him drink from me.

"Eleanor," Raj said. "If you don't stop that particular line of thought, I might not be as patient as you need me to be."

I tried to redirect my train of thought, but from the red flashes in his eyes, I wasn't doing a very good job.

"I should go," he said.

I wanted to tell him not to go. I wanted him to stay with me, to hold me while I slept, but I knew as well as he did that it wouldn't stay platonic for long. We were dancing dangerously close to a line I wasn't sure I wanted to cross, and it wouldn't take much tonight to push me over the edge. So instead of grabbing him and kissing him, I closed my eyes and said, "Okay. I'll see you in the evening for the next leg of our journey?"

"I'll be back before then. I need to feed, though."

I ignored the stab of jealousy and nodded. I felt a feather-light caress on my face as he exited the hot tub. I kept my eyes closed until I was sure he'd have had a chance to dress and then opened them and looked around. He was gone and I was alone.

"Never alone," his voice whispered to me. *"If you need me, just call."*

I sat in the hot tub and finished my wine. I tried not to think about my complicated relationship with Raj, or my missing mate, or anything more confusing than whether or not there was any pizza left. I got out of the hot tub and wrapped myself in the large robe that Raj had left by the tub. I finished the pizza and made a nest of blankets in front of the fireplace. I added enough wood to hopefully last through the rest of the night, then huddled into my blankets and fell asleep.

I KNEW I was dreaming because it was summer and I was warm. I stretched out and felt wings grow along my back. I dropped forward onto all fours and slowly morphed into a dragon.

When the transformation was complete, I launched myself into the air and surveyed my surrounds. The Earth was barren but beautiful. Browning scrub grass dotted the canyons that were at the base of impossibly high cliffs dotted with holes. When I flew in closer, I realized that the holes were doorways. I was somewhere in the southwest, then. I felt a hot updraft rise up off the canyon floor and spread my wings to catch it. As I soared upwards, I felt it. The gate energy was unmistakable. I flapped my wings to get out of the heat stream and turned towards the gate. I flew over a circle of stone foundations that marked an old village. I wondered who lived in that village and who lived in the cliff-side village. Did they have people afraid of heights?

Or were the easily accessible homes reserved for the elderly and the pregnant women?

Then something caught my eye that ended my idle speculations. A figure crept out across the desert floor. I was high enough up and its back was to me, so I couldn't see if it was male or female, but the way it kept glancing around marked it as someone hoping not to be seen. I flew in closer, operating under the assumption that since I was dreaming, this figure wouldn't be able to see me.

Once he—for it definitely appeared masculine now that I could see the lines of his body—reached the inside of the foundation circle, he began laying down items in an elaborate pattern. He remained crouched in one position for a long time, his hands stretched out and then the items slowly sunk into the ground. He dusted his hands off, then rose to standing. The setting sun caught his hair and in flamed a brilliant red and then he turned to face me. It was Finn.

In an instant, I forgot that this was a dream and I dove towards him, claws outstretched. I flew right through him with no effect. He didn't even flinch. He surveyed the area, concentrated for a second, and then the ground smoothed out; looking as if it had never been disturbed. Then he backed slowly away before turning and disappearing.

I landed in the very center of the circle and shed my dragon shape. I carefully found the spot where one of the items Finn had buried was and dug it up. I had a flash of wonder that I could effect my dreamworld when I couldn't touch Finn, but it faded quickly as I examined my find. It was a small disc, about four inches in diameter and less than two inches thick. I turned it over a couple of times and then saw the pressure plate on one side. It was a land mine. I laid it down and sank into a cross-legged position. I didn't know how to disarm a land mine. Now that I knew they were here, I knew I could fly into the center where Finn had NOT placed any mines, but that would leave me isolated.

The worst, though, was that this was not the next gate. That meant that it was going to be a minimum of three months before we got here —maybe even longer if New Orleans was between the mystical rocks and the cliff village. Tourism had probably dropped off some in recent weeks, but the effects of the cataclysms were less in the southwest, and there might still be tourists coming through here. Or national park rangers. Or lost hikers.

The more I thought about all the innocent people that could get caught in Finn's deadly booby traps, the angrier I got. I transformed back into a dragon and roared a great wave of fire at the ground, blackening it beneath me, but having no effect on the one visible landmine.

Fuck.

I flew back to the cliff where I'd started my adventure and once again shifted back to my human body. I concentrated on leaving the dream world behind and waking up, and slowly the blue sky, purpling to dusk in the west, faded into black. I struggled for a second; feeling suffocated after the recent freedom of heat and flight, and realized I was cocooned in my nest of blankets.

"Let me help," Raj said, and he was there, untangling the blankets from around my arms and legs and freeing me from their claustrophobic confines. I sat up in front of the fire that was still burning and shivered a bit, although more from the memory of my dream than from any real chill. The room was pleasant.

"Do you want to talk about your dream?" Raj asked.

"We need to, but we'll need Florence, too. What time is it?"

"Nearly dusk, probably about five."

I sighed. "It's probably time to get going, then."

"I have coffee for you," he said.

I smiled at him. "I'm not sleeping with you."

He laughed. "That wasn't my aim. I merely desire civility."

I grabbed the proffered cup of coffee. I wanted a shower, but there was no hot water other than that from the hot spring. I settled for a refreshingly brisk face wash with a hot coffee chaser then made Raj turn his back so I could layer on my clothing.

ABOUT THE AUTHOR

AMY CISSELL IS an urban fantasy and paranormal romance writer. She grew up in South Dakota and received her BA in English Literature from South Dakota State University. That degree has carried her far in her career as a financial administrator.

Her first exposure to fantasy was when she picked up her father's copy of The Hobbit while in elementary school and an enduring love affair was born. Although Amy reads anything and everything, her first love is fantasy.

Amy is the author of the Eleanor Morgan series. Visit Amy online at www.amycissell.com and sign up for her newsletter. In addition to receiving deleted scenes and excerpts from her upcoming releases, you'll get the newsletter-exclusive serial following the origins and first millennium of Raj Allred—everyone's favorite sexy vampire.

facebook.com/acissellwrites

twitter.com/acissellwrites

instagram.com/acissellwrites

ALSO BY AMY CISSELL

The Eleanor Morgan Novels
The Cardinal Gate (February 2017)
The Waning Moon (June 2017)
The Ruby Blade (October 2017)
The Broken World (March 2018)
The Lost Child (February 2019)

Oracle Bay
It's Not in the Cards (October 2018)
First Hand Knowledge (November 2018)
Belle of the Ball (December 2018)
Wing and a Prayer (January 2019)

Made in United States
Troutdale, OR
03/09/2024

18317403R00224